THE WAR

a novel

THE CERISTEN SERIES
BOOK FOUR

VERITY A. BUCHANAN

The War

The Ceristen Series, Book Four

ISBN: 978-1-64960-352-4
eISBN: 978-1-64960-369-2
Library of Congress Control Number: 2022943349

Cover Design by Hannah Linder Designs
Interior Typesetting by Dentelle Design
Edited by Susanna Maurer

AMBASSADOR INTERNATIONAL
Emerald House
411 University Ridge, Suite B14
Greenville, SC 29601, USA
www.ambassador-international.com

AMBASSADOR BOOKS
The Mount
2 Woodstock Link
Belfast, BT6 8DD, Northern Ireland, UK
www.ambassadormedia.co.uk

The colophon is a trademark of Ambassador, a Christian publishing company.

DEDICATION

To Vanna

This is Jeddy's book

Being a map of
Legea
The KNOWN WORLD,
Showing the lands north of the FALLEN CONTINENT
as far as EDEL HARTHE and the HAVGEN MOUNTAINS
THE GREY LANDS
EDIVERNEL
EDEL HARTHE
FEARNISH MOUNTAINS
FEARNLAND
THE GREAT WASTE
HAVGEN MOUNTAINS
EVENA MOUNTAINS
ORDEN
EDERAN
DIRION
RODRON
GALTHA RELGA
GONTLAND
RAESIR
HARLALAN
RIVER FALLAHN
MENEVACE
HAROTHA
SEA OF PHERITRA
ERAHAR
CASCADE MOUNTAINS
EDU RIVER
REHIRNE
ELERIAN MOUNTAINS
VELIA RIVER
MATTADOR
Territory of the NORTHERN SUNSTERS
Territory of the SOUTHERN SUNSTERS
SATHDEL ARON
RAESTR MOUNTAINS
MESOREMN
DIRION RIVER
RUNNICOR
TERRAGERE
GLUMINTOR
STRAITS OF GLUMINTOR
ENYDHWYN
HAELOR SEA
COASTAL SUNSTERS
BAY OF ARAHAD
ARAHAD
WALIA RIVER
ZAGHA BOWL
TO HAVIS
N
W
E
S

CHAPTER I

THE TWELFTH OF APRIL DAWNED clear.

Sunlight glinted on the needles of Thiranu's pine trees, and cascaded through empty boughs of birch, oak, aspen, and maple. Under its heat the snow-drifts of winter thinned into the air, the vapor forming trailing white shrouds amid the quiet trees of the forest. As the light hit them, they glittered like the breath of dragons and unraveled slowly into weak, wisping strands that dissipated with silent sighs.

The houses of Ceristen stirred. Morning meals warmed over the fire; men fed their animals and walked the fields, gauging the days until the planting could begin. Around the village, news circulated that the yearly horse sale was on the move northward; it would arrive at Thiranu in less than a se'ennight.

Winds sailed over the little mountain, coming down cool and fresh from the high Elerien peaks to gently stir the lowlands that flanked the West-Gate road. In glades and valleys the first crocuses of spring pushed their pale leaves through the drying ground, and clinging vines showed sparks of green on bare grey trees.

But the quiet serenity of the morning was lost on the young man galloping grimly through the streets of Orden City. Sun-seared and disheveled, he pulled his horse up at the east end of the capital and looked up at the dark, gleaming pinnacle overshadowing the outer wall: Mitheren, Tower of Kings. A silent symbol of bygone austerity, a steadfast vigil pointed eastwards to the old threats. Its imposing make seemed to touch the rider for a moment even in his haste, and he stalled, the reins loose in one hand and his dark eyes wide. Then he swung off his mount, led it over to a nearby tree where he tied it securely, and exchanged some low, hurried words with the guard at the door. At their nod, he rushed within. He had a message for the king; he would not wait.

~

. . . that eight hundreds of the army should depart at the king's discretion to accompany and protect the embassy to Arahad. Also that with them should go Captain Keyes and the lords of Calen and Halingir, and many gifts besides, and it is hoped by this to renew the alliance, which has been uneasy these two generations past. All these proposals were approved and carried, and the embassy is to depart the fifth of April. (Further note appended at the request of the General Derek Winston: the embassy departed as designed.)

Lord Darethin protested sending so great a force into another country's territory, calling it "questionable policy." He was overruled by Captain Rhodes, Captain Keyes, and the representative from Grinaz Hall on the grounds that Arahad values display and opulence, and regards small embassies, especially from greater countries, as a disrespect and a potential threat; and that furthermore, they shall be passing through the territory of the barbarians. Lord Darethin requested his displeasure noted.

The next assembly was set for the fourteenth of April.

The council was dispersed.

Chronicle of the second council meeting in the season of Luenna, on the thirtieth day of March, by the hand of Culhas the secretary, complete.

Further note appended at the request of the General Derek Winston: That the state of the army is growing rapidly poor, due to the manifold skirmishes on the north border with Wild Men of late. Though at present we are surrounded by allies, it may nonetheless become a danger. Let not the time of peace be used as an excuse to lie in sloth. We must see to the strengthening of our defense, whether by a conscription or—

"My general?"

"Aye," the general answered, lifting his head from the papers he was reviewing. "Captain Rhodes?"

"My general." Captain Rhodes entered and bent his head in a swift bow. There was a darkness in his eyes like doubt or concern. "Below there is a man who has ridden here in great haste. He bears an urgent message, he says, for the king's ears."

"The king has ridden south to Lake Dracaman."

Captain Rhodes swept his hand dismissively. "So I told him. He says he will speak to you."

The general nodded. "Send him in."

Captain Rhodes returned shortly, a young man behind him of perhaps twenty-five. The stranger's bearing was wary, one leather-clad hand curled in a half-gesture as though reaching for the security of his sword. He met the general's eyes with a dark and fiercely determined gaze, and directed a swift glance at Captain Rhodes. "He can be trusted?" he asked, his voice rough and low.

The general held those piercing eyes searchingly. "I would trust him with my life," he answered. "But what do you bring, that it must be so secret?"

The man sent another quick glance around the room. "I bring tidings," he said, dropping his head in a courtesy to the general; "tidings of war."

Captain Rhodes drew in breath sharply; but the general looked at the young man intently with narrowed eyes. "What do you mean?" he said. "War where, and with whom? Explain this to me."

The man hesitated, uncertain as it were how to speak. "I am Grant Eagle, of Runnicor formerly, a wanderer by trade," he began at last. "Four months since, I was traveling through the Grey Lands to the north of Harotha and near the sea, and I came upon a place where there were many men encamped—I could not say how many, for they were interspersed among the trees and valleys, but it was a great host. Because I wondered at such a sight, I slipped among their tents. And the gist of the conversations I overheard between their leader and his lieutenants, my lord, is this: Runnicor in her envy of Orden has laid a plot for her utter and irretrievable overthrow.

"For years they have laid their plans, my lord. They have spared no expense of caution or mercilessness. I was nearly slain by their scouts; if my Runnicoran tongue had not spared me, I doubt any would have warned you before the crisis came. Even their march they plan to chart north of Edivernel and across the Great Waste, so as to avoid all eyes on their approach. And their spies are ever coming and going with word of Orden's military affairs—how many they employ I know not, but some of them correspond with informants in very high positions of state. For this reason, my lord, I was compelled to ask the loyalty of your captain."

He paused and looked pleadingly at the silent face of the general. "You believe me—do you not? I cannot have ridden across Legea to be disregarded. I beg you, my lord, heed me. They were already making sure to depart when I headed east; they cannot be more than ten days from your borders by now. Orden is on the brink of destruction."

The general stood quietly to his feet and held the man's eyes with his own. "There is no lie in your face," he said. And with a movement of swift passion he struck the table with his hand, sending the records fluttering down like a flock of frighted birds.

"My general," said Captain Rhodes softly, his voice trembling like a man touched with sickness. "What are we now to do?"

"What indeed?" murmured the general. He turned to Grant. "No word came to us before, and none surely would have come but for you. Though ten days of preparation be but little, it is more than none. And you surely risked your life to so warn us. What of their spies? Is there any that you have recognized or might recognize among this court?"

Grant shook his head. "Among their own men they are bidden to walk masked or otherwise concealed. There might be some that I could know again by their voices or walk, but it is hard to be certain. Nonetheless I will serve you how I may in that regard."

The general took a pace forward and laid his hand upon the young man's shoulder. "Know that you have my thanks," he said. "You say that you came from Runnicor, and yet you chose to warn us against an army of the same. That is not something done lightly."

Grant looked down in answer. "I was born in Runnicor," he said, "but I have not lived there for near twenty years. I have no country. When I met my father after a time of long separation, he had departed that land himself and was traveling north to Orden, for a life he thought might be better than the one he knew. But I spoke harsh words to him, for he would have called himself my father again, and I wanted to be alone; I did not want to be his son. I left him in anger.

"He never reached Orden. He died on the border of Rodron and I found him and buried him. It is for my father's sake that I came."

The general looked at the young, rugged face, still harsh with a grief that was not yet old. "*Mari*," he said gently, using the old tongue for *son*, "you have done well."

He turned to Captain Rhodes. "Send out a dragon to overtake the king. He must return at once. And make preparations to send another after those who went south towards Arahad—we must call off that costly embassy at once, and pray that they return in time. I need not tell you to use care in the men you select."

Captain Rhodes nodded and whirled around to the door.

"Captain Rhodes. Tell this news to no more than you must. If they can play at stealth, then so can we. They may find us more ready than they expected; and what little advantage we have we must use to the fullest."

He sat down and began to write quickly. "Send Captain Murray to me," he directed Captain Rhodes, and motioned him from the room. "And you, Grant, I will lodge you in Mitheren this night if you have no place as yet to go. Tomorrow I may have a thing to ask of you, if you are willing to undertake it."

"I will undertake whatever you ask, my lord," answered Grant.

The general gave him a smile of thanks.

But when Grant was gone, his pen faltered and slipped from his fingers. He dropped his arms onto the table, and his head sank down on them. Orden, a country proud and beautiful, suddenly cracked within and beset without. His people's confidence in him misplaced—their trust betrayed . . . a cruel darkness coming upon them, and nothing he could do to stop it.

~

The dragon banked steeply in the evening sky, wheeling about as it dove towards the small party which was preparing to set their camp for the night. The rider dismounted the instant his mount settled and headed for the stoop-shouldered figure in the lead.

"My king, King Conrad!"

The king turned his long, worried face towards the comer; always solemn, it appeared pale and sad in the gathering gloom. “What is it?”

The man gave him a folded parchment. “From the general, my lord king.”

A torch was lit and shone upon the letter as the king read it. The color left his face, and he looked at the messenger, whose somber countenance confirmed the letter’s words.

He slipped the papers into his tunic with shaking hand. “Tomorrow we turn about. We are needed in Mitheren.”

~

“Grant Eagle.”

Grant bowed his head and shut the door. The general was evidently waiting for him; a sealed scroll rested in front of him on the table where the sea of papers had been the day before, ring and dark-hued wax beside it. The seated man’s face was grave and composed as yesterday; but a deep sorrow throbbed beneath his eyes. Meeting those dark eyes, an impulse unbidden stirred in Grant—never had he owed a man fealty, but for an instant he felt that this man might ask him to enter the Cleft of Lynnel and he would gladly do it.

The sensation, unfamiliar to him, ebbed an instant later yet did not wholly fade. Such a man must Thireler the Conqueror have been, Grant thought, a man who could command with a word, a look—

“Yestereve the council met,” the general said, rising. “Our situation appears desperate indeed. We have sent a rider to Fearnland in the north, who is our strong ally, but that will take a month or more to reach the king, and twice that time for him to muster his men and return to us. Whether we will even be able to hold out so long I do not know. But we have a nearer place to look for aid, our sister country,

Dirion. She has never yet failed us, nor is the King Ahearn a man to withdraw from others in time of need. He will undoubtedly help in whatever way he can."

"You wish me to go to him?"

"If you are willing. You have done much already; naught compels you to do more."

"I am willing," said Grant simply, but at the compassion in the quiet face he quailed again and burned with that foreign zeal. Too great was the love in this man's eyes, too staggering in its measure, given too freely to one he scarcely knew. Grant could not meet that gaze.

"My lord," he said, his heart aching to burst out and express itself in broken words, "my general—I would serve you in any way you bid."

The general nodded. "So be it." He picked up the scroll from the table and handed it to Grant. "If he doubts you, give him this, but speak first; these matters are more urgent when heard from a man's own lips. How soon can you depart?"

"At once, my lord. I have no need to stay."

"That is well. And now, is there anything more you desire to say before you go?"

"Only a warning which I forgot to relay to you yesterday. In your caution, my lord, take care not only for disloyal men within your circles, but also watch for birds."

The general glanced toward him, eyes narrowed in that intent, questioning way.

"The Runnicoran general employs the *eraris*, the soulless and masterless ones that bear the form of crows. They often bear messages, but they can also overhear words spoken between men who think nothing of a bird perched on the limb above their heads."

The general nodded, his brow clearing in comprehension, though his eyes grew heavier. "I have heard of the *eraris*-kind."

"In either case, it is better to intercept or slay one if you suspect its nature."

"We will surely take heed. Again, Grant Eagle, on behalf of the king and this land, I thank you." He came forward, gripping Grant by the shoulder. "Now, go with speed. Ride to Ederan. Ahearn must be reached."

Words never came easily from Grant's lips, and though he longed to prove himself with them they did not now. There was nothing he could say to give utterance to his new-found servitude. Instead he knelt and departed, his quick pace turning to a run through the dark stone halls, a commission branded behind his eyes.

Dirion—Ahearn—he must be reached . . . he is not a man to withdraw from others . . . he must be reached . . . he must be reached . . .

He saddled his mare with fumbling haste and leaped onto her back, trotting across the courtyard, urging her into a gallop as they left Mitheren behind.

He must be reached.

CHAPTER 2

THE SUN SHONE DOWN ON Orden: on the thick foliage of the East-border Forest, on her glittering lakes still bordered with the last of winter's ice, on the harshly chiseled terrain of her north country, and the lower swells and wide rivers of the south. Beyond the Elerien Mountains, the Western Guard of Orden, its rays had risen high enough to touch the Dirion River, and further still the Great Waste. They beat down hot upon the small figure of a man riding hard south and west.

Towards Dirion.

Grant Eagle pulled his horse in from full gallop, tensing in the saddle. The mare reared and whinnied in protest.

"Whoa, my Lady," Grant murmured. "Whoa . . . "

With a final prance she settled beneath him, and Grant leaned forward, senses on the alert. Just a moment ago, on that rise, he thought he had caught a movement ahead of them. Or had he been mistaken?

Then he heard the hooves, faint but clear enough. Someone else was coming along this road towards them. The slow, rhythmic beat indicated a work horse, maybe pulling a wagon. It was the first sign of humanity he had seen for hours, ever since he had left behind the morning buzz around the city, and despite the harmless indication of a farmer bringing his goods to Orden's market, an uneasy frown creased Grant's brow.

The mare had heard it, too. She shifted sideways, her ears flicking forward, her nostrils flared.

"No worries, Lady," Grant muttered, sending her into a walk. "We need not speak to him, not more than a greeting."

Her ears swiveled back, hearing his voice.

"And what if he asks me questions, you say? Nonsense, Lady. A traveler on the road keeps to himself, and those who wish to keep their skins do not pester the ones that carry swords. I should be surprised if our stranger speaks to me at all."

Lady snorted and strained at the bit.

"Now you wish to run again? Nay, lass, it were best to pass this traveler, whoever it may be, at a walk. We want to do nothing that will attract notice, and all the less when there be fear of spies . . . nay, even then it may be safe enough, but I do not wish to leave any man with questions turning in his head. We'll keep this pace for now."

Lady neighed indignantly.

"Aye, there he comes over the hill, cart and horse. I'll talk to you no more now, my Lady."

Grant held Lady down to a steady trot as they approached the slow-moving wagon, with every intention to ride straight on past—for there was no reason he should stop, nor anyone try to stop him. Perhaps in the true wilderness, where a human face was a chance for valuable tidings, but here, in this narrow no-mans-land between the civilized communities of Orden and Dirion, a grim-faced wanderer was unlikely to carry any news that a busy workman would care to hear. And Grant looked grim-faced indeed as he drew abreast of the placidly walking horse and the wiry farmer striding beside.

To his surprise and annoyance, however, the farmer stepped into his way with a cheerful hail. "Good day, sir! And where might you be bound to this fine morning?"

"South," Grant replied curtly, drawing rein on Lady so that she did not run the man down. The fellow should leave him alone now.

But the farmer scratched at his wide-brimmed cap and did not move. "Any one place, laddie?" He spoke lazily, his words broken into one another.

"What business is it of yours?"

"None, only I like to know sometimes. Got me a curious mind, maybe."

The dangerously impertinent boldness of his manner stirred Grant's unease. He made to nudge his heel into Lady, but the farmer was still half-blocking the way.

"What's that a'peeping out of your pocket there, now?" the other remarked, and Grant followed his gaze to see with alarm the letter the general had given him half-visible with the seal in plain view.

"Riding down to Dirion?" said the farmer, with a sly sort of softness.

Grant reined Lady to the side and attempted to gallop past, but the other man leaped and crashed into him, knocking them both heavily to the ground.

"Thought I recognized you from some place," said the man with no trace of his countrified accent, steel hissing as he whipped out a knife. "That spying little mercenary by the Iron Heights." Divested of the shadow of the cap, his pallid, contorted features bore a passing similarity to Grant's own despite the tawny hair falling around his shoulders. A Runnicoran half-breed.

Grant seized at his wrist, trying to wrench the blade out of his hand. "Maybe you are mistaken," he panted.

The man's grip strained against his. "I think not," he growled. "But 'tis no matter. Whoever you are, you will die now and your message with you." All at once, with his free hand, he jerked a second knife from his boot, and for one terrifying instant Grant saw it catch the light above him. He heard Lady's shrill whinny.

Then he saw her—saw her leg flying forward—and the man lurched forward with a groan at the full impact of a horse's kick. Instantly Grant jerked the knife from his slackened hold, parried a frantic swing from his adversary, and thrust it home.

The man sagged, and slumped to the ground. Grant shoved him aside and rose.

He unharnessed the cart-horse and turned it loose; the dead man he dragged away from the road and laid his weapons by him. Then he turned, mounting Lady, and spurred her down the road once more.

~

The heavy gates of Ederan, capital city of Dirion, were swinging slowly shut as the red sun sank below the horizon. Then a horn blast rang out from the walltop, alerting the soldiers below that there was yet one traveler desiring entrance. The gates ground to a creaking halt, and those whose duty it was to close them waited as the horse and rider drew closer.

A weary horse, its head drooping and trot slow, covered in dust. A dull-eyed rider, rising and falling limply in the saddle. But they both brightened as they neared the high walls of the city.

The rider checked as he was about to pass through and turned to the captain of the guard who stood nearby. A young man, observed the captain. Under the dirt and sweat the face was blunt-featured and even grim, though not unhandsome. The gaze that met his was keen and filled with a burning, intense resolve. The captain cast a glance down the road whence he had come, wondering with a stir of uncertainty what had brought this man here and in such haste.

The traveler seemed to hesitate, as if searching for words. "Is this . . . Ederan?"

"Aye," replied the captain.

The man nodded, a tired half-smile forming on his face. Then he urged his horse on into the city.

~

The bedroom of King Ahearn of Dirion was no greatly magnificent affair. The stone floor was adorned only with a soft braided rug. The furniture displayed good make but little ornament; the tall bed was canopied with velvet draperies, perhaps the most expensive item in the room, but a far cry from the stiff, brocaded, gold-embroidered cloths which old King Hiartho had preferred.

The only light in the chamber this evening issued from the lamp which sat on the writing ledge, shedding its radiance over parts of the room and throwing others into shadow. Nor did it shine without reason; for Ahearn was busy.

The soft gold sheen played over the young monarch's thoughtful features, the level grey eyes and the expressive, thin-lipped mouth that was framed in a clipped dark beard. His slim fingers guided his pen in brief marks, but his attention seemed to wander from the tax records in front of him, and he let his head slip tiredly into his other hand, his gaze drifting elsewhere. Thoughts filled his head—faces, dim at first, growing clearer, faces he longed and dreaded to forget—an arrogant, handsome face, tight with anger, lips closed and eyes as icy as a winter's storm—the heat of his own anger and confusion, the lashing out that had turned into an irreparable gorge—

"What could I have done?" he murmured, unaware that he spoke aloud. "What if I had been gentler . . . "

His voice broke off short as someone rapped on the door. Ahearn lifted his head. "Come in."

The steward of the castle entered, inclining his head respectfully. A delicate note of disapproval tinged his words.

"My king, there is a man waiting below who has ridden hard, these past two days, he says, from where and for what purpose he will not tell. He insists that he must speak with you; the matter is 'terribly urgent'. Moreover, he desires to have with you an audience of total privacy."

Ahearn glanced at his desk. "Can he not wait until morning?"

"It seems he cannot. You would think that a man swaying on his feet from exhaustion—"

"He will not rest first?" This time Ahearn's question was more uneasy than annoyed.

The steward made an expressive sweep of the hand. "He will not so much as seat himself."

The king looked troubled, and rose. "Very well; I will receive him in the throne room."

"King Ahearn," the steward began hastily, "I am not at all sure that this is wise. Such a man, who will not say who has sent him nor why he comes (indeed he says he has proof, but it appears he will show it to none but you), such a man, I say, my king, permit me—seems more likely to be an assassin than . . . "

Now he was hurrying after Ahearn, down the dim hall.

Ahearn sighed. "You may be right. I promise that I will not concede to his demands if it can be helped. But if he is an honest man, no doubt he will have a good reason for keeping his business—whatever it is—from everyone else."

"No doubt!" the other muttered. He paused at the second door from Ahearn's chambers and disappeared inside, coming out shortly with the royal mantle and crown; these he arrayed on Ahearn, and stepped back with a satisfied air.

"There, my king. Go now to the throne room; I will fetch him."

~

Grant Eagle, staring fixedly through sleep-blurred eyes at a high, slitted window, felt a pressure on his arm. The voice of the state-robed man who had met him in the outer court addressed him again, brusque and formal, saying, "King Ahearn will receive you now."

Grant blinked and roused himself, feeling the desire for rest ebb away. He followed the speaker with quick steps through a long corridor and a pair of carved wooden doors, and, keeping to the left, strode resolutely forward to the very feet of the throne where sat the king of Dirion.

King Ahearn spoke. "Who are you?"

"I am Grant Eagle." He glanced back at his guide who stood with arms crossed and two more servants standing at the door behind him. "My lord, I would rather speak to you alone."

The king's expression did not change. "So my steward has told me." He looked sternly at Grant. "Why do you wish it?"

The hostility in his voice bewildered Grant. Had they never need of secret messages? The castle steward in particular had only dogged his footsteps since he entered, and Grant had no wish to share his news with such a pair of clearly eager ears. "Can you guarantee them, my lord king?" The frustration filtered in under his tired voice. "Would you disclose to them all secrets? If you desire another witness here, assure me that he is beyond even the question of reproach. I will not disclose my burden without a surety."

Ahearn sat quietly, seeming to consider. “Trethan,” he said at last, looking at the steward, “bring me Edar and *Hiaro* Cevra.”

The steward nodded curtly and departed, and a strained silence unfolded in his wake. King Ahearn sat with lowered eyes, running his hand slowly over a signet ring on his left forefinger. There was a firmness, even a forcefulness, in his face, despite his gentle and unassuming features. His grey eyes were deep-set and perceptive, set under straight brows and an unlined forehead. He was very young, Grant realized, scarcely more than twenty—and his heart sank a little.

When the doors swung open again, announcing Trethan’s return and shaking Grant from another near-doze, the steward was preceded by two older men clad like high-ranking nobles. One cast a sideways look at Grant, silver hair swishing over the shoulder of his tunic. They positioned themselves on the opposite side of the throne.

Ahearn nodded to Trethan. “You may leave,” he said, and the steward exited with the two guardsmen, their footsteps echoing down the hall.

Ahearn then turned to the older men, whose gazes silently questioned the circumstance of their summoning. “This man arrived here with a message that he wished to deliver at once, in secret. Grant Eagle, I have no doubt of these men. Speak freely.”

Grant surveyed the king’s intent, quiet face and was assured; with a surge of will he squared his shoulders, the general’s words burning again to the forefront of his wearied thoughts. Deliver a message, no, he was here with more than a message. He was here for the distress of a people not his own.

“My lord king, I come to you on behalf of your sister country. The General Derek Winston sent me to beg your aid. Orden is in gravest danger.”

The two nobles' eyebrows shot up in tandem. They exchanged glances and turned doubtful if not suspicious eyes to Grant; but Ahearn stood sharply. "Danger! What danger is this?"

"Runnicor has mustered a great army against her in the Grey Lands," Grant answered, and saw startled comprehension alter the taller noble's countenance. "Even now they are marching to her borders."

Ahearn shook his head, aghast. "Why? What reason?"

A quiet cough from the tall nobleman. "My lord."

"*Hiaro* Cevra?"

"The gold dispute was well before your time—some four generations ago now—but that it should be the cause of a Runnicoran attack is almost beyond doubt. There was strong grudge, and the Runnicorans had the worst of it."

"The gold dispute—I know naught of these things, Cevra. Tell me."

"There is little enough to tell. Orden simply secured sole trading rights to the gold mines of Arahad when they first sealed their treaty, and has held them since. Runnicor, being not only closer to Arahad but a longer ally, took hard to that. They started raiding and pirating Ordenian ships during the early days of our King Hiartho and Derin II of Orden, and there were . . . harsh words that came nearly to war, especially when one of Orden's captains slew a high-ranking Runnicoran noble in the aftermath of one such sea-skirmish."

"They say that the kings made a peace after that," said the second man, Edar. "But a peace made in the wake of a killing is a skittish thing. I marvel it did not turn to war sooner than this, except that they must have known they would stand no chance without careful subterfuge."

"Edar speaks true enough," said Cevra. "Besides, my lord, Orden is a powerful nation, powerful and rich—all know that—and not a few covet such wealth. Little, grasping countries need small quarrel with their betters to pursue their mastery."

Ahearn sat down, hands tight about the arm-rests of his throne. When he spoke again, it was not to the lords but to Grant. "How large is this army, emissary?"

"I know not its full dimensions, my lord, only that it is vast and they have added to it for years. Their leader has called crushing Orden an easy matter."

"Surely he spoke in over-confidence. Orden's army—"

"Nay, King Ahearn, it is smaller than you know—"

Grant broke off, searching for the right speech, more bereft than ever in his fatigue. He reached in his jerkin, drew out the sealed letter, and offered it to Ahearn, who took it silently and examined the seal before breaking it open.

Again as he read it he looked young—alarmed—vulnerable. Grant's heart tightened. Had the general been mistaken? Would Ahearn be afraid and refuse? Would he put the letter aside, to deal with another time, only to have that other time never come?

The king creased the letter closed, gaze lowered. "I must confer with the council," he murmured slowly.

He looked to Cevra. "Have you any estimate of the military strength that we can spare?"

"Avrulin would know that, my lord king."

"Of course. Be sure that he is present tomorrow—we must give whatever aid we can."

They spoke on, but they were distant and immaterial now. Grant cared not of cavalry barracks, or the number of weapons that were permitted into a secret committee. He had fulfilled his charge, he had not failed; no words mattered more than that. Head bowed, he dropped to one knee before the king and thought wearily that he would not ask or wish to move again.

"Please, rise," said Ahearn, in his tone an awkward trace of one unused to the homage of others. "Rest tonight; you shall be refreshed in whatever way you wish. Trethan!" he called, and the steward appeared shortly in the doorway.

Grant stood, relief still slicing through him, and followed Trethan silently to the waiting bed.

~

Dawn was breaking over Ederan. The city hummed with all the early-morning activity: children shouted, mothers scolded, peddlers hawked their wares. But no daylight penetrated the chamber in the heart of the looming castle, where the king, his most trusted advisors, and the emissary from Orden were holding council.

"How much time do we have?" Ahearn asked, turning to Grant Eagle.

Grant shook his head. "Six to eight days is a thought, but we cannot be certain. As I said to the General of Orden, they were preparing to leave when I set out east. If they came across the Great Waste as intended, unless they traveled very slow, they will not be long behind me."

"Then we cannot waste time," said Ahearn. He turned to the tall Cevra. "What is the council's advised selection for the man who leads the relief?"

Cevra folded his arms with a frown, as if perhaps he had expected Ahearn to make a suggestion himself. "It is seemly, my king, for you to go."

"I had thought—but then, the country may need me."

Avrulin, general of the armies answered instead of Cevra. "We are not troubled ourselves. If the Runnicorans turn their attention here, then you should return, but when a sister country is in need, and sister goes to sister, it is right that the kings meet one another as brother to brother."

Ahearn nodded slowly. "The thing reads well. So be it, then; I go over the armies, and leave the country to the charge of *Hiaro* Cevra till my return. How long, Avrulin, before you have ready our force?"

"The summons began yestereve after we received the word. Six hours yet, my lord king."

"Six hours, then we ride." Ahearn's voice gained an edge of firmness, pressing for an answer.

The general bowed his head. "We ride."

~

Shadows lengthened over the empty plains of the Great Waste: shadows of a thousand horsemen, the light glinting off spear and shield and helmet and the ground shaking under the ceaseless impact of the drumming hooves. Not a word was spoken among the whole company; even had they been able to hear one another over the clashing and the thundering, the need for haste was too great, too keenly felt among them.

A little apart from the left wing rode Grant.

Someone had made a passing suggestion of placing him up front with Ahearn and the captains, a suggestion forgotten in those last harried minutes before they departed Ederan. And Grant, to whom it made little difference where he rode, guided Lady to the outside. There the dust and the heat of bodies was less intense, and having found a place which suited him, he was content.

Now a horn-cry was sounding, signaling the time to breathe their mounts. As the noise died away into comparative quiet, and peace washed over them, Lady's ears suddenly flicked sideways. Her head went up, her nostrils widened, her neck tensed.

Grant, her master since she was foaled, needed no conscious effort to read her warning language—something out of place, something new that had been drowned in all the uproar before. "What is it, my lady?" he murmured. "What is it?" He rose up in the stirrups, listening. Almost he thought he heard something.

And it might be—

Grant leaped from Lady's back and lay full length on the rocky ground, his ear pressed against it. When he stood, his face was pale. He mounted Lady again and kicked his heels into her, galloping up to the head of the company.

Those nearby King Ahearn watched as the Ordenian messenger exchanged hurried words with him. Their king shook his head decidedly, giving a reply which seemed to not please the other man. He spoke again, earnestly, fiercely.

Ahearn hesitated still, and finally he shrugged in consent.

The captains turned to each other and also shrugged in bewilderment.

But Grant Eagle reined Lady and sent her into a light canter westward into the wilderness.

He could hear it unaided now, an indistinct rumble in the air, growing louder with every passing minute. It could have been a band of feral horses, if they had been in the steppes of Runnicor.

It could have been a flood, if it were coming from the east where the Dirion River lay and not the emptiness of the waste.

The ground was changing under him, a subtle but telling slope, and he knew that he was on one of the broken hills of the Great Waste: a slow, slow rise ending in a drop-off and a sheer cliff. Not far beyond it, he guessed, lay the source of what he followed.

Grant reined in, for he dared ride no further up the incline, not knowing whether he might be seen. His quick gaze scanned the brown wasteland and caught sight of a stony outcrop a little to the northwest. If he headed for that on foot, he could remain unnoticed, and assure himself for certain what roared so close at hand, though his suspicion already knew and dreaded it.

He swung off Lady and turned to look into one limpid eye, repeating words for her sensitive ears alone. "Stay here."

She shook her head with a whiffling snort, those brown eyes studying him contentedly.

Grant smiled, patted her side, and turned away to continue on foot.

By the time he dropped to a crawl, the noise was tremendous, louder than all the hoofbeats of Ahearn's men had been before. Its blurred growl had expanded into separate sounds: the quick staccato of trotting horses, the creak of wheels, the steady pulse of marching feet. Grant, who knew quite well what it had to be, yet found himself driven by something beyond common sense to prove it with his eyes, reached the rocks and slipped between them to the very edge of the drop.

And under its shadow, he saw the army.

They marched fifty abreast, the shining-helmeted river of men, in steady, clean movements, hazing darkly into the dun colors of the land at their tail end, their head already out of sight. He had seen them in camp, but he had not seen them on the move like this—a single magnificent thing with a breath all its own, their own breath and humanity lost under the crushing noise and ferocity and grace. A column of horsemen flanked the infantry on either side, troops of enlisted men, standard bearers, and officers set apart by their dress and harness. In the wind of their passing, the white-on-red banners eddied and writhed.

Grant watched it all for a moment, unwilling eyes riveted by the sight, and suddenly, out of the urgency, he knew fear.

Fear for himself; for the men from Dirion; for the grieving man who had called him son not three days ago, and for the country he loved.

Then the driving urgency returned, swallowing up the sliver of fear, and he tore his eyes from the gleaming river, and turned and ran to Lady. On her back he jumped, and rode, for now there was no time . . .

~

The soldiers had begun to whisper. Why did they not move on? What was afoot?

Several of them had heard the low rumbling like thunder coming from the west, and guessed or suspected the truth. Many of the horses heard it and snorted, tossing their manes and stamping restlessly.

Ahearn, too, heard it, and had little doubt as to what it was. Anxiously he scanned the horizon for Grant. Why did he not return? What kept him? Had he been seen—slain?

They could not wait for long.

But at last he saw the returning rider, hurtling over the ground at a frantic pace; and he knew that the tidings were not good.

Grant reined in before him, gasping out, "We must ride with all speed. They are many, my lord—so many—but they cannot overtake us, with their foot soldiers—only we must ride, now . . . "

Without delay Ahearn spurred his mount forward. The horn rang out, and the cavalry sprang forth as one. On they sped, over the darkening plain.

CHAPTER 3

"'TIS SPRING," MURMURED THE SMALL young woman whose long braid was reddish-blonde, and whose gaze swept slowly over the glorious vista of Mount Thiranu's greening slopes below.

"Aye," agreed the tall, dark-haired man beside her.

Laufeia Kenhelm brushed a wisp of wayward hair back from her face, and glanced up at her brother. His face was quiet, the look in his eyes closed.

"Mordred," she said, struggling not to let the desperation show in her voice, "your mind is not on spring."

He looked down at her in turn with a wry, teasing smile. "Is it not?" he said easily. "What a pity for vivacious sisters."

If she closed her eyes, she could almost think it was the same Mordred. Perhaps it *was* the same Mordred . . .

She looked at him again, and the sober, closed look was back.

When would she have her brother again?

~

"So the work on the castle is finished, but the Earles and Staffords both are willing to hire men during the time between now and the harvest."

Fred nodded. "That is well. After the horse sale, then, you and I shall take turns in clearing and planting our own land, and working for either Mr. Earle, as you say, or Edric Stafford."

Daren returned his brother's smile, but after a moment it faded and he faced him fully, laying one hand on Fred's shoulder. "Fred . . . it is not too soon to say again that I am glad that you are with us. When one remembers the weeks of long worry—even after weeks of reunion—it is good to have you here."

"Aye, Daren."

No more words were needed between them to express their thoughts to one another, and silently they walked up the path to the house.

Inside, Sandy was poking up the fire, whistling between her teeth. Her long, fair braid was dangling over her shoulder, and her cheeks were flushed with the heat. Isabelle was at the window, her mouth puckered in a whistle as she endeavored to coax a cautious chickadee to the dusting of crumbs in her outstretched hand. Cecelia was mending a shirt, her eyes grave and the graceful fingers moving in and out with a pensive slowness. Gwenda was on her knees with a small dog.

"Look, Fred!" she exclaimed as they came in. "Filian came by just a short while ago. The blacksmith's dog has had her pups, he said, six of them, and he brought this one for us. Is she not beautiful?"

"She is that," Fred agreed and bent to ruffle the small pricked ears.

"See how large her feet are! But Filian says they will even out when she grows bigger. Hold her, Fred. She is softer than down feathers!"

Daren laughed quietly. "You will find her teeth are not so soft if you hold your finger by her mouth much longer, Gwenda."

Gwenda laughed back and withdrew her hand. "What shall we call her, Fred?"

Fred stroked her hair with a smile. "Let us ask Daren. He has named more creatures than I."

Daren shook his head at them. "Now he must be teasing you, Gwenda. I have named a horse or two, but never a dog. But we had a dog with us in Dirion for about a year. Her name was Shep, because she was a shepherd dog breed and had done her share of flock management. This little girl is of the same strain, it looks, and while Shep is neither long nor fancy, it will do for everyday life. We'll call her Shep."

"Isn't Shep no more than 'sheep' gone wrong?" asked Gwenda quite solemnly, with dancing eyes. "Shouldn't we call her Sheep?"

Daren shrugged in feigned frustration. "Oh, call her what you like."

Isabelle turned around. "Call the dog Sheep? I never heard of anything so outlandish!"

Fred's lips twitched in his invisible smile and he motioned to his little sister. "Ask Gwenda."

~

They were having their private jokes at her again. Isabelle shrugged good-humoredly and turned back to the window.

Sandy joined her shortly, having got the dumplings bubbling at their proper rate again. "Is it a new one?"

"Yes, a new one," answered Isabelle, and screwed up her face in dismay as the small bird fluttered away to a higher branch of the ash tree. "Oh, I may as well give up. It won't come. Oh!"

For the chickadee, with a sudden, swooping movement, had dived back to Isabelle's hand and perched for the barest of seconds, as with a swift peck it salvaged a pittance of the crumbs. Then it was gone.

Isabelle dusted her hand off and leaned her elbows on the sill, and the two of them watched the bird's flight till it darted under the fringes of the wood and out of sight.

"Do you suppose," said Isabelle in a conspiratorial undertone, "that Cecelia is . . . pining?"

"What?"

"*I* think she's pining."

Sandy folded her arms and stared down her nose at Isabelle, which came off rather well, as she was nearly three inches taller. "For what on earth? For Dirion?"

"For a man, you goose. And keep your voice down." Isabelle peered back at Cecelia's dutifully sewing figure.

She might as well have said a flock of thindran were flying overhead. Sandy blinked once, opened her mouth, and shut it. "Cecelia's *fifteen*."

"Fiddle! She's more a woman than most girls of twenty, and don't think I haven't seen the signs. I'm going to talk to Fred about it, one of these days."

"If you know," said Sandy, "Fred's probably known for twice as long."

Isabelle's own mouth fell agape, but even she could not argue with that.

~

Cecelia was in love; but she was not minding much about it. It was not so different from the days when she had watched and admired Jared before he went to Delgrass, admiring him for his steadiness, his rare, succinct contributions to a conversation, and his quiet reliability. Now he was older, deeper, his boyhood vanished under the confidence of a man grown, and she was conscious of her admiration in a deeper way herself; it had become something warm and full and longing; but that was all. And she was prepared to wait quite a long time, if need be, for when Jared had been broached on the matter, first by her and then by Fred, he had asked to wait. Cecelia was his almost-girl, and someday it might come to more, and for now that was enough.

At the moment, she was thinking more of her youngest sister and a set of knitting needles.

"Gwenda," she said as she stood up, turning the mended shirt right side out and folding it on the table for Fred. "Have you finished that scarf you wished to make for Marjorie?"

Gwenda leapt up from the puppy's side, face bright. "I have, Cecelia."

"Then you should take it to her. Come, fetch it, and I will walk with you to town."

The sunshine was cool, fierce, and whole against them, and the earth unwinding with new things. Gwenda carried the new scarf very carefully, a fat, folded bundle in her small hands. She broke into chattering now and again, about the dog, or the old, woody vine winding its cords across the tree-trunk, or about how glad she would be to see Marjorie; and Cecelia nodded and responded gravely, and contented silence fell again. No observation was too small to spare an answer for; for though Gwenda spoke her observations more often than did Cecelia, they were wise and thoughtful and Cecelia was determined that her younger sister should be treated with the respect she herself had wished for as a child, and not tut-tutted or gushed over every time she opened her mouth.

They passed out of the empty, half-wild countryside and into the town. Lucas Boccin's figure, working busily around the half-raised supports of a new partition on his northwest wall, raised a hand in greeting to them, and Marianne Denholm called a hello from the other side of the street.

Further down the road, Marcus Segelas bounded up under the shadow of the eaves by the blacksmith's shop. He dropped a knock on the small, crudely paneled door and stepped inside. Evidently, they were not Marjorie's only visitors today.

~

Marcus was not in love.

It was that, he was reasonably convinced, that made it so awkward to stand in the same room as a couple who were definitely in love.

Marjorie Delaney leaned up, planting a kiss on her husband's cheek as he shouldered his bag of blacksmith's tools. "Good-bye, Charles."

"I shall see you at noon, my dear." Charles plucked a wisp free of Marjorie's dark bun and let it dangle by her cheek as he went to the door.

"Now," said Marjorie, turning to Marcus and tucking back the stray lock, "what is it you needed, Marcus?"

Marcus glanced around the white, clean walls, and the four-legged table with a posy of very early grass and snowdrops resting in a flask at its center. He ought to ask where she had found the snowdrops; Peony would like to know. "The ladies of the house wish to inquire if there are special wedding traditions in the Thorne family that ought to be observed by one marrying into them."

Fiona and Fred, now—they were an entertaining pair to watch, what with Fiona's blushes and Fred's occasional forehead kisses and their grave self-consciousness towards their mutual affection. Marjorie and Charles were disconcertingly . . . matter-of-fact about it all.

"Oh!" Marjorie laughed at his inquiry after traditions, seeming startled. "I think not. At least none I know of! Is that really all you came for, Marcus?"

"Rather, ma'am." He swept her a low bow. "I think that Peony wanted me out of her kitchen for a while."

She laughed again, sympathetically, and packed him off with half a bread-roll. A sweet sort of person to have for a sister, he reflected as he made his escape, though the thought that she would soon be his sister was more disconcerting still.

He was turning into the yard when he realized he had forgotten to ask about the snowdrops. "Well!" he murmured, with a philosophical shrug.

The windows were wide open, and he could hear Peony humming from the house. A flash of bright hair moved further back in the trees, telling him Fiona's whereabouts. Someone was with her, a shorter, half-glimpsed figure. Laufeia must have come to visit.

Marcus sauntered into the house, whistling.

~

"Are things well with you?"

Behind the two girls was the Segelas cottage; before them the ground dropped steeply away and leveled out into ground where a field might be visioned.

Laufeia twitched a strand of hair away from her face and let the wind blow it back. "Are they well? I suppose so. I feel settled in my own home again; we are surrounded by a happy village. How is your own family?"

"We are well." Fiona shook her head gravely, dismissing it. "Laufeia, the village may be happy, but you do not sound happy. And I think you have not been happy for some time."

"Have I?" Laufeia hesitated, surprised. "Oh—maybe I have not. If so, it is because Mordred is not happy either."

"Mordred," Fiona repeated, her dark eyes sober, half-guessing Laufeia's meaning.

"Not in the way he was before the—the Delgrass business. Maybe no one else has seen it, but he is my brother, and oh, Fiona, I can see it all too well." She broke off, and started again.

"It has hurt him very deeply, Fiona. Maybe deeper than he realizes. He never talks about it; I fear to mention it—and he acts almost as he used to. More gentle even, especially to Fenris. But there is something missing, some part of him is dead, as it were. He never laughs, Fiona. Never."

Fiona put a hand on her. "Time may mend it, Laufeia. Do not worry too much about it now."

Laufeia managed a wan smile. "Fred has no such trouble, I hope?"

Fiona shook her head again. "I see nothing in him save joy and contentment. And the Thorne family has spoken of no concerns to me."

Laufeia put a hand to her cheek, feeling the heat of her own worry. The wind rushed past her, fresh and heavy, swaying her braid and skirts.

Fiona's hand stirred on hers. "Laufeia, I do not know if there is any easy way to help, but this I can do. I shall ask Fred to speak with Mordred some time soon. Perhaps after the horse sale, and all this flurry around it, is over. Fred, too, suffered, but he seems to have found peace. Maybe he can show Mordred a path to healing."

Laufeia was silent, her mind flying back to the long voyage up the Dirion River. Mordred and Fred had had ample chance to speak then, if they had wanted, but they had scarcely seemed to notice one another's presence. Would Mordred really consent to share his troubles with the other man?

But it could hardly do harm, and Fred, too, had suffered; and if she feared to speak to Mordred, perhaps someone must. "Aye. After the horse sale."

CHAPTER 4

THE BLACK STONE OF MITHEREN gleamed dully under a sky filled with gloom, and the wind blew back the dark hair of the man who stood on the high parapet of her tower.

The general leaned against the breastwork, his hand on the hard stone, faint rumbles murmuring from the dragon run directly below him. His face was sad and anxious, and his gaze roved ever westward as though seeking to pierce the mountains and see the Great Waste and an army spread over its brown plains. And he fancied that he might see a second army as well, headed by a young king quiet of face and grey of eye . . . but that one lay still in hope and not reality.

Another figure came up out of the dimness of the dragon run behind him and paced softly till he stood a few feet behind the general. "My general," he said soberly after a moment.

The general turned to face Captain Rhodes. "There is no word from Dirion yet?"

"None," answered Captain Rhodes; and after a moment he stepped up beside the general and narrowed his eyes into the wind, looking toward the Elerien Mountains, the Western Guard. And they stood there silent, waiting.

But not from the west was the news when it came.

~

"My general!"

Captain Rhodes came running up the double row of steps as the general turned to meet him. Captain Murray strode behind him, his eyes grim and lips set.

"My general," gasped Captain Rhodes, halting to catch his breath. "There are tidings of the messenger sent to the Arahadian embassy—"

"The dragon was shot down before it reached the southern border," Captain Murray said, voice hard. "They found its body and the rider's slain two leagues south of Dracan, between the lake's border and the mountains, but the message was not on his body."

"They must have guessed its aim, or were told; but the damage is done." Captain Rhodes lowered his eyes and winced as though in pain. "They are watching in the south. Do we send another dragon?"

"Send messengers on foot." The general placed a hand on the younger man's shoulder. "Even if those are caught, word may reach them nonetheless."

"And when?" Captain Murray's voice cut harder than before. "Word passes slow outside our own borders. They are already ten days gone, and moving ever further beyond the current of rumors. We dare not presume on their return."

The general hesitated a moment and dropped his head in a slight, final nod. "May Ahearn come," he murmured. "Else, we truly are alone."

~

Inspector Dickson knelt and kissed the flabby hand outstretched to him. "My lord king," he murmured, withdrawing a respectful distance. He had never met his monarch, who was little more than a figurehead in the severely equalized system of Delgrass' government. Officially, the man held power to gainsay any law or decision passed by his cabinet, but for the most part he lived in luxury and ignored them.

"Wilhelm Dickson, Inspector of the Peace," the king intoned. "You are late in answering my summons."

"I assure you, my lord king, I came as quickly as I could."

"Stop!" The king flung up his hand, jewels winking in the light. "I will not have my subjects contradict me. I understand you supervise one of the two riverside precincts?"

"Yes; the norther—"

"Stop! I don't want to know which one; I don't care which one, do you understand?"

"Yes, my lord king," replied Inspector Dickson between his teeth. He wondered for the thousandth time why he had been summoned, and when he would be told the reason.

"Now," resumed the king, "in this precinct of yours, I have heard, there was an incident involving a . . . werevulture. Interesting, really. I thought they were extinct." He paused, perhaps for appreciation of his wit, but his intractable subject could not force a laugh. "H-em! And we were rid of this werevulture by the timely intervention of Orden's general himself."

"He slew the creature, sire, if that is what you mean."

"Excellent!" The king's hands splatted together in a burst of applause. "Excellent!" he crowed again. "And you, as my loyal vassal, will deliver to him this letter of appreciation which I have written. Think of it! The connection to Orden! Invitations, gifts, prestige!"

Of all the things Inspector Dickson did not want to be, the bearer of a missive saturated with all manner of flattery and servility was presently heading the list. "Your Majesty," he protested. "Surely there must be many more qualified than I to—"

"Silence! Do you question the mandate of your king? Do you scorn his generosity?"

Inspector Dickson, who could not truthfully answer no to either of these questions, kept silent.

"Now you will go, will you not?" The smile beamed down on him, benevolent, pale, and repulsive as a rot-wood grub.

"I will go, Your Majesty."

~

East of Orden City about twenty leagues, where the Kathira Mountains began, was Mivena, a crowning ornament to the beauty of the peaks above. Tower of Light, the Thiredanians had named her, for in the sun she stood a white and slender pinnacle underlaid with gold and touched with star-fire, and even in the night, she gleamed as snow does after dark. But perhaps another meaning was veiled in the name; of old she was made a watchtower for the men of Orden, and he who stood in her topmost chamber could see far.

In these days, a city had sprung up about the tower, and over it was a governor. This day, on the evening of the sixteenth of April, the governor stood in a darkened chamber high in Mivena, gazing out into the star-spattered night. His face was thin, the forehead high and pale, the nose hooked and a little large; black hair, streaked with grey, was combed straight back and fell to his shoulders, which made it appear that he was balding—as indeed he was. Still as a statue he stood; his right fist was clenched, and he was looking west with a peculiar hate in his hooded black eyes.

Almost noiselessly the door opened. The governor heard it, but he did not stir. "Word from him at last?" he asked tonelessly.

"Aye, my lord Mirden."

"Send the messenger in."

"Aye, my lord Mirden." The servant stepped aside, and a large crow fluttered into the room, like an oversized, ungainly moth that had found its way inside.

"My lord sends his compliments to Lord Mirden," she shrilled in accents of the most high-pitched order, all sound and no breath, and which left the ears ringing.

Mirden wheeled. "How many times have I told him not to send me the females!" he exclaimed thunderously. "They are obnoxious and thoroughly detestable, and they weary my ears with their endless prattling!"

"Apologies, O my most excellent—"

"Oh, have done, old crone, and give the message!"

She extended one claw, around which was looped the ties of a parchment roll, and Mirden seized this impatiently and scanned its lines. His nostrils flared with suppressed excitement—his eyes brightened; he crumpled the parchment in his fist and dropped it carelessly to the ground. "So soon!" he murmured. "So be it then; we will march upon Adun Cerien. He must be close—four days from the border, maybe?"

"Two by now, Lord Mirden, most illustrious—"

"Can you not keep silent! Leave at once!"

Alone again, Mirden stared out at the stars. A smile like a snarl curled his lip. "Truly, our triumph is near . . . "

~

Inspector Dickson stood in the antechamber, tapping his fingers against the hated roll of parchment. King Conrad might be busy, the servant had said. How long would the interview be put off?

It was vexing enough, having to wait after he had steeled himself to get the thing over with, but mingling with the impatience was a deeper discomfort, one that had begun the moment he stepped into Mitheren's gate. He did not like the somber, quiet halls, the stiffness of the guards at the gate, the uneasy sadness in the manservant's eyes and manner. Even now the gloom seemed to drip off the very walls over his head.

Inspector Dickson was tired of politics, of palaces, and of waiting in general.

He looked up with relief as the door reopened into his gnawing thoughts. "The general, sir," said the servant, bowing, and stepped aside.

Anyone but the general. Visions of laying down his missive, and dashing out the door before the man he so highly respected could recognize him and associate him with its contents, danced through Inspector Dickson's head. He held out the roll wordlessly.

The general approached with his light, steady step. "Inspector Wilhelm Dickson!" he exclaimed, seeming taken aback. "What is this?"

"I—" stammered Inspector Dickson, bemused at such a reception. "I bring a dispatch from my king, sir; that is all."

"You should not have come," murmured the general, taking the message. "The king is in council at the moment, I fear; I will see to this." His dark eyes softened with a deep sorrow. "Ah, you should not have come."

"Why?" demanded Inspector Dickson, struck with fear. "Why?"

The general strode across to the window covered with a heavy curtain, reached up, and tore the draperies aside. "Why do they cover the windows?" he muttered. "This is no house of mourning yet."

He turned again to Inspector Dickson. "The Runnicoran army marches upon Orden, and even now closes about her borders."

“An army!” echoed Inspector Dickson in astonishment. “How is it possible? We have heard no rumors at all.”

The general shook his head. “There was little reason for anyone to suspect. It has been long since any outward strife existed between us, and they have gone far to ensure secrecy—for they are a small country, though their military is strong and valiant. We ourselves almost did not hear of it at all.”

“So I cannot go back,” said Inspector Dickson, grasping at last the main point of the general’s words. “But, sir, I arrived yesterday in safety enough.”

“That was yesterday,” answered the general sternly. “Even now, it would be a risk; by the time we have a fitting response for your dispatch, I fear it will be too late. You ought to know how jealously the safety of an ambassador is guarded, for your king can hold us responsible for any harm that befalls you between your going and returning. Only when we can find a sure and safe way to transport you from our borders would I or any of the council let you depart.”

Inspector Dickson nodded. Half his mind was still in protest that such a bother should be made over him—the other giving in, realizing with touch of wryness and selfish relief that this was, in a way, an unsought reprieve from the task he so despised. “In the city,” he muttered, another thought shooting out to perplex him. “Even in the city, no one spoke of it to me. No one mentioned war.”

“It has not been disseminated to the people as yet, and indeed we have not known long ourselves either; the secret has been kept in Mitheren but four days. But they must know, aye, and soon. I ride out tomorrow to Orden City and the surrounding lands to tell them.”

His face was unlined, his hair dark and thick; yet as he spoke he seemed old with grief.

Such a man, thought Inspector Dickson in wonder. He had felt, from the moment he first saw the general, the man's magnetism, the stern pull of awe. Yet only now, as he saw him bowing under failure, did he feel that he truly saw the man. In that transparent grief, in those unshed, weighty tears, was greatness.

The general roused himself. "We must arrange your quarters," he said. "I shall call a man to see to your room."

~

It was a very red sunset that fell over Orden that night, shadows velvet thick perforated by glowing, incandescent rods of crimson. The guards at the West Gate of Orden stood at their posts and watched in silence. It was shut, the gate, and no men waited at its base as was customary, but only patrolled along the top, grimly watchful.

Captain Rhodes, hurrying with a lighted torch in hand down one of the towers' circling stairs, was accosted by one of his men. "My captain—"

"What, Dares?" He marked the man's pale, agitated face and urgent manner.

Dares beckoned him swiftly and led the way out onto the open wall with the twilight breeze brushing their faces. He gestured to the open plain. "Listen, my captain—listen—"

A faint growling, like thunder but incessant, swept up from the brownness of the Great Waste.

Captain Rhodes in one swift stride came up to the parapet and leaned out over it, his eyes straining into the gloom as the sound grew nearer. A dark mass slowly solidified on the dimming horizon and gained in bulk; and the captain turned to hold the tense, fearful eyes turned on him, knowing that there was no more confidence or courage in his than theirs.

They waited for his command.

"Weapons to hand," he said tersely and turned about to stare again through the gathering night.

A horn rang out, and the vast clamor came to a slithering halt, the fore horsemen drawing rein close before the gate. Again it sounded, a question.

Captain Rhodes caught his breath.

"Do we reply, my captain?"

Above them, in the pinnacle, two sharp trumpet notes challenged the horn call. Captain Rhodes bent down, thrusting the torch vainly at the shadows below. "Who seeks entrance at the West Gate?"

Lights sprang out below them in response, and in their flickers a white face-blur upturned. "King Ahearn of Dirion and Grant Eagle emissary from Orden, with one thousand horse behind us to the aid of she our sister country." And the fire gleamed on the slender, dark-haired man who spoke and the gold upon his brow.

Captain Rhodes whirled about, snapping his fingers for two men to follow, and sped down to open the gate. "My lord," he said gladly, bending head and knee to Ahearn in his gratitude. "It is good to see you here."

Ahearn swiftly dismounted and raised him up. "As it is good to be here," he said, embracing Captain Rhodes. And there were tears in the eyes of Captain Rhodes, though few saw it, and none who did counted it a shameful thing.

CHAPTER 5

SPRING'S SCENT HUNG COLD AND clean in the dawn air as the Thornes left their house and headed north. Mist melted slowly among the pines at the fiery touch of the sun.

There was already a gathering of people in the square by the time they reached the town. Strangers were herding their animals into rude corrals, leading them past prospective buyers, while peddlers of all sorts moved through the sparse crowd with their wares on tantalizing display.

"So this is a horse sale," said Sandy, her eyes bright with interest. "How fun." She sped off towards the pottery table.

Fred exchanged a look with Daren. "What to do now?"

Daren raised his eyebrows. "Look around, I suppose. If we can find a horse at a fair price, that will be of great help in ploughing. A cow however would likely be cheaper, and just as much worth. What we find, we find."

Fred laughed slightly in assent and moved aside, searching the pens of horses.

~

"What do you think, Mr. Earle?" Mordred lifted his voice to the older man nearby and ran a hand down the neck of the horse, stroking its muzzle and lifting the lips away from its teeth. It was a strong, young stallion: fourteen hands and greyish in color, with well-muscled neck and hind-quarters and a compact build bordering on stocky, but a delicately formed head and large, sensitive nostrils.

"A sturdy animal," was Mr. Earle's comment as he approached. "About four years old?"

Mordred nodded.

Mr. Earle gave the lead rope a light tug and the animal shook its head doubtfully, planting its forefeet before giving in and stepping forward.

"He will need a firm hand," Mr. Earle said, stooping to lift its hooves one by one. "He's sound though," he continued, straightening, "and healthy; he'll serve whatever purpose you need. Aye, he would be worth your money in the end. You've a good hand with horses, lad," he added, his steady eyes scrutinizing the easy, rhythmic way that Mordred was stroking the horse's neck and withers to quiet its restive movements. "Accustomed to them?"

Mordred met his gaze and shrugged. "Not much, sir; but thank you."

Mr. Earle went his way, and Mordred turned to the horse's owner to ask about the price.

Laufeia watched her brother as he spoke, the relaxed set of his shoulders and his animated face. He seemed to have forgotten himself for the moment, forgotten his pain, and she felt her heart lift a little. In time, yes—Fiona was right. In time he would mend.

" . . . He's a fine animal," said the scruffy, spindly man whom Mordred was questioning. "He's naught to sniff at, and that we will take into account with the price."

"He will do well for what I want," agreed Mordred, "or I would not have chosen him, but he's not a palace horse. And as for sniffing, I'll sneeze in a moment with the dust rising off his coat. I think it's grey, but at the moment it's nearer brown."

The man guffawed cheerfully in acknowledgment of the remark. "Well, looks isn't everything, you'll recall. I price him at twenty thira."

"*Twenty* thira?" repeated Mordred. "A fancier way of saying, 'more than a recenna'? I haven't a king's purse. I'll give you three."

Losing interest, Laufeia drifted away toward a rickety wooden stand arrayed with cloth dyes to let Mordred finish alone. At least, she thought, he was enjoying himself.

"Are they not lovely?" said Fiona's voice across the table, and she lifted up one of the glass flasks so that its deep red contents caught the light of the sun. A wistful appreciation glimmered in her eyes. "I could hardly bear to use it, it is so beautiful in the light like this—like a jewel."

"I like this one." Laufeia touched a pale, new green like unfolding birch leaves. "It makes me think of a dress I had when I was a very little girl, before the orphanage. The tavern keeper's daughter had worn it, but she died and her mother gave it to mine. I remember feeling that she loved me when she put it on . . . " She hesitated, and let the sentence fall. "So you prefer the red?"

"I have always loved the deep colors," said Fiona, her hand lighting over a vivid cobalt, a glowing amber, and a warm violet in quick succession. "But red is the one that draws me most, and Peony always said that crimson becomes me best of anything." She laughed lightly. "I have not worn a crimson kirtle for three years now. Maybe sometime . . . sometime soon."

They stood in silence, looking over the manifold hues. Shortly they were joined by the owner of the merchandise, who took quick note of their interest and plied his wares on them with skill. But Laufeia, much as she would have liked to, felt that she could not in good conscience purchase something so needless for herself without Mordred's approval. Fiona must have thought the same; neither of them yielded to the man's persuasions, but walked away at last and wandered down by the lakeshore.

~

The sun of high noon was beating down, turning the lake's surface into a blazing glory. They took the food that Isabelle had prepared and sat down to eat beside the flicking waves. Daren's purchase, a shaggy roan cow with beautiful, limpid dark eyes, stood picketed beside them and nosed out the new blades among last year's dead grass.

Fred sat with his hands clasped over his knee, feeling the brisk wind coming in over the water. His gaze traveled from the white huffs of cloud to the cool sapphire lake, the mist of leafing trees around it and the grazing cow nearby.

Never had he felt such contentment. Never had the world seemed so full of promise, so glad and fair. And when he heard the step behind him and turned to see his lady with the sun on her hair and light in her eyes, it was fairer still.

He stood and took her hands gently. The steady radiance in her face set a quick yearning in his heart. "My love," he whispered.

They were silent a moment, while the sunlight shone down.

"I asked you if you would marry me when the trees of spring budded, my lady Fiona. Will you be my wife tomorrow?"

Her hands were warm in his. She met his gaze steadily. "I will be your wife."

"That is well," he said, and drew her into his arms. "This is not the time for waiting any longer."

She rested her head lightly on his chest, and moved with the passion that did not come quickly to him he kissed her hair, then her brow, and held her close.

~

"How much there is to do at the horse sale!" sighed Linda Boccin, lying flat on the prickling grass and staring up at the hazy color of the late afternoon sky. "Why, we have ogled cloth and dyes and pottery and trinkets, and eaten lunch, and splashed one another in the lake—"

"I did not ask for that," Lia Earle cut in, shivering dramatically. "Linda, that water was freezing!"

"—found a toad in the reeds—"

"So disgusting!" Lia cried.

"—bought chickens, chased them over the whole village green, caught them again, watched our fathers haggle to *no end* over livestock and livestock and more livestock . . . "

She paused and looked at the third figure of their group, who was lying with her cheek propped on one hand and her green eyes staring dreamily into space. "Marianne!"

No answer was forthcoming. Linda pulled up a handful of grass and threw it at Marianne's prone figure.

Marianne Denholm tossed the sprigs back at Linda. "What are you after?"

"Naught." Linda giggled. "Just wanting your attention. That is harder to get these days than a splinter out of a horse's hock."

"Oh . . . " Marianne looked off dreamily again, and transferred her attention to Linda. "I suppose I was thinking of something else. You see . . . Linda . . . I shall be having a baby."

"Oh!" Linda gasped, suitably astonished and ecstatic. "Marianne, that's wonderful! When?" Her gaze traveled hopefully to Marianne's unremarkable waist.

Marianne giggled in her turn. "Some time yet, Linda! October or November, I think. I told Kenneth this morning."

"What is going on here?" asked a curious but hesitant voice, interrupting their laughter and babble. They looked up, surprised, to see Laufeia Kenhelm with her long braid swinging over one shoulder and her clear-cut features highlighted in the afternoon sun.

"Marianne's going to have a baby," answered Lia brightly, and at Laufeia's appreciative—"Oh!"—they were suddenly all part of a tight-knit circle that enfolded and laughed, and was much bigger than the quick, happy embrace they shared together.

~

Setting rays of sun were shooting out over the reddened lake waters, and a warmly bluish twilight gathered in the east as the last few tradesmen packed away their goods and herded their animals down the beaten road, leaving the villagers to linger behind and savor the last moments of a full day.

"So this was a horse sale," said Laufeia, combing her fingers through the tangled dark mane of the fiery little stallion that Mordred had named Smoke; and those tired words summed up all the mad whirl of events in one.

"It was a good day," said Mordred surprisingly, his face lit by the dying red sun and his eyes looking clear and unafraid. He rested one arm on Smoke's neck and lightly caressed his muzzle, and his other hand found Laufeia's and closed over it.

There was a dark thing winging past the sun, a heavy beating overhead like giant bats. Mordred let Laufeia's hand slip away and leaned forward, his eyes narrowing in confusion as the thing alighted and the dispersing people came curiously back.

The dragon shook its head, seeming to set itself proudly above the lesser beasts around it, and the general dismounted from its back.

His shoulders were bent, as one carrying a great weight. As one after another recognized him, exclamations of surprise murmured among them. But he lifted his hand, commanding their silence, and stood looking upon them with love, love great and tender, as though he would encompass the whole of Orden in that gaze.

"My people," he said and was silent a moment. He drew a breath; his gaze moved over them again, slowly, marking out individual faces in the small, waiting crowd. "We are under attack."

~

Mordred felt the coldness of the words settle over him, while the heat of alarm pounded in his bones. He saw in searing flashes death, and blood, and burning, swords and spears, while the lake water lapped quietly on the shore and he was acutely aware of all the still evening about him.

In the next instant another thought veered his mind aside, and he thought that surely he had been too swift. He repeated the general's words to himself, tore them apart one by one.

We are under attack—under attack—

Who were *we?* Where was the attack, and from whom? He must have been too hasty, his assumption unfounded. Could not his instinct be mistaken? Surely the flash of seeing had been a lie?

What do you mean? he thought silently. *Speak plainer. Tell me I have erred.*

All this happened in the space of a few fleeting seconds, which seemed an age of agony. The general's voice fell like a tolling bell upon the lake's shore.

"Encamped before the West Gate this very night lies an army greater than has ever faced Orden's borders at one time. To you this is a sudden word, to your king and leaders scarcely less so, and yet already they have loosed their first arrows on our watchtowers; the conflict is begun. This is war, a dark and evil war."

Dark—dark—the word whispered like a chant of hopelessness. A cold stillness reigned, and then the general's voice rang out again, sharp and clear like a hammer onto the anvil, though filled with sorrow.

"Know that we are not yet without strength. They have found our borders guarded and prepared, and yestereve we welcomed our sister-country's warriors within our gates. Yet outnumbered we remain, yea, outnumbered to odds that make a hardened soldier quail. My people, I do not wish to ask this of you. No man should wish it. You do not know war; you may have never touched a sword. Spring is upon you, the time of ploughing and planting, and your family is dear to you.

"But you will know war—whether at one end of a weapon or the other—and if you love these fields you have not yet ploughed, and if you would keep that family, I do ask it of you. As of now, we have signed no enlistment edict. I pray we will not need to. But men of Orden, should you come to take up arms, we will not turn you away. The army is small, and the threat is very great, and tonight, hope is very small.

"You who come, present yourselves at Mitheren swiftly tomorrow. Now is not the time for slackness."

The last echo of his words fell on the dead air. The general turned and mounted his dragon, and the heavy wingbeats sounded in their ears, and faded.

~

The awful quiet broke, like a thin pane of protection shattering. The muted buzzing of tense whispers was all around, sounds of feet hustling down the road. Linda Boccin was crying.

Laufeia could not cry. She was too dazed, too afraid.

Mordred stood beside her, his frame tall and rigid, his face pale in the dusk and very set. He seemed not to know anything around him, not even himself, and when Laufeia spoke his name he did not answer.

"Laufeia Kenhelm." It was Kenneth Denholm, hastening up to them. "Have you seen the Thornes?"

She shook her head, incapable of forming words yet.

"They must have left earlier," he muttered. "The Segelases, too. Someone will have to tell them. Braegon!" he called, moving away.

Laufeia turned back to Mordred and took his hand that was closed about Smoke's bridle, prying his fingers slowly loose. He started slightly and shook her away, glancing down from her to Fenris.

"Mordred?" she said.

He picked up the bridle again and turned, leading the way down the road toward home.

~

"Is it such a ceremony to milk the cow for the first time?" asked Daren with a wry grin, looking up at the crowd of five surrounding him. Lantern-light made a golden circle in the darkness of the old, musty barn.

"I have never seen a cow milked," pronounced Gwenda gravely. "Of course it is a ceremony for me."

Fred laughed. "Go on, Daren. You will acquit yourself well, I do not doubt."

"My prowess is not as great as I fear you believe it to be," returned Daren with a sigh, feeling for the teats. With a careful rolling motion he sent a squirt of milk flying against the side of the wooden bucket, and the cow with a startled movement jerked away from his hand and sent the bucket tipping over.

"I see we will all have much to learn about this," said Daren ruefully.

"Madam Cow included," added Sandy, and grinned as they laughed.

Daren bent to retrieve the bucket, but as he straightened he cocked his head with a frown to the door. "Someone coming?"

Fred listened and nodded. "It sounds like hooves," he said and stepped out as the horse came cantering up to the cottage door. "Kenneth!" he called, recognizing the rider. "What is it?"

Kenneth Denholm took a husky breath and met his eyes. "War."

~

War.

The dreadful tidings swept through Ceristen, while time continued in its relentless path and the night wore on.

~

Peony had not expected the sudden storm of shaken tears that overtook Fiona. Fiona, so quiet-tempered, so composed—but not now. Peony held her like a child, and Fiona wept herself out in her arms, while over her head Peony watched Bardrick and Marcus talk in low voices.

". . . down to Mitheren . . . tomorrow morning . . . so few soldiers . . ."

It was men's talk, she thought quietly. They were moving in another world, now, her brothers, a world cut out of spears and long, long waiting. A world from which they might not return—and all at once Peony understood Fiona's tears. She swallowed back her own and held her younger sister firmly.

~

"They may not need so many, Arad." Mrs. Earle's plump, inquisitive face showed distress and worry. "Please do not go, not yet, not unless you are certain you must."

"I will not yet, my love," he said. "But what of Jared?"

She bit down on her trembling lip. "Jared is a man. He may choose himself. If he wishes it . . . I will not forbid him to go."

~

"But they have an army." Filian's voice rose, and his dark eyes met his older brother's accusingly. "Why do you have to go? You might be killed."

"Little brother," said Braegon, "I was in an army once. It is for that reason I must go. They have an army, Filian, but it is too small. They will need soldiers, and they will need the ones who can fight. I must go, Filian. You will be the man in my stead."

~

Mordred stood by the house under the moon, head bent and gaze far away. He twisted a dead twig off the laurel growing by the wall absently but did not let it go; he rolled it between his fingers again and again, as though seeking the ribbed bark that had sloughed off its stem long ago. At last he let it slip, almost noiselessly, to the ground below.

The rustling of Fenris' approach over the weak new grass made him look up. The younger brother halted as Mordred saw him.

"Aye, Fenris?" Mordred asked gently.

Fenris gave a soft, uncertain shrug in answer and walked to stand beside him.

Mordred lowered his eyes and touched an opening spray of the laurel bush, staring at its slim delicacy under his hands. Another dry twig snapped off and tumbled to the grass. "So sudden," he murmured. "So cruel—one moment we have a farm, a horse, the promise of a life—the next it means nothing." He laughed shortly. "For what? For the whims of kings."

"Will we go down tomorrow?"

Mordred looked at his brother, at the question. "Aye," he answered. "Aye, of course we will go. How can we not? You heard the plea in the general's words. It is fight or perish." His face lit; the tightness dropped away for a moment. "But who would not fight—for such a man?"

"Mordred . . . " Fenris' voice faltered. "Please stay safe."

Wind whispered softly in the trees. Moonlight glimmered on two young men, the clear grey eyes of the elder saddened by the suffering he could not spare his brother, the younger's dark and fearful of the end. "Fenris, I would promise you anything. How can I promise what I do not know?"

"Mordred." There was desperation in the plea.

"Oh, Fenris." Mordred laid a hand upon his brother's shoulder. "It cannot be that bad. We shall care for one another, you and I. We shall keep one another safe and survive many a foolish soldier who thinks to cross our paths."

At his light, almost teasing words, a smile came hesitantly to Fenris' face.

CHAPTER 6

EARLY ON THE MORNING OF April nineteenth, before hardly a soul in Orden was awake, a lone figure knocked at the gate of Mitheren and demanded to see the general. The sleepy guard eyed him doubtfully, refusing to unbar the gate, until the stranger leaned forward and whispered something into his ear.

The guard jumped and took a second look at the man standing before him. Fumbling in his haste, he loosed the chains. The gate creaked open, and the man slipped, catlike, through the gloomy shadows of the courtyard and into the Tower of Kings.

~

The general had not slept. Letters sealed and incomplete, ink-bottles, and scraps of candle-wick littered the table before him. His head rested in his hands.

The door creaked softly on the admittance of another, who took a single, respectful step into the room and halted, eyes dark with apprehension. "Someone to see you, my general."

The general's shoulders straightened, his head lifting in acknowledgment of Captain Rhodes' word, but he did not turn.

"Shall I tell him to wait, General?"

The general stood, facing the captain with a shake of the head. "Let him come in."

In another span of minutes, the door reopened to admit a tall figure, cloaked, features shielded under the hood. He came forward quickly with a lithe, panther-like grace, and the general took a step back, hand straying to his sword-hilt.

"There is no need for that," said the man, sounding a trifle annoyed. "*If* I were going to murder you, which I'm not, you would never be able to best me anyway. Let alone kill me." He shook back the concealing hood, and the first rays of daylight fell upon his face.

It was a face which every man of Mitheren knew.

The general gasped, dropping his hand from his sword. "Jedediah Crayes!" he exclaimed.

"Precisely," Jedediah Crayes retorted. "I suppose you thought I was going to miss out on *this*."

The visage was striking rather than handsome that addressed the general so irreverently: lean, strong-jawed, narrow-eyed, and a jutting, almost hooked nose reminiscent of a bird of prey. Despite a weathered appearance, he presented few lines of age, and his wiry hair was dark as a crow's wing; men incorrectly put him nearer forty than fifty. He was, in fact, forty-six.

"Well, if you've no better greeting for me than a horrified exclamation," Jedediah Crayes resumed in his disdainful, almost derisive tones, "I suppose we must get on to business. I daresay you would love to know how I got here so soon, and how I know everything about this war that's going on, and more than that, why I'm here at all. Unfortunately, I'm not going to answer the first two. In respect to the latter, as a senior member of the Legean Association, I'm here to assist the authorities in the usual—or unusual—manner. You have my services and my fealty for the duration of this war, though naturally there is to be understanding that this state of affairs is *only* for the duration of the war, and does not bind me in any lasting way to Orden and her concerns."

"We are grateful for the aid of the Legean Association," the general answered, inclining his head in an acknowledgment. "And you are welcome, Jedediah Crayes, to give your services wholly and in whatever regard you choose."

"Excellent, excellent," Jedediah Crayes purred. "Most wise of you. If you had not accepted—well, then I would have assisted in spite of you and that would have been positively irritating for all concerned."

He strode casually across the room to the window, and peered out it at the quiet courtyard. "What? No streams of devoted youngsters flocking to your gates yet, ready to lay down their lives for their beloved general? No councils organized? No-one blaring the trumpets and calling the soldiers to arms? You're all practically asleep, aren't you. A wonder the Runnicoran general isn't sitting on Mitheren's throne already."

The general came to his side and looked out as well. "They will come soon," he said, a sorrow in his voice. "As for the council, you may come with us below shortly if you wish."

"Come I shall," retorted Jedediah Crayes. "What do you think, that I came to lie on a couch and nibble sweetmeats all day?"

The general sighed a little. "Should you desire anything in the way of mail or helm, it shall be provided for you."

But Jedediah Crayes snorted irritably. "I can get along without those very well, thank you. Save them for your pet warriors. I should think you'd find better use for me outside combat anyway—not to say, of course, that I would *mind* dazzling your recruits with a display of actual swordsmanship, but I'd prefer to have my intelligence exploited while you're at it. And I really don't like armies; nasty places full of rules and rules and more rules.

"Besides"—the glance he cast at the general was shrewd—"you have little to spare, I'll warrant. I can get by well enough with a leather jerkin; give the armor to a poor volunteer who can scarce wield a sword, let alone last five seconds in a battle."

With an elegant movement he wheeled and left the room.

~

The sun was still peeping out like a line of fire traced across the horizon when Mordred and Fenris reached the base of the mountain. A throng surrounded them as they came out onto the road to the city, a steadily moving mass like a silent, mighty river that straggled out for miles behind them.

Though Mordred was in a sense aware of everything around him—the jostling people on every side, the cool air of dawn, the uneven line of the city and Mitheren's dark silhouette ahead in the distance—another part of him was still living in the small, sharp, sweet memories that he had left in the cottage on the mountainside.

Laufeia's wide, firm green eyes holding back her tears. Her lightness as he held her. Her soft "Goodbye, Mordred." The darkness of the shadows all around them, and the hazy grey-golden first light fluttering in at the window. A strange pull holding him to the ground, even though it was time to leave.

"Go," Laufeia had said simply, looking back at him. She must have known that if she did not tell him to, he could never have forced himself to move away. Her eyes, so steady, so quiet, locking all the tears within—how strong women were!

"Hi, you! Come back with that! Thief!"

A dirty man shoved through the crowd, another, better-dressed, close on his heels. Mordred thought in relief of their own hard-earned coins, safe in the cupboard at home.

And then, before he meant it to happen, they were there, looking up at the colossal blocks of dark stone that made the outer wall of Mitheren. A long slow line was forming up ahead—two armored men stood there, and a third who wore a long dark cloak of some velvet material and took down the names of each man who passed him, and directed him afterwards in one direction or another.

The first wave had passed; they were standing in the wake of it. Stragglers pushed past them, up to the waiting men at the gate. Mordred glanced at Fenris beside him and moved slowly forward over the empty stones.

Hooves clattered on stone behind them and Mordred halted, edging out of the way as the rider cantered past and drew his horse up to a blowing stop at the gates. The nobleman—he was a noble by his garments—dismounted with a swift, easy motion and turned briefly to the dark-cloaked man by the gate, exchanging some pleasantry-words with him. Then he glanced briefly around and flung a quick, gloved finger at Mordred. "You—boy—take care of my horse."

Mordred balked, staring at him, about to say that he was not a palace servant. But the next instant the reins were lying across his hand and the horse was snorting gently by his ear. Mordred flung a pained look at Fenris and said quickly, "Wait." Reaching up with a light hand to rub the horse's head, he guided it away to face the gate again.

He had been worried that it might shy away from him, since he was not its usual caretaker, but perhaps the horse was used to having different men stable it; at any rate it let him handle it easily, and paced at his side through the gate, stopping and nuzzling his shoulder when he halted. He did halt, just inside, for he had no idea where to find the stables.

"Are you waiting for someone?" asked a voice, and he turned to find a young-faced man at his elbow, dark-haired and eyed with a long, shallow nose and a lean jaw. "But," he added, "this horse has already been ridden."

Mordred nodded. "I was bidden to see to him," he said, "but I did not know where to find the stables."

Understanding lighted the other's eyes, and his face, which had been sober and even sad, smiled ruefully for an instant. "Oh—did the Lord Darethin happen upon you? It is his habit to saddle the first person he sees with duty of his mount—'tis his way of asserting his command over the world."

Mordred shrugged with an answering smile of his own. "It matters little to me; only direct me to the stables, if you will."

"I am Captain Finley Rhodes," said the man, leading the way through the busy courtyard.

And that, with the smile, fitted together the puzzle in Mordred's memory. "Then I remember," he said, "that you came to see the work at the castle once."

"Do you?" Captain Rhodes frowned at him, and then his face cleared. "You—you are of Ceristen, yes! But I think I never heard your name."

"Mordred Kenhelm, sir."

"Kenhelm." Captain Rhodes frowned again, a pondering look. But he shrugged it away. "And so, Mordred Kenhelm, you are here to join with the army?"

"I and my brother, sir."

"As a footsoldier?"

"I am nothing better, sir."

"Are you not?" Captain Rhodes' face glinted in that quick, boyish smile. "I do not know—there is something about you, Mordred. I hope we shall meet again."

With a brief bow he turned; they had reached the stables.

"I thank you." Mordred returned the bow and led the docile horse in, removing her saddle and harness, and, studying covertly the actions of another stableboy close beside him, rubbed her wet flanks down and curried the ruffled hair along her flanks and belly.

"You were having a long time of it, were you not, lass?" he murmured to her as he made her comfortable, and at last settled her with hay and water at her nose. With a final pat to her side, he turned away to find his path back to the gate.

Hurrying through the press of people—why need they take up so much of this huge courtyard?—dodging this basket and that elbow, he did not see the sharp stir; the first thing he knew was a backhanded swing at his face, and a voice barking, "Out of the way of the king!"

Mordred's instinctive thought was that he had impeded the way of Conrad III. He flung his head up to look, and for one painful, horrific second, his eyes locked with Ahearn Kenhelm, King of Dirion.

The next instant he was dropping to one knee, drawing all his arrogance and coldness about him like armor, hoping desperately against all certainty that Ahearn had not recognized him in that one moment. Then he heard the sudden, loud cry. "*Mordred*!"

He heard the footsteps coming; they were stopping at him; the fine leather boots were before his eyes. "My lord king," he murmured stiffly, holding the arrogant armor fiercely close.

"None of that," said a voice just as sharp and fierce in his ear, and Ahearn's arm was hauling him to his feet.

Mordred pulled away.

"No!" hissed Ahearn into his ear, so close that his close-cropped beard tickled it and Mordred started away. "Do you want to make more of a scene than you have already? We are getting you out of here."

Mordred wanted to spit at him that *he* had made half the scene, and held it back with difficulty. He let Ahearn drag him away from the turning heads and the questioning eyes into a small side-door in the huge black spike of Mitheren; then through a few blurred halls and doorways until at last Ahearn released him with a shove against a small niche in a wall.

"Fenris is waiting for me outside," said Mordred.

He saw the pain flash through Ahearn's eyes. "Fenris—"

"What did you want me for?"

"I needed to talk to you."

Mordred's face hardened. "What is there to say?"

"There is everything to unsay! Everything that I said that night. Mordred, please—I—I did not want this separation—I did not want—"

"Of course you did not," said Mordred dully, suddenly finding that all his anger he had ever had against Ahearn was spent. Maybe it was that he had been hating Inspector Dickson so much that—but he flinched from even the name of Inspector Dickson. "Of course you did not want it. I did. I am sorry."

"Mordred." Ahearn caught his hand. "It is done. It is erased. Forget it—I know not what you have endured since then, and I vow, it will all be made right—"

"There is nothing for you to make right," said Mordred flatly. Because Inspector Dickson was so close in his thoughts, he reared up again, but Mordred pushed him away. That thing Ahearn could never make right. "We found a good place, Ahearn. We do not suffer there."

"Well, no matter. That is good, and now you will come—will you not?"

Mordred flung himself away from Ahearn's touch. "No," he said, more roughly than he had meant. "Ahearn, you cannot ask that of me now; I am not ready. I have not thought on that. I have scarce thought of you for months. Please understand, Ahearn"—now he was pleading, with the brother that he had told he would never ask anything of again—"please, it is nothing you have done—do not think I am angry with you. I am done being angry with you. You must see I can give you no answer yet."

Ahearn was silent, his face half-turned away into the shadows that the wall cast. "Yes," he said at last, in a stifled, regret-filled voice. "I see that."

"Let me go," said Mordred softly. "Fenris is waiting for me."

Ahearn nodded. He stood aside and remained there, very still, as Mordred went away down the hall.

~

A hand touched Ahearn's shoulder. "King Ahearn."

Ahearn started and lifted his eyes. "General Derek Winston."

"I have been seeking you." The general hesitated, studying his face with those quiet, commanding dark eyes. "You are troubled."

"I have seen my brother," said Ahearn in a low voice.

"That was the commotion in the courtyard, then. It was . . . Mordred?"

"Aye." Ahearn leaned heavily against the wall. "I spoke with him. Who knew words could drive us so far apart?" But he shook his head as he spoke. "We were never as close as we ought to have been—as we thought we were. It was the orphanage; somehow we were always separated from one another. I was older, I was given different tasks, I had other companions. Mordred held onto Fenris, would not let him go; he loved him too much. But he and I—we drifted away. And now . . . "

"Did you quarrel again?"

"Not this time. He—he is sorry for it, he told me. But there is still a rift, and I thought a reconciliation would heal it. It has not. He said he would think on it, but I feel that there is something of him that—that seems to think he belongs here, and it is too strong for me to break."

"He has found a home," said the general quietly. "That is a thing like to strike a man's roots very deep, especially when he has never had a home."

"You—" Ahearn frowned at him suddenly. "You know him?" He did not wait for an answer. "You have known all this time that he was here! And you never told me?"

"Peace." The general put a very firm hand upon Ahearn's arm. "Peace, King Ahearn. These days have been long and filled with much darkness and little thought of the family of Ahearn of Dirion. Maybe I ought to have sent word to you as soon as I learned of them. But it is done now."

Ahearn gave a small, tired nod.

"Strong as that pull might be," said the general gently, "do not think he is lost to you. His life is not an easy or high one. The love he still has for you, and the thought of content and riches, might yet persuade him to come."

Ahearn let out a sharp and slightly bitter laugh. "That is just the difficulty," he said. "Mordred is one to whom riches are less than nothing. It is not any humility that makes him so; it is just the way he is. Wealth he scorns, gold he laughs at; he wishes only to make his own life and keep food on his table, and cares not how simple it is. When I—when they told me who I was, he could not see why I would accept the kingship; he thought I was greedy and self-serving, that I only wanted money to pile in chests—" He broke off, breathing quickly. "It is best not to dwell in the past."

"Yes, I know." The general's hand was still firm on his arm. "He is very proud, your brother. And he loves deeply. I think there is more love for you in his heart than you know. Do not give up hope, Ahearn."

~

When Mordred reached the outer gate again, there was another massive line going slowly by. He pushed through, looking anxiously for Fenris, but found him soon enough where they had parted; he was waiting by the wall. Mordred worked his way up to his side, and glanced at the line, wondering where they ought to join it. But a peremptory voice caught his ear and he looked to see the cloaked man beckoning to him. "You were here earlier—come."

Mordred came, keeping a hand on Fenris' arm. The man was younger up close than he had thought, perhaps thirty; he wore his cloak with a carelessness that was neither graceful nor slovenly. His face was stiff, even harsh, with lines bitten into it that did not belong with his years, and he spoke in a grim, indifferent tone. "Your name."

"Mordred Kenhelm. My brother is Fenris."

The man noted it down briefly. "The barracks are that way, to the left," he said, pointing. "You are under Sergeant Garin."

They went where he had directed, along the crowded road that wound around the edge of Mitheren and then continued going eastward. The barracks were near; it was impossible to miss them, great, dark structures frowning over the side of the paved street. There was building after building of them, massive blocks stretching back in an unending labyrinth. Which one?

Mordred hesitated an instant, and then strode forward to the nearest structure and went inside.

It was dim, and noisy; there were men everywhere, crouched on the ground tossing dice or talking against the wall, but no-one seemed to notice his entrance.

He caught at the shoulder of one burly man, and a forbidding, bearded face turned to his. The voice that spoke was surprisingly pleasant. “Aye?”

“I am seeking Sergeant Garin.”

“Garin Hawke? Down that way”—the broad thumb jerked—“and all the way down to the end, the one furthest east. You one of the new lads joining up?”

“Aye, sir. Thank you, sir.”

The cheeks moved up in a half-hidden grin. “You’re brave little ones. Coming by the scores, the hundreds, you are, and scarce one in five of you knows how to swing a sword. Aye, well, who wouldn’t answer the general’s call? We’ll handle this enemy all right yet. Send them back home like beaten curs.”

“They say the future is bleak.”

A shrug was his answer. “No one got anywhere by despair, boy. Trust to the worst, hope for the best.”

Mordred left the building and rejoined Fenris.

They followed the man’s direction without difficulty. At the very eastern end of the barracks was one last building, an open field stretching out beyond it, grey with last year’s grass; by the weathered wall were stacks of wood. Something very blue was thrusting itself out of a nest of dead grass at the corner, and Mordred knelt to see it closer. The flower was a bluebell, the tiniest of its kind he had ever seen, and it was blooming so early. Already its petals looked dry and wan at the edges. Mordred ran one light finger over the soft open blossom.

"You—speak up. What are you doing here?"

Mordred straightened quickly and wheeled to face the sharp, inquiring countenance of the tall, square-shouldered man who stood there. "Sergeant Garin?"

"Answer the question."

Mordred stiffened, a dozen biting replies springing to his lips. "I was told to report to Sergeant Garin, sir," he answered as quietly as he could. "I am Mordred Kenhelm, soldier in the army as of this morning."

A smile lit unexpectedly over the man's face. "Very good. I am Sergeant Garin Hawke, to answer your question. Remember that here, you do not ask before you have answered the inquiries from your superior."

"Aye, sir." Despite the clipped, curt tone, Mordred sensed that the man was not angry with him.

"Call me Sergeant Hawke. Have you a weapon?"

"No, sir—Sergeant."

The other sent his eyes rolling upwards. "And they expect me to get you one!" He turned, saying, "Come on."

He disappeared into the building and came out moments later with two sheathed weapons, one of which he handed to Mordred. "Here you are. He's with you?"—with a tip of his head to Fenris.

"Aye, Sergeant."

Sergeant Hawke tossed the other to Fenris. "Find a place in there to make your bed," he ordered, motioning to the barracks, and set off into the maze of buildings behind them.

Mordred drew the blade slowly out of the leather hold. The light glinted prettily off the bright surface, highlighting the pits and nicking near the hilt, and he wondered how many people had died wielding this sword. He was very keenly aware that he was holding Death, that to use this would be to irreparably snatch the life from another man like himself, and in the pit of his stomach he was sick about it.

Yet it felt good in his hand all the same. There was a rightness to the balance, the way it moved when he swung it from side to side. It needed polishing, he thought abstractedly, rubbing at the traces of rust.

"Mordred!" cried a voice in his ear, making him jump.

"Marcus," he acknowledged shortly, seeing who had startled him. "Is there any other way of getting my attention?"

"Well, I was, you know—so happy to see you here!" Marcus grinned awkwardly at him and shrugged. "So you are with Sergeant Hawke?"

"Yes."

"Wonderful! We'll be together." Marcus cast a dramatic arm wide.

"Who else from Ceristen is here?" Mordred asked, suddenly curious. He sheathed the sword.

"Just Bardrick and Therelane. Oh, and I think Jared Earle. But who knows? We may have more before the day's through."

Footsteps drew near, and Sergeant Hawke materialized out of the shadows again, carrying something over his arm. "Put this on," he said, dropping one of the leather jerkins at Mordred's feet.

"Is that our uniform?" Mordred asked, picking it up.

"It's your armor. And all the armor you'll get."

"Not very much armor," Mordred observed quietly as he pulled it on.

"You can be glad you have even that," returned Sergeant Hawke as he strode off.

CHAPTER 7

INSPECTOR DICKSON PACED, RESTLESS AND disgruntled. The walls of Mitheren were too close, confining like a prison; though he knew that he was being held here to keep him safe, rather than to harm him, it still felt a prison. He ached to be away, out of this mess. Why had the king chosen him? He stared around at the hall he had been wandering down, its shadowed walls and high arched ceiling looming all around. Everywhere were the dark walls, sentinels saying in their silent vigil, "We are a guard—a guard from what lies beyond."

And could they keep out what lay beyond? It was no secret that Orden had been utterly unprepared for this devastating attack. Inspector Dickson was afraid, afraid of the words uttered in his hearing, afraid of the somber, hopeless faces that he saw all around him. Even now that the aid from Dirion had come, there was little confidence.

"A thousand horsemen," the general had said, his clear eyes anxious. "I had hoped for twice that number at least—yet it is no blame to Ahearn. He readied what he could spare, and it seems that was all. But a thousand! It is too, too few . . . "

Inspector Dickson left the tower and found his feet taking him to the gate. After all, he thought, staring at its tall bulwarks, why not? Maybe he was bound here in Orden for now, but he need not endure the pressing silence of these prison walls.

He addressed the guards. "Will you let me out? If anyone asks for the ambassador Wilhelm Dickson, say he is gone out for a breath of air and will be back by noon."

Moments later, the gates were creaking open for him, and Inspector Dickson stepped out with a sense of relief and freedom onto the open road.

He passed by the army barracks, the vast buildings bustling with movement and sound. It was only the second day since the call had gone out now, and already so many had come that they had set up tents on the training ground for those who had no room left.

He continued on, passing out of the city and walking down the road with the scent of new grass and fresh-turned fields filling his nostrils. Here—yes, here was peace. One could almost forget that there was a war, back beyond him in that high tower. He knelt by the side of the road for a moment, studying the little buttercups and daisies springing up amid the grass.

He would have gladly walked far, very far, but he knew he must not be away too long, at least not, he suspected, until he had got the general's sanction on the matter. Not much further on, he turned about and began an unhurried walk back.

The sun was warm over his head as he drew near the city again. He turned away from the paved highway and walked curiously down the long rows of the barracks, watching the soldiers as they moved to and fro. Bent on their own errands, no one noticed him; he wandered among them like an inquisitive ghost, until someone finally did notice.

"Hi, you! Who are you with?"

"Who?" stammered Inspector Dickson.

"What division? Who is your sergeant?"

Inspector Dickson gathered his wits and spoke with courteous dignity. "I am not in the army. I am an ambassador from Delgrass.

Forgive me if I have intruded." He made a hasty retreat from the scowling officer.

Several buildings away he leaned against a sunny wall, gazing out over the broad, empty fields and a thin line of forest on the horizon. Somewhere beyond them a little prick of light glinted—what was that? A snowy mountain?

Raised voices and clashing brought his attention back to his surroundings and he went around the corner of the building to see a group out on the bare training ground, wielding a motley collection of weapons and responding to the orders that a sergeant was barking out. It was so painfully obvious in their awkward, disorganized movements that they knew nothing of formation—of fighting, of war—Inspector Dickson almost looked away, it was so pitiful to see.

"Enough!" came the ringing command over the commotion. "That's all for now. Take a breather."

The knot broke apart into singles and twos, the men walking away or lowering themselves panting to the dust. Inspector Dickson, sitting with his back against the warm wall, found his eyes absently following one. He was a tall man, lean and broad-shouldered, who walked with the graceful gait of youth. His hair was dark—he was so like—

Inspector Dickson stood slowly, a dread rising up in him as the young man turned straight towards him and their eyes met.

An awful paleness passed over Mordred's face—whether of shock or anger, Inspector Dickson knew not and could not guess. All he knew was that his own heart was rushing in his breast like a hunted deer and he was feeling a strange sick combination of guilt, anxiety, and startlement.

Mordred moved first, breaking that frozen moment. He bent his head in an incline that was full of coldness and scorn. "Inspector

Dickson of Delgrass," he said. "May I ask why you have sought me out all the way to Orden?"

"I did not seek you out," snapped Inspector Dickson, his tongue springing to life without his bidding. Anger started building in him, an anger that he thought he had been done with weeks ago. "What makes you think I would come here for *you*? The world is not centered upon you, Mordred Kenhelm."

"Is it not?" uttered Mordred in a sarcastic tone. "I should never have guessed."

He tilted up his chin a little. "Nonetheless you have no reason, to my knowledge, to come here of all places and leave your work behind. Or are they so short on crime in the northern precinct, that you must seek more to gratify your tastes?"

The goading insinuation set a bitter taste in Inspector Dickson's mouth. Well, if Mordred could play the game of infuriation, so could he. "Hardly," he answered between his teeth. "Orden, I assure you, is the last place I should willingly have chosen to come, but it was not my doing that my king selected me as ambassador. I at least know to heed the bidding of my monarch."

It was a blind shot, going off all the half-statements and hints he had ever heard about Mordred's relationship with Ahearn of Dirion. But Mordred inhaled a sharp, broken breath and Inspector Dickson knew the accusation had struck home. "I congratulate you, then, Inspector Dickson," he said softly when he had gained control over himself, "on your promotion. A pity it has landed you in so unpleasant a place."

"It is not so bad," returned Inspector Dickson, coolly.

"Oh—indeed? Certainly you have little cause to fear for your own skin. After all, the enemy is hardly likely to put himself at odds with

Delgrass by killing her emissary. No, I can see how *you* would feel yourself quite comfortable here."

Inspector Dickson felt his cheeks heating as he realized that Mordred was none too subtly contrasting their situations. "Thank you for your heartening words," he spat out, and spun away before Mordred could speak again. He could not bear another second in the company of that unendurable man.

Why must he mock and provoke him so? Why could he not let the past lie? Why could he not, like Fred, forgive and harbor no grudge? He even—Inspector Dickson seethed—why, he blamed him for the whole business!

His innate sense of justice cried out in outrage. The werevulture was at fault, not he. He had acted on the evidence, done nothing consciously wrong. When he had realized the truth, he had done all he could to make it right! And yet Mordred still hated him. What had he done against him?

Unwillingly other memories tickled the edges of his mind. His own hand slapping Mordred out of his panicked thrashing—no, he had been warranted in that. His voice uttering barbed responses—always when Mordred had irritated him first . . .

Then came the one against which there was no answer, the one he hated and dreaded most of all. *"There you lie, murderer."*

Inspector Dickson winced unconsciously as his own voice echoed harsh in his head. He shut his eyes in defeat. No matter that he had thought him a murderer at the time. No matter the provocation. No taunting, no goading, no ridicule could justify that cruelty. He tried but could not shut it out, could not erase Mordred's dreadful, stricken look. There—there he had been wrong . . .

And Mordred's pride, oh, so hot that pride—and for an instant Inspector Dickson began to see, strangely, inside Mordred's way of thinking, and it hurt so much that he sprang away from it and walled himself off with that quick, welcoming armor of resentment. He did not want to see the gap that lay between them. He did not want to regret its existence.

~

Mordred watched Inspector Dickson go, the burning anger in him constricting his breath away. His hand clenched at his side until the nails tore into his palm, but he did not feel it. He could scarcely think—he knew nothing but the fearful, blazing anger.

Wounds were ripping open that he had struggled to bury for weeks. How he had held his composure through that whole time he knew not, except that it was the only thing he could do. Inspector Dickson had torn every other protection away from him; a mocking facade was the only defense he had left.

"Mordred." Fenris was gently touching him.

Mordred turned slowly, like a swimmer coming out of deep water. Fenris' eyes were wide with worry. "Fenris? I—I'm all right."

Fenris could never verbally contradict his brother. And yet those dark grey eyes gave the lie to his silence.

Mordred drew in a gasping sigh and some of the strain in him released, leaving weariness in its stead. "It was—only Inspector Dickson, Fenris."

Fenris started at the name. An understanding trembled in his face—the deepest kind of understanding, one only he could give and one Mordred did not want to see. Fenris knew; knew what Inspector Dickson meant to Mordred; knew Mordred's heart, though never a word of the

Claw had passed between them. Mordred looked down, away, avoiding his brother's gaze for the pain that Fenris felt on his behalf.

"Why is he here, Mordred?" The quiet question broke into the dark sea of his thoughts.

"I—don't know." He stared at the ground, noticing the furrows churned into the scuffled dirt. "He said—something about an ambassador. Being an ambassador." The words of their conversation were seared into his mind, running through one another and mingling in the wrong order.

All at once he whirled violently away. "Don't talk to me about it, Fenris. I don't want to talk about him, ever again."

Fenris did not answer. No hurt was in his silence, only deep concern and a silent plea.

Mordred turned and walked blindly away to rest his head against the corner post of the barracks. Fenris was worried about him, suffering for him, and there was no way for him to alleviate that worry. The hurt was just too deep.

Forget it, he told himself, clenching his teeth. *Forget it, before it destroys you . . .*

He could not forget. But he could almost forget. He knew he would have to see Inspector Dickson again, and that he would not be able to live with the torture of such emotions every time he saw him. So all the pain and all the anger he pushed far away inside—all day long he pushed—until the pain was quite buried. The anger was not so buried; it lay latent for now, until they should meet again, but he did not mean to let it go. It was all that kept the pain at bay.

~

Inspector Dickson had thought little of the king of Dirion since he had arrived. But when he saw him after the conversation with Mordred, he was possessed of a sharp consciousness of Ahearn Kenhelm's connections. He saw the resemblance in him that he had not bothered to trace: the wide, sensitive mouth, the upspringing dark forelock only restrained by the royal circlet, the broad and open forehead. In feature, he was actually more like Fenris, with the thinner, narrower planes of his face and cheekbones less prominent, the eyes more thoughtful and pensive than Mordred's guarded look.

But any resemblance was enough, Inspector Dickson found. He begged to be excused from the council that the general invited him courteously to sit with that afternoon. All thought of Mordred was simply—too much. He wanted to forget about him, forget about everything . . . the thought of alcohol crossed his mind, and for the first time drinking oneself into a stupor seemed a likable prospect.

The cold sense that over a decade of law enforcement had drilled into him kept him from considering that road. He knew where it led.

Still, Mordred continued to dog his thoughts, and in spite of all Inspector Dickson's endeavors he persisted there the remainder of the day.

~

Late afternoon was falling golden, the shadows possessed of a peculiarly velvety darkness. Mordred, looking at the slowly westering sun, saw the clouds banking thick in the north sky and the way the wind teased them towards the sun. Fingers of grey reached out to leaden the glowing brightness.

"Again!" the curt order snapped.

Mordred swiftly brought his thoughts back to the moment and held his sword as Sergeant Hawke was bidding them to do.

"And again. Sheathe blades. March forward ten paces."

He heard the weariness in the sergeant's voice, the dismay at trying to make a cohesive fighting unit from men who had "never known how to swing a sword"—the old soldier's words from yesterday morning spoke themselves in his mind.

"Turn! March back!"

Mordred could sense the weakness among their group, the lack of coordination; and he knew he was as much at fault as the next person, too. But he had not the least idea how to mend it.

It was only for the worse that there was another eye on them at this moment. Captain Murray, the dour-faced man who had been at the gate of Mitheren, had come by the training ground and stood at the side with arms folded in a forbidding manner.

"He's a cold one, is Captain Murray," one of their fellows had remarked to Mordred yesterday—Golin, an older man of thirty who had done some time of army service years ago. "Never a smile for any man, nor much of praise either . . . "

"Groups of two"—Sergeant Hawke's voice cut sharply—"practice with the man beside you."

The person next to him was Fenris, of course. Mordred gave him a light smile and set his own sword in a defensive position. "Further up, Fenris," he murmured as his brother attempted an overhead cut.

The sky was clouded over, cooling the air, offering a welcome breeze as they labored on. Sweat dampened Mordred's hair, stuck his shirt against his back. The sword was irritatingly clammy in his grasp.

Then the hooves came, a threatening clamor, pounding in a ceaseless urgency, drawing nearer. The men slackened their work, sensing to the last one the abrupt, imminent danger thickening the air; they peered down the line of buildings at the rapidly nearing rider until he and his foundering horse came into full view.

The man reined in before Captain Murray, gasping out, "Treachery in Mivena, my lord—Lord Mirden betrayed us—marching for Adun Cerien—must intercept him, before he can move on!"

Captain Murray wheeled, his grim face grimmer still. "Sergeant Hawke, ready your men."

"Captain—" protested the other. "They are farmers, not soldiers. They have scarce trained two days."

Captain Murray's expression did not change. "Let be, sergeant," he ordered. "If Orden wins this war it will not be by her *army*. How many does he ride with?" he asked of the messenger.

"Six hundred march upon Adun Cerien, but he has many within her walls; it is estimated another seven score, my lord."

"They cannot spare me more than three hundreds," muttered Captain Murray. "'Tis a hopeless venture; but such is all the war. Sergeant, I will return within the hour. See to your men."

Mordred sheathed his sword and turned to his brother. "Did you hear, Fenris, how he called us farmers? A fine thing, don't you think, for those who have never plowed a furrow in their life?"

CHAPTER 8

THE WALL OF ADUN CERIEN loomed against the clouds, dark, grey and solid, immovable, impenetrable. On either side the mountains reared over it, darker and more threatening like twin thrones. The city was not idle; noise resounded dimly within, the walls crawled with movement, and armed men stood upon the bulwarks. The red-bordered banner of Runnicor floated above the gate.

Captain Murray reined in and stared up silent at it, the white insignia dull in the sunless light. The same light lent a harsh, bleak cast upon his face, and he might have been carved out of the brooding stone of the mountains whose knees they trod upon. "Spread out and encircle the place," he directed, turning sharply. "We were too late to keep him from taking the city, but he shall get no further—he must not!" he added in a bitter undertone. "Well did Lord Mirden make his strike; if he crosses the pass, then he has only Mianu in his way, and if she should fall, our defense is wholly breached! The Runnicoran man will be able to march in all his troops at will."

"We shall regain it, my lord," said Erunmar at his side, a higher-ranking lieutenant.

Captain Murray made no answer but turned his mount aside and trotted over the rocky ground.

So they made a ring around Adun Cerien, and Captain Murray and Erunmar his lieutenant camped on the west side of the city; and dawn deepened, though the sun did not shine.

Scarce an hour had gone before a man was brought to the captain's tent, a straggler who had fled the city.

"What do we face?" Captain Murray asked of him. "Did they lose many numbers in the fighting?"

"There was scarcely any fighting, my lord," the man answered grimly. "The garrison meant to defend the city was almost half Lord Mirden's choosing. Before we knew a thing, our own men were slaying one another and the other dwellers were left to ward the walls as best they might. We held out only a few hours."

Captain Murray bent his head in bored agreement. "And the inhabitants, what became of them? Were they all massacred?"

"I do not think they were killing many, only the ones who resisted."

The captain dismissed him.

"We are at a standoff for now," said Erunmar, "for we do not have the numbers or material to breach the city. Unless he comes out—"

"He will come out," said Captain Murray. "It is his duty to open the pass of Adun Cerien for his new master, is it not? And we are blocking that endeavor with our three hundreds. He will come out, most surely, thinking that he will break through us with ease, and march on to Mivena."

"And he must not break through," said Erunmar, firmly.

Yet his voice was more convicted than his face, and all at once he burst out, "All the odds are against us, Captain Murray. We have ill-trained men and less than half his number. Well might he think he will break through with ease! One charge out of that gate and they will shatter."

"Say not that all the odds are in his favor," said Captain Murray shortly. "We have one element, perhaps, for us, and that is that we are expected to crumble quickly. If we manage not to do that, we may strike doubt into the enemy, which is always a valuable thing."

"Expected to crumble quickly," said Erunmar, growing frustrated, "because they will crumble! From your own lips, my lord, 'We are fighting with ploughmen, not warriors.'"

"We have one contingent of trained fighting men to our hand," said Captain Murray. "When Lord Mirden should show himself, we will place those, our strongest, where they will take the brunt of the charge. He will most likely give us an arrow formation."

"When do you think he will attack?"

"Soon, I doubt not," returned Captain Murray. "He knows that we are here."

~

"It is called Cias Ath on the left, and Isiod Gareo on the right," said Lanerad, lifting a hand to the vast, immutable mountains shadowing them; a black-haired young man with a face too thin and a nose too large, and very dark eyes set deeply in his too-small face. "They built Adun Cerien as a guard for Mianu, in the days of Thireler when they held only the western edge and the land was still rife with foulness."

Mordred looked up at the monstrous, towering heights with eyes tired from the ten hours' march. The cold wind battered wildly at him. "They are very great mountains," he said.

Lanerad nodded, and there was something terribly wistful in his face as he looked up at the immensity beside which even the city was dwarfed. A wistfulness, Mordred thought, that he knew, for he felt it in himself—a sorrow for the things that were breaking and blackening in the grasp of war; but in Lanerad's intense, brooding features there was still more, because these were not just his mountains, but rather mountains that had been his from birth. A land that he had spent his life knowing and loving he now watched darkening under his eyes.

Mordred touched Lanerad's shoulder. He said nothing, nor did Lanerad, though his mouth worked a little, and they stood silent on the broad knees of Cias Ath.

~

The tents were pitched on the stone, but Sergeant Garin forbade his men to lie down and take their ease. "We shall be fighting soon enough," he said curtly, and told them to sit outside if they wanted a breather for their weary legs.

"How soon is 'soon'?" Marcus queried uncuriously to no one in particular, lying full length on his back and squinting into the grey sky. He had not spoken a word of complaint through the hours of marching, though when they halted he voiced a dramatic if quiet moan about the state of his legs. This drew laughs from the older men; they all liked Marcus.

"Careful, or you'll fall asleep yet," said Braegon, his grin flashing white and creasing his face into its unexpected, joyous abandonment. "Even a bed of stones will lull a man when he's marched from sundown to sunup."

"I'm not that tired!" protested Marcus.

Mordred's attention flickered to Fenris at that. Fenris, too, had held up through the night without a murmur, but his head was drooping forward as he sat with his arms across his knees. Quickly Mordred got up and went over to him, shaking his shoulder lightly.

"Fenris," he said in a low voice, "you can lie down and sleep a little. We might be here for hours, or we might not; it all depends on when the enemy comes out. I'll stand by and wake you when I must."

He thought he might get his brother to lie down directly, but Fenris was not so tired as all that. He lifted doubtful eyes to Mordred.

Mordred gave him a reassuring smile. "Go on, Fenris. It will be fine."

"But, Mordred, you won't be able to—"

Mordred overrode him with a slight laugh. "We can't both do it, Fenris. I'm very much awake at the moment; more than you, at least. Rest."

Fenris yielded and lay down, his breath rising and falling steadily within moments. Mordred stood above him with folded arms, his gaze fixed keenly on the high-walled towers in the shadow of the mountain.

He found soon that though he did not feel drowsy, his body had a strange trick of muting sound and vision if he stayed still long enough. He paced back and forth and in a little circle around his brother, springing instantly to his side if anyone made a move in Fenris' direction.

Golin laughed after this had happened twice. "Lad," he called, "you're as edgy as a panther over its kill, and look it, too."

"Methinks it's his cub he's standing guard on," said another, joining the game.

Mordred tilted his chin up and ignored them.

The morning wore on. Once the sun glanced through a rent in the sky's dark shroud.

Then, distant, clear, a trumpet-call rang out within the walls of the city and lingered on the still air. A faint hustling and clamor grew.

"That will be the muster for the soldiers," said Sergeant Garin quietly.

Mordred bent to rouse Fenris.

Doom was over them, thick in the air, a wordless tension inescapable. Only one emotion was seen plainly in the eyes of those who looked to the wall-tops: fear.

"Form ranks." The sergeant's voice snapped out clear but low over the quiet. He looked over them silently, his face pained behind the stoic visage, as though he would have spoken to hearten them, but he must have realized there was nothing he could say that would prepare these men against an ordeal of which they had utterly no comprehension. Words would have been inadequate, a lie. What did courage mean to them, they who were faced with what they did not know? And yet how could he lead men so full of fear?

"Remember for whom you fight," he said brusquely. "After this time, it will be better."

"Garin Hawke!" Erunmar, the lieutenant, trotted towards them. "Take your men up into the pass. Your contingent is directly behind Madiren's." And he was past them and gone.

"March," said Sergeant Garin, and he led them across the hard ground towards Adun Cerien and Captain Murray's tent.

Mordred did not feel anything; or perhaps he simply did not know what he felt. His head was light and his mouth dry, and he thought that if he tried to swallow his head would explode into a thousand pieces. But he was not afraid either, for too near was the danger, too near the death. One could not dread a death that was rushing up so quickly, that would be over and gone in a moment.

Fenris was not beside him.

He realized it suddenly, and he was afraid then, blindingly afraid, afraid for Fenris—he could not leave Fenris alone, he must keep him safe—

But he could not keep him safe. For the first time in his life Mordred could not even try. And he knew it; he did not lunge through the men, trying to find him, he did not call his name. This was not the time. He was sick and dizzied all through for one instant, and then he had control of himself, and there was a fresh hardness in his face as he set his hand on the hilt of the scarred, pitted sword.

Erunmar appeared again, cantering past their ranks and up to the front lines. Captain Murray joined him, and then came a silence awful in its continuity and totality.

The trumpet sounded again, and this time the gates opened to it and a wedge of men flooded through with great drumming and a shout. They ran across the small space of separation, more and more pouring out behind. Mordred waited, bracing unconsciously, the smell of the clean, thin wind in his nose. Then the arrow-head punched into them like a breaking wave, and everything shattered into a sharp-edged blur of noise.

~

"Remember," said Captain Murray to Erunmar beside him, "we are to hold the pass. We seek to move neither forward nor back for the present; at all costs we are to hold the pass and not let him through. Lord Mirden is not to reach Mianu."

Erunmar nodded, his eyes fixed on the opening gates and glimmering through his helmet. "And let us hope for as little blood on our part as may be."

Captain Murray laughed dourly. "Mark what I say, we will buy our victory with a slaughter if we buy it at all."

Erunmar made no answer. The enemy pierced them with a crash, and the battle of Adun Cerien was begun.

~

Lord Mirden stood on the rampart, cloaked in black. The pitiful number of the Ordenians barred the way, their forces spread thin like a ribbon across the low reaches of the pass. What, could they meet him with no better than this? The general must be a fool. And Lord Mirden laughed, because he knew better than anyone the situation of Orden's army, and that the general was no fool.

The dark line wavered, dissolving as Lord Mirden's men breached it, but the impetus failed and the fighting, instead of moving all the way through, broadened out, lapping at the edges.

Mirden was mildly disappointed, but undisturbed. He had not gambled on an instant victory. His troops numbered seven hundred fifty, not counting the archers on the buttresses, and he feared no defeat from the paltry few that faced him. The only thing that irked him was that the quick arrival of the Ordenian forces had cost him another day's wait. And he had waited long enough; seven years since the contract with the Runnicoran general, and generations before that . . .

A quarter of an hour passed. The first heated brush of confrontation was over, and the Ordenians were slowly giving ground against the onslaught of men more and better trained than they. Still, they were not yet faltering or scattering, and Mirden steeled himself to patience, patience, had he not been patient those seven years? But the frustration was rising in him, working on him, a lust for destruction that only slaughter might satisfy. Had he had a bow releasing between his fingers, he would feel better. His eyes burned angrily as they raked over the men who were too far a range and too intermingled for him to dare a shot.

At last, at some rallying word or action, the Ordenian line ceased to move. They held taut, refusing utterly to give ground.

Lord Mirden's pent-up rage turned cold as a burnished dagger. He now saw that he had made an error in sending only half his men to meet them. They had not been able to breach the line directly, and because they had failed in that, the Ordenians were able to hold their own long enough until the battle was evenly joined.

So he had mistaken the needed margin. Very well; he could double it, twice over.

"Send out the remaining soldiers," he ordered the captain beside him.

"Shall I keep a hundred in reserve?"

"No," Mirden ground out. "Unleash them all." He whirled back to stare at the battling soldiers. "I shall make them fear me."

~

The fighting was all about them, an endless, eddying whorl of death. Captain Murray hewed down the man before him, one of the dozens he had already seen whose faces he knew from a glimpse or chance-meeting, but who now disported the white and red of Runnicor. As he lifted his eyes, he saw that the gate was opening and knew that Lord Mirden had loosed his remaining men.

"Erunmar!" The lieutenant was still close to him. "'Ware the gate. Hold them steady."

Erunmar looked to the men streaming out, his eyes widening with horror. "They will not hold!"

"Hold them!" shouted Captain Murray grimly, and wheeled his horse away to face the next enemy.

The enemy side was drawing back a little to meet the reinforcements, gathering to meet them in a second charge. They were not forming an arrowhead this time, but the broadside that was coming would be shock enough.

They sucked up like a wave, and came plunging. With a roar they struck against the battered Ordenian soldiers. The line crumpled, retreated . . . and held. Incredibly, wonderfully, it held.

But it was not joy for Captain Murray. He knew they would not last long. The charge, no, that had not broken them. Yet the numbers would. They could not win against the numbers. Already, they were buckling, cracking, peeling apart.

Perhaps, he thought, their death would secure some respite for Mianu, if they had managed to weaken Lord Mirden's forces by any significant amount. But still, Mianu was not expecting this, she had no word, and none would reach her now. Adun Cerien had fallen, Mianu would fall, the enemy would stream in, and the war would be over before it had begun.

If I had thought what hung on this battle, he said sourly to himself, *I would have pressed for five hundreds.*

He saw for an instant, in the scathing fury of the battle, with the clarity that comes unlooked for in unlikely moments, a young man's face, eyes filled with fear, gone in the next second. It was a face to stick in one's mind, so clear-cut and proud, with an odd vulnerability about it, and it came to him that he had seen it before among the volunteers.

Then came a sound that blotted all other things from his mind, made him rein in sharply so that his horse reared up whinnying. It was a horn call, one that did not come from the city or the pass behind them. And beyond the edge of the fray the pennant of Orden, the white mountains crowned with silver stars, rose and fluttered in the wind.

~

Mordred knew none of these things, and would not have cared if he did. For him, there was nothing but the horrendous noise and increasing stench, weapons flashing everywhere and every one seeming aimed at him. He saw horses falling dead, men collapsing who would never rise again, and so overwhelming were the sights and the din that he felt torn out of himself and left a shell that could not think or act.

A hundred times he thought someone was coming at him, thought it and was powerless, even paralyzed. But when at last someone did come for him, he *knew* it, saw the concentration and the intent in the man's snarl as their eyes met, and he did not want to die, and at once his limbs were free. Their blades clashed with a jolt that shuddered his arm.

He did not know what to do. His eyes darted from the crossed swords to the other face so near and so ready to kill him. The man's eyes were smiling with a dark purpose; he knew he had easy prey. Mordred was suddenly cold all over with a fear that made his hands shake.

Suddenly the man lurched, and retched, and fell face-first to the ground. Something had slashed him open in the back and side, and there was blood pouring out, and more than blood. Mordred thought he would be sick, but he knew he could not, and he turned away from the sight and was swept away next moment in the tides of fighting. He did not see what or who killed the man, nor did he ever know.

After that things became a strange and almost monotonous haze of moving back, and forward; always being confronted with another face, another enemy, warding off attacks, and feeling horribly exposed and defenseless. Once, he saw Braegon, and almost did not recognize him because of the swiftness and intensity of the moment. Then, oddly, he found that young, silent Lanerad was beside him, his face locked in the same brittle, high-strung calm as Mordred's own, only a little more steady. "I've got your back," said Lanerad, and a wonder and gratefulness stole through Mordred's tense body.

And so they battled together, back to back, and someone was fighting with him and for him, and though he wielded his weapon no better than before, to Mordred it made all the difference in the world. He was not isolated anymore.

He could tell that it was almost over. Somehow the fighting had petered away, spreading into scattered knots, no longer a mad striving press. "Lanerad," he said. "It's growing quieter."

Lanerad twisted his head around and nodded with dawning understanding. "Who won?"

They did not know. It did not even seem to matter, amid the still-heated struggle and the lifeless men and pools of blood. Mordred raised his sword as another man approached him.

Beside him Lanerad gave a grunt, and Mordred turned as he fell against him, neck rent asunder. Mordred stared blankly for a moment at him, and let him fall. He could feel no more horror, there was no room for it in the world now. He turned again to fend off the coming foe.

One, two—a third was in front of him. But this man was not attacking, not even coming closer; he was laying down his sword. And Mordred realized that they were all doing that around him, and that Captain Murray was astride his horse nearby, his adamant features redly lit in a fleeting gleam of sun and his hands locked around the pommel of his now sheathed blade.

Up the rising ground came trotting a second horseman, with another behind him holding up the banner of Orden. The man in the lead was helmed, but he removed it as he halted in front of Captain Murray.

"Captain Rhodes." Captain Murray's voice spoke more harshly and coldly than usual.

"The general feared you would fail to forestall Lord Mirden, and bade me take three hundred to barricade Adun Cerien," said Captain Rhodes in the tone of one vindicating himself to an enemy.

"Your aid is accepted with thanks," said Captain Murray, but it was plain that he was angered.

"I did not seek to be chosen," said Captain Rhodes sharply, between his teeth.

"Nor did I say aught against your coming."

They looked at each other in silence, dark eyes challenging dim ones, holding, flickering, dropping, returning.

"We have retaken the city," said Captain Rhodes at last, twitching the silent contest of will behind them. "It was a simple matter; they had turned out nearly all their men upon you, as it seems."

Captain Murray's lip lifted in something like a sneer. "Truly you leave a trail of success behind you."

Captain Rhodes made no answer to this. His gaze, sweeping away, suddenly lit on Mordred and that bright, boyish smile flared out. "Mordred Kenhelm!" he exclaimed.

Mordred answered the smile, with the sense of coming out of sleep. The wind beat on his brow, stirred his hair. The sun was sinking toward the west. So much was in the world that he seemed to have never felt, or had forgotten from the time he was a child of two or three. He lived, and lived unscathed at that.

But others—Mordred remembered Lanerad, remembered piercingly now, the blood falling all over, everywhere, and the mangled neck and shoulder, and *Fenris*—where was Fenris?

As Captain Rhodes wheeled his horse toward the city, Mordred turned and sped over the dull, bloodied ground.

"Fenris!" he called, raising his voice higher, louder. "Fenris—Fenris!"

It echoed lonely and answerless off the mountains.

"Fenris—" he cried, again and again, crossing and recrossing the gruesome field.

And then a slim figure was moving in the distance, calling back to him, and Mordred had leapt across the space and was clasping his brother close, holding him back to look for injuries, drawing him close and tight again.

Fenris was safe and whole. For the present, all other fears faded and the world was still.

CHAPTER 9

QUIET WAS THE CAMP AT nightfall. Men had taken lives, seen lives taken, many that day for the first time; silence and sobriety reigned over each one in his tent. Into one of those tents Captain Rhodes came unnoticed, and strode across to a young soldier who sat kneeling on the ground and staring intently at his sword drawn before him on the stones.

"Mordred."

Mordred started and looked up, and rose to his feet. "Captain Rhodes?" he said softly, the statement framed as a question.

The captain hesitated, uncertain or unwilling to speak whatever was on his mind. "The general . . . the general said to me, before I left Mitheren, that spies are being chosen to go among the leader's army. Jedediah Crayes is to be one, of course. He did not say it in so many words, but I believe, Mordred, he had you in mind."

Silence hovered between them, for the time it might take a man to draw a breath.

"Only if you are willing," Captain Rhodes said quickly. "You need not, Mordred. The danger is terrible. If they should catch you, it is torture . . . "

The word hung, ugly, twisted, in the air.

" . . . and at the last it will be death—no matter what you tell them it will be death, for it is always death for spies. None will think the less of you if you should choose against such danger; warriors of long seasons tremble at the thought of it."

"I do not fear danger," said Mordred.

And it was true. He was young, strong, and quick in mind and body. And while he had no delusions about war, and hated passionately its wastage and cruelty, at Captain Rhodes' words his heart stirred, his pulse quickened, and a strange excitement gripped him. "I do not fear danger, Captain Rhodes. Tell me what I must do."

Captain Rhodes surveyed him. And fearless he looked as he stood there: young and tall, his head high, his grey eyes gleaming proudly. "A swift horse you must have; it is near forty miles from the pass to Orden City, and you will do best to see the general before another day is past. And, Mordred—" But the captain broke off short, and the two men's eyes met.

"I can tell no one," Mordred finished quietly. "Is that not what you were about to say, Captain Rhodes? Very well; I can bear that, too."

Presently he continued, "I should leave now, then, before Fenris senses anything amiss. Find me this horse, Captain Rhodes, and I will depart."

Captain Rhodes put a hand on his shoulder in concern. "You are willing to go immediately? I confess, I had hoped you would be, but are you certain?"

Mordred looked away sharply. "I am certain," he said. "Let us go."

Several men looked up as Mordred left the tent with Captain Rhodes, but none marked it as important. He will come back soon, they thought.

But he did not come back.

~

Jedediah Crayes was sitting on a handsomely carved wooden chair, its back padded with cushions and hung with fine damask velvet. That is, if sitting is the word for reclining at an outrageous angle, with one's right foot on the floor and one's left leg draped over the armrest. Jedediah Crayes' black brows had met over his eyes in a scowling V, and he was tapping his fingers on a small table at his side. "A nuisance," he muttered. "A perfect nuisance."

What exactly was a nuisance he left to any possible eavesdropper to try to fathom.

In fact, the nuisance was presently that the general wished the man of the military council's choosing to accompany him in his spy work. Who this man was, however, and when he would turn up, nobody would inform him. As if he needed an assistant! As if he had the *time* to sit about waiting for the Runnicorans to knock the Elerien Mountains down and ask for a cup of tea! As if any of these refined, over-cautious little Ordenian lordlings had the time. What an absolute, blithering nuisance.

Another nuisance, now that he was thinking about them, was this police officer from Delgrass. Plainly the fellow had heard of Jedediah Crayes, and whatever he had heard, it had not been of the down-to-earth variety. He treated Jedediah Crayes with a nervous awe that almost amounted to servility, and Jedediah Crayes, who despite the soothing touch on his vanity despised people making fools of themselves, was deeply vexed.

Grumbling under his breath, he rose lightly, paced to the window, and turned to walk the room with the quick, coiled strides of a caged lion. His mind had moved on to the council last night.

"Defense will not win the fight," the general had said. "But for now, it is our only path. Though defense may not secure us victory, attack will lose us the war before we know what has come upon us."

"And you'll all be running around like chickens with their heads chopped off," Jedediah Crayes had put in, and sat back savoring the startled, sidelong looks that he usually received upon his rare contributions to the councils.

A pleasant memory, but an all-too-likely scenario. The more reason for him to be on his way to the Runnicoran army in short order, eh? Jedediah Crayes repeated his question peevishly to the room in general, settled himself by the window, and tapped his boot against the floor.

It was several minutes later that he heard hooves, and glancing out beheld a lathered horse flying over the stones two stories below, slowing to a stop beside the stables. The rider dismounted and led it in, reappearing shortly and heading with long, graceful strides for the tower. He was tall and dark-haired, and easily marked out as an infantryman by the leather jerkin he wore—scant protection, but stamped with the insignia of Orden's flag.

Interesting, thought Jedediah Crayes.

He got up and left the room.

~

"A Mordred Kenhelm, footsoldier, General," said the servant.

The general's head jerked up, and he nodded slightly. "Admit him." He stepped aside from the table and greeted Mordred as he entered.

But Mordred crossed the room swiftly at once, and drawing his sword knelt before the general. "You have my service, my general, in whatever way you choose to use it."

The general bade him rise, and searched his face deeply. "Captain Rhodes has told you, I see," he said at last. "Your presence alone shows that. Tell me, have I forced your decision in any way? I do not desire that you enter into this against your will."

Mordred lifted his head in an unconscious, proud gesture. "I chose it, my general, and I do not wish to turn back."

The older man nodded. "So be it. Now I had thought thus, if you came, that I would assign—"

He broke off short. Mordred stared at him curiously.

"Jedediah Crayes," said the general, "you may join us if you wish."

Mordred followed the general's gaze, and one eyebrow shot up his forehead. For either the person reclining negligently against the wall had been in the room before, unnoticed, or he had entered and shut the door with no noise whatsoever. "Well met, Jedediah Crayes," he offered, courteously enough. "I have heard something of you recently, I think; it is evident you are highly thought of. Who are you, and what do you do?"

The general's eyes widened.

Those of the man called Jedediah Crayes started half out of his head. He inhaled between his teeth and took a deliberate pace forward. "I am," he said menacingly, "the greatest person in the world."

Mordred's eyebrow soared again; his lips twitched. "The greatest person in the world," he murmured with an utter lack of expression. "I see."

Jedediah Crayes' mouth opened soundlessly, his face reddening. After several failed, seething attempts at speech, he resumed in tones carefully articulate and trembling with indignation, "Many people in my life, nay, a great many, have failed to recognize me, but I have had yet to meet a grown man of twenty *ignorant* of my existence. What kind of brass impertinence—"

"I am sorry, as you must be well-known indeed," Mordred replied, the amusement running through his voice plain to hear. "However, I am not from Orden; I have only lived here for a few months."

"Orden!" shouted Jedediah Crayes.

"Mordred," the general interposed quietly, "the name of Jedediah Crayes is renowned throughout Legea. Suppose you tell us how he is unknown to you."

There was no rebuke in the general's words; Mordred nodded in quiet compliance. "Renowned throughout Legea? Maybe so, but the orphanage is a place where toil comes first and news second, if at all. It is possible that I heard his name before; but I thought nothing of it, and he certainly was not widely noised. Besides"—his tone stirred with an edge of scorn—"it is not often that the people of Rehirne take a care for the things they do not know, still less what they dislike. And I doubt they would have liked you." And suddenly Mordred turned a smile on Jedediah Crayes—a wide, impulsive grin, wholly genuine. And the general looked at him in wonder, thinking, *I have not seen him smile so before.*

"Rehirne!" Jedediah Crayes demanded like a kingfisher diving for its prey. "*That's* the wreck where you grew up?"

"Aye," Mordred acknowledged, the traces of the smile lurking suspiciously about his serious face.

"Bah! Rehirnish." Jedediah Crayes waved his hand dismissively. "Idiots, the lot of them. 'Let's lock up all the orphans and make them do the dirty work!' But good grief, I didn't know they'd taken to raising them in perfect ignorance! 'Let's lock up all the orphans and make them do all the dirty work and pretend Jedediah Crayes doesn't exist!'"

He pulled up short and fixed Mordred with a shrewd stare. "But if *you're* Rehirnish, I'm the daughter of the Man in the Moon."

Mordred returned his gaze with an almost mocking light in his eye. "And supposing I were Rehirnish?"

Jedediah Crayes, once again, sputtered.

But the general spoke now. "Jedediah Crayes, it is good that you came. This young man, Mordred Kenhelm, I would have be your fellow spy if you are so willing. He is possessed of integrity and great courage, and is moreover intelligent, quick-witted, and in all ways highly suitable for . . . "

"What?" Jedediah Crayes howled. "This impudent rascal, this arrogant brat—this disrespectful beggar boy—my partner? My assistant? You must be mad! I won't put up with this—I won't, I tell you—and that's that!"

Mordred winced as the door slammed violently behind his lithe figure. "Well, that is rejection for you. A pity; I think I should have enjoyed working with him."

"I must get you food and lodgings for the night," the general murmured, bending over his desk a moment, "that you may rest; for you must be sorely wearied and Jedediah Crayes will want to leave at first light."

"Leave . . . " Mordred stared at him. "But I will not . . . "

The general shook his head. "I cannot say that I know Jedediah Crayes well, Mordred Kenhelm—I think there are none who do—nonetheless, I should be much surprised if he has truly rejected you."

~

Jedediah Crayes barged into Mordred's room as night was drawing near.

"I suppose you have nothing to pack," he said unceremoniously. "Well, what are you sitting around in *here* for? What possessed the general to slap you off to the nether regions of the castle instead of to me, who is, I might add, supposed to be instructing you in the ways of this job? It would be one matter if you were experienced in espionage!

But no, they saddle me with a country brat of eighteen who knows next to nothing, and, in the bargain, hasn't got a civil tongue in his head . . . "

Mordred noticed that Jedediah Crayes had mentioned his age correctly this time; but he made no comment on it, only remarked, swinging his legs over the bed and following Jedediah Crayes from the room, "I shall soon be nineteen."

"Indeed," Jedediah Crayes returned with a shocking degree of civility mellowing his tone. "And what is 'soon'?" The sarcasm returned.

"The seventh of May."

"That is soon," Jedediah Crayes conceded grudgingly. And then, "Oh, drat."

It was Inspector Dickson coming down the corridor toward them. At first he had eyes only for Jedediah Crayes, whom he gave a wide and respectful berth, but in so doing he came straight by Mordred, and when he saw him pulled up short.

"What are you doing here?" he asked.

Mordred tilted his chin, the anger surging up like poison into a festering hurt. "I have not heard that I need answer to you for all my comings and goings, Inspector Wilhelm Dickson."

Inspector Dickson's lips tightened. "I only thought that your garrison was gone away to Adun Cerien," he said in a low, angry voice.

Mordred shrugged insolently. "They were," he said. And he brushed past Inspector Dickson down the hall.

In Jedediah Crayes' quarters, Mordred watched the other man wander in an exceedingly aimless fashion around the room, kicking furniture in and out of place and muttering to himself. Suddenly he rounded on Mordred. "Too much, I suppose, to hope that you can read and write?"

Mordred made no attempt to conceal his amusement. "Is it too much to ask why you consider me an unlearned barbarian?"

Jedediah Crayes glowered at him. "I take that to mean you can."

After a minute he muttered defensively, "I can't be too careful, you know. Don't have a high opinion of these Rehirnish orphanages." Abruptly and completely switching tone and manner to that of amiable inquiry: "Speaking of that, if you aren't Rehirnish, what are you?" In a menacing parenthesis: "None of your sauce, either. I know you aren't."

Mordred's mouth quirked slowly in a wry, laughing look. "I believe my family's descent is in the old houses of Thiredanian nobility."

"Oho! Now that's a fine tale to fleece on me. Nice try, Mordred Kenhelm."

"Oh, I assure you it is far more credible than the other half of the truth."

"Tell away," said Jedediah Crayes, looking amused in his turn.

Mordred shook his head.

~

Jedediah Crayes narrowly studied the young man across the room. A prettier enigma he'd never seen. Those grey eyes, laughing at him so infuriatingly a moment before, were suddenly cold and closed. Who was this absurd creature? He looked—and acted—the part of a penniless young lord, had supposedly grown up in Rehirne and those ridiculous orphanages, possessed more than a nodding acquaintance with the General of Orden, and on top of the lot claimed to have never heard of Jedediah Crayes. Certainly he spoke more audaciously than anyone had spoken to him in *years,* and that included peasants, who were too awed, and lords, who were too dignified.

Now he was refusing to give the 'other half' of this half-cooked tale of noble heritage. When you came right down to it, they all were the same, these poor young men: they wanted to impress. But no, Jedediah Crayes was not impressed. Look at him, the fine young actor! Showing an appropriate level of hesitancy, proud but fearing not to be believed, and obviously itching all the while to let it out. "Go on," Jedediah Crayes invited. "Go on; give up the other half like a good boy."

"No," said Mordred, with a quiet, final stubbornness.

Jedediah Crayes' short temper ran out. "Why not!" he shouted.

"Because you will assuredly laugh at me, and I don't care to be laughed at." Mordred's voice remained cold and quiet.

Jedediah Crayes looked at him again, somewhat taken aback. The statement had less the ring of a youth who realizes his bluffing has gone too far than one who has told more than he wishes and intends to tell no more. "I see," he said. "No, I won't laugh at you; but now I should truly like to know what is this your family history."

"So be it," said Mordred, his chin lifted arrogantly into the air. "You may inquire into it if you have doubts, for he is in Mitheren now. I am brother to the king of Dirion."

Jedediah Crayes stopped himself in time from whistling, from snorting, from laughing, from any number of things that he wanted and had promised not to do. Mordred was correct; he could verify it whenever he desired because Ahearn of Dirion had come to Orden City with a thousand horses to the aid of his sister country. Now, he leaned forward and scrutinized the young face.

"That's it," he muttered. "I thought I traced a resemblance when I first saw you there."

He relaxed back into the chair. "Mordred, I'm prepared to give thorough credence to your story, for a number of reasons, but one and one alone would suffice. And that reason is, I am the man who discovered that your brother, Ahearn, was the rightful king of Dirion."

"You!" Mordred stared at him. "But why—"

"Simple enough; I was trying to find a closer heir."

"You were—trying! But why—"

Jedediah Crayes lost his temper again. "Why would I try? Why would I try? It's what I do! Don't you know who I am? Don't you know what my job is?"

"In case you had forgotten, Jedediah Crayes," Mordred answered with perfect cool, "no, I do not."

"Very well! Allow me to introduce myself again. I am Jedediah Crayes, *of the Legean Association*!"

A strange expression crossed Mordred's face. "The Legean Association!" he breathed. "So they do exist still, then. And you are of them! Tell me about it, please."

Jedediah Crayes went limp in his chair and gaped at Mordred, only able to exclaim, "Those Rehirnish!" at intervals.

~

Mordred could see that he had scandalized Jedediah Crayes with his ignorance yet again. He leaned back in his seat as the man regained his composure, listening to his furious outburst, which as far as he could tell accused the Rehirnish of unmitigated incompetence, and him of multiple lies, and which ended triumphantly, "So! If the Rehirnish taught you anything about the Legean Association, why are you pretending they didn't—and if they didn't, how do you know about it at all? Ha! Answer me that!"

Mordred heard him patiently to the finish. "Jedediah Crayes, the orphanage taught us nothing. Reading and writing I did learn on my own, before I was orphaned, or I surely would not have learnt it afterwards. Work was all that we were for, in their eyes. Some of the orphan homes, I heard, gave their children a sorry semblance of education, their version of history and such, as though to further the public image of their own benevolence and delude their charges into thinking that their treatment was natural and proper. Ours did no such thing. But—"

He straightened up, alive with the memory.

"But the headmaster had a library, a marvelous library; he was always adding to it, the richest and fattest books he could find, only for show, for he never took a step in there except to impress his visitors. And I slipped in there by night, every night I could, and sat amid that glorious sea of writings, and I read it all—even the great tomes on the shelves . . . "

~

Jedediah Crayes looked into those grey eyes, intense now, blazing with unconscious fervor, and thought, *No, he is not lying. About this, at least, he is not lying.*

Mordred recollected himself and continued on. "And there was one scroll that said thus: that 'in the days of Veno Thir there lived a certain man, who, foreseeing evil days ahead for Legea, decided to form such an assembly of men as would aid and protect all countries of the world who were not allied in any way with werevultures; and these would assist the authorities in any way that was good and proper'.

"So I wished to learn more; but I had to be careful in my questions, for the only reason we were not forbidden to read the headmaster's library was because they did not dream that we would want to. And when I so much as mentioned the Legean Association, the older men turned their backs on me; the younger ones jeered at me and threw stones; the matrons boxed my ears; and when the headmaster heard about it—though I assure you I never intended my inquiries to reach *his* ears—he ordered me a flogging. I told them they were making me more curious, not less, but the head matron shrieked 'Sass!' loud enough to deafen a stone dragon, and cuffing was all I got for my pains."

Jedediah Crayes roared with laughter. Then he said, sobering, "You know, that is very good, what you quoted there, and was written by a man who knew the Legean Association well. For that is what we are: an assembly of men formed to aid the countries of the world, assisting the authorities as is good and proper."

"But," Mordred protested, "that I already know, and I wish to know more. What sort of things do you do? Give me examples, not a generality."

"We do anything we need. Often a situation that the local authority cannot deal with, whether because of poor management, lack of men, or busyness. Or this very war that Orden's dealing with right now. We do prefer not to get mixed up in war, I might add, but Runnicor marching twenty-five thousand on Orden over a trade dispute that happened fifty years ago—frankly, it's an overreaction. Or the rather knotty issues that crop up around the concept of slave trading. Now, in some countries slavery is legal and there we don't interfere, particularly where the slave system acts as a debt-payment function—highly integral to the society. The difficulty comes when someone tries to set up actual trafficking in a country where it *isn't* legal.

"Aha, see, there's a concrete example for you. Five times I've dealt with this over the past thirty years, down south in Mesoremn. Mesoremn borders both Terragere and Arahad, both slave trading countries, while not—ostensibly or legally—dealing in slavery itself. And there's a good many in both Terragere and Arahad who wish they could have easy pickings out of Mesoremn . . . but a very sturdy and valuable trifold alliance stands in their way."

"So they can't send in bands to raid Mesoremn," said Mordred, his eyes bright as he followed where Jedediah Crayes was leading.

"Exactly. Instead, someone in Mesoremn sets up an underground working, does the kidnapping, and makes a pretty profit. As I said, it pops up every couple years or so, despite my long-suffering efforts toward the contrary. The stupid government of the country needs to either make it legal or fire all their rich and incompetent nobles."

Mordred laughed, tossing his head up, his mobile features alive in the firelight.

"Then of course," Jedediah Crayes went on, "there was your brother. What a gem of a problem. What a little beauty. Tricky, asking for a delicate hand, tough but not too tough; quite a fun exercise for me. The most exciting thing was, I knew there was only one right answer, only one opening for another heir. But I will say, I hadn't expected to find my answer so quickly; I'd only been at it for a few days, and I was expecting to concentrate my search outside the country because I suspected my quarry—your parents—to have fled it. As it turns out, of course, they had.

"I recall hearing wind of some siblings," he went on; "but I never took notice of you; I had to leave directly." He appraised Mordred with a quick stare. "I daresay there's an interesting story of how you came to be here, instead of eating off the fat of the land in Dirion's palaces—but never mind that now," he said with a laugh as Mordred's face stiffened. "I expect I'll find it out soon enough. Where do you live, or where did you, before this nuisance of a war took place?"

"My home is in a little village on Mount Thiranu," Mordred answered.

"Ah! The one they are trying to 'reinstate'!" Jedediah Crayes smiled at his vast stores of knowledge and peered covertly at Mordred's inscrutable face. Bah! He was laughing at him behind that mask, he knew it.

Well, he thought, what an enigma. What an intriguing person. Why *was* King Ahearn's brother living in a nondescript village like any other hopeful newcomer, too poor to buy himself a decent position in the army? And how had he met the general? Had he any other siblings, and if so, were they in Dirion or not?

Jedediah Crayes stifled a yawn, whereupon it occurred to him that his protege should be getting to bed. Then a certain memory recurred. "I see," he said, "you're on less than good terms with that Delgrass Inspector."

A startling look tore through Mordred's eyes, so swiftly that Jedediah Crayes all but missed it. It was white-hot anger, and searing pain, and bitter sorrow all at once; and what replaced it was a cold, cold impassivity that seemed deader than a winter sky.

"Do not speak of him to me," he said.

"Let's go to sleep," said Jedediah Crayes.

~

April twenty-third's morning was cold. Frost lay thick on the ground, melting at the sun's touch, yet showing that winter had not quite let go her clutches on the land. The earth warmed as the morning passed into afternoon, though the air still nipped at face and hands. And as the sinking sun spread its failing light over the enemy encampment and the great mountains behind, two Ordenian deserters approached the lines of tents: one a tall young man with arrogant look and keen eyes, and the other a paunch-bellied fellow of middle years who slouched and sat poorly on his mount. His grizzled hair was untidy, an unsightly scar across his face, and an ostentatious display of wicked knives graced his belt.

"It unfortunately can't be helped," Jedediah Crayes informed Mordred in the hours before daybreak, as he thoughtfully smoothed a nameless mixture onto his cheekbone and speckled whitewash into his hair with a practiced hand. "I've been in Runnicor often enough that someone in that mammoth army is bound to recognize me if I don't take precautions."

"Runnicor?" Mordred questioned.

"Yes, Runnicor. And you can be glad it's them and not the Arahadians."

"Someone said that we are allied with Arahad."

Jedediah Crayes snorted. "Barely. The Arahadians think you lot stole their dragons. Why don't you make yourself useful and fray the cuffs of my shirt for me—and don't cut my hand off while you're at it!"

As they rode away amid the early birdsong, Jedediah Crayes instructed Mordred further. "Although you don't need any disguise, you ought to have an alias to be on the safe side. What do you say to Gerald Richardson?"

Mordred was suspiciously quiet for a time, and looked as if he were biting the inside of his cheek repeatedly—at, Jedediah Crayes suspected, the clash of his uncouth appearance and clipped, haughty voice. At last he said, straight-faced, "Gerald Richardson will do very well."

"Good. But"—he lifted a finger—"it is not enough to approve of the name. You must fix it in your head, be primed always to answer to it, never stumble when you are asked to give it. Never. Blink a moment, apologize that you didn't hear, do whatever you need to recollect before answering, but do not fumble over the name itself. A slip-up is deadly.

"Of course, I'll have an alias, too; I'm not proclaiming myself as Jedediah Crayes, all the worse since I probably look at present like most of them imagine me. I am Mog Dremmag, and see to it you remember that as well."

"Mog Dremmag," repeated Mordred dubiously. "What on earth does that mean?"

"Old Ordenian, means wild sorcerer of music," said Jedediah Crayes snappishly. "Be quiet."

And he had spent the rest of the day drilling Mordred in the use of both names.

"Expect a challenge," he warned Mordred now as the endless lines of tents came closer. "I shall be surprised if we don't see a patrol of some kind soon."

Indeed, even as he spoke a wedge of mounted men thundered out on the open ground towards them.

Jedediah Crayes looked to Mordred, wondering if it were now he was realizing how close was the reality upon him, the first test, the first terror—how if he failed, there was no second try any more.

Mordred was a little pale, perhaps; his face was closed and set. His eyes followed the horsemen as they drew near, and his fingers gathered the reins in steadily, pulling the horse to a stop.

He'll do, thought Jedediah Crayes approvingly. *He'll do just fine.*

The soldiers formed a half-circle around them, and the one in command snatched a spear and leveled it at Jedediah Crayes. *"Etti rai! Ca corrik etti?"*

"Ittik atti Ordeni," Jedediah Crayes answered in the same language. "We wish to serve your commander, rather than perish with our fellows."

"You speak our tongue well," the man observed.

"I have traveled in Runnicor," Jedediah Crayes returned equably.

"And what of your companion—does he also speak it?"

"No, he is a foolish youth ignorant of such things," Jedediah Crayes said contemptuously, "though I have told him he will have to learn his fair share here!"

The captain guffawed scornfully. "And is he kin to you?"

"Nay, no kin of mine; merely a tentmate who shares my views about the fate of this war. Excuse me," Jedediah Crayes added, glancing at Mordred's white, strained face. "I had best let him know you mean us no harm."

Returning to the common tongue, he muttered to Mordred, "You may cease looking like an idiot, Richardson; they have no desire to spit us like pigs yet." But he lowered his voice to a barely audible level and murmured in Mordred's ear, "You are doing beautifully. Keep your chin up."

Mordred's shoulders relaxed; his taut fingers loosened on the bridle-rein. Submissively he answered, "Aye, Mog Dremmag."

There was an almost teasing lilt to his voice as he pronounced the last two words.

CHAPTER 10

SOME OF MORDRED'S TENSENESS RETURNED as he stood with Jedediah Crayes outside the tent, a great black tent with red designs of an eagle tearing at its prey, and above it the Runnicoran standard flying.

The soldier had continued speaking with Jedediah Crayes as they were escorted to the camp.

"They will take us to their commander," Jedediah Crayes translated to him. "He will approve us to the army and assign us our place here."

"Do very few of them speak the common tongue?" Mordred asked with a sinking heart, thinking of the difficulties for him as a spy and even in his assumed role if the only people he could talk to were Jedediah Crayes and a few deserters.

Jedediah Crayes put the question, and the man answered with a laugh and a stream of Runnicoran which Jedediah Crayes translated.

"Most of the men have command of the language, but they prefer their own. The officers on the other hand generally speak ours, for it sets them apart with a mark of learning and superiority."

Now, at the tent, the captain dismounted and the others rode away. "Here we are," he said, speaking so that both could understand him. Mordred noticed a marked absence of *h* and a rolling of the *r*'s.

He steadied his mind, and followed Jedediah Crayes in.

The tent's interior was spacious, and several well-placed torches mounted on iron stands spread their light from the middle almost to the far ends. Pacing between them with quick steps was a man clad in shirt and tunic of fine-woven black linen; his leggings were of dark red wool, his boots of red-dyed leather. Silver gleamed at his waist, and a sword hung from his side. He wore no helm, nor armor, nor distinguishing mark of any kind; yet by his bearing, and the deferential attitude of those who stood around him, there was no doubt in Mordred's mind which man in this tent they sought.

He saw them then waiting in the shadow of the entrance, and with an imperious gesture summoned them to him. "What, Captain Alétun, more Ordenian deserters?"

Captain Alétun inclined his head respectfully. "Aye, *Paraki*."

He turned to them as they drew near, and looked straight into Mordred's eyes. They were like his voice, his eyes, Mordred thought. Dark, dark grey they were, almost black, like the evil smoke from a burning building, like the sea under a sky with no sun nor hope of a sun. Ruthlessly they raked through him and moved on to Jedediah Crayes.

"Your names," he ordered them at last. There was no trace of accent in his voice as there had been in the captain's.

"Mog Dremmag," Jedediah Crayes supplied ingratiatingly.

"Gerald Richardson," said Mordred.

He gave a curt nod. "I am Cern Dersturi, general of these forces. My men call me *Paraki*, that is, 'Leader' in your tongue; so may you call me."

"Aye, Leader," Jedediah Crayes was quick to answer.

"Aye, Leader," Mordred echoed.

"Captain Alétun?"

"Paraki." Captain Alétun bowed.

"Put them wherever it is convenient." And with a sharp wave of his hand they were dismissed.

"He did not keep you long," Captain Alétun remarked as they walked through the fresh night air. The smell of spring and the chirping of crickets was all about. "He must be much occupied with the war councils."

"Doubtless," said Jedediah Crayes, a peculiarly dry note in his voice that no one except Mordred seemed to hear.

He felt Jedediah Crayes lean up against him, murmur softly in his ear, "First evaluation tonight. Follow me when I signal you."

~

Mordred strained his eyes into the blackness and groped blindly at the rough tree-boles. He had lost him, this time he was sure, and yet he dared not call out . . .

The moon came out, its pale light shining dimly at first, and gradually stronger. Mordred saw the shadow-dappled figure ahead of him turn and beckon impatiently.

"Good grief," Jedediah Crayes grumbled when he caught up. "It's like dragging a two-year-old around with me."

Several more minutes passed before he decided they were far enough away. Then he leaned against a tree with an expansive sigh, his lean, hungry face sharply chiseled in the moonlight. And he began to laugh, soft, almost hysterical yet quite controlled chuckles, under his breath. "Well, *that* was something," he said finally, and laughed again. "What a coincidence. What a coincidence. I tell you, Mordred, I thought I was prepared, but that near knocked me off my feet." He tilted his head back, looking up through the bare tree-branches at the stars. "I met that leader, that Cern Dersturi. I met him face-to-face, aye, and worse still, *talked* to him. Ten years ago, but neither of us much changed—and me, me nattering on about 'one of the soldiers in that mammoth army—"

Again he laughed.

"But the funniest part is that I was right. I was right about him, all along. When I saw him those ten years ago, a captain in Runnicor's army, I thought to myself, 'He has high ambitions, this fellow Cern Dersturi.' He wasn't satisfied with the promotion he had just received, no, he had only had a taste of power and he wanted more. 'He'll go for more,' I thought, 'and he'll unfortunately get it.' Well, get it he did! Hasn't improved him, by the look of things.

"Well, well. A turn it gave me, I'll own; and I wasn't sure he wouldn't recognize me under all my guise for a moment there. But it all smoothed out, and you acquitted yourself splendidly, so let's try to keep it that way."

~

Mordred leaned drearily against a tent pole.

In one morning he had discovered that there was nothing for a soldier to do, save an odd task here and there, and to hobnob with fellow soldiers.

How untrained they must be!

Nay, they were quite well trained—so much so, in fact, that they needed only to drill once every three days.

Still then, 'twas the ideal situation for a spy.

Aye, the ideal situation, thought Mordred bitterly, if that spy but spoke the language! He must have roamed half the camp by now. Everywhere it was the same.

They despised him.

In different degrees, in different ways, they all scorned his failing, from open derision to genuine pity; and though they understood him perfectly, speak to him they would not. Nor was Jedediah Crayes at hand; Mordred had not seen him since the early dawn, when he had departed on some mission of his own among the labyrinth of dull-colored tents. So the hurt of loneliness, and the hurt of rejection, and the hurt of failure, with his weariness from last night, all weighed upon his spirits. Tired and despondent, he slid to the damp new grass and slept.

When he woke, a voice was speaking in his ear, low but distinct. " . . . so that they maintain order in the . . . "

Startled, he sat up.

The sun was nearing noon; he had been asleep for some two hours. Staring all around, he saw and heard no one; and when he pressed his ear against the rough tent canvas, nothing more fell on his ears than a light babble, a mere susurration. He sat up again and frowned down at the place where his head had lain. And then he saw it: a small rip close to the base where a corner of the heavy fabric had been torn away. He held it with his fingers, guided his ear to it, and the words jumped out at him with startling clarity.

"So. What have you to say?"

Mordred knew that implacable voice from the red-patterned tent last night, and the image of a dark, sunless sea swam into his mind. But the unpleasantly smooth one which answered was a stranger.

"It pleases me well, Paraki. As you say, I have done work for you in Orden before, and no man can find an accent in my words to betray me. Naturally it is different under actual warfare, but considering the heightened danger I go into, as well as the long years of service behind me, the wage might be raised . . . by a third again?" The question tailed off suggestively.

"Your price is the same as all the other spies I employ, Blackthorn," replied the leader with a peculiarly chilling dryness. "And you will take it if you wish to continue with your 'long years of service.'"

"Aye, Paraki," the man called Blackthorn muttered.

"You have always been an apt learner, Blackthorn. I commend you for it."

Silence fell for a while, and then the leader spoke again.

"Do you understand your directions, then?"

"I slip into the refuge city Mianu, disguised as an outlying farmer driven from my home, and from there travel to Orden City and present myself as another straggler joining the army."

"Precisely. Save that . . . "

"Save that I bring with me a recommendation from a lord suggesting to promote me at once to lieutenant."

"Not 'a' lord. Lord Archlas of Grinaz Hall. Men bringing testimonials from lords of high standing are not vague."

"Lord Archlas of Grinaz Hall," amended Blackthorn sulkily.

"Speed is crucial. With every day that passes, fewer will grow the recruits and greater will suspicion be on the remainder. Take a horse and ride speedily; you may sleep in Mianu tonight if you depart at once."

"I hasten, Paraki," returned the other.

Two sets of footsteps walked across the tent.

Mordred sprang to his feet and ran, afraid with a blind and unreasoning terror lest one of them should come around and find him there. His heart flailed like a wild thing trapped within his breast, its thundering driving out his thoughts. He dodged around one—two tents, ran past several more, rounded another, and found himself facing the broad, placid Dirion River with its ceaseless flowing waters. The nightmarish feel of being hunted faded.

He could think again, and he was thinking, with a quick, shaken process, but quite rationally.

Where was Jedediah Crayes? No, there was no time to look for him. The leader had spoken in ignorance, or else sarcasm, when he said that the man might sleep in Mianu tonight; it was scarce twenty miles from the place, and he might be well on his way to Orden City by sundown if his plan unfolded well.

With purposeful strides Mordred made his way to Captain Alétun's tent. He buckled on his sword, and picked up the small Runnicoran crossbow by his bed. He led his saddled and bridled horse until the camp was long out of sight.

~

Mianu, called the Refuge City, had been built in older days by Thireler the Conqueror, when the threat of werevultures was great and the inner parts of Orden were still rife with evil things, and it was from the inside that the attack was feared. Adun Cerien had not been a walled city then but a squat tower, garrisoned to fend off and hinder attacks on that city. Now, on the west side of the Elerien Mountains, with all her fair towers facing the old threat to the east, Mianu was the most vulnerable point in Orden's defense, and the one at which any enemy would throw his most concentrated force. The leader had already tried once to open the passage from within, by way of Adun Cerien and Lord Mirden's treacherous assault. So Mianu's inhabitants were chary of those whom they let within their walls.

The guards on the rampart first saw the rider when he crested a hillock and came galloping over the plain. They watched him drawing near, reining in his horse and hammering on the gates. The sun was not far past its zenith; as he tilted up his face to look at them, they saw that his garb and equipment were as a soldier of Runnicor.

The wind bore his words up to them.

"Gatekeepers! Have you no entry for a traveler in haste?"

One man strode to the edge, cupped his hands around his mouth and shouted back. "Who are you, Bold-tongue, who come to us arrayed as one of the enemy? We are not such fools! Try the West Gate of Orden, where they will shoot you for your pains!"

The rider swayed in the saddle, and remained there a moment with his head bowed. Then he raised it again and called, "Will you not come down and hear me face-to-face? Surely there is a hatch in this gate that may be opened. See, I am taking off sword and bow, and my knife as well. I will meet you unarmed."

So several went down and opened a barred hatch in the wood of the gate. The man, having dismounted, came swiftly over and gripped the iron rods in his hands.

"I am no Runnicoran," he pleaded, "nor yet a deserter from Orden. My name is Mordred Kenhelm, and it is the general's business I am on. I beg of you, let me in!"

"Business of the general, aye," one of them muttered. "Maybe the business of stabbing him in the back!"

"Peace, Ceth," commanded the sergeant. "Look you, boy. You have given us no explanation of how, if not a soldier of the enemy, you come to appear as one of them."

The young man's face became grimmer. "Look then, sergeant. If I am not of Runnicor, nor one who has joined them, then what am I?"

The sergeant's face changed. "There is . . . another thing you might be," he said cautiously. "But you should have given us a password, if you are—that."

The man's dark head dropped, pressing wearily against the bars. "Jedediah Crayes meant to teach me last night, but we had no time," he murmured. "Fool that I was to forget . . . " Suddenly, proudly, he lifted his countenance. "Now you will not let me pass. But I tell you I mean to pass all the same."

"Nay, nay!" The sergeant held up a hand. "I tell you truly, sir, that if you are what you say I do not wish to hinder you. But answer me this: if you have seen Jedediah Crayes, how is he in appearance?"

"He is about two inches below my own height, sir, and of lean build. His hair is black, as are his eyes, and his nose is thin and curved, so that his aspect reminds one of a hawk. In his face there always seems to be an eagerness, or perhaps it is better called a hunger."

"And his manner?"

"That is difficult to say, sir, for it is constantly changing. He is terribly short-tempered, but can regain his cool in the blink of an eye. He has an enormous vanity and makes allusions often, though sometimes veiled, to his own intelligence. He can be irritable, pleasant, angry, sarcastic and smug in the space of a minute. Some people, I daresay, find him unbearable; but he is quite amusing really, and not bad when you get to know him."

The sergeant whistled and moved to undo the heavy chains. "'Tis as good as a password for me; though I'll own I never heard any call him amusing. Maybe he has mellowed in the last six months."

The young man, Mordred Kenhelm, retrieved his weapons and led the horse through. "Thank you, sir. Is there one of high authority in this town?"

"Captain Rhodes took charge of the defense preparations yesterday. You can find him in the tower Mithissa, which is that way, along the Street of the Nobles. Anyone can direct you to it."

"Again, I thank you." He swung up into the saddle. "One thing more—have you let anyone else through the gate today?"

"One man, an aging farmer whose lands the enemy took and burned. That is all."

"Was he riding?"

"Aye, he was riding a horse. Tired, it was, but finely bred."

"Ah." The young man's face was tense with a hidden strain as he nudged the horse's side and trotted down the street.

~

"I must send to the general immediately," said Captain Rhodes as soon as he had heard the news. But he frowned and something plainly troubled him.

"What is it, Captain Rhodes?"

"It is . . . it is that I cannot go myself, and I know of none I can trust enough with the message."

Mordred took a pace so that he stood directly before the captain. "Send me."

Whatever protest the captain was going to make he stifled, and finally he said, "As you wish. You will need a steed of swiftness. Take one of the dragons from the runs in the southern quarter."

Mordred's eyes shone with an eagerness he could not conceal. "I? A dragon?"

"A dragon," Captain Rhodes assented.

"How would I—is it hard? Should I know aught?"

"Nay, save that being much like a horse in handling, they are still bigger than the biggest horse, and thus more dangerous. Other than that, it is not hard. The beast must know you are the master, that is common sense. It has a harness to fit over its head, and will be trained in steering with a bridle like any land-bound mount. The motion is different, to be sure, from the gait of a horse, but it is far from uncomfortable. Nay, you can have no difficulty with a dragon."

Half an hour later, Mordred sat in a leather saddle cinched to a black dragon's back between the stubs of two spikes. Behind him was the warm interior of the building where they had found and harnessed it, above him a dimly blue and ever-dimming sky.

"Nudge her with your heel," said the stableman.

Mordred dug a heel tentatively into the hard, leathery skin of the creature, so different from the soft flank of a horse. Against his calves and underneath him he felt a powerful surge of muscle, and suddenly the ground and the dragon run and the stableman were all below, and there was only the vault of darkening sky about him and the world spread out like a living map beneath. He felt the beat of the great wings on either side, the steady rhythm of the toiling muscles, the stream of air in his face.

To ride a dragon, he realized, is a glorious thing.

And he was glad. It would be a pity, he thought, to ride and not to realize.

~

The stars had not yet come out when he landed in the courtyard of Mitheren. He hastened inside, and by a miracle was able to see the general almost immediately. Quickly he outlined to him the message.

"He will most likely come here directly after his arrival; he may be calling himself Blackthorn, but perhaps not. I know not what he looks like. You will know him by his letter, which purports to be from Lord Archlas of—I cannot remember the name."

"Grinaz Hall?"

"Grinaz Hall, that is it. It will contain a recommendation that he be promoted to lieutenant."

The general nodded. "Aye, he is a well-known man and a trustworthy friend of mine. I would have accepted any request of his. Well, 'twill be but a simple matter to check the seal, and if they have managed to get that aright we may put several questions to him. Sooner or later we shall trip him up. You expect him to arrive tonight?"

"Very early tomorrow at the latest," Mordred answered.

"You shall testify as well, then, before you leave. You did not see him; but you would recognize his voice, I hope?"

"I would recognize it, my general."

"Good." The general smiled and clapped Mordred on the back. "Well done, Mordred Kenhelm. Two days and you have already foiled one plan of this leader's. You must be careful, or Jedediah Crayes will begin to grow jealous."

Mordred laughed. "We shall see."

~

The sun of early afternoon glanced across a distant bank of trees folded around Mianu's white turreted gleam, striking some with golden-green fire and leaving others to linger in a sober contrast of dark grey-green. Ahead, in the direction that the horse was steadily cantering, the Dirion River shimmered a deep, royal blue, and its surface glitter was like a starry crown.

Yet the mounted patrol hurtling towards him as an arrow to the mark seemed to have naught to do with the beauty of the day, with the trees or river.

Mordred reined in, and waited for them.

~

Flanked by soldiers, his weapons confiscated, Mordred walked behind a stiff-faced Captain Alétun into a small tent distinguished as the private quarters of an officer by the scarlet pennant affixed to its ridgepole.

The man seated within looked up—a stout individual with deep-set, narrow eyes. "This is the one, Captain?"

Captain Alétun jerked his head in a nod. "Aye, Lieutenant." He wheeled and stood to the side.

The lieutenant stood. "Give your name, boy."

"Private Gerald Richardson," Mordred answered distantly, tilting his head in a deliberately provoking manner and wondering with a detached part of himself if he could be the same person whom the general had smiled at in the warm rush-lit room in Mitheren.

The man frowned. "And what have you to say, Private Richardson, concerning this breach of conduct? Your captain accuses you of an entire day's absence when he had given you no leave."

Mordred lifted his shoulders in an insolent shrug and pointed to his bow which another soldier was holding. "Are your men not allowed to hunt for their own pleasure?"

The officer's cheeks reddened. He sucked in a slow breath, and the yell he gave made even Captain Alétun wince. Most of what he said, Mordred could not understand, as it was at least half in Runnicoran, but none of it sounded complimentary in the least.

And I would be appalled, too, he thought with that distant, cool part of himself, *if I had been just sassed by an absolute prig a third of my age.*

Knowing it would do no good, he said simply, "My apologies, sir."

The lieutenant glared wildly at him. "Your apologies!" he roared. "Captain Alétun!"

"Aye, Lieutenant."

"Five lashes for unsanctioned departure, and ten for insubordination." His chest swelled angrily, the red spreading down his neck. "Now get this *werevulture* out of my sight!"

~

Jedediah Crayes glanced in all directions and stepped into the silent tent, pacing noiselessly as a cat over the matted grass.

Mordred was lying on his stomach, head pillowed on his arms; his shirt was stained dark across the shoulders. His blanket lay carelessly half across him. "Little fool," muttered Jedediah Crayes.

He bent down on one knee. "Little fool. *I* could have talked myself out of it."

He tapped him on the arm and Mordred's eyes flickered open. "It's all right, there's no one in here; they're all out at the drill. By the time they're done, I shall be back with them. Now tell me, what on earth was that for?"

"Insubordination," said Mordred and winced involuntarily.

Jedediah Crayes waved his arms in disgust. "I know why you were flogged. I even managed to hear an account of your conversation with that lieutenant, and it's a wonder you didn't kill him with an apoplectic fit. I am Jedediah Crayes. What I want to know is why you left!"

"It was . . . a spy. The leader sent a spy into Orden."

"A spy. And you just up and left? For pity's sake, why didn't you let me know? I could have made up a perfectly good excuse for you to be gone. I could have gone myself—I should have gone myself!"

"There wasn't time."

"Huh. And what about getting in? I didn't teach you a single password yet! Don't tell me they let you in without one!"

Mordred smiled faintly. "They did."

"Really! How about you do some—never mind. Did you actually manage to succeed in this rash endeavor?"

"Aye."

"Well . . . that's good, I suppose," said Jedediah Crayes with a grudging note of praise. "You did well, all things considered. But did you *have* to sass the lieutenant?"

"I knew they would ask me straight away why I was gone, and I dared not give them the chance to press me. There's a great deal in a tone. If I had said, 'I was hunting, sir,' in an ordinary respectful way, it would have looked queer to them, especially because I was gone for so very long a time. And they would have remembered I am Ordenian, and the game would be all but up. At the very least they would be suspicious, and there would have been questions and more questions. But if a man is insulted, he might not stop to think of those little things. So I—I used my newness to the army to my advantage instead, and played the role of a stupid lord's son who has known nothing but having his own way. And it worked; I am rather good at acting proud." Mordred gave a slight, wry smile.

"Huh," Jedediah Crayes said. "I'm glad I don't have to emulate your method of turning away questioners. But never mind. You did rather well. I'd still like to know how on earth you got in without a password—but never mind. Never mind. We'll cover that another time, when you're feeling better. How are you doing now?"

"I'm fine."

"You are *what*—Listen, this is not heroics school. I am your employer. I need to know when you are going to be up and around again. I need to know how you are!"

Mordred sighed. "A bit more than uncomfortable. I'll be up tomorrow." His eyes drifted closed, leaving a face that looked suddenly very young and exhausted. He did not speak again.

Jedediah Crayes felt his forehead when he was sure that Mordred had gone to sleep. Clammy, warm. The unruly dark cowlick was damp with sweat. "Touch feverish, I shouldn't wonder," he muttered. His face softened imperceptibly. "Little fool . . . "

Mordred did not stir. Jedediah Crayes sprang up lightly and left the tent.

CHAPTER 11

"**IF THIS IS ALL THERE** is to war, I can handle it." Marcus stretched on the cot with an innocent ecstasy. "While the beds may not be quite as comfortable as those of home, they are a sight better than no bed at all."

Sergeant Garin's men had expected that they would return to Orden City after Adun Cerien was won. Instead, they had been marched on through the pass to the tall, white-turreted city of Mianu. After four peaceful days stationed in the barracks there, Marcus was—or claimed to be—resigned to a life of boredom.

"In fact," he declared, "I am content with it, and that is so much the better."

Bardrick shook his head with a slight grin, pretending not to be amused by his younger brother's prattle. Others, knowing Marcus less well, took him literally.

"There'll be fighting yet," said one young man. "Haven't you heard all the officers talking? Even Sergeant Garin. How great a simpleton can you be?"

Marcus only laughed and folded his hands behind his head, staring up at the ceiling.

"Marcus, there's an ant on you," said Bardrick, looking at the black insect that was making its way over Marcus' arm.

"Oh?" Marcus said placidly. "How interesting."

"On your sleeve. Get it off."

Marcus twisted his head to one side and studied the creature. "To oblige you, my dear brother." He flicked it away. "You know, after a battle, a few ants are nothing to fret about."

Bardrick shrugged and was silent.

"It happened well for all of us, really," Marcus remarked softly after a moment. He glanced around the damp, dark room. "You and I, and Braegon, and Therelane and Jared, and Fenris—we all made it out alive."

"And Mordred, don't forget," said Bardrick. He looked at Fenris. Fenris' eyes were on the ground.

No one knew what had happened to Mordred. Some people had seen him with Captain Rhodes the night following the battle, but it could not be found out why or where he had gone. All Sergeant Garin would say was that he had been called away by the captain, and they were left to wonder. The most logical guess was that the captain had reassigned him to a different division, and so they generally assumed, but why? What had they, or he, done wrong? It was then that Marcus had said to Bardrick, vehemently, "I *hate* the army."

"Hush," Bardrick had said, aching for his little brother. *You are too young for this, Marcus . . . sixteen, too young for war, for death.*

As for Fenris, he had taken it quietly, but everyone knew it had cut him hard. He ate little, and barely answered when spoken to. Maybe it would not have been so bad for him, Bardrick thought, if he could have said farewell to Mordred and known where he was going . . .

The painful silence that descended at Mordred's name was broken only when Marcus said, "I wonder if anyone else from Ceristen is posted here in Mianu? We ought to have a look around, while things remain this quiet."

"Aye," said Bardrick; "that's a fine idea, Marcus."

One of the few older men among them spoke up obligingly. "You can go about the city most any time that's not training hours. Just be back by sundown. Check the taverns; that's where soldiers go in lee time."

"Thank you," Bardrick replied. "Braegon, Jared—any of you coming?"

Jared shook his head. He had taken a gash along his forearm in the battle at Adun Cerien, and since then he had been more laconic than ever.

"I think I shall come," said Braegon, swinging his legs over his own cot. "Come, Therelane, we'll make it a four of us."

Therelane's eyes lighted, as they always did when he was included among them. He came forward eagerly and joined them as they left the building for the blinding sun and keen spring wind.

~

With a rush of wings, the dragon made a delicate landing on the white paving of the courtyard. Mithissa rose up in the center, one among the many fair towers of Mianu, built after the style of Orden's earlier periods which favored tall, slim pinnacles and scant outer facings.

The rider dismounted in an easy spring and strode within.

"I am here but briefly, only to verify that the defenses here are adequate and that all preparations are being carried out," the general explained after he and Captain Rhodes had greeted one another. "You will accompany me out later?"

"Aye, willingly."

The general paused, a frown gathering itself between his eyes. "In Captain Murray's report, he said that Lord Mirden was not found in the city after you recaptured it. Is that so?"

"It is, my general. He must have escaped it when he saw the reinforcements arrive."

The general's eyes were narrowed in anxiety and doubt. "It is ill news, for he ought not to be still at large. I fear of what he may intend now. But it is done; and we can do nothing until we hear word of him."

Captain Rhodes nodded. "Tell me, my general," he said, "did Mordred Kenhelm reach you safely in time with his message?"

"Concerning the enemy spy? That he did, and we were able to apprehend the man directly."

"So, that is well . . . " Captain Rhodes sighed, his face still troubled. "I hope that I did right in sending him on with the message. I had none others to relay it by, and he offered at once without my asking. Yet I fear that he will suffer something for his eager service, unless he has a solid tale for such a long absence."

"He has a quick wit, and Jedediah Crayes at his back. Do not fear, Captain Rhodes." The general smiled. "You care much for him, I think."

Captain Rhodes hesitated. "Aye. There is a love in me for that little village of Ceristen, from the day I first saw it: an admiration for such hardy, close-knit, welcoming folk. But Mordred . . . he is strangely as a brother to me, though I have now met him but thrice. I would not readily see him hurt."

~

Kenneth Denholm pinched the old, softening wood of the squarely fashioned table, not listening to the rambling of his comrade beside him. He was thinking of Marianne, her cuddling close to him and whispering with shining eyes and irresistible smile about *the baby*; then, barely a day later, seeing him off in the grey dawn, her eyes huge with fear and the sleepless night, face pinched and taut with the effort of not crying.

"Try to smile," he told her pleadingly, cupping her face between his hands in the old lover's way. "Sometimes. For the baby."

She suddenly looked more scared still. "Kenneth—what if something happens—to the baby?"

"Hush, hush." He placed his hands gently on her lower belly. "Nothing is going to happen to the baby. He's going to be grand, big, strong."

"Maybe it will be a girl." She was almost laughing now, one tiny dimple half-visible in her beautiful smile. He caught her, crushed her in a quick hug, and turned and hurried out the door before either of them could cry . . .

"Kenneth!" The shout jerked him out of memories, and he looked up at Marcus Segelas' winsome, infectious grin. Startled, and then delighted, he leaped up and met Marcus halfway in a somewhat rough hug.

"You—and Bardrick—land, how many of you are here?"

"We left two back at the barracks," said Marcus, eyes dancing. "Anybody else with you?"

Kenneth blinked and recollected himself. "Fred and Daren Thorne, as a matter of fact. But they're back in our own quarters. Not here."

"Well, then, we can go there!" said Marcus cheerfully.

Braegon demurred. "Without warning, I shouldn't like to do that. A barracks are the nearest thing to home a soldier has, and unannounced visits are not always welcome."

"Oh, very well—" Marcus shrugged.

"Another time," said Bardrick. "Come, Kenneth, tell us how it has been with you."

So Kenneth told them of going down to Mitheren, how his division had been sent up to the West Gate. There had been some mild attacking there, half-hearted, the sergeants called it. "More probing the defenses than aught else. They never laid real siege to it and drew off early. I did nothing but fire a few arrows down myself."

"Then we have you beat," said Marcus, grinning. But his gaiety was tempered by an unusual gravity, and Kenneth, looking at his friends, saw a weary, burning look in all their eyes. They had been seared by war. They were not the same.

~

At first, it had seemed like one could not carry on.

How were ordinary things to continue? How, when the world had come crashing down? When brothers and friends had torn themselves out of the village's peaceful framework to leave jagged, irreplaceable holes? How, when the eve of *one's own wedding* had been stamped upon and blackened, and the betrothed had gone to a place whence he might never return?

But as the days went by, and the sun still shone and the trees began to leaf out, and no ravaging soldiers entered the village with axe and sword and fire, Fiona found that one could carry on. It was not quite the same. The holes were still there. A strange invisible shadow seemed to be cast over every moment. But it was a shadow that they could live with, that could fade only to the very edges and lie forgotten.

She walked with quick steps along the road, reveling in the greenness that was everywhere and the pure life that seemed to radiate from the trees, the ground, the whole world. Sixteen springs she had seen in Erahar, but this was so different from Erahar's pale, austere springs that she felt like a child seeing for the first time, and everything was new and vibrant.

It would have been Fred's first spring here as well.

The shadow deepened, and she walked on with sober face.

She had not seen Fred after the news came; in a way she was glad of that. The last memory she had of him was the glad, shining one of his face filled with love and peace and his strong arms holding her in a net of security.

Oh, if she could have one more moment like that with him, she would never take it for granted again . . .

Fiona came out of the trees and the open slope of the mountain was all around her, swallowing her up in a sense of vastness and might, the empty sky a thing of intangible, weightless, wild freedom. She shifted her bundle under one arm, picked up her skirts, and ran.

The Earles' home was a comfortingly placid environment, warm after the brisk wind outside, and it almost seemed at first that the war had no place here at all. Fiona explained to Mrs. Earle why she had come—to return the carding battens that she had loaned to the Segelases—and Mrs. Earle accepted them with thanks and sat Fiona down by the fire with bread and butter and a warmed cup of cow's milk, rambling cheerily on this and that.

"Aye, and the Staffords are looking at another young one this autumn, come harvest time or a little later, about the same time as Marianne's, 'twill be."

"That is nice," said Fiona, a smile breaking out as she thought of a fifth infant in Mrs. Stafford's arms. And then the hurt constricted in her heart again, and she said no more.

" . . . but you know Irene Grey, of course?"

"Know her?" Fiona hesitated. The Greys were so secluded, the only one she could say she knew was Therelane. But Irene—yes, Irene was the one who was able to sense ailments. "I remember her. What is it?"

"Why, she's leaving! That's what."

"Leaving?" Fiona stared in perplexity at the other woman. "Why?"

~

"I—don't—understand." Fourteen-year-old Lewis Grey panted as he lengthened his steps to keep up with his sister's surprisingly quick stride. The last thing Therelane had said to him was, *"You and Adolphus are the men of the house now, you know; be good to Mother, and keep Irene company."* "I don't understand. Why are you going?"

Irene whipped coolly on him, her dark hair swishing. She was short, but her eyes were still barely on a level with him. "I have been hiding up on this mountain for sixteen years, Lewis, with the rest of my crazed family. Haven't you been doing the same?"

Lewis did not know what to answer. He shrugged and scratched behind his ear.

She swept his hand down. "Don't do that. Now, some of the family has a real excuse for hiding up here—like our father and Ledelia. I never did. And now that there is a war, I truly don't."

Lewis frowned. "But you have the curse, too, like them. Therelane and Adolphus and I are the ones who don't."

Irene's eyes snapped with impatience. "Of course I have the curse! But I'm not mad, am I? Nay, the curse gave to me a gift, if gift one can call it. For a long time it was almost dormant, because I didn't care to use it, but lately I have been testing; and the more I test, the more powerful it grows. Pains and ailments that used to be a vague blur because of distance are now clear to me from a mile away. I can focus on a particular person and block the others out with greater ease than I could before.

"Now you see, Lewis?" Her cold, abrupt tones were almost gentle. "I have to use this. I can help the world, and I must. It has been my calling since I was an infant, and I ignored it long enough. I am going out to the cities, to the hospices, wherever there is the most sickness and wounds; and while I have no gift of healing, my gift of sense may prove its worth yet."

Suddenly to Lewis his strange, cynical, sharp-tongued sister seemed a whole new person, wonderful and brave. He gulped back the babyish lump in his throat and told her so.

She looked like she might snort, or roll her eyes; instead she sighed and gave a light pat to his head. "You little, idealistic dreamer-boy. Just like Therelane."

CHAPTER 12

"RICHARDSON! OVER HERE, BOY!"

Mordred came across the dim tent and stood before his superior, waiting for whatever tongue-lashing or reprimand Captain Alétun had in store. But the man merely handed him a letter, and said sharply, "Deliver this to the Paraki at once."

"Aye, sir," said Mordred, taking the folded paper and walking carefully out of the tent. It was the second day since the flogging, and his shoulders and back still smarted fiercely and threatened to break open at the least sudden movement. It gave him, though he did not know it, a still prouder look than usual as he walked through the camp.

The leader was, surprisingly, alone when Mordred found him—quite alone, staring into the dimness of the shadow beyond the torches. He turned about swiftly as Mordred entered, and fixed him with those grim dark eyes, holding out his hand for the note. "Who sent it?"

"Captain Alétun, sir," Mordred answered.

He started to read it, but checked, the paper fluttering in his fingers as he studied Mordred. "You are not Runnicoran by your face or speech."

"No, sir." Mordred wet his lips, willing his eyes to meet the older man's.

"What is your name?"

"Gerald Richardson, sir."

He waited for some sign of recognition, but the leader made none and Mordred realized in relief that there was no reason for him to recall one boy out of possibly dozens of Ordenian deserters in the past se'ennight. The leader transferred his attention to the letter and read it through at a glance. When he was done he rubbed his thumb over it and began to feed it in a detached way to the candle-flame beside him.

"Shall I carry back a reply, sir?" said Mordred.

Cern Dersturi halted and looked at him, then shrugged and continued burning the parchment. "A captain's petty concerns are not mine. There will be no reply."

Something of a wholly new nature seemed to strike him. He dropped the smoldering paper on the grass and turned to the side, frowning in thought.

"Did I not dismiss you?" he barked suddenly at Mordred.

"Forgive me, sir," Mordred started, but Cern Dersturi cut him off.

"Can you read and write?"

"In the common tongue, sir, and in my birth language—but not Runnicoran."

The leader waved it aside. "No matter. You are educated—you are intelligent."

Mordred stood quite still, having no idea what to say. The entire conversation was bizarre, unreal; did the leader somehow suspect him of—of . . .

And then came the questions, a great number of them, sharp and quick on the heels of one another, and Mordred was quite sure that he was being tested, though he did not know why. Quick they came and quick he answered them, a taut silvery dance where the balance might fall wrong at any moment. Some questions he knew he could not answer with the truth, and an answer would come just when there could not be another millisecond of waiting. The balance never slipped.

At last the questions stopped; Mordred could not remember what a single one of them had been.

"What do you want with me?" he asked, the words bursting painfully out of him like the small, hard breaths of a winded horse.

The leader smiled. It was not a pleasant sort of smile, but a disarming one all the same. Then the smile vanished, and his eyes became cold. "I had a man who was lost to me," he said. "One Blackthorn. Just yesterday the word was brought of his arrest. His value lay not in soldiering but in spy work; and his service will be sorely missed."

A heartbeat of silence.

Mordred dropped his eyes, sure that his face would betray him.

He heard the leader's voice, speaking coolly again into the echoless quiet. "I think that you would make a good replacement."

The astonishment that seized him rendered him mute, and then as the horror began to creep all over him he stammered out, "I—I could not, sir—I could not—"

"No?" That disarming smile again. "You do not fear danger, surely. There is nothing of the coward about you."

Desperately he tried. His words were as empty and impotent as clods dashed against a wall of glass. "I cannot go back, I deserted—now, sir, they would recognize me, they would kill me."

White and sharp like a cat's glinted the leader's teeth in the torchlight. "Naturally. You think I did not know that? We need not return you to your old division; all the same you will go under a disguise, to be safe. Does that suit?"

Mordred had no argument or plea left—he stared back dumbly at the leader.

"Now, you have a tongue still. You are not still thinking of refusal?"

And that dry question told Mordred that there would be no refusal. He remembered Blackthorn's sullen but submissive "Aye, Paraki."

"Aye, Paraki," he found himself uttering unconsciously, and then he was dismissed, panting in the cool evening air outside the tent.

Jedediah Crayes.

~

"What?" Jedediah Crayes stared at Mordred as though he had said the Ruler of Night himself had come to the camp. *"What?"*

"He asked me to spy." Mordred's face was taut with strain in the moonlight.

"Impossible! What? What did you do?"

"I did nothing—only delivered a letter from Captain Alétun, and he—he noticed me."

"Impossible! He must be crazy—mad—what a *mess*! Right, we've got to get you out of here first thing. At once. Before dawn, in fact, so get your belongings and whatnot together."

Mordred's head whirled dizzily as Jedediah Crayes ranted in an incessant storm of sharp, irascible upset. "How will you get out of it?"

"I'll think of something," Jedediah Crayes snapped. "I always do. Outrageous, unthinkable, good land, what a horrific turn of events, what a travesty . . . "

"Must I go? Is there no other way out? I—I've done nothing yet."

"Nothing?" Jedediah Crayes snorted. "Don't sell yourself that short! Oh yes, catching an enemy spy was 'nothing'. Anyway, it shan't be discharge for you, only relocation. We'll find somewhere else to send you, the general will see to that; word has it a number of the Runnicorans are marching north. Still! What a stupid, annoying thing to happen . . . "

Mordred did not know why, but the thought of leaving seemed to close a cold, lonely hand around his heart. "Could we not try to—if the leader—" He broke off both times. None of the ideas would work. The leader would never relent, certainly would not forget, to press for a change of mind would be too dangerous. He did not say again, “I don’t want to go,” though his heart cried it; that would change nothing . “Don’t accompany me out of the camp, Jedediah Crayes. I can find my own way well enough and you will be in trouble if you and I disappear together.”

But Jedediah Crayes’ yowls were changing from protest and denial to acceptance.

“It just might work, you know,” he said slowly. “It’ll be a risk, of course. Double spy is always a mad risk. But if you play it right—and you’ll have me to help you—you can string the leader along all right, while you’ll be in a position to hear quite-a-lot of the enemy plans. *And* there’ll be no more of this mishmash of trying to sneak you away from the camp and back again without kicking up a fuss—asking for a flogging, or a hanging.

“It’s your say, Mordred. I could get you out of here and back to Mitheren before the leader knows a thing. And if you make a slip, you’re dead. There’s no guarantee that I could get you out of *that* mess. But, as I said . . . it’s something of an ideal wave. Don’t get this thrown your way every day.”

Mordred stood there, conflicting thoughts scoring through his mind, one part of him wanting to pull back. But he knew what his answer would be.

“I’ll do it.”

~

Again, he stood in the hot, muffling tent with red and black designs. But this time it was not only himself and Cern Dersturi, but a small convocation of high officers and one man who, Mordred gathered, was the leader’s second, Dovurti Atta by name. And it was not only the leader’s dark eyes boring into him, but all the men. Measuring him, assessing him. Asking this question or that.

"Enough," said the leader with a wave, after the discussion had gone on for a tedious time. "He will serve. Now, Richardson, we must discuss how to properly integrate you into the Ordenian army, and where you would best be assigned. You will, naturally, need a disguise and a false name; for the disguise, find Igurst the metal-worker when we are finished here. Tell him to alter significantly but nothing too elaborate, for complicated disguises fail easily, and you will need to sustain yours for some time. I need not tell you, I am sure, to avoid anyone who knows you by sight."

"Aye, Paraki," said Mordred with a respectful nod.

The leader smiled; Mordred's use of the Runnicoran term seemed to please him. "You know where Mianu lies—what is called the 'Refuge City'?"

"Aye, Paraki."

"And you surely know it is a weak point, perhaps the weakest, unless we marched our army all the way to the eastern side of the country. I believe I shall send you there; for we shall soon launch an assault upon it."

Mordred lost the next thing he said in a rush of lightheaded exhilaration. Jedediah Crayes had been right: he was in a place where he could hear anything, everything.

"Well, Richardson? Richardson!"

"I—I did not hear."

"You were not listening. This is no place for daydreams! You will find out for me while in Mianu the figures of the army, how it is defended, and relay them to me. Have you a good memory?"

"I think so, sir."

"Commit as little to writing as may be; such things give away a spy quicker than anything else. But be sure of your information, for mistakes are worse than a jotted number."

"We cannot send him in by the same method as Blackthorn," said Dovurti Atta. "That would be suspect now."

"Quite true. But there are other ways." The leader halted and frowned heavily. "Nay, we will discuss it later—"

"I can get into Mianu." Mordred broke in, impetuously, almost panting in his excitement. "I know I can." He met Cern Dersturi's sharp gaze earnestly and without fear, willing him to assent.

Cern Dersturi did not look displeased, though several of the other men were murmuring doubtfully. "You are sure."

Mordred nodded eagerly, face alight with conviction. If the leader would not press him on *how* . . .

"So be it," said the leader after a long pause of scrutiny, and Mordred knew that he had satisfied him in some odd way. "Once you are in, it should not be hard for you to join the army. I cannot get you any high rank, however; you will have to manage to fulfill my orders as best you can in the guise of footsoldier. But I daresay that you shall manage it; you are, I think, inventive."

"There is still the matter of his name," said another lieutenant.

"Certainly. You will want an Ordenian name, of course—does Sinethar suit you, Richardson?"

"Sinethar," repeated Mordred. The name was strange, but it rolled easily off his tongue. "Aye, sir."

"Good. You are Sinethar. Remember that. Go to Igurst and see to the disguise; then report back to me by evening. You will leave tomorrow at dawn."

"Aye, Paraki."

As Mordred left, he saw one of the men who had been largely silent the entire time, of silvering hair, a balding forehead, and a large and hooked nose. His eyes were very dark and sinister, and he was watching Mordred intently.

~

"What the blasted—blithering—blazes—did you *do* to yourself?" Jedediah Crayes squinted at Mordred with priceless disbelief.

Mordred laughed.

"*Hsst*! You idiot, keep it down. This is supposed to be a secret meeting."

Mordred laughed again, but softer. "What do I look like?"

Jedediah Crayes took a long and judicious breath. "Like you lengthened and thickened the reach of your eyebrows, scarred yourself thrice along the cheek, and acquired a most unbecoming wart below your lip. Other than that, you look more or less like the annoying brat I'm accustomed to seeing."

"If I didn't linger around and talk to you, could you pass me on the street and not know me?"

Jedediah Crayes considered with arched eyebrows, and nodded. "I believe I might. I might, at that . . . Think about growing a beard and you'd be better off, though."

Mordred's mouth worked in another grin. "I'm afraid that's something I'm not very good at."

"Oh well!" Jedediah Crayes snorted and tossed a stick into the air. "Well, you smug little double spy, I suppose you're off shortly. Behave yourself among the Great Ones. Congratulate yourself on deserting me—not that I need your help to do my job. In fact, I'll be a lot better off without your uppity nose and pert tongue making you an hourly nuisance."

Mordred sat down and folded his arms over his knees, staring up at the half-formed moon. "What does Sinethar mean, Jedediah Crayes?"

"Hmm? Thiredanian Sinethar? Translates to 'little knife', I believe. Oh, what a dratted nuisance. He had to give you another alias, didn't he?" He laughed drily and flicked another stick away. "I think he's taken a shine to you, Mordred. Make good use of it."

~

The forest was awash with fog drifting up from the lowlands and the river. The moon had set, and sunrise was not far off as the rider galloped over the last furlong before the city.

Mordred wondered whether the guards on the wall would be the same as the last time he had come. He would have liked to see the sergeant again, but he realized that not only was it unlikely, but also if they recognized him under his guise there would be awkward explaining to do, and secrecy to be demanded. Anyway, it did not matter; he had the password.

He was outfitted merely in the clothes that he had arrived in the enemy camp with, and a cloak to ward off the chill. Besides his sword and knife he had one more small dagger that the leader had given to him, saying, "It will be a token, if you should need to prove yourself to any of my men."

His horse slowed as the wall loomed up. Mordred drew rein before the gate, and for safety's sake pulled the hood of the cloak low over his brow.

Stirrings sounded above in answer to his knock. "Who goes?"

"A rider from the west, with tidings—*very* urgent tidings." Mordred waited tensely and with relief heard the footsteps coming down in answer. The hatch opened with a clang and the man said softly, "Well?"

"The stars shine in a circle, and the mountains are red," replied Mordred in the same quiet tone.

"Ah!" murmured the other, and with a grunt of satisfaction he moved to unbar the gate. "Go on in, sir, and good speed to you."

Mordred answered with a nod and spurred his mount quickly in, through the narrow streets, up to the tower Mithissa.

"I must see Captain Rhodes," he said to the servant who greeted him at the door.

"Captain Rhodes is not here," was the answer. "The general has taken over command of the city; shall I take you to him?"

"Yes, thank you. At once." Mordred dropped his mount's reins and followed the man within.

"Yes?" was the general's question as Mordred entered the room and shut the door behind himself. There was no recognition in his face.

"Do you not know me, my general?"

The general started and looked closer. "Mordred Kenhelm! I do know you, indeed, but how is it you come here in such a manner?"

"It is very simple," Mordred answered, "and yet not simple at all. I have been forced to take on another role; and I will need your help."

He explained himself, as clearly and briefly as he was able, and the general listened without question or interruption. At the end he remained silent and stern-faced, his head lowered, seeming to withhold judgment.

"Do you think that I did ill, my general?" Mordred asked at last when he could not bear the silence any longer.

The general raised his head, surprised, and laughed. "No! No, *mari*, you did nothing amiss, and indeed you handled it as best as could be done, I think. If you are willing to take on this burden as you have others, let me not dissuade you."

Mordred could not contain the glad smile that broke across his face at the warm praise. "My general, you will find me a place then in the army? Make sure it is not with anyone I know. They would see through my disguise soon enough."

"I shall see to that, aye, at once. And I will give you a list of numbers that you may take back to the leader—small enough so that he will perhaps muster fewer against us, while not so small that you are indicted later on. Do not take it to him too soon, however; he will wonder how you came on the answers so easily."

"Aye, my general. And you will care for my horse? I shall need him again, I suppose, when I ride out, but I will not be taking him into the barracks with me."

An hour later, Mordred stood silently to the side, waiting as the general spoke swiftly to Sergeant Galbert Corass.

"He will be often absent and may return at irregular and unexpected times. You will not question him on these absences, nor permit your men to do so. He will keep to himself, and will not be required to yield any information to you. If you form any guesses, you will keep them to yourself. Know that if you fail in these regards, and I hear of it, there will be recompense."

Sergeant Corass nodded throughout all this, his eyes flashing curiously towards Mordred. "Aye, General."

The general turned to Mordred, pressed his hand, and went out into the early morning.

Sergeant Corass folded his brawny arms, tore his gaze resolutely from Mordred, and opened the door of the small, private room to gesture into the main barracks. "Welcome, Sinethar. Make yourself at home."

CHAPTER 13

"WHO ARE YOU?"

"Sinethar," Mordred replied curtly, folding his arms. He leaned against the wall, shifting away from the inquirer.

"Where are you from?"

"Whence that scar?"

The amiable questions spurted out, guileless and well-meant, but the sergeant had already taken note and was striding over to them, barking out the command, "Hold!"

He reached them, looked them over, and said briefly without rebuke, "There's to be no questions asked."

The men drifted away, puzzled but obedient, while Mordred slowly brushed over the false scars along his cheek. He caught himself—unnecessary, if not dangerous, to draw attention to any part of the disguise.

He suddenly realized what a lonely time it was going to be here. He must not even make friends, lest in closer intimacy he make an unguarded fumble.

Against his will a great torrent of longing rushed upwards; the faces of Braegon, Marcus, and Therelane flooded his mind—and *Fenris*. Why had he ever left them?

Again, he reined himself in harshly to a halt.

Sink into Sinethar, he thought. *You must be Sinethar, and Sinethar is cold and distant and answers nothing. Sinethar has no friends, and if he does he certainly does not remember them. Sinethar is no more feeling than the distant moon.*

Mordred crossed his arms and set his jaw in tight resolve.

~

"The days drag by so," muttered Kenneth.

Fred looked up. "But it is already nearly the first of May."

"The first of the new year," said another man, Curith, with a small, explosive sigh. "Much rejoicing there shall be in these streets!"

"No time for rejoicing, for celebration, or for respite," said Daren grimly. "Only war."

"Only war," echoed Fred, and he ran the polishing rag with a slow circular movement over the blade across his knees. "But there has been little of that for us as yet. So far Mianu's streets are quiet."

"The war will come," said Curith. He bent over Fred's work. "A fine blade, that; but it has seen wear. Is it a family sword?"

The edge of Fred's mouth worked a moment, and he held up the blade. "Perhaps it is now. I secured it from an old merchant in Harcalan."

"Harcalan! Not the Ordenian fasting by the skirts of Edivernel?" Curith whistled. "You are a further traveler than your appearance makes you, Fred Thorne. Have you had it long?"

"Not long." Fred lowered the sword as though it had grown heavy on him, and stared at it. "Some six or seven months. Even now it has not yet drawn blood by me. I think—the wish is not yet in me to take the life of any man . . . "

"Nor is it in many of us," said Curith.

"Orden has known peace too long," said another, raising his voice from where he sat, though his eyes did not leave the ground. "She has forgotten the ways of war. Nonetheless the lust to kill is one more quickly learned than one might guess."

"Peace, Ellas," said Curith, rounding on him in a tone of annoyance. "One need not be gripped by the lust of it to kill."

Ellas shrugged. "It is quickly learned," he said.

~

Mordred traced his finger over the raised whorl on the hilt of the leader's dagger.

A group of men was heading out for one of the taverns. "Care to come, Sinethar?" one of them called.

Mordred shook his head. Slowly, he traced the patterns on the dagger. Someday they would understand that he was never going to accept their invitations, their ready inclusion. He liked them for it; if only he did not have to ignore it. If only it were safe to befriend them—if only he did not have to worry that he might meet Fenris in one of the taverns—

He stopped himself, fiercely. It was no good wishing; in fact, it was bad. This might go on for weeks, and he must learn to bear it. Almost savagely he thrust the dagger back into its sheath and walked across the barracks. It had been two days; he had waited long enough to see the general.

The general was in Mithissa, but to see him was another matter. He was closeted with several lower officers and Mordred stood in the soft-white, thick-shadowed entrance hall for an hour before a servant summoned him.

"My general," he said quickly. "I think it is time I am returning to the leader. Do you have my numbers?"

The general withdrew a paper from among the tumbled documents on the table and handed it across to Mordred. "Take it, memorize it if you can, and then it had best be burned. Neither among your side or the Runnicorans' would it be safe for any to find you with this."

Mordred nodded, and folding the closely marked sheet stowed it in his jerkin. "My general, how ought I to leave the city? Is there another way besides the gate? It may be noticed by unwanted eyes, and if Mianu is attacked shortly I will not be able to use it at all."

"Yes!" The general pushed back his chair and stood. "I ought to have remembered that. Yes, there is another way out—let me show you."

After a quick traversal of the city, Mordred found himself high up on the outer wall where it hugged the shoulder of the mountain, feeling very small between the massive earth-born stone on one side and the vastness of the man-shaped city on the other. A slender white bridge ran the width of the gap between wall and mountainside, as though sprung there by hands not human.

"Go," said the general, pointing at the bridge. "It is not a way made for many, but for one, and even so it will not be without difficulties. Follow the ridge until you reach the forest. There the path is marked out, though rudely; you had best tread it in daylight until you know it well."

"Aye, my general." Mordred stepped up onto the foot of the bridge and laid one hand on the carved rail, feeling the slight unevenness and pits under his fingers where it appeared to br smooth, white-flecked stone.

"There are guards there—up on that tower." The general gestured up to a watch bastion looming near on the eastern hand. "If they should see you, they may accost you, but give them the password and all will be well."

Mordred glanced up at it, narrowing his eyes against the brightness of the climbing sun. "Aye."

"Go in swiftness and in safety." The general's hands were closing over his, and then he was running lightly across the bridge, the free, thin wind in his nose and the general's figure still waiting dark and small against the sun-struck city when he looked back.

The ridge was treacherous—slippery and full of crumbling stones. But he worked his way gradually around the shoulder until he found that the safe ground was broadening out and a lightly beaten track curved around an outthrust arm of rock and into thick trees.

Noon came, and he broke free of the winding, tree-choked path into the open plain. The mountain was behind him, the city hidden beyond it, and he set his face northwards to the fifteen miles that still separated him from the leader's camp.

The hours fell away from him, leaving the memory of timeless walking, wind ever ripping and rustling across the land, pausing in a little grove of spruces to memorize the false list of numbers and setting the scrap of parchment alight, watching it curl and blacken; then timeless walking again, a fresh smell in the air of sharp new grass and earthiness mingled. The sun sank and darkness settled. Dusk was still lingering when he slipped among the tents.

"Richardson." The leader looked up in that keen, detached way, one finger holding his place on the records that he had been bending over. Mordred had not once seen him sitting down.

"Sinethar, Paraki," he said as he lowered his head in courtesy. He could not help it.

His effrontery was taken well; the leader smiled that odd, disarming smile and his eyes glinted bright. "Very good; you have not forgotten. I trust that your quick return is from success and not failure?"

"Sinethar has met with success indeed," answered Mordred. "Twelve hundred garrison the city. Two hundreds are regularly posted on the walltops, in divisions of five to ten, while a patrol of forty makes a circuit every eight hours. A company of ninety archers arrived this morn . . . " He released the information steadily, pausing as the leader noted down each figure, glad he did not know how much was true and how much was false.

When he ceased the leader set the quill down and stoppered the inkwell. He examined what he had written for a long time, nodding on occasion to himself, and finally stepped back from the table with a sigh. His gaze drifted and sharpened on Mordred.

"You have served me well, Richardson. Tomorrow we shall muster what is necessary and march on Mianu. I trust that you can get back into the city before we reach it?"

Mordred nodded. "Aye, sir."

"You will keep me informed of any further detachments of men that enter Mianu. Also, I request that you find out for me if there is another way into the city—any secret way whereby we may infiltrate unexpectedly."

Excitement surged into Mordred's blood and he took a slow, steadying breath. "I will search for such a way, Paraki," he replied.

The smile curled the leader's lip up again, a little more sardonic this time. "Excellent. I do not doubt that you will."

A short silence fell.

"It will be inconvenient for you to get in and out of the city during the siege," said the leader. "Perhaps you can find a way, but I think for the most part, unless I summon you, we will communicate by—" He broke off, stepped to the side and leaned out of the tent, releasing a shrill two-note whistle. Moments later a dark bird came winging cleanly through the opening as the leader held the flap for it.

"By these," finished the leader evenly, stretching out his hand and allowing the crow to settle on it. It blinked rapidly in the light, spreading its wings as it regained its balance, and tucked its head modestly against its breast to regard Mordred with one sly black eye.

"They are *eraris*," said Cern Dersturi. "They can speak and think as men. I have many of them in my service. They are suitable chiefly for transmitting messages, and in such capacity they will serve between you and me. I will send one to find you now and again, and you will tell it what you have learned."

"Aye," said Mordred, looking at the *eraris*-bird with curiosity, waiting for it to make some evidence of human intelligence. But the crow only stared unwinking at him, and preened a little.

"So your guise is managing well?" said the leader in an almost conversational manner. "Have you anything to report other than the numbers I demanded of you?"

"It goes well," said Mordred with a slight shrug, knowing he must not give away much of his actual situation, and also knowing that he must not seem slow to answer. "The sergeant is lax; he has not remarked on my departures thus far and it is easy for me to roam the city."

The leader's eyes narrowed. "Be sure you do not risk his good will unnecessarily. That is a fickle thing to hang one's assurance on . . . you seem to be favored with a peculiar luck, Richardson, but do not carry it too far."

"Paraki." Mordred bowed his head with what he hoped was an appropriate level of meekness.

The leader snorted, and looked at him. "You are as cocky as a young colt, so do not try to deceive me! If your sergeant is taken in by you, he must be as blind and deaf as a headless mole."

Mordred broke into a smile. He was enjoying himself; he could not help it.

"Come out here with me," said the leader abruptly. He shook his wrist to dislodge the bird and it fluttered away cawing.

Mordred followed him out and into the deepening night. He had difficulty keeping up with the other man's rapid, twisting route through the rows of fallow tents, but did not dare fall behind or ask him to slow, and eventually they came into the open and the leader halted beside a rude three-sided corral. The fourth side was bounded by the Dirion River, and there were at least twenty shapeless lumps standing within.

Mordred was wordless with perplexity. Surely they would not have brought cows with the army?—but the lumps were too large for cows anyway. Low snarls sounded from within the corral, and one black mass stirred.

"*Mogra,*" said Cern Dersturi, a faint tone of triumph in his voice. "Or in Runnicor we call them *Adorti.* The trolls of the mountains, now found in few places of the world; but a little gold will do much in securing negotiations with even the most backward yokels. Have you heard of them, Richardson?"

"Yes," said Mordred, breathless and a little sickened.

"With these I shall break the walls of Mianu."

"How—how do you control them? I thought they were wild beasts."

"Wild, that they are, but they are no more beasts than you or I. Their intelligence is on a level with the *eraris*-birds, though, granted, they are more brutish in nature. It is necessary to keep them enclosed and guarded, for they are wont to rampage for scant reason."

"Yes," said Mordred again. He did not care, and suddenly he realized that he was shaking with weariness, and that he had not eaten since a piece of bread in the dawn.

"You are wearied?" Cern Dersturi's cold voice cut into his dread and exhaustion as he stumbled against the fence.

Mordred bit his lip almost to the point of blood and straightened. "Perhaps—a little."

"Come, there is a tent for you. Rest and eat. Do not sleep too long; you will need to leave before noontide."

~

"He is marching here as we speak. He will be here by evening today. I was not able to discover the quantity that he plans to detach from the main body of the army—"

"But?" said the general as Mordred hesitated.

Mordred took a swift breath. "He has the mountain trolls with him."

The general stifled his own gasp. "*Mograre*?" he uttered, and at Mordred's nod dropped into his chair, bowing his head in his hands. "May the Ruler of the Worlds sustain us," he murmured. "I have no strength to face this. How many?"

"Twenty to thirty I saw. I know not if he has others. My general—" Mordred sprang to his side, kneeling by the chair and grasping those steady hands as gently as they had taken his yesterday.

The general shook his head and stood, withdrawing his hands from Mordred's clasp. "Go, *mari*," he said softly. "You have done well, but you can do no more for now." And going into the next room he shut the door.

~

Kenneth and Fred were together on the wall guard when they heard the rumblings. Darkness poured over the horizon, outlined stark against the greying sky, and separated into divisions of men, each flying the Runnicoran standard. The whole company halted a bowshot or more beyond the walls and began the ordinary business of pitching camp.

Kenneth was counting rapidly under his breath, and when Fred turned to look at him his face was pale. "Six thousand," he said.

"There's more," said a voice, and they both whirled to see Braegon King staring out over the enemy forces. He was panting; he must have run up to the walls as soon as the word spread.

He turned to face them now, that odd alert, clipped attitude about him though his face was near as white as Kenneth's. "Those great creatures in the rear—perhaps you didn't notice them—the trolls. I saw one of those once."

"You fought it?" Kenneth said.

"Among others I did." Braegon shut his lips tightly and stared down at the torches pricking out against the darkening sky.

At dawn the first arrows began to shoot, a slow, tentative fire returned in like manner by the defenders. Then the siege ladders began to move.

~

Mordred stared over the crawling lines of soldiers, the ladders rolling amid them like sticks stuck into a milling bed of termites. He did not need to be here—in fact he knew he should not be here. Jedediah Crayes would scold him for it. A spy's business was to stay alive, not get killed on the front lines. But he could not stay away. He *had* to see, at least for a little while. He gripped the stonework and stared until his eyes ached.

There was a stir somewhere down the walls—"What is it?" Mordred murmured to the nearest man. And then he saw, it was the general, and he darted guiltily for the wall steps, knowing that the general would send him back if he saw him—and he might as well go back now anyway, there was nothing he could do . . .

But he lingered on the steps as the general passed, and watched him as he touched this man and that, and spoke low words of encouragement. He walked erect, and his voice never faltered, but his face was drawn with great strain. Yet in his wake men's heads lifted, and fear was driven out.

Mordred watched until he could not see him, trembling with the pain of the agonized man of yesterday. Then a violent tremor shook the wall, and he turned and fled down into the city with unashamed tears falling down his cheeks.

~

Ladder after ladder thudded against the outer wall. Dust was shaken up into the air, and already the noise was growing to a bewildering height. Grant Eagle leaned into the protection of the bulwark, firing arrow after arrow down into the men swarming so quickly up the solid wooden framework. His accuracy was fair, and he dropped them grimly and without remorse.

Grant Eagle had found what his heart had unconsciously sought all his twenty-five years: a man to serve and a cause to serve him by. Grief and duty had brought him to Orden. Now he cared nothing for Orden as Orden; but Orden as the land his father had sought and never reached, and Orden as the land beloved to the general who had called him "son," was a thing for which he would gladly live, and gladly die.

Perhaps he wanted death. He had no strong wish to live. Instinct kept him pressed to the shield of the rampart, was alert to the sounds of anyone approaching behind him, but he would welcome death if it came as a way to repay all he owed those steady, loving dark eyes, which had given him a love he did not deserve.

Grant Eagle had seen the mountain trolls, and had known what they were. He could see them now, their ugly, greyish, half-human forms, and when he squinted he made out that they were carrying clubs or some such weapon. Small they were from this distance, but they towered over the men nearby them.

He guessed why the leader had not released them yet. They were rare weapons, as rare and valuable to the Runnicoran side as dragons were to the Ordenians, and not to be thrown away lightly. The leader counted on their use to take Mianu, but he would hold them in reserve until he was sure he needed their strength.

The enemy rippled up like a steady tide. Here and there the defenders with spears flung a siege ladder backwards to the earth, but they could only stave off the inevitable, and the trickle of Runnicorans became an onslaught, overrunning the walltops. The time for arrows was over.

Grant unstrung his bow, strapped it to his quiver and whipped out his sword, hurling himself into the rush of fighting.

He battled like he had shot: with a grim abandon, looking only to kill and not survive. Time passed over him like a cloud, and he did not know when he was carried toward the very edges of the fight, which had spread out along the spurs leading toward the city's center, lapping into alleyways. But he became aware, distantly, that it was growing quieter.

Felling the man in his way, he spun around on the one he had sensed behind him, just too late. The blow that would have struck his neck clipped him on the shoulder and he staggered backwards, twisted on his heel and lost his balance altogether. He was clearly conscious of fumbling for his knife, knowing that he was too slow and seeing the Runnicoran lunge at him sword-point first.

And then the Runnicoran was dead. It was as sudden and confounding as that. Grant scrambled up to his knees automatically as the red knife emerged below the breastbone and withdrew again before his eyes, and the enemy crumpled with a quick moan.

Where he had stood was a very young man, eighteen at the most, short, lean and wiry, with a soldierly carriage and a strangely wide, unaffected smile. It flashed very white against his dark eyes and dark-toned complexion as he bent to give Grant a hand up. "Him or you."

"I thank you," said Grant slowly, taking in the awareness that he was still alive and that he and the young Ordenian were the only ones in the small lane.

"That looks like it'll be causing trouble in a minute," said his savior, nodding to Grant's shoulder. "Shall we get you to the hospice?"

"Why not rejoin the fight?" said Grant, uncertain even now why he was talking to a man instead of lying dead on the ground.

The grin flashed out again, amused in denial. "Because you shall be bleeding like a pig soon and won't be able to use that arm, and because it seems the fighting has left us two behind. You won't do the world much good if you die in this battle instead of staying alive to fight another."

"Maybe there will be no battles after this one," said Grant as he followed the young man's lead down the street, something in him mulishly determined to argue a point that he did not care about.

"Mianu's not the last stronghold," said the young man simply. "I am Braegon King; you?"

"Grant Eagle."

"Well met, Grant Eagle."

A part of him softened and untwisted. "Well met to you then, Braegon King."

"Haste your steps a little," Braegon observed, "or I shall have to bind up that shoulder myself, and I warn you I am little good at that."

~

The battle was over, for now. It had ended in a stalemate and isolated skirmishes all throughout the edges of the city, and finally the Runnicorans drew off. They had not yet deployed the trolls.

Therelane was hurrying to the hospice for a gash on his forearm that was shallow but bleeding with a frightening persistency. He did not know whether he were dizzy from blood loss or simply anxiety, but he was glad to sink down on a bed and wait for one of the surgeons to see him.

It was a girl who came over his way, small and quick-stepping, with dark hair bouncing soft and loose over her shoulders. She looked startlingly like Irene—why, she *was*—

"Irene!" Therelane cried, and stared speechless at her as she seized his arm and began applying numbing pressure to the wound.

"Don't squirm," she said with stinging briskness.

"Irene—you're here!"

"Yes, and I arrived just in time, it seems," she answered. "Don't squirm, I said. You're a grown man, or you ought to be."

"But why on earth are you—"

"Don't be such a distraction," she said shortly, cutting him off. "There's two men coming in here every minute. I really don't have all day. Hold this here, and I'll be back in a moment to bandage it up." She whipped away like a humming-bird, tiny and fierce and no-nonsense. As Therelane waited for her to come back, he realized he did not need to ask her why she had come. It made perfect sense for her to be here.

"Irene," he only said, urgently, when she reappeared and began winding a cloth tightly around his arm, "you know, you might get hurt."

She stopped short and regarded him with pursed lips. Then she laughed, dryly, and after knotting the bandage ruffled his hair.

He was too shocked to be embarrassed.

"You're absurd," she said. "Don't worry about *me*, young soldier."

CHAPTER 14

MORDRED RAN IMMEDIATELY FOR MITHISSA when the attack drew off. How long the lull would persist he did not know, and his question was urgent.

"Is the general within?" He caught the arm of the nearest man as he tore into the courtyard and skidded to a halt.

The man shook his head. "Boy, he rode out to the walls before the battle started. He's not returned."

Mordred spun around, ready to rush out and scour the walls and streets. But even as he did so the gate creaked, and a horse trotted in with the general astride. He leaped off at once on seeing Mordred, and motioned him within.

"What is it, Mordred Kenhelm?" he asked when they were alone.

Mordred wet his lips. "The leader said to me—he bade me find another way into the city, a small secret way." The excitement welled up in him as it had two nights ago, shot with uncertainty. "My general, I thought of the little bridge and the mountain path, and how if—if I were to tell him of that, and promise that it would be unguarded at a certain time, he could lead a number of men in as he had planned. But we would lie in wait for their coming, and their surprise attack would be surprised."

"How many would he bring?" the general asked slowly.

"Not very many. I would advise him no more than fifty because of the difficulty of the pass." He was speaking rapidly, the words tumbling out that he had sorted and mulled over for long hours. "I believe he intends this as a mere sortie, in order to open the main gate from within. My general—" he faltered, his voice fading away as he waited for the older man to speak. "Is it too great a risk, do you think?"

The general lifted his head and crossed to Mordred in a swift stride, laying a hand on his shoulder. "*Mari*, it is a risk to you."

Mordred flung up his head, his smile as fearless and confident as he felt. "I can manage it. He will think I made an error in the message, and he will reprimand me; but this once I think he will overlook it. My general, is it not my place to risk myself, if I must, when we can gain by it?"

"You are so full of courage," murmured the general, shaking his head a little in wonder. "Aye, if you are willing to take the chance then send to him. No gain is too small to be counted in this war. But, Mordred—take care for yourself." He paused, his hand firm on Mordred's shoulder and his eyes keenly searching. "There are times to think of one's own well-being."

Mordred hesitated—and dropped his gaze, and bent his head. "Aye, my general."

The general smiled. "There, it is past. Go, and bring to me the details of your message when you have sent it. How fare matters with Sergeant Corass and the men?"

"Sinethar is a dull character," said Mordred lightly. "But at least he is an easy act to play."

The general did not laugh. He was no more taken in by the lightness than the leader had been by the humility. Mordred felt himself ache as that dark gaze scraped over loneliness and hurts beneath. Suddenly he did not trust himself to endure it any longer without something breaking, and he whirled and without so much as a farewell left the room.

~

He saw the bird as he approached the barracks. It landed on the road in front of him, cocked its head on one side and fixed an eye on him with strange intensity. Then it stirred its left wing, as though beckoning him closer.

Mordred glanced up the road, and behind him, and saw it all empty. Striding over, he bent down on his knee beside the bird. "Well?" he asked at last, snapping the endless silence.

The bird—it was a crow, perhaps the one he had seen in Cern Dersturi's tent—looked extraordinarily smug. "Cern Dersturi wishes a report," it said in a gravelly croak.

Mordred pulled a cool, authoritative mask over the thrill that sped through him at hearing a bird speak with human tongue. "Tell Cern Dersturi that no reinforcements have come to the city yet. I have not yet ascertained how many men were lost in the first clash this morning. Tell him also"—he lowered his voice—"that I have discovered an excellent way into the city." He jerked out his knife and began to scrawl in the dirt beside the road, replicating the mountain path as best as he could. "It is a dubious path, especially on the ridge; he cannot send large groups along it, but for his purpose it should serve."

"Is this path guarded?" the bird demanded shrewdly.

"It is guarded at the bridge." Mordred thrust his knife at the point in the rude map, wiped it clean, and sheathed it. "There will be no guards on it *at sunset this evening*." He stared hard into the crow's beady eyes. "You understand?"

"Yes," the bird sniffed. It put its head so disdainfully high in the air that it looked liable to topple over in a moment, and Mordred struggled not to laugh at the foolishness.

"You can replicate for him this?" He indicated the map, and, when the bird assented, scuffed it out with his hand. "That is all, then. Farewell, *eraris*."

"Farewell, O favored spy," it returned bitingly, and launched itself into the air. It did not look back to see Mordred gazing after it with a delighted smile. *What excitable, easily offended things they are! And so sharp!*

Reluctantly did he turn away to set his steps again toward the barracks.

~

"Sunset," the leader muttered. "So, that does well. I had indeed hoped to release the *Adorti* at night. Where is Rasakt? Dovurti, send Captain Rasakt to me."

Lieutenant Dovurti Atta was back shortly with the captain in question.

"Captain. The spy has sent back word. Take forty men up the mountain, and into Mianu by the bridge—here. It may take you some time to negotiate the path, so leave soon, but do not attempt to cross the bridge or expose yourselves before sunset."

"Paraki. And once we are in the city?"

"I shall send out the trolls shortly before the time you enter it. They will have to call out all their forces to resist that attack, and you should be able to make your way through the city with little or no opposition. Of course you may lose some men; it matters not. It matters not if you lose all." He leaned forward and spoke grimly, his eyes like harsh stone. "Whatever the cost, only get to the gate, and *get it open*."

Captain Rasakt bowed. "We shall succeed or perish, Paraki."

The leader uttered a short, sarcastic laugh. "There is no 'or', Captain. You shall succeed, regardless of the perishing question."

"Understood, Paraki," returned the captain.

~

The shadows stretched long over Mianu, flinging themselves backward in tangled black spires across the mountains, and the light was golden, rich and dark. One hundred men waited amassed on the north-west wall.

"You know your orders?" said the general to the man commanding them.

"Wait in hiding until they have crossed the bridge," came the ready answer. "Come after them and take them by surprise."

The general nodded, and then as horns and stirring sounded distantly from the enemy camp he wheeled, his face taut. A nearer horn sounded, within the city, mustering the soldiers. A deep, growling bellow, like the rumbling of doom, drifted up to their ears.

The men stirred, unease swelling. The general glanced back to them with resolute countenance though tense and anxious. "It is not your concern. Fulfill your duty, and fight with honor." He whirled and ran down into the city.

~

The guard had been doubled since the beginning of the siege. Therelane and Bardrick were already on the walls when the call to assemble rang out.

Familiar faces pushed towards them. "What is it?" panted Kenneth, alarm wavering in his eyes.

Bardrick lifted a hand against the fading sky, his forefinger pointing sober and dark towards the camp. "See, down there—" So shaken was he, that he gave his answer in the guttural accent of Erahar.

"They are huge," said Marcus, eyes wide with awe and fear.

The *Mograre* were gathering before the city, grunting and roaring in a bestial manner. Twice the height of a man, some of them that much and half again, their squat, bulky forms were covered in leathery hide the color of shale on the mountainside, the color of dulled iron or a clouded sea. Their heads, sunken low into short necks, thrust forward like angry bulls as they stormed back and forth, jostling one another.

"Archers!" The general was striding along the walltop, lifting his voice whip-clear and steady for all to heed. "Archers, to your places! Prepare to shoot!"

The command was taken up and passed along, and the defenders grew more orderly and quiet, though the noise from below still continued. For ten minutes it persisted. Then—perhaps at an unseen command—the trolls craned their heads upwards in a simultaneous gargling howl, and lunged for the walls.

"Fire!" rang out the general's voice. And "Fire!" echoed on down the wall. The snap of releasing arrows thrummed the air. Into the advancing line they hissed, and fresh roars rose up of pain or anger, but not one of them fell or even stumbled.

"Again! Fire!"

This time one of them did drop, with an arrow straight through the eye of its ugly, creased features. But next instant they were all hurtling against the stone, tremoring it with the ferocity of their impact, some of them snatching up the fallen siege ladders and leaping up them in fearful agility, others climbing up the walls by sheer strength.

"Fire at will and prepare to defend yourselves!" And then the general's words were lost in the tumult.

Therelane, lost in a mad, pressing crush of people, did not know where he was or when it would end. He saw a dark shape of a *Mogra* heave itself over the top of the rampart against the fast-blackening sky, and wondered bewilderedly if this was how he would die—crushed under the foot or the club of one such thing, like a candle flame dashed out. A coldness pressed around his heart, and he felt no battle madness or excitement, only terror and a longing to go home. Half-heartedly he drew his sword, aware that around him others were doing the same.

Torches flared out into the descending night. Therelane saw a sickeningly clear moment of a troll hurling a man's form over the battlements, and another brief but vividly lit instant of one's jaws closing around a man's throat, and then red, horrible red—

The stones vibrated under his feet, and a low, endless growl sounded close at hand as a dark hump burrowed through the mass of bodies. Therelane with a surge of panic struck out blindly at it as it came at him, again and again, feeling the jar as his blade sunk solidly into the troll's leg. And it was past him, stamping further down the wall. Therelane staggered, his hands shaking violently.

When his head cleared, he noticed that high on a bastion several dark figures, highlighted dimly by the torches below, were shooting down at the *Mograre*. A steady and persistent fire they kept up. One troll fell under the relentless rain, then another. And Therelane, seeing those cool, regulated shots, felt a measure of calm return; not all was lost, not yet. His hand tightened upon his sword's hilt.

The trolls began to bore their way down from the walls and into the city below, swathes of carnage following them. "Oh—stop them!" shouted Therelane helplessly, his words empty and lost in the battle-noise. But now they faced a new trouble, for in the wake of the trolls came enemy soldiers, climbing up the ladders. And Therelane flung himself into the fight, glad at least he was able to do something. The Ordenian side was holding its own; despite the numbers of the Runnicorans, they did not break through like the *Mograre* had done.

The air around him trembled with a thud.

More and more came, resonating in Therelane's ears, in his bones, as if the wall below him was being battered into shreds.

"Down!" Someone's voice was shouting, hard and loud above the clamor. "Down, to the gate! Brace the gate!"

Therelane ran, his breath hot and loud in his ears and his legs heavier than they should have been. It occurred to him that they had left the wall abandoned, and he looked back; but the struggle was still ongoing. Some had remained. Therelane turned again and kept running.

Rivulets of battle followed them, but they outdistanced the bulk of it in their rush. Where the trolls were now, Therelane did not know. And he did not want to wonder, either.

As they drew up to the gate, Therelane noticed that the assaults came with marked irregularity, sometimes two at once; though there was one much louder crash that seemed more regular. "What's going on?" he grunted breathlessly, finding Braegon beside him as they shoved themselves against the timbers.

"Going on where?" Braegon returned.

"Out there—the pounding on the gate." Therelane stumbled as the gate shivered under another barrage.

"Last I saw the mountain trolls were hurling rocks against it, and they were bringing up the ram. Now save your breath." He did not say it reprovingly; his voice was only short and rough with weariness.

Again and again the ram struck. Then there were many cries from without, and the blows came no more.

The men at the gate waited, suffering under anticipation and ignorance, not daring to leave their post of defense. The uproar was dying away into an almost eerie quietude.

At last footsteps sounded, drawing near to them. The sky, to Therelane's astonishment, had begun to pale with dawn and as the figure came down towards them they could see that it was the general.

"Well done, men," he said, his words heartening and full of candid cheer despite the exhaustion in his face. "You held them off through the night; they have drawn back now." And with a quick smile he passed on, leaving the gladness reflected on their faces and tired relief springing in their hearts.

"We lived through it," said Therelane in wonder, to no-one really but himself.

"Come," Braegon was saying. "We'd best return to the barracks, and rest while we can."

He and Therelane found the others congregating at the edge of the building—Fred, Jared, Marcus, Bardrick . . . They all simply stayed there, talking about everything and yet nothing much, mentioning the battle now and then in a half-marveling, half-wary manner, as if to speak of it would incite another attack. They all knew it was coming, eventually; this was but a respite.

"Where's Kenneth?" asked Marcus suddenly.

Therelane looked at Braegon. He did not know why—except maybe it was that Braegon had remained quite still when everyone else started and broke into murmurings.

"Kenneth's dead," said Braegon simply, his flat tone cutting under all the questions. "He never reached the gate."

~

Though the Runnicorans had retreated into their camp again for now, the streets of Mianu were not safe. The *Mograre* ran rampant through them, appearing in unexpected places and wreaking destruction; and wherever one was reported, it had fled by the time soldiers arrived. A few had been killed. At a guess, ten or more remained at large in the city.

Mordred, aware of the danger, went carefully when the general summoned him to Mithissa. By cutting across back ways, treading light and soft and listening to every sound, he reached the tower without incident.

"Mordred Kenhelm." The general greeted him with his customary sincerity. "I thought you would like to know that the matter of the bridge went well and as planned. By it we certainly frustrated Cern Dersturi's plans and forced him to play some of his tricks that he would have liked to keep in reserve. It is not a sore blow in his numbers, perhaps; nonetheless I think he will take it hard, particularly the *Mograre* that he has wasted to little purpose."

"And the rest of the battle?" Mordred asked. "How did that go?"

The general shook his head, the movement so weary it was more of a drop. "Ours the city remains, yet the cost is grievous. They assailed the gate for hours, and would have broken through, I doubt not, but that we managed to pour oil on the ram and set it afire. They retreated then, for we targeted the trolls as well and several were severely burned, perhaps slain. Yet the gate is now weakened, and our numbers have fallen by half." His breath shuddered as he released it. "I have sent a plea for more soldiers, but they will not arrive before tomorrow; and that may be too late."

Mordred said urgently, "But the leader does not know that. I am his spy for Mianu; he depends on me to know how many men are here and what numbers fell in the attacks. If I can perhaps give the impression that there are many defenders yet for the city—more survivors than he expected—it will give him pause. He may wish to restructure his plans, and thus delay his next assault."

The general's face lighted. "It is possible," he said slowly. "Do what you can."

~

Mordred waited in a hungering strain and anticipation for the *eraris* to return. Terrified that the attack would begin afresh before he could reach the leader with his desperate gambit, he paced feverishly over the barracks, peering constantly out the window and not caring that all eyes were directed at him for it. He would have liked to stay outside, but he dared not—not with the *Mograre* still loose. And besides, he had glimpsed a figure that he was almost sure was Fred's on his return from Mithissa, and now he knew that one at least from Ceristen was in the city. How many more?

He forced his pacing to a halt and stood by the window, his forehead pressed into the frame as he clenched his sweating hands and struggled to calm himself. Worrying would not help, worrying would not bring the attack one second sooner or later—and then he saw it. A black flutter of motion passed the window, vanishing into the shadows of the next building and then reappearing in the open to settle on the ground.

An instant later Mordred had flung the door shut behind himself and knelt in the dusty road beside the crow. "Well?"

"Cern Dersturi wishes to know if you can leave the city, Richardson. He desires to see you as soon as may be. You are to give your report in person."

Mordred's heartbeat tripped sharply. "Tell him I shall come at once," he said and rose. He went with a slow and irresolute step into the barracks.

He told the general that he was going first. Then he crossed the slender white bridge that forty Runnicorans had trod the night before and made a swift descent. There were no fifteen miles to traverse this time; just a brief walk around the base of the mountain and the difficulty of discovering the leader's whereabouts in the busy camp. He would have liked more time; time to think, time to prepare. But at least he had less in which to wonder and fret.

The leader greeted him curtly but made no mention of the failed infiltration. He demanded to know how many of the trolls were in Mianu and still alive. Mordred replied honestly that he did not know.

The leader turned back to the papers he had been studying. He seemed in an ill mood, and Mordred was almost certain he was deliberately making him wait.

He knew it would be unwise to cross him or push him to speak, but he could not bear the frightening silence, and at last he said, softly, carefully, "I am sorry that the attempt on the gate did not succeed."

"Oh?" said Cern Dersturi in an unreadable voice, looking up. "Well, you should know that is the reason you are here. Much as I hoped to make use of the *eraris,* I think that our communication will fare better without the garbling of a third party in the middle."

He laid the blame on the crow. Relief seeped cool and welcome into Mordred's hot, pounding blood.

"What further reports have you? Any fresh troops?"

"A detachment of four hundred men arrived in Mianu this forenoon, compensating for the loss sustained in the attack last night," answered Mordred, and unconsciously stiffened as he waited for the reply. The bait had been tossed.

"Four hundred!" The leader ground his teeth, and spun away so that his back was to Mordred.

"So be it, then," he muttered, wheeling again, his face dispassionate. "I will be drawing off from Mianu; it has cost me far too much already, and I cannot continue to waste men and time on it while it feeds on a steady stream of incoming soldiers. 'Tis time to regroup and reconnoiter. If I plan quickly enough, perhaps I can startle them while they are recovering and testing for trickery."

He was saying—he was saying—Mordred could barely make sense out of the words for his disbelief. A great joyous release fell on him.

"Return to the city," the leader continued. "I shall still need your services, though we will see if you can be moved shortly to a more profitable location."

"Aye—aye, Paraki."

"Go." The leader dismissed him with a wave.

As Mordred turned towards the opening, someone else entered, the pale-faced man with silver-streaked hair who had looked at him so intently the day he had become Sinethar. Their gazes met, and the other man's locked on Mordred's, his dark, malignant eyes probing with a snakelike menace. Then Mordred broke away and went out into the night.

He wanted to go, wanted to bring the tidings to the general *now,* but night had fallen and he did not yet wish to attempt the mountain pass in the dark. He found a place and slept. In the morning with the first pale gold-haze of sun-rods he rose, and left the camp.

~

The night was past, and with it the time for grieving. Therelane had not shed tears; the words had hit him and numbed something inside of him that would not wake up no matter how hard he hit it. Braegon had wept; Marcus had cried as unashamedly as a boy half his age; but Therelane could not. And while the rest had one another, he felt apart again, severed, lonely. He wanted Mordred; and with all the selfishness of his heart he hated whatever power had taken Mordred away from them.

He walked recklessly through the streets, forgetting the danger and ignoring it when he did remember. He simply wanted something to happen, something that would liven the terrifying numbness inside him, something that would tell him Kenneth was alive and would see Marianne and Jerithan again.

The sun rose on him, and all the streets and buildings around caught the pure, untainted fire and were gilded almost tangibly by its light. Detached still, with that sickening, tight, dead feeling inside him, he wished the sun would not rise.

But nonetheless, watching it rise, he knew a measure of peace and it was as though warmth came back to the very edges of his heart.

I do not want to go on, he thought rebelliously.

But you will go on. You will go on, and you will still be glad of the beauty and the goodness in the world.

There is not enough goodness.

There is enough.

He let out a small, tired sigh, and hearing it he did not know which side of himself had been defeated. But the peace was still there, uncertain, yet tenacious.

Again he sighed, feeling very much more tired, and realized it was time he was heading back. He should not have gone out, at all, really.

He had entered a dim, small alleyway when he heard the sound—a low, stirring, rustling noise accompanied by grunts and clanking. As he lifted his head in alarm, a flicker of movement glanced by the corner of his eye.

He whirled about, and saw the last person he had expected.

CHAPTER 15

MORDRED LEANED OVER THE RAILING of the narrow bridge and drank in the vista of the yawning space below, the crevice between city and mountain, the mountain itself, sun-touched in the early morning, shadows knife-like and light keen. Unwillingly he turned and continued on, but his steps quickened as he remembered the words pressed within him for the general's ears, longing to spring off his tongue. *He is drawing off from Mianu . . .*

He forgot himself, forgot Sinethar, Richardson, and the evil still lurking in Mianu. His only thought was the message he bore. As he worked his way deeper into the city and left the shining heights of the city for the lower shadowed alleys, he ran freely, his head and shoulders thrown back, even humming softly to himself.

Something checked him as he turned into a quiet lane, sudden and chill, a prickle that shot over him and centered at the nape of his neck. He glanced around and his eyes fixed directly on Therelane Grey.

All fear of imminent danger vanished from Mordred's mind—there was only *one* imminent danger, and that was the one staring at him. He knew it was too late to turn, to run. Therelane's mouth was opening, forming the shocked cry that would come a moment later.

Only it never came.

A rending growl rolled through the air, and Mordred, gripped with the earlier dread again, saw a large, dark thing charge out from the buildings straight between him and Therelane. He saw Therelane's face, drained of color, saw the *Mogra* hefting a huge mace in its misshapen hand as it took a lumbering step towards Therelane. Therelane reached for his sword, tripped, fell—

Mordred cried out and lunged forward as the troll swung its mace.

It whirled on him at once, with terrifying agility, and he hacked at it again and again, rage and desperation driving every strike, fighting harder and better than he had ever used a sword. Again and again he felt the wind of the mace whistle past him, but he was never in its path—he was always dodging, diving, lashing his blade into it every chance he saw.

He overreached a stroke and tripped, like Therelane had, and sprawled backwards on the stones. But he did not die. Shouts came, that he heard as from a great distance, and suddenly a spear protruded from the troll's side, and Mordred as he picked himself up saw that four or five other people had joined the fight.

After that it was a blur. Slashing, thrusting, mace flailing inches away, falling, getting up, cries, roars—and then someone yelled, "Get back!"

Mordred lurched to the side as the troll with a rumbling groan swayed and pitched earthwards, unmoving. Dead.

But Therelane—

He sprang forward, leaping over the twisted limbs of the monster, to the crumpled figure with soft dark hair tangled across his forehead. Therelane, he struggled to say, but the name would not come. Then he saw the chest lifting, faintly, and he sank to his knees in relief.

Where had it hit him? Not his head, not his neck, not his chest—had it cleared him altogether? Maybe he was only stunned in the fall, Mordred thought.

Then he saw it. His stomach surged up into his mouth, and as he swallowed back the sickness he felt weak and dizzy, and the world for a moment went white.

The mace's brunt had fallen entirely on Therelane's left hand. A hand that was dark and mangled beyond anything that looked like a hand, or ever would again.

~

"It's Sinethar!" said one of the soldiers in surprise. For it was Sinethar, kneeling there beside the unconscious young man.

Sinethar got up, his knuckles white around the hilt of his sword and his face whiter. "Get him—somewhere—to a hospice," he said, tersely, half-coherently, and set off into the streets at a hard run.

"Where has he been, anyway?" demanded another man. "Where does he go?"

"We're not supposed to ask," said the first. "Come, he was right; this man needs a surgeon."

They took Therelane gently up between them and bore him to Mianu's hospice. The girl in the ward that they entered took one look and snatched him from them, carrying him with a strength extraordinary for her slight frame.

"My lady, let us—if we can help?"

She thanked them curtly, dry-eyed, and told them to leave.

~

Mordred ran fiercely through the streets of Mianu. He ran until all he could think of was the next step, and the next, and the next, and so there was no time to think about Therelane Grey.

The general's glad greeting gave place to anxiety as Mordred entered the room in Mithissa. "*Mari*, you are weary and your clothes are bloodstained," he exclaimed. "Are you wounded?"

Mordred shook his head, words refusing to come.

"What was it, a skirmish in the streets?" The concern deepened in his face. "Or is it possible you have been discovered?"

"No—no," he stammered, and after that the words came, though in short bursts and gasps. " I—no, I have not been discovered. Let me—tell you the news from the camp . . . before I explain this."

"If you must, then. But sit down. Your legs are shaking under you." When Mordred did not move, the general drew out his own chair and guided him forward, and Mordred dropped into it without protest.

"The leader is drawing off from Mianu," he said flatly. The joyful news that he had thought to bring was stale and worthless on his tongue.

But the general started and leaned forward, wonder breaking over his face. "You are certain?"

"Yes. He believes the cost is too high . . . " But while Mordred mechanically narrated the details of his exchange with the leader, his mind was seeing again Therelane's face, the fear in his eyes, his fall as he tried to defend himself, and finally the dreadful hand. The hand that was not a hand.

"Now tell me, Mordred." The general's voice, clear and urgent, broke in upon his inner turmoil. "What is this, that you would not speak of it to me before?"

"Nothing." Mordred was ashamed of the tremor in his voice. "You would not remember Therelane Grey—one of us from Ceristen."

The general smiled, shaking his head. "I remember you all. Therelane is the quiet dreamer of the family that is cursed."

The sickness was coming back, the quivering in his limbs. "He—was—injured."

The general reached out as if to steady him. "Say on."

Mordred's stomach contracted again. He wondered if he would be able to get the words out. He shut his eyes for a moment and thought about nothing, and slowly let them open again. "One of the *Mograre* came upon him. He tripped and fell and I ran forward to attack it. Maybe I deflected its blow with mine; at any rate I distracted it after its first strike, and then others came and we killed it. But—Therelane's—hand—is crushed."

He said no more. He did not think he could.

The general rose. "I will see him," he murmured, reaching for his cloak. "You may rest here until you need to leave."

"I should go now." He stood, dizzy with tiredness. "Some of the men saw me; they will be wondering why I am not back at the barracks."

"Do not worry about the men at the barracks. I will arrange things." The general's hand was on his shoulder, guiding him back into the chair.

"No," Mordred insisted, rising and fighting the tendency to reel forward. "You have enough to manage without making excuses for me, my general—I will go."

He went out the door, pace as steady and back as straight as he could manage, until he knew that the general could no longer see him. He was walking almost blind by the time he reached the barracks.

~

"General?"

"Lady Grey." The general was struck with wonder at how near kin to the young Therelane she looked, and yet how unlike. It seemed as though she had acquired all the shrewdness and firmness in her girl's body where Therelane had the soft uncertainty. There were small, hard lines of fatigue around her young mouth; despite her petite figure, she appeared neither lissome nor frail.

Yet she was weary. It was in the set of her shoulders, and in the circles beneath her dark-browed, cynical eyes. Her hair hung loose and heavy over her shoulders, damp at the temples with sweat.

"Aye?" she said curtly. He realized that she had no time to spare for niceties.

"Tell me, where is Therelane, your brother? He was brought in not long since, is it not so?"

The taut lines deepened around the mouth. "Yes," she returned, still shortly; "it is so. What is it to you?"

"If the physicians will permit," said the general, "I would see him."

She shrugged and beckoned him to follow as she sped down the hall and wheeled into a doorway on the left. Past groaning men, men tossing with fever—"Here," she said, and jerking a finger at one cot near the far end of the ward, she halted. "He's sleeping, you know," she added with her customary abruptness.

"Sleeping?"

"Unconscious, if you like."

Therelane lay with a coverlet drawn all the way to his chin, his face still and of a ghastly paleness. *I have seen men die after looking like that,* thought the general.

"He may come out of it," said Irene, as if she had read his mind. "It is too early to tell. He was half awake when they brought him in, but after—" She snapped off the words with another shrug.

"I have heard only of the one injury—I do not know if there were any others—"

Irene was shaking her head. "It left him unmarked, save that one blow."

"And the hand?"

Irene Grey said nothing. She lifted aside the thin blanket for a moment, and the general saw the blood-stained, shredded sleeve, and what protruded beneath.

"It will go hard on him, if he wakes," he said quietly.

Still Irene said nothing. No tears were in her eyes, yet the general saw the grief behind them.

"It will go hard on all of them who love him," he continued. "There was no other way?"

"It would have killed him to keep it," she said simply. "The work grows more, and not less. I must away." She spun on her heel and strode back down the ward.

~

Sinethar was always withdrawn, taciturn; the sergeant, bearing in mind the mysterious orders from the general, made no comment on his broody nature or his frequent absences. But when Sinethar returned that afternoon swaying with exhaustion, scarcely able to speak, clothing bloodied, he was almost tempted to break the rule.

As a matter of fact he found out the truth soon enough, though it was not from Sinethar but several other men, who explained that Sinethar had been in a brief skirmish with a mountain troll in the city that morning. So that was an end of that matter, and no one seemed to be the worse.

Sinethar himself slept for several hours, and it seemed to the sergeant that after he woke he was in a stranger mood than he had ever been. Refusing to talk, avoiding all people, an odd pain in his face—indeed, it occurred to Sergeant Corass that he was grieving.

~

Mordred hated Sinethar. With a passionate, anguished hatred he hated him. It was Sinethar who barred him from open suffering. It was Sinethar who would not let him go to the others from Ceristen, because of Sinethar that he could not even see Therelane and comfort him. Every word that Sinethar must speak came as gall out of his mouth, and he thought he would choke on it.

The word came from the general that evening, in the form of a small missive delivered by a soldier: *Therelane Grey still lives. They were obliged to amputate his hand.*

Mordred had known it already. He had known that sickening, mutilated thing would never be a hand again. It made the tidings a very little easier to bear. He did not shudder or cry out but turned his face against the wall, the tears burning behind his eyes.

Sergeant Corass came to him some hours later. "Sinethar." He shook him lightly by the shoulder when Mordred did not turn.

"Yes." Mordred said the word between his teeth, afraid that if he did not his voice would start to shake.

"Sinethar, you are on guard duty at the outer wall, midnight till dawn. Can you manage that?"

"Yes." His voice sounded strangled in his own ears. The tears were close, too close.

"I know not what is amiss, I fear—was it something in the letter—" The voice hesitated, uncertain, gruff, kind.

Mordred's hand closed around the letter in a taut fist. Was it so plain? He summoned all his will into a desperate front of his most distant, cold politeness, knowing that at all costs he must keep away further advances of friendship and sympathy. "Nothing is wrong. I will thank you to keep your questions out of where they are not needed." He rose stiffly and strode out of the barracks.

~

The night stretched out long and cold. Movement rustled and wavered below in the enemy camp, but nothing approached the walls. Mordred longed for a distraction, for a skirmish, and he watched until his eyes ached for something that would take his mind away from the deathlike face of Therelane, the lightheaded memory of splintered bone sticking out of a mash of fingerless, meaningless flesh, swimming in the acrid blood; and then all that *gone*, tossed into a drain somewhere, and Therelane would never have a hand again.

He stared at his own hands in the dark: faint white blurs that sharpened as he brought them closer, lean, whole, beautiful things that flexed and bent at his command. With a shudder he buried his face in them and wept, unable to hold it back any longer.

The sobbing breaths were the only sound he made; no-one heard him except the nearest of the guards, who put a swift arm around him with a murmured, "Brace up, lad." Mordred, lost in misery, did not care.

The presage of dawn came in a strange, pure silence and an imperceptible lightening of the air. Mordred leaned over the breastwork, worn out with spent tears and sleeplessness. A fluttering by his ear beat the air, and he turned his head slowly to meet the bright eyes of a great crow that settled with the gentlest snick of claws on the rampart.

It preened its breast feathers, scrutinizing him all the while, and tapped a single claw secretively against the stone. At that Mordred was sure, quite sure, that it was *eraris*.

"Cern Dersturi?" he asked in a low voice, careful of the soldiers who were standing so close by.

The crow nodded once.

"Does he have a message?" Mordred scarcely moved his lips.

It shook its head this time, deliberate, unwinking, and with a violent swivel stabbed its beak downwards in the direction of the camp.

"He sends for me, then?"

It tipped its head in a light nod, and instantly flapped into the sky again, darting downward across the plain of grey tents.

Mordred watched it go dipping and wheeling, and noticed how light the sky had grown. Scarcely a minute later their relief arrived, and amid the banter and jesting complaints Mordred departed and hurried through the city: first to Mithissa to apprise the general of his absence, and then to the north wall.

~

Because of the withdrawal, the leader had ridden back to the main camp. It was evening before Mordred reached the red-woven tent.

He lifted the heavy flap and ducked under, his feet scuffing lightly over the trampled grass. "Paraki?"

The leader turned from the map-strewn table at the side of the tent, his eyes narrowed in a calculating way that made Mordred suddenly apprehensive. "I wonder that you should call me that when you have made it plain where your allegiance lies."

Mordred did not move. Like a bird struck, he could not.

All at once, everything was over.

"You played a pretty game, did you not? It is like playing with a knife—a lovely toy, but very dangerous."

Mordred's instincts begged him to run, but there was no call from his will in answer. He knew that if the leader were so sure, he would never gamble on taking him without a struggle. Wherever he had placed his men, they must be close at hand and Mordred refused to degrade himself before those hard eyes by fleeing further into the trap.

"Still you do not speak? You did well, Richardson, or I might call you *Mordred Kenhelm*. It was long before I began to suspect you. Only after the faulty attack did I suddenly wonder—of course it could *easily* have been misheard information, or a change of plans, but I realized that the opposite was quite a viable possibility. You were an Ordenian, you had shown reluctance to spy, and now this blunder. No, I did not quite suspect the double spy part. I thought maybe that after deserting you found the Runnicoran side not so much to your taste.

"So I sent an *eraris* to follow you, a spy upon my spy. And he tracked you to a tower in Mianu yesterday morn and there overheard certain words between you and the General of Orden. So I discovered that you had betrayed me twice."

He looked up from a small knife that he had been handling ever since he spoke of knives. "I might salute you, as a most clever opponent and one worthy of esteem. But I do not take kindly to being played upon. And I fear you will have to learn that I, though exciting as a knife, am likewise sharp and unpleasant in the end."

"Thank you for the advice." Mordred found his tongue suddenly, his head very cool and steady. "I fear it is late in coming, for I shall not have long to practice it."

Cern Dersturi's mouth curled up on one side. "Not long indeed. Although I hope a little time will suffice to persuade from you the secrets that you are still concealing."

"If they should catch you, it is torture . . . "

He made some motion that Mordred did not quite see, and several seconds later a stream of men came through the rear entrance to the tent. "Take him," he ordered briefly.

Mordred let them surround him, did not evade or lash out as they seized him, though he hated the hold on his arms. To struggle, that would be useless by this time, an entertainment for the leader which Mordred had no intention to give.

They took him to a small empty tent and led him in. *"Stag,"* snapped one, jerking his finger at the middle, which Mordred took as a command to go there. He obeyed slowly and sat down, crossing his legs under him and resting his chin on his clenched hands.

The soldiers—there were five of them—posted themselves around the tent in various poses of vigilance. They watched him with unfriendly eyes, rather as though they expected him to shoot fire from his fingers and decimate them.

Mordred was tired, so very tired. Muddles of thought swam through his head—Therelane, caught, the general, torture, Fenris—Fenris would hurt so if he died. Jedediah Crayes—*"I can't guarantee getting you out of that mess."*

With a drowsy sigh he lay down. Jedediah Crayes might not even be in the camp any more, and if he were he could not try to rescue Mordred without great danger to himself. That was all right; he would manage. Somehow, he would manage. Torture could only hurt for so long—one must pass out eventually.

~

Jedediah Crayes scowled into the flame of the candle beside him. He grumbled, very softly, to himself. "That boy! Got into trouble again, has he? Oh yes, we always leave it to Jedediah Crayes to fix things up. He never has important work to do. Nothing better to occupy *his* time."

He stretched out on his back, his mind whipping over the aspects of main importance. Five men in the tent with him. Ten more posted outside. Hands might be bound. All manageable issues.

As long as he himself could stay in the clear—but Jedediah Crayes was perfectly sure that he could do that. Cern Dersturi had no idea who was infiltrating his camp, and he was not going to find out.

Little fool, he thought, but did not say it aloud. He blew out the candle in an irritable burst of breath, relaxed again, and waited for the murmuring around him to deepen into stillness and snores.

CHAPTER 16

MORDRED STIRRED, A ROUGH HAND on his shoulder dragging him persistently out of dreamless, exhausted sleep. He struggled to remain there, his body yearning for the rest that it had lain in deadened and content, but the hand tightened, shaking him, until his eyes drifted open.

He did not see the leader, as he had expected to; the man in front of him was the balding, pale-faced one he had seen twice now. And something in him began to be afraid, and his drowsiness faded. "Is it morning?" he asked.

"No," said the man. "It is only a few hours past sunset." He shifted his grip to Mordred's face, eyes narrowed, and Mordred writhed away with a violent shake of the head. The icy, bony fingers pinching his skin were too much like the werevulture's claw-hand. Memories poured over him, and he began to tremble in spite of himself. He shrank away, knowing that contemptuous eyes were on him, vainly trying to stop.

"Has the Paraki sent for him, my lord Mirden?" asked one of the guards.

Lord Mirden! Mordred sat up in astonishment.

"Nay, I came of myself." The man seized Mordred again and studied him, and Mordred clamped his jaws together, desperately forcing a mask of impassivity over his features. "I wished to see him and speak to him."

He addressed Mordred. "You, Sinethar, Richardson, Kenhelm, I suspected you early on."

"How perceptive of you." Mordred felt easier; here, on the ground of insults and word-gamery, he was safe.

The bottomless dark eyes narrowed again. "I suspected you, as I said. There is something strange about you. I wish to know what it is, and that is why I have come."

Mordred almost laughed. The shivering had passed, he was awake, and this man was making all the most exquisite blunders. "Pray be more specific, my lord. I am sure there are a dozen things strange about me, but I cannot be expected to know any of them, much less which one you are referring to."

"I do not know what it is." Lord Mirden was growing angry. "And I wish to know."

"Perhaps we should find a third party who is more clever than either of us," suggested Mordred.

His face stung with the slap. "Silence your impertinent tongue! I tell you, there is something about you foreign to me, something which is opposed to all that I am—from which my senses recoil."

"Is it that I have hair where you do not?" Mordred arched a wondering eyebrow.

"You foul little *zarhiss*—"

The torrent of harsh, hissing invective that he fell into was unintelligible, alien, yet it rang on Mordred's ears with a strange familiarity, for he had heard such sounds before. At last the man fell silent, and quietness settled over the whole tent; but his eyes never left Mordred. And Mordred stared back, scornful, cold-faced, a new fear beginning to grow in him.

~

Rustlings came from without, murmurings. A guard lifted his head and said something in Runnicoran.

"Someone comes," muttered Lord Mirden, rising with an irritated scowl and retreating into the shadows of the tent.

Mordred heard the footsteps scuffling the ground outside the tent, and the flap swishing open, and a figure stepped in.

A slouching, paunch-bellied figure, with an unsightly scar across his cheek and snapping, very much alert black eyes.

"Fine night for guard duty!" said he by way of greeting, nodding to them.

"Mog Dremmag," mumbled one, recognizing him. "What are you here for?"

"Orders were to relieve you." The keen eyes drifted over the tent. "Looks like I'm the only one who decided to show up on time, eh?"

With a rueful shrug he sat on the grass and produced a bottle from the satchel at his side, handing it to the nearest guard. "Dirty little slackers. Well, they ought to show up soon. Have a drink to pass the moments?"

The atmosphere became suddenly much more cordial. The soldier accepted the bottle and drank deeply, passing it around, even offering some to Mirden, who came forward and took it stiffly.

Minutes passed. A sluggishness grew on the soldiers, a lethargy, and the bottle lay forgotten and almost empty between them. They sat with drooping eyelids until finally they slumped over, one and then another, while Mordred watched so tense that he could scarcely breathe.

The relief guard eased himself up delicately as a cat and prodded the nearest man thoughtfully with his boot. There was no response. With a sly, satisfied grin he turned leisurely and winked at Mordred.

"It pays to learn the components of a sleeping draught," said Jedediah Crayes.

Mordred stared at him, speechless, an ecstatic smile widening his mouth.

"Well, don't just grin at me like a recently birthed idiot," Jedediah Crayes said irritably. "Get up and let's see about getting you out of here. I hope you appreciate what an inconvenience you're being."

Mordred did not answer. The smile died away from his lips, and his hands grew cold, as Lord Mirden rose from the ground with no sign of drowsiness, shrugging his hair deliberately back and coming up behind Jedediah Crayes with a knife—

"Jedediah Crayes," he gasped.

Jedediah Crayes whipped around, a knife sliding into his own hand as if he had conjured it from the air. It clashed ringing on the first. Then, with a shriek, Lord Mirden hurled himself on Jedediah Crayes in the form of a great white-headed vulture, wings flailing, spitting and screeching in its own tongue.

Mordred sprang to his feet, shaken, eyes riveted helplessly on the sight. For a bare few seconds they were on the ground, locked snarling and tearing into one another like two animals, but Lord Mirden suddenly returned to man-form and with a hiss snapped his hands around Jedediah Crayes' throat.

But Jedediah Crayes answered with an instant, solid punch on Lord Mirden's own throat, and as Lord Mirden reeled, choking, he slipped a second knife out of his belt and stabbed him between the ribs.

Lightly he leapt back as the dying werevulture staggered, and sheathed his knife, breathing quickly. His eyes were bright and he looked more than ever like a cat.

"Well," he remarked. "A near shave, that." Amusement twitched his face as he regarded the dead body. "If it isn't the turncoat Lord Mirden. Ha! I fancy that's a tidbit that will please the general. Mirden discovered, apprehended, and executed." He uttered a short laugh, nudging the lifeless form. "Old, he was; he shouldn't have tried that. Old, stupid, and slow. Wonder what he was really up to?"

"Did the—draught have no effect on him?" Mordred gazed down at the white, hook-nosed face.

Jedediah Crayes snorted. "He wasn't that stupid. No, I'm quite sure he never took a sip of it. Fool that I am, I didn't check to make sure that everyone actually swallowed who put it to his lips. I should know better." He grumbled softly to himself as he picked up his other knife and sent it with a snick into his belt. "No, he wasn't that stupid. Just stupid enough to think he could take me on at his age. He must be at least a hundred twenty; past his prime, at any rate."

He glanced at Mordred. "Anyway. Back to where we were before that little incident. Let's get you out of here. If we hurry we can get to Mianu shortly after dawn, though we'll have to be wary of Cern Dersturi's retreating troops."

"It's all right," Mordred began. "I can go alone—"

"No," Jedediah Crayes snapped. "I've had enough. I don't trust you two feet out of my sight, you rascal. Next minute I turn my back you'll be in the Runnicoran's clutches again, or maybe another werevulture. I am accompanying you to Mianu's gate and that's an order."

"I understand." Mordred could not quite manage to keep a straight face.

"And I hope you don't think I'm doing this because I like you or anything. It's because you're useful, very useful, and I'm too smart to let something useful go to waste." Jedediah Crayes shot Mordred a menacing look under his brows. "Understood?"

"Yes," said Mordred. "I see."

Jedediah Crayes led the way out of the tent and through the camp with his expert discreetness and speed. Mordred followed with difficulty, only breathing easier when they had left the Runnicorans behind and were walking through the fringe of forest, whereupon Jedediah Crayes slowed his pace to a lazy amble.

"Stupid," he muttered on one occasion, and on another, "Absurd—ha!" Mordred, accustomed to his casual, unannounced verbal expulsion of emotion, did not ask what he was thinking about, nor did he care. He was quite simply happier than he had been since—since he had said good-bye to Jedediah Crayes upon becoming Sinethar.

"Jedediah Crayes," he said, comforting night-whispers in his ears, "What was Lord Mirden doing with the Runnicoran side? He must have been helping them for a very long time. I thought werevultures hated all men."

"What?" Jedediah Crayes laughed. "Of course they do. And there's nothing they love better than to help pit two countries against one another! As long as there's bloodshed for the 'nikorss' in it, you can bet a thousand recenna that a werevulture will want to get his beak involved. Of course, he'll place himself strategically on the side that's most likely to win, which in this case was Runnicor.

"Werevultures!" He snorted softly, gazing up at the sky. "They are never done making trouble. Cunning, strong, long-lived—one of them will stir up more havoc than a dozen men. But after all, we have at least this advantage: they cannot work together, as they once did. They walk alone."

"I read that tale," said Mordred, memories stirring in him. "A long time ago, in the orphanage. They were cursed in the fall of Serndol. The queen doomed them to never have a ruler from their own kind again. And ever since, they have been scattered and disunified."

"Exactly. Very kind of the queen." Jedediah Crayes' eyes glinted with laughter that he did not utter. "Who could stand against an entire army of werevultures? Goodness knows they cause enough headaches for us as it is."

He broke off speech abruptly and dragged Mordred behind a low bank of fallen tree and bracken. Mordred, crouching with thundering heart and Jedediah Crayes' hand tight on his shoulder, listened as the tramp of a couple dozen men passed them and faded.

Jedediah Crayes rose and stretched, and beckoned Mordred to move on again.

"We're on the run from the law—so to speak," he remarked, a glitter of excitement lingering in his eyes. "Isn't it fun?"

"There is no law in war." The phrase came back to Mordred, a phrase he had heard or read somewhere, and he uttered it aloud.

"That's not true," said Jedediah Crayes sharply, with unexpected rebuke. "Don't you ever say that. There is always law, in war just as there is in peace, and the one who abides by the law just the same is the one whom the men in future years will hold up to their sons and say, 'Be like him.' The ones who don't abide by it—well, they're the kind that start wars like this in the first place." He strode on, his eyes glinting moodily under the black V of his brows.

As the first warm hints of the dayspring touched the mountains, they glimpsed Mianu in the distance, her white turrets sparkling as they found the light.

"*She's* free, anyhow," Jedediah Crayes said, somewhat cynically. "Thanks to your game of touch-and-go with that prig of a Runnicoran Paraki. Do you know what a horrific risk your tactics were?"

Mordred wondered idly how Jedediah Crayes was so well acquainted with his actions. He only said, aloud, "I am sure you devote yourself to avoiding risk, Jedediah Crayes."

Jedediah Crayes sputtered, his mouth opening and shutting in inarticulate outrage. "You—you—how dare you, you saucy—"

"I suppose I shan't have to be Sinethar any more," said Mordred, the realization breaking on him.

Jedediah Crayes tossed a look of quick scrutiny his way. "Well, that's good news, because it looks like you don't have much disguise left on you."

Mordred laughed outright. "I guessed it was wearing off, and I planned to ask Igurst to touch it up last night, but that never happened after all . . . and I suppose Lord Mirden managed to slap away what little was left."

"The little . . . " Jedediah Crayes paused and whatever epithet he had been going to assign Lord Mirden remained forever unknown. "Whatever he hit you for, I daresay you provoked him to it, you unspeakable brat."

Mordred tossed his head with a disrespectful grin. "It's very hard to say nothing to stupid people."

At the gate, Jedediah Crayes fidgeted in impatience as he waited for the guards to come. "The-stars-shine-in-a-circle-and-the-mountains-are-red," he gabbled rapidly, and when the loosing of the bolts seemed to take too long for him, he nipped a small pendant out from around his neck and dangled it in the guards' faces.

"What is that?" Mordred asked as they walked into the city, motioning to the coppery object.

Jedediah Crayes slipped the chain over his head and handed it to Mordred. "This? Just a medallion, engraved with a tree. Serves to identify members of the Legean Association. We use it as proof of our authority when necessary."

Mordred handed it back. "Did you really have to show it to them for them to let you through?" he asked, a suggestion of teasing in his tone.

Jedediah Crayes harrumphed and said nothing.

"Not seeing the general yet?" he observed after a time.

Mordred looked at him questioning.

"I notice you're heading for the barracks."

Mordred nodded. "Unless they were moved, my division is here. I'm going to ask after Sergeant Garin."

"You still consider yourself part of that division?" Jedediah Crayes barked with laughter. "You're not even in the army right now."

"My brother is there," said Mordred. And there was so much in those words, so much that could barely spill over into speech, and so he repeated them, his heart bursting with love and longing. "My brother is there."

A short time later he approached the building where he had been directed, Jedediah Crayes still trailing behind him. He came towards the door, but before he even reached it Marcus came at a run towards him, his face shocked, exclaiming, "Mordred!"

"Yes, I'm back." Mordred could not manage a smile for Marcus. He suddenly felt strangely, deathly tired.

"Mordred!" Marcus still stared at him. "Mordred, Kenneth's dead."

He understood, perfectly. "Kenneth is—dead," said a voice that must have been his own, but the words made no sense. All the balance in the world seemed suddenly, completely gone—

~

Jedediah Crayes snatched Mordred as he pitched forward. "Look, I don't know who you are, or who Kenneth is, but it strikes me you could have found a slightly more appropriate time to bless our ears with the information. The stupid boy doesn't know how to take care of himself and he's half dead on his feet. Get him to a bed before he passes completely out."

He really ought to let the general know that the little fool was back safe and sound. And, furthermore, start thinking of possible ways to explain himself when he got back to the Runnicoran camp. Jedediah Crayes directed his steps toward the tower Mithissa. He wondered momentarily what Mordred's other brother was like.

CHAPTER 17

"MORDRED, WHERE *WERE* YOU?"

Mordred stared doggedly at the stew on his knees and ignored Marcus' honest, curious question. He knew, if he ignored the questions long enough, they would stop asking them. But that did not make it any easier to ignore them while they lasted.

He felt betrayed inside. He had yearned so to come back, to have the companionship of the people he loved, and he had not anticipated the crushing blow that met him, that destroyed all the joy of the reunion. Nor had he thought of the silence he still must keep, and the strain that put between him and them. For he still was in service as spy—as far as he yet knew—and it remained a danger for the truth to leak out to anyone's ears.

"What happened last night? And who was that man with you?"

"Marcus, let me alone," he said tightly.

"Marcus." Bardrick got up, and drew his brother away.

Mordred stared at his bowl of stew and let it slip disinterestedly to the floor, leaning forward to rest his arms on his knees. He wished he had never come back—never, never. It was all wrong, it was no use, nothing was the same anymore.

"Mordred, eat." It was Braegon who came up to him and retrieved the discarded bowl to set it gently on Mordred's lap again.

"I cannot." He loathed the stiffness in his words, yet it was all he had to keep his pain from spilling over.

"Why?"

"Do not speak to me!" Mordred cried in agony, and hurled the bowl away as hard as he could. "Do not hound me with your questions!"

He sprang to his feet. "Where is Therelane?" he demanded accusingly, his pain and desperation forming themselves into an anger that needed to lash out. Not wanting to hear the answer that he knew already, he spun around and fled the barracks.

When he stopped running, his legs were like water under him and he panted fitfully. He looked up at the tall, smooth pillars that ornamented the front of the hospice building, and after a time walked forward and went inside, and asked after Therelane Grey.

It was quite some time before he could find anyone who recognized the name; and more time before anyone could direct him to the right ward. But at last he approached the cot where the figure of Irene's young brother was lying.

Therelane's eyes were shut, but his mouth was set in a way that indicated wakefulness. His cheeks seemed sunken in, his hair sweat-matted and rough.

"Therelane," said Mordred gently.

The eyes snapped open, fixing on him. "Mordred?" He sounded astonished, disbelieving.

"Has no one else come to see you?"

Therelane's look of surprise faded into listlessness and he gazed dully into the distance. "Irene has not let anyone come before now. She said I was too ill."

"Irene, your sister?" Mordred was surprised now. "She is here?"

"Yes."

Something in Mordred cringed at the horrible flat indifference in Therelane's voice. It was—it was like the way he had been once, when nothing seemed to matter, but only because there was so much pain far beneath . . .

He knelt by the bed, casting aside the empty surface inquiries. "Therelane, let me see."

Therelane's wall of lifelessness snapped. "Look then," he said quickly, roughly, almost sullenly, and turned his face into the bed.

Mordred turned back the blanket. Therelane's left sleeve was a chewed mess; out of it emerged a scarred, bloodied, swollen stump that looked as repulsive as the ruined hand itself had been. Burns seared across it where they had pressed an iron to stop the bleeding. It was not a sight at which one wanted to look for long.

Mordred looked. He forced himself to look at it as long as he could bear, and longer.

"I'm sorry, Therelane," he said quietly.

A convulse shuddered Therelane's rigid body and he began to weep, the tears running in a silent stream down his half-hidden face.

Mordred caught Therelane's one hand in his own, and held it, steadily, fiercely, clasping as though his grip could transfer vitality and comfort by its strength. He did not let go all the while that the tears flowed, and even when they stopped, still he held fast.

"I missed you, Therelane," he said.

Therelane stirred, and turned his head. "Me?"

"You and everyone."

The soft, light eyes studied him, clouded with weariness and but no longer void of life. "Mordred, you look—you look like you ought to eat something."

Startled, Mordred stared at him and shrugged it off with a quick smile. "I'm all right."

Therelane's face cracked into a weak, shaky laugh. "Mordred, d-don't be ridiculous."

Mordred tossed his head. "Well, I'm sure I can't look worse than you do."

"Mordred!" Therelane sputtered into another laugh.

"You're grinning like a sheep again," declared Mordred smugly.

They looked at one another for a short while, and Mordred was aware that the thought of going back to the barracks did not seem half so bad anymore, now that Therelane was all right.

"Mordred," said Therelane slowly, "one more thing, if you would not mind."

"Yes, Therelane?"

"Would you let go of my hand?" Therelane wiggled his fingers feebly in Mordred's crushing grasp.

Mordred glanced down and loosened his fingers, realizing they ached. "Is it all right?" he asked, with a slight feeling of foolishness.

"A little numb." Therelane flexed his hand with that reassuring, silly sheep-grin.

"I have been away a long time." Mordred got up. "You know I'll come back, Therelane, as soon as I can."

"Aye, Mordred."

~

Braegon feared and worried for Mordred all the time that he was away from the barracks. He had not seen him so truculent and unstable since Fenris' scar and illness. But when Mordred returned, there was a measure of peace in his face.

He helped himself to a portion of stew, and ate three bowls of it straight without a pause. A small, contented smile lifted ever and anon the edges of his mouth. And when Fenris approached him, he did not avoid him as he had done before, but clasped him in a tight, loving hug.

~

"Come," said Irene briskly, "let me see it." She whipped the blanket away from Therelane's arm, and Therelane, who had been relaxing rapturously in an unwonted lack of self-consciousness about his injury, felt his chest tighten and the twisting dread return.

His sister's capable fingers seemed like they must belong to someone else, a stranger who did not care about him, as they painfully probed the stump. "There's no dangerous infection—not yet. To all appearances, you're making a proper recovery. That doesn't mean it hasn't the potential to turn foul, of course."

If only Mordred had not gone, he thought wistfully, shutting his eyes, waiting for Irene to finish and leave him alone. If only—

Then a coldness as sharp as Irene's voice checked him. It was selfish, very selfish of him, to fret because Mordred could not stay.

It's not. I am lonely, and I want to be happy. His self was quick to retaliate against his conscience.

To sulk because you want something you cannot have? To ask the world to bend every way for your own wants? It is selfish enough. You know the resentment in your heart. Prove rather that you can be patient and enduring without every wish met. Bear yourself like a man.

He saw his innate selfishness a little more clearly than he ever had, and it was not pleasant; it made him defensive, and frightened him. But he refused to hide from it or cover it up again.

~

Mordred was back the next morning, with a ready-springing smile, and was quick to tease Therelane that he needed to wash his face.

"Well—you look like you need to sleep," said Therelane. He meant it. Mordred seemed cheerful, but there were unusually dark shadows under his eyes.

Mordred shrugged it off with his usual, "I'm fine."

Therelane gave up. It was never any use to argue with Mordred.

He wanted to ask if Mordred had been in Mianu the day the troll had injured him. He thought he had a memory of seeing Mordred's face right before the mace fell. But he half suspected it was a false memory, or a delirious dream, and he did not want to ask and be disappointed.

"Therelane." Mordred's voice broke in, clear and suddenly grave. "I'm leaving Mianu again."

"Oh." Therelane took this in silently. "Is everyone else going back to Orden City?"

"I'm not going with them. I have to go—away."

"Why?" Therelane was bewildered, more bewildered than he was sad. "You just came back to us."

"I—have to." Mordred's voice and face were strangely tight, as though he were stifling what he wanted to say. His eyes seemed to be looking on a world of things that Therelane could not see. "I need to." He sighed and looked back at Therelane. "I wish I could stay. I will come back."

And with that swift, pleading promise he rose and strode out of the ward.

~

"Men, we're leaving," said Sergeant Garin, entering the barracks. "Get together your belongings and form ranks."

A scattered response of "Aye, Sergeant" murmured throughout the room, and men bestirred themselves.

"Where are we going?" asked someone.

"With the city safe for now, the general's orders are for half the troops to be withdrawn again to Orden City," answered the sergeant.

They were a more organized group than they had been a fortnight ago; it was a bare quarter of an hour later that they marched out of the barracks quarter and through the city's streets.

Fenris' mind was not on the road under him, or the sheer walls of the pass on either side. He was lost in the painful, tearing memory of last night.

"You will be all right without me, Fenris? You must." A strange strain had lain upon Mordred's face; it seemed sharp and hollow. He had not slept the previous night, Fenris knew. He had seemed content at first after seeing Therelane, but an unexpected restlessness soon swallowed up the peace, and he had been distracted and ill at ease.

"Are they making you go, Mordred?"

"Fenris, you mustn't ask me that question. Nay—no-one is making me do anything."

"But you want to stay."

"I can't." And Mordred would say no more.

"Where are you going?" Fenris asked in one last, desperate plea, so puzzled and helpless that he felt as if he would break.

Mordred shook his head, caught Fenris firmly in his arms, and whispered, "Goodbye."

And Fenris watched his older brother walk away, the one he loved more than anyone else in the world, and though he did not understand Mordred's departure, he knew that Mordred was hurting. And he knew why.

~

It was the second day before the soldiers reached Orden City, Captain Murray at their head. As they passed by Mitheren, a horseman rode out and intercepted them, bringing the march to a halt.

"Captain Rhodes?" said Captain Murray with a stony incredulity.

"I was watching for your return," said Captain Rhodes. "Is there a word from the general for me?"

"Aye. There is report that the Runnicorans are moving up towards the Thesta, and he is riding northward. He wishes you to take command of Mianu."

"Very well." Captain Rhodes wheeled his horse aside.

"What lies between them?" muttered Braegon as the column began to move again.

Golin overheard him. "Aye, the captains? Well, the whole story is anyone's guess, but at least one root of the problem lies in their backgrounds. Finley Rhodes acquired his position as captain the way our general did, by the hereditary office. But Captain Murray came of poorer stock. He worked his way to where he is now, and as far as anyone can see he resents Captain Rhodes, because though Rhodes seems to have great favor in the general's eyes, Murray sees him as a stripling not worthy of his place. They're rivals, really."

"Rivals over what?" Braegon shook his head in wonder.

"Over the general's favor, of course. They both see him like a father—do not we all? But they are the youngest of the captains right now, and he oversaw their training, so—" Golin shrugged. "They have more reason to look up to him than many."

Braegon nodded slowly. "It is foolish."

"So it is." Golin laughed shortly. "Men of high degree can afford to be foolish like that. Would that I had the luxury of fighting over the general's approval with another!"

Braegon did not laugh at the jest. "They are no children," he said. "They must be closer to thirty than twenty. They should not be making such childish enmity."

"Watch your tongue," said Golin with raised eyebrows. "Not but that I and many others wouldn't agree with you, but it's hardly wise for a private to voice such words."

They reached again the building that they had left behind weeks ago, with the training field behind and Mount Thiranu vividly green and high on the near horizon. If Braegon looked long enough, he could imagine that he saw the houses of the village mingling among the trees.

"Fair, is she not?" said Golin, standing beside him and looking at the furrowed slopes. "Not so grand as the Elerien Mountains, but more homelike."

Braegon only nodded assent. There was a thickness in his throat too great for words.

~

"The city is now in your hands; send word to Mitheren at once if there is any sign of the enemy returning."

"My general." Captain Rhodes bowed. The formalities over, they stood without speaking for a time.

Captain Rhodes inquired at last. "Have you had further word from Mordred Kenhelm?"

"Indeed," said the general. "He played a valuable and dangerous part during the siege of Mianu. However, he was found out several days ago. Nay, fear not, he escaped very quickly. Let me give you the account as Jedediah Crayes told it to me."

And so he told Captain Rhodes all that Jedediah Crayes' report had been, ending, "He has gone back now—in a different guise."

Captain Rhodes' mouth opened in perplexity and even disapproval. "My general, you would not send him back. Not after all he has done. He deserves a long rest."

"I did not send him back," said the general, and his voice was weary and sad. "He returned of his own choosing. He begged me to send him despite my urgings for him to stay."

"My general, why?"

The general hesitated and answered with a certain deliberation, "He said that Jedediah Crayes was alone in the camp, without help, and would need him as assistant."

"But, my lord, he must know that Jedediah Crayes is well able to handle the spy work on his own until we find a replacement—or even without one altogether." Captain Rhodes looked at the general. "You said such to him."

"He is running from something," said the general softly; "I think he does not even know what himself."

The younger man's dark eyes flickered with curiosity. "Do you then know what this thing is, my general?"

The general was silent. "If I know," he said at last, quietly, "it is not mine to speak or share."

He did know; for it was bound up in a murder accusation, and a Delgrass Inspector, and a werevulture two months dead. But there was nothing he could do to ease the pain and the hate burning poisonously in the young man's heart. And so he let him go.

CHAPTER 18

CERN DERSTURI, GENERAL OF THE Runnicoran forces, had called off his troops from Orden for the time being as he bethought himself of a new way to break her borders. Idle was the army, with little to entertain or do; and it was with interest that they passed along the growing word of a Rehirnish peddling merchant who was already making a name for himself among the soldiers.

Damachrus of Ralecurn was his name. Exactly when and where he had come to the army no-one seemed to know; but he had come up from the south, and was working his way through the Runnicoran lines ranged along Orden's west border, going wherever he found room to sell his wares. He was of middle age, said the reports, tall but a little stooped in his walk, dark-bearded though his hair was grey. And he was a kindly man; among his merchandise were such things as headache tonics, and wound salves; and often he offered his services as assistant to the surgeons in the sick tents, without request of payment.

So the word spread of Damachrus, and he grew to be quite popular among the men, even in the places where only rumor of him had come. And it happened that one day he arrived in the area where the Paraki himself was camped: in the forested land between Mianu and the West Gate.

~

Mordred tugged carefully at the full, dark beard; the unusual sensation made him itch, even now after days. He peered into the still forest-pool, trying to see if his hair wanted any more white.

"If go you must," the general had said, "you will need disguise. And good disguise at that; for do not think Cern Dersturi will be quick to forget your face. Also, when you go, circle around secretly and come up towards the leader from the south. It would sound questionable if anyone should realize you came out of Orden, and the further you backtrack, the less they will suspect.

"You will not be going as a soldier this time; your role should be something you know. What do you know?"

"I know Rehirne," said Mordred. And the idea came to him, rapid and wonderful, and he told the general what he would need.

So when he had a horse and cart, and a load of supplies, and his disguise, he set out. The disguise was good indeed, but tricky nonetheless, mostly in the area of his hair, which needed the powder rubbed into it every few days. And he had constantly to remember to shuffle as he walked. It took more concentration than playing Richardson had, or even Sinethar. Yet he enjoyed it; for the first time he was acting a character who could be anything he pleased, any way that Mordred wanted him to be, and he was happy. He had grown to like Damachrus, the blunt, eccentric, gentle soul who doctored cuts and pains and offered trinkets "for the wives back home."

But now he had reached the leader's camp again; and Mordred was beginning to be afraid. Afraid that his disguise would not hold up. Afraid that he would be caught, tortured, and hanged.

With set jaw he turned away from the pool, gave a clap to his splotched mare, and strode beside her through the trees. After all, he need not see the leader much, if at all. Furthermore, being here meant that he would see Jedediah Crayes soon . . . very soon. A slight smile uptilted Mordred's lips, and an anticipatory light began to dance in his eye.

He found Captain Alétun's tent without difficulty again. Entering, he was immediately spotted by several soldiers who asked his business.

"Damachrus," said Mordred easily. "Traveling peddler. Salves, ointments, ink and parchment, twine, ribbons—and a couple razors and bars of lye soap. The cart's outside; care to have a look?"

The spirit of the tent burst into life and the men eagerly followed him out. The sun was setting, and when the time of flocking around the wagon was over, they invited him into the tent to sup and talk with them.

Mordred regaled them with stories of what life was like in Rehirne, and things he had seen in his wandering life—the latter largely drawn from tales he had heard of other peddlers in his childhood, with his own fanciful additions and remnants of truth added in. But his eyes stirred away at odd moments to the man called Mog Dremmag, who was lounging near the rest and scowling at him intently. And in a slack moment, when the soldiers were laughing and talking amongst themselves, Mordred slipped up to him and murmured softly, "Don't you know me yet?"

Jedediah Crayes' eyes goggled. His mouth fell agape and he took a second look at Mordred, and a third. Then he regained control of himself, and did not even glance Mordred's way again the rest of the evening.

But late that night, when Mordred went to their old meeting place, he was there—and his howl was one to wake the dead.

"What the *blasted blithering blue blazes* did you think you were doing? What makes you think this was a good idea? Was one brush with death not enough for you? No, you come prancing back into Cern Dersturi's camp with an impossible background and alias, touting a false beard that's probably going to fall off in a minute, and smirking at me like you think this was the most brilliant brainwave of the last century—"

Mordred tilted his head at him. "Aren't you the least bit glad that I came back?"

Jedediah Crayes bestowed on him a glare of burning outrage. "*No.* I am most emphatically, thoroughly *disgusted* that you came back."

"Did you recognize me before I spoke?" asked Mordred.

Jedediah Crayes' glare deepened. "I *knew* there was something wrong about you. My instincts never fail me in that regard. I *knew* you were not who you pretended to be. But I did not know what you really were, and I fully intended to find out before you shocked me out of my wits like that." He shook his head ferociously. "Scandalous. Idiot. I ought to send you home."

"But you're not going to, are you?" Mordred smiled impudently at him.

Jedediah Crayes heaved a breath which was probably meant to sound impressive and frustrated, and was actually neither. "Much as I hate to say it, you are, well, useful to have around. So no. I'm not going to send you back—this time. It had better not happen again!"

"What? Me being stupid?"

"So you admit it!" said Jedediah Crayes triumphantly.

"I admitted nothing," returned Mordred, unruffled, "save what you clearly consider me."

"Bah," said Jedediah Crayes.

~

"Jedediah Crayes"—Mordred's infuriating, teasing cheek was gone, his tone earnest and inquiring—"Did you manage to get suspicion off yourself after you helped me escape?"

Jedediah Crayes grinned. "Oh, I had to do a lot of talking. It was touch-and-go, but I've got a silver tongue in my doddering head yet—I am Jedediah Crayes, after all—and they eventually swallowed the idea that you had gone on an insane rampage, killed Lord Mirden and put the guards to sleep, and meanwhile I alone escaped and went after you. Of course I failed to catch you, but I did it with such bravery, and returned with such a convincing painful lump on my head, that they were compelled to acquit me. I was forced to sit through a long yowling lecture, however, concerning the need to go for help next time rather than trying to play the hero."

Mordred laughed, that clear, alive sound. "They clearly don't know you, do they?"

"Of course not!" Jedediah Crayes leaned back on his hands, pleased. "I was born to play the hero."

The little fool was enjoying himself with this new disguise, quite plainly. Well, far be it from Jedediah Crayes to interfere with his fun. Fresh-faced boy—reckless brat—Jedediah Crayes' mind enumerated self-righteously the various appropriate names for such a maddening, useful, useful, er, acquaintance.

Jedediah Crayes scowled to himself. Was the word "friend" acquiring a new tastefulness for him, somehow? Nonsense. He had no friends. People were potential criminals, attachment was ridiculous and perilous. And *brats* were annoying. Satisfied, Jedediah Crayes brushed the idea aside and stared smugly up at the moon.

"Jedediah Crayes."

His keen ears caught the odd, too-careful steadiness in the tone, and as he looked down at the young man he saw the vulnerability trembling on his face. Only once before had he seen that look crack open the shield, when an inquiry about the Delgrass Inspector had birthed such drastic results.

"What is it?" he asked bluntly, without facade or sarcasm.

"Has a—a werevulture ever hated you before?"

Jedediah Crayes let out a bark of amused laughter. "Me? They all hate me. I'm Jedediah Crayes, a legend whose life is devoted to stamping out all the things they love best to propagate. Affiliated with the organization that is an abomination to them all. And as of a fortnight ago, I'm werevulture's bane twice over, which is more than I daresay any man alive today can boast. Why do you ask?"

His eyes rested on Mordred, slowly appraising, sensing the pieces begin to fall together. The general's recent absence from Orden. Rumors of a werevulture slain east of Delgrass. The Inspector Wilhelm Dickson whose name had meant so much desolated anger in the eyes of that proud, valiant-hearted young man beside him.

"Now why would a werevulture be pitting himself against a young Kenhelm living harmlessly in an Ordenian village?" he asked, not unkindly. It was clear the boy needed to talk about it.

Mordred's hands clenched in the grass. His voice was tremoring slightly but almost toneless. "Thedral Kenhelm, who was my father's brother, slew a werevulture. The cousin of the thing sought for his vengeance, and he found it in me. He sought to kill me indirectly at first, by conspiring to accuse me of a murder I did not do. He succeeded—almost. But when the general came and I was released from prison, he took me captive and held me for nine days."

And the Inspector Dickson is the one who imprisoned him, Jedediah Crayes guessed shrewdly. But he did not ask it aloud. Best to let that matter lie for now. There was more, much more, beyond Mordred's words that he was not telling, and Jedediah Crayes could only hazard vague amplification on it. In any case, capture by a werevulture was not something to be passed over lightly whatever the circumstances. Their vindictive cruelty toward all men was dark enough; a blood feud would make the matter that much worse.

"I am sorry to hear it," he said quietly, and the words were not empty, though a little brusque. "There is much evil in the world, and more than a man ought to see without scarring. Only some of us were born to bear the face of evil with ease."

Mordred shuddered, and drew in a breath. "Let us speak no more of it tonight," he said.

~

Cern Dersturi cut through the camp, halting for no-one's question or call. He scorned escorts and bodyguards, as was his wont; believing his own sword quite sufficient for protection, he complained that such men were more a hindrance than an aid.

He was making for the edge of the camp, where just within the skirt of the trees a small faded green tent was nestled beside a sturdy cart and a brown-and-white mare. There resided this traveling merchant, Damachrus . . . and Cern Dersturi had business with him tonight.

The man was bending over something when he came in, a tray suspended on a light wooden framework containing various small vials. He turned around, and Cern Dersturi saw in the wavering firelight a tall man, not long past middle age, for though he came towards him with a stoop and his hair was whitened, his beard was still dark. He met the leader's gaze with keen, undimmed grey eyes, seeming surprised at the intrusion.

"You are Damachrus?" said Cern Dersturi curtly.

"I am. What does my lord desire?" He spoke in a faintly rasping tone, with an accent of Rehirne, but the leader thought there was something familiar in his voice—something that nagged at him until he brushed it aside, unsolved.

"I am Cern Dersturi, general of the army. An impediment has lain before me these past many days, as I searched for a path by which to penetrate the mountains of Orden. It has been a bitter gall in my mouth, and though I have diligently sought, closed were the answers to me. Yet now, it seems, a way has opened—or it shall, if you are not afraid of gold, and have as little love for Orden as you have shown thus far."

"Explain yourself, my lord."

"I understand that you claim to have traveled long and often in these parts. You know the land well."

"Yes, my lord." He sounded puzzled.

Cern Dersturi leaned forward, his tone grating like rock on rock. "*The pass of Mirech.* Is that name known to you?"

Damachrus blinked at him. "Aye, of course."

"I am in great need of one who can lead my army in safety through the pass. You say you know it. Have you traveled it?"

"Aye."

"Are you confident you can guide four thousand men through it surely and knowledgeably?"

There was silence for three counts. Then—"I can do that," said Damachrus quietly.

The leader stood back. "Then you will be as my guide two days from now. It is a small thing I ask of you, Rehirnish-man; serve me well and you will be rewarded, to go on your peddling way a little richer than before."

"Willingly, my lord. I thank you for requesting my assistance; it is a great honor."

"Save your words of blandishment for after you have fulfilled the thing I exact from you," returned Cern Dersturi coldly and left the tent.

~

"I hope you had a good reason for demanding a meeting tonight," Jedediah Crayes grumbled as he heaved himself over a fallen tree with the light crackle of underbrush. A bat flew by in the soft moonless dark. "I was looking forward to some solid hours of sleep for once."

"It's urgent," said Mordred.

"That's what you'll always say. 'Jedediah Crayes, I got a thorn in my finger. It's urgent.' 'Jedediah Crayes, I don't know which outfit I should wear to my fancy dinner with Ahearn. It's urgent.'"

Mordred stopped as they reached the little half-clearing and leaned against one large, seamed tree. "What is the pass of Mirech?"

"It means pass of danger. If you know the river Zarethir, that flows past Orden City and into the Dirion River. Well, in order to get to the Dirion River it's got to cut through the mountains. Easy to get through by boat, if you're a halfway decent sailor, but on foot—well, you've got to know your way to get there on foot. I've been through it myself; it's a tricky mess, full of cliffs and rivulets of water and dozens of dead ends. You—" Jedediah Crayes stopped his rapid output of information and stared hard at Mordred.

"You can't be saying that Cern Dersturi means to march his men through there. That would be practically suicide. Not that I'm opposed to slimming the size of his army, but good grief, I thought he was smarter than that! Surely he knows what a menace the pass is. He would need a guide, so unless he has one—"

"He does," said Mordred. "I'm the guide."

"What," said Jedediah Crayes.

Mordred had never seen him so shocked.

After his first utterance he was perfectly speechless for at least a minute, only uttering half-articulated noises that attempted to express the depth of his wrath. Finally he exploded into a rant of pure indignation, railing at Mordred for his idiocy in every inventive way imaginable, demanding to know over and over again what he thought he was doing.

"Jedediah Crayes," said Mordred calmly when he was done, "it's the perfect way to spring a surprise trap on him. You would have said the same thing."

"The difference," said Jedediah Crayes, seething, "is that *I* know how to get through there!"

"And all you have to do is tell me how."

"Easier said than done!" roared Jedediah Crayes.

"I'm sure you can manage it." Mordred flashed him that teasing grin, knowing that he would flick on the raw of Jedediah Crayes' vanity. "Don't worry; I won't get hurt."

Jedediah Crayes spluttered in discomfiture. "The last thing I'm worried about," he blustered, "is whether you get hurt or not. I don't care two straws about your welfare, I don't have any friends, and you're definitely not one of them. All I'm concerned about is that I don't lose a heretofore extremely valuable fellow spy."

"All right," said Mordred pleasantly. "Unfortunately I don't think the leader is going to look at things your way. Would you please start telling me how to get through the pass of Mirech now? I have to lead four thousand men through it in two days."

Jedediah Crayes growled and mumbled under his breath as he lit the lantern and began to scrawl in the dirt. "This is bound to fail. It's your neck. You got yourself into this. Don't expect you're going to get out of it."

Mordred leaned over his shoulder, watching the map take shape. "Can you bring word to the general for the counter-attack? I shall not want the leader to miss me and grow suspicious."

"Always asking, never giving," Jedediah Crayes complained unjustly. "Yes, I will. As Mordred wants. Always obey Mordred. I hope you can pull this off, you little idiot."

"I think I can." Mordred studied the jagged lines, his eyes bright with the scent of danger. "I think I can."

CHAPTER 19

"SEE, I'VE GOT IT DOWN." Mordred gestured to the map that he had replicated in the dirt without once looking at Jedediah Crayes' handiwork. It was the evening following his commission, and Jedediah Crayes had been schooling him relentlessly in the intricacies of the pass of Mirech. "Not a line wrong."

"It's not the same," said Jedediah Crayes flatly. "Young man, you've got to make some pretext to get out of the camp. I don't care what you feed the leader, you're not crossing the Mirech Pass without a trial run."

So Mordred found himself on the feet of the mountains again, beside Jedediah Crayes and the swift, shadowy waters of the Zarethir River, the pass opening above them in a forbidding, cavernous fissure full of grinning rock-teeth.

It had actually been quite easy to explain to the leader that he had not been over the mountains in a long time, and would need to familiarize himself with the route again and be sure it was still passable. The leader bade him go—"Only not alone," he said. "I shall send a man with you to be sure all is as you say."

Mordred did not ask how Jedediah Crayes had arranged things, though he was quite sure whomever the leader had intended to accompany him, it had not been the slippery, unreliable Mog Dremmag. But Jedediah Crayes was himself; and that was really all the answer necessary.

Jedediah Crayes was squinting thoughtfully up at the cleft. "Yes, up that way and around the prong should do. Come along." He waved

Mordred forward. "What are you waiting for? It's not like this is the Fell Pass of the Galtha Relua. Now *that* would be disastrous for you to find yourself in."

"Has anyone ever survived the Fell Pass?" Mordred asked as they began to climb the slippery, spray-dampened rocks.

"Most people don't go in the Fell Pass. The smart people." His black eyes narrowed with a dry grin. "No, I never heard of anyone surviving it . . . but oddly enough there was one time that I *saw*. I was prowling around the northern end of the pass, for my own reasons—don't ask, you endless spring of curiosity! About twenty years ago this was. Some man came out of it. Shocked me to no end, I must say. He looked pretty wild-eyed himself, and he leaped away from me when I said a polite hello like he thought I would tear him into pieces. He didn't know who I was—ignorant boor." Jedediah Crayes sniffed. "Nobody did, back then. The loss to them it was."

"What was he like?" Mordred asked.

"Hmm? Oh, nothing outstanding. Looked like he would be a steady fellow in everyday life. But he had a restless air about him, like a wanderer or one seeking something. Whatever he was seeking, I wouldn't have recommended he look for it in the Fell Pass! Well, he was quite the curiosity to me, naturally, and I pried him for more information, but he was as tight as a clam shell. Not a word of explanation or even a vague hint, *if* you please. Not even when I waggled my Legean Association pendant in his face to prove I was trustworthy."

Mordred laughed. "He probably thought you were a wraith."

Jedediah Crayes muttered under his breath. "A wraith. Me? I'd still give a pretty penny to know what he saw in there. Not many places in Legea so perilous as that one. The Death-Mere, maybe. Morarn—Morarn's unpredictable. Not recommended for a pleasure trip."

They were on the very edge of the gap now. Peering in, Mordred could see dim, scraggly lines of trees and a bewildering labyrinth of cliffs and ravines. The water roared below them, and the mist of it rose up to cloak the valley.

"Looks quite a bit different from the map, doesn't it?" came Jedediah Crayes' voice dryly behind him. "Don't worry, after we've gone through it you'll be able to piece the two together with considerable ease. But I think you can see now why Orden doesn't keep much of a guard on this road."

He forged ahead into the shadow of the frowning abyss and Mordred followed.

Jedediah Crayes did not permit him to follow very long. "Lead the way," he ordered. "See what you can apply of that map you memorized to solid earth and stone. Come on, stop dawdling. I'll tell you if you go wrong."

He kept his word, mostly. Once in a while he held back to see if Mordred would figure out the mistake on his own. Mordred longed to prove himself and not fail once; but somehow it was not shameful to blunder in front of Jedediah Crayes. This despite his vociferous and at times lengthy castigation, none of which Mordred minded in the least.

They seemed to be detached from all the rest of the world, in that silent, lonely place with the rocks towering over them like a safe enclosure, the trees arching their feathery branches in unstirred peace, and the spray and fog sifting down onto them cool and gentle. Mordred forgot that he had a role to sustain, obligations to fulfill, danger to walk amidst. Out of his mind he pushed them; they seemed so far away, so muffled and superfluous.

"I hope you're remembering that you have to get through here by yourself tomorrow," said Jedediah Crayes apropos of nothing. "Eh? What are you laughing for?"

"It's just that I almost *had* forgotten," said Mordred, happily. "How much farther, anyway?"

"Use your own judgment, guide," retorted Jedediah Crayes pointedly. "How far have we come? How many miles have we covered? Oh, fine," he relented, too impatient to wait for Mordred's hesitant answer. "I should say we have another two hours to go, as long as neither of us missteps into a gorge."

"Let us try fervently to avoid that," said Mordred.

Time and road dropped away from them, until they found themselves coming out of the precarious path and treacherous footing onto flat, even, forested land, and the Zarethir River swam lazily on their right, no longer plunging amid sheer precipices.

"All right!" said Jedediah Crayes briskly. "Time to go back."

The return journey was easier. Mordred began to feel quite confident that he could get through on his own tomorrow morning. This did not slip Jedediah Crayes' eye; he, apparently thinking that Mordred had no business to be so cheerful and cocksure, proposed such lugubrious omens as, "Don't count your chickens before they're hatched."

Mordred only laughed at his preposterously dour mien, and Jedediah Crayes seethed in silence and insulted dignity.

And there was the moment when Jedediah Crayes laid a very tight hand on Mordred's arm, and said in a calm, flat voice, "Don't move." And with a delicate inclination of his head he drew Mordred's eye up to the ledge above them, where a mountain lion was coming out of a fringe of trees. Its soft buff-grey color nearly blended in with the darker rocks behind it as it stalked in silent, graceful movement along the brink and vanished into a deep crevice.

After that Jedediah Crayes hummed softly to himself. "I prefer wildcats above the tame variety," he remarked to Mordred once, and that was all he said. But his eyes were alight and deep, a slight smile on his lean face; the tense, exquisite moment had stimulated him, and he seemed very much alive.

At last the pincer-arms of the pass opened before them, and they came out into the open, windy sunshine, and parted ways at Jedediah Crayes' injunction lest they be seen returning together.

"Get yourself back to the camp safely, if you can possibly help it," said Jedediah Crayes rather snappishly. "Do you hear?"

"Yes," said Mordred. "Jedediah Crayes, I hope—that is, Captain Alétun's men aren't going through the pass tomorrow, are they? It won't be a good place for you to be—they'll all be cut to pieces in there."

Jedediah Crayes looked at Mordred with some wonder and a grim sobriety which was the closest thing to tenderness he ever showed. "Doesn't he know he's got more to worry about there than *I* do?" he muttered, as though to himself.

Mordred realized, in startlement, what Jedediah Crayes meant. No, he had not thought of how he would be there, in the front of the line, when the attack was sprung and everyone cut to pieces—

He tossed the thought aside. "'Tis no matter," he said quickly, reassuringly. "Truly, I'll be all right."

"It's not like I *care*," muttered Jedediah Crayes. But he sounded like he very much did care.

Mordred reached out a hand hesitantly toward him, withdrew it, and turned to go swiftly down the hill.

~

Mordred rubbed the piebald mare's nose. "I don't suppose I shall be seeing you again," he murmured, letting her nuzzle his fingers. "They'll take good care of you—put you into army work, most likely. But it doesn't matter to you, does it? One side, then the other. You only want to be well looked after, and you will be, I promise."

He stepped away from her with a small sigh and picked up his walking stave. With a final scratch at the prickly false beard, he headed for the main body of tents. The sun was an hour away from rising.

"Damachrus." The leader's short greeting, and a wave of the hand to indicate where he should be, was all the acknowledgment given him.

Mordred stepped up with dry lips beside Cern Dersturi and the other high officers. He had not thought of being so close to the leader, and that during the whole journey. Suppose his disguise would not hold up? Suppose he fumbled in something, or the leader took a closer look, saw beneath the white hair, the crude lines of aging, and the beard?

He clenched his hand around the stick, as though the action would feed him with steadiness and confidence anew. *You must not fail; you dare not. The general is waiting, there, where the pass widens into a green vale and broad-leafed trees, and you will bring the army into his hand, as you vowed . . .*

"Forward," came the leader's voice, dark and cold over the dawn. "To the pass of Mirech."

I am tricking them, the voice echoed in his head—a sudden, breathtaking fear of the enormity of the trick he had played, realization of the consequences, and a touch of guilt. *I am tricking them, and it will be a slaughter.*

But it was long past the time when he could do anything about it.

The air was pale around them by the time they reached the great cleft. Perhaps the sun was lighting houses on the other side, but here under the mountain's shadow not a sliver of it could yet be seen.

"Do we go forward, Damachrus?" inquired the leader's dry voice, reminding Mordred that from now on he was completely, terrifyingly in charge.

He was silent for a moment. Then he answered, "Yes, my lord." And shifting the stick in his sweat-dampened grip, he set out up the steep hillside in the forefront of all the company.

"Remind me again," said the leader as they passed into the split—"what sort of a watch do they keep upon this way—or do they fail to guard it altogether?"

"As I said to my lord," said Mordred, "I saw a small outpost a short way down the road, though I do not know if it were garrisoned. Even if they have not abandoned it, my lord can overcome them like one crushes an ant."

He spoke stiffly; the strain of keeping up his facade with the one he dreaded while dredging the path from memory was heavy, and he hoped the leader would not address him again.

He went slowly, carefully. The most mortifying thing, and possible giveaway, would be to have to backtrack. Never did he change direction without a pause to order the map in his mind.

Even so, he led them wrong once. There was a time when in his pause of recollection, he could not remember which way to turn—not though he tried, and tried. And at last he went right, when he should have gone left. He remembered, suddenly, several rods down, and said so to the leader at once.

"You mean we must go back?" said Cern Dersturi coldly.

"Yes," said Mordred. "Not far."

It was a dubious and nerve-wracking moment, but the leader let it pass. Things could have been worse, Mordred told himself, much worse. He might have led them into a gorge or a mountain lion's den.

"How much further?" demanded the leader impatiently some time later, even as Mordred himself had asked the question yesterday. And this time there was no Jedediah Crayes to answer.

"About an hour," he answered.

He knew where he was now. The last few miles were burned clearly in his mind. The firs slipped past him, becoming interspersed with thicker, greener trees; the walls were widening out, the cracked, broken cliffs resolving themselves into knobbly, half-bare ground.

"At last," the leader breathed beside him. And Mordred looked away, his heart thudding rapid and sick inside him. The victory in the Runnicoran general's eyes was too avid, too fierce; finally, he had within his grasp what he had been seeking to achieve for over a month—or so he thought. And already Mordred's waiting ears could hear the stir of the ones concealed near at hand in the trees . . .

Now. It came to him, in a flash of knowing. *The time to run is now.*

And as the first of the Ordenians sprang out of the trees, he ran.

~

The Rehirnish peddler had done well. Cern Dersturi turned towards him to tell him that he was now free to go, only to find that he was not there. A sharp curse broke his usual restraint, and he wheeled to Dovurti at his side. "Where has the scuttling little merchant taken himself?"

But Dovurti did not answer, nor did the leader wait for one. His head snapped up, hand flying to his sword as a wave of Ordenian soldiers rushed upon them. And in that instant he knew, as though it were a sword in his mind, why Damachrus of Ralecurn was gone.

Burning, coursing anger filled him, razor-like and terrible.

The peddler had given him a trap, and he had entered it. Like a fool.

"*Nitta.*" He seized Dovurti's arm. "Call a retreat and let us escape on our own."

"Few will survive the retreat, if there is any," said Dovurti when they had barreled out of the fight and were picking their way back through the dim, dripping pass.

The leader ground his teeth. "I know," he said harshly, and his voice echoed off the stones. "That is why we are fleeing alone."

Harder and harder clenched the rage within him, and the more it honed itself the deeper and greater it grew. He was completely thwarted, and not in some passing, trivial matter either. This he had set all his weight and anticipation on, and his loss was total. He was without recompense. He had lost a fifth of his force there behind him; he knew not more than a handful of them would ever return.

"If ever I see that *Damachrus* again," he said, and in his controlled tone there was more hatred than a thousand words could tell, "*he shall pay.*"

~

Mordred flung aside his cloak as he ran, hurled the walking stick away. He unbelted his heavy outer robe, useful for concealing his build, now an impediment, and tore it off. Clad only in his ordinary garb, he covered ground like a deer. The noise and chaos were escalating behind, but they could not overtake him.

Pursuit he feared. Yet he heard no sound of it, and when he had gone maybe a mile he looked back over the stony, wooded land and saw no one. He hesitated, his hand on a tree as though he might leap behind it at any sign of movement, but none came. Shaking, spent, he lowered himself to the ground and sat watching a little beck cut its way through the rough earth.

His face stung, and there were welts on the back of his hands; he must have run into a dozen branches during his crazed flight. His beard was long gone.

He could still hear the battle-sound in the distance, spreading out towards him. He could not stay, not here.

Mordred pulled himself up to his feet, and set off at a light, steady lope over the hills.

~

The fighting did not cease till dusk. Heavy the losses on both sides, but the Runnicorans' were far the greater. About two thousand were dead or taken prisoner; the rest had fled into the pass of Mirech, and from there only a few hundreds returned alive. An orderly, careful retreat would have saved more; but their Paraki and lieutenant had deserted them, and it was a terror-driven mob of every man for himself in the treacherous Pass of Danger. The water of the Zarethir River at the site of battle was red and riddled with bodies.

"It is victory for us today," said the general quietly as he stood with Captain Murray as they stood overlooking the death. "Yet it is hard for me to think of it so, when I see a thing like this."

~

Mordred's spy term was over. The general was quite plain about it.

"But do not think it is a punishment toward you. You leave not in disgrace but honor; not in expulsion but in well-earned reprieve. If the war should end well for us, you will be recognized and rewarded.

You have done much, Mordred Kenhelm, more than I or any other can truly thank you for. But there are others who can take your task, and I will not have you court danger a third time. You are due for leave."

"Aye, my general," said Mordred. He did not argue. He did not want the commission of spy any longer. It would be a long time before he could subdue the thought in his mind that two thousand deaths were laid to his charge, some of them men he had spoken to, and laughed with. They were very ordinary men—some of them had been as young as him, some had not cared about this war at all . . .

And yet—and yet, what did he have now? To go back to the army, that would mean facing Fenris and everyone else, and he would not be able to hide from the memories that lay so threateningly near his consciousness. It would mean more killing, and he did not want to kill anyone or anything for a very long time.

All doors had been closed in his face. He felt himself beginning to tremble inside, afraid to face the pain that was peeling the locked sheath away without his asking. "Can I do anything else for you?" he pleaded, not caring that the desperation bled into his words. "Anything—else?" His voice broke, and he looked down, ashamed, the tears starting in his eyes.

He felt the general's eyes on him even though he did not dare meet them, and knew that they were seeing steadily, clearly, more clearly than he wanted them to. "What do you want?" the general asked gently.

"Something that does not involve killing." He was trying very hard to force back the tears, and just managing it.

The general's hands were on his shoulders. "I have but a moment ago finished writing a letter," he said. "It is to the king of Fearnland. We sent a rider to him a month and a half ago, before the Runnicorans arrived, but we have had neither word nor sign of his coming yet. While it takes time to muster and march an army, still it is best to take the precaution of sending to him again; any number of things may have happened, and we would not know of it for quite a time, perhaps never. So I have written again our plea for aid, and I will give it to the secretary to make copies; and I shall send out three riders in the dawn to bear word to Fearnland. That way, if two should fail, perhaps the third will make it safely away. Will you be one of them?"

Mordred lifted his eyes to the general, and he could not speak for the gratitude in him; but his eyes spoke for him.

"Go in the dawn, then," said the general.

Mordred bent his head. "I will go."

CHAPTER 20

"PLEASE," SAID INSPECTOR DICKSON FOR the second time. He felt like a child whining for a petty reward, and despised himself for it. In front of the general's grave, stern eyes at that. But he could not bear to be adrift any longer. The need for a purpose in his life was driving him sleepless, and all day he paced the hateful halls of Mitheren, vainly fending off the horrible sense of indolence.

"You know why I cannot permit you to fight."

"You let this Grant Eagle join the army," said Inspector Dickson, the irritant that had been rankling at him finally letting itself out. "He is no more a native of Orden than I myself—he comes from Runnicor, at that. He, too, served as an ambassador."

A sadness entered the general's eyes at Grant's name. "Grant Eagle is following his own path," he said simply. "He has cast himself upon Orden as one who has nothing else to bind him. You are bound to your king, and neither you nor I have a right to throw your life away before you can return to him. The answer, Inspector Dickson, is no; I cannot let you join the ranks."

He was right. Inspector Dickson was not so foolish as to fail to realize that. "Then let me do something else for you, anything else. I am done with sloth while everyone around me dies. Please, my lord."

The general watched him a moment longer, another, peculiar look in his eyes. Then a light came into them, and he said, "Inspector, you may give yourself, if you have a mind to do it, to the hospice in Orden

City. The physicians there are overwhelmed with the sick and wounded who come to them now. You will be safe there, and to assist them is the greatest thing you can do for us."

"Then I will do that," said Inspector Dickson. He was not afraid of blood, or of the sight of wounds and death. "I will do whatever they bid me."

The general smiled, and turned aside to stamp his seal beside that of the king's on a closely written parchment.

"What is that?" said Inspector Dickson, nodding to the letter.

"It is the second plea to Fearnland. The riders go out within the hour." Again that look in his eyes that Inspector Dickson did not understand. He crossed to the window and looked out into the greying darkness; the light of the tall, glimmering candle played over his quick hands as they knit themselves behind his back.

"Go, Inspector Dickson," he said. "Seek out the physicians, and serve them well." Inspector Dickson almost did not hear the final words, spoken so softly as the door shut. *"Would that I might help all with such ease."*

Inspector Dickson went down into the courtyard, the words running ceaselessly in his mind. Lantern-glow was streaming out of one stall as he passed the stables, and he glanced toward it to see a tall, very familiar figure saddling a horse. Mordred's face, even from the distance of several yards, was set like flint, the lean, instinctive fingers intent upon his task.

Inspector Dickson stared for an instant, frozen, and then he withdrew as hurriedly as if he had come upon a snake. His curiosity sought to flag him and turn him back, but he would not listen. The ugly warnings stirring in his belly were deterrent enough. It was no matter what Mordred was doing. No matter at all.

~

Therelane was tired.

He had been walking since sunup. It was only mid-morning, and three weeks ago, it would have been different. But his body was still healing, and it had taken him three days to walk from Mianu to Orden City. Now at last he entered it, just another sun-browned, ragged, worn soldier returning to his regiment. The left sleeve of his shirt dangled empty.

He paused by the great front of the hospice, much like Mianu's, broad and built of stone with the emblem of knife and leafed branch carved above the lintel of the door; but this one had shallow steps at the front, and looked larger.

Halting made him realize how heavy his legs felt. The barracks were not too far off, he thought. He could spare a rest.

So he sat down against the warm stone, settling his head on his arms, and let the sun beat comfortably down on him and the breeze wobble past his ear. The warmth of summer was coming; May's days were nearly spent. The humming of insects whirled by him, there and gone, and he breathed in the scent of stone, a smell so elusive it was hardly smell at all. In the peacefulness he began to doze.

"Are you hurt? Come, let me help you in." The light, clear voice pulled him back from sleep.

"No—no," he said blearily, shaking his head as the drowsiness lifted. "I'm coming back—to the army; I just stopped a moment to rest." He looked up at her—wide, limpid blue eyes, springing curls, a brow puckered in concern, a wicker basket overflowing with linen bandages on her arm.

But then the frown washed away and her eyes widened further. "Therelane Grey!" she cried.

He took another look at her, and recognized the face, but he could not put a name to it. "You're—"

"I'm Mirda King. You remember me, don't you? Braegon's sister. I came down here to help nurse the wounded, but—well, it was mostly a hope that I would get to see Braegon somehow."

Therelane nodded. "I've seen him recently. He's all right."

Her face beamed on him at the words, full of earnest, transparent joy. But the motherly concern pushed back. "You *are* hurt. You don't look well, Therelane. Where is it? Come, show me—" And she saw his hand.

"Oh," she said. And, "Oh, Therelane."

He was very careful not to look at her. He knew her pity was not of the unpleasant, condescending kind—Mirda was too bright-hearted and genuine for that. But he was not ready for pity, not now, when he was just learning how not to pity himself.

"Thank you," he said, and was relieved that his voice sounded quite ordinary and steady. "I have to be going."

"Good-bye, Therelane Grey. You'll greet Braegon for me and Filian if you see him again?"

"I will." Therelane dared to lift his eyes to her face again and met that frank blue gaze. Suddenly something in him was lost, and as he went on down the road there was only one face and one name in his mind.

~

The barracks murmured with low, lazy talk. It was cool and shaded inside the wooden walls, a pleasant change from the fierce sun on the training ground.

Braegon came over to the corner. "How is it, Fenris?"

He did not need to explain what he meant. Fenris stared at the dusty floor. "Why did he have to go?"

He meant it not as a rebellious outcry, but as the broken, bewildered plea that was in his heart. Mordred had always been there for him, separation an unknown thing. And now he was *choosing* to go.

"Whenever he leaves me, he becomes hurt." Fenris lifted his eyes to Braegon's. "I am afraid for him. And—more than that—" His voice trembled a little."You know what happened at Delgrass."

"Aye." Braegon was waiting, his kind eyes full of sympathy.

"He has not been like himself since then—ever. There is so much pain inside him, and it is getting worse and not better. I could see it when he was with us for those two days. He tries to hide it, and he cannot"—Fenris struggled to speak past the tears rising in his throat—"and it is killing him."

"Aye, Fenris." Braegon put an arm around his shoulders. "Would that I could help."

"If only I could see him," Fenris whispered. "If only I could know where he is."

~

Mordred touched his heels against the horse to goad it into a canter. Catching a hint of motion and the sound of hooves to his right, he swung away from it. They were not to ride together, the general had ordered, so that if one of them were seen the other two would remain undetected.

The trees made him uneasy. In an hour or so he should come out onto the bare stretches of the Great Waste, but for now the forest was all around him and anyone might be hiding in it with an arrow trained on him.

He told himself not to be foolish; the leader's camp was south of here anyway. What chance was there that a patrol would be riding twenty miles to the north?

But they would. He knew that. They would very well be patrolling in this area, watching for riders such as him, watching for anyone who left the West Gate . . .

The arrow whistled past his cheek. He twisted in the saddle, caught a glimpse of several horsemen behind him, and kicked his heels into his mount, urging it to a gallop.

"E, turta!" came the shout, and Mordred had been among the Runnicorans long enough to know what that meant. "Halt!" the man shouted again, this time in the common tongue. "There! Who are you, and where are you going?"

Mordred only leaned low over the horse's neck and spurred it on harder. He had been on horseback much in recent times, and was a better rider than he had been a month ago, but this was a speed beyond his experience and he was quite sure that he was either going to fall off, or hit a tree—and then he would definitely fall off. Chancing a second look back, he saw a blurred flash of the horsemen again, more than ten. Maybe twenty.

The arrows were whining around him in a rain now. The horse shied, and Mordred clamped desperately to it with knees and arms. He could not fall, he *dared* not fall.

"Faster, lad," he murmured, even though he was already blinded and almost out of control by the speed. "Faster, if you can. If they catch me, there are only two others."

Onward he galloped. Whether they were gaining he did not know, but they could not be falling behind, for the arrows still hissed past.

Suddenly the horse arched with a shrill whinny of pain and reared up, thrashing its forelegs. Mordred's grip on the reins was too slack; they tore themselves loose from his hands, and as he snatched for them, his balance betrayed him and he tumbled backwards. He remembered an instant of fearing that his feet would catch in the stirrups, and then his head struck the ground and all was black.

~

Something in him knew the danger he was in and forced him awake in bare moments. His eyes came open and he staggered up to his knees, tasting blood in his mouth. Shooting pain danced through his head, and subsided.

He wrenched himself to his feet and ran, a part of him realizing that he was finished, as good as dead, and he wove side to side, desperate to throw off their aim, another part of him thinking that maybe, maybe he could lose them. He panted raggedly for air, the sounds behind him were closing in, and then—

Like a blow from a fist, something smote him in the back of the leg and he went flying forward with the cruel force of it. Beaten, and a little dazed, he pushed himself up from the ground and looked down at the long arrow-shaft protruding from his boot.

It hurt. It hurt very badly, and every second it hurt more, a pinching, grinding throb that sent queer feelings into the pit of his stomach. His breath shook unevenly as he struggled to swallow back the nausea.

The enemy soldiers approached through the trees, surrounding him. Mordred realized that all their bows were trained on him, and wondered if a dozen arrows could hurt more than one, and if it would be a very long time before he was dead.

"Stay!"

The bows lowered.

"You, boy," said the clipped, accented voice with sharp recognition. And Mordred raised his eyes to the face of Captain Alétun.

"Private Gerald Richardson," Captain Alétun said with grim distaste. "The Paraki will be pleased that we have caught you after all."

"He is a spy," said another. "hall we not shoot?"

"Nay," said Captain Alétun briefly. "Cern Dersturi will wish to see him and have him executed in his own time." He swung down from the horse and drew his sword.

The sickness had subsided enough that Mordred, with a sharp, resolute breath, forced himself to stand. His leg seemed twisted in a thousand contortions of pain under him, but he stumbled back to the nearest tree and it braced him so he could stand on his unhurt leg. He reached for his own sword and pulled it awkwardly from the sheath.

Captain Alétun strode towards Mordred, shaking his head. "Put it down, Richardson," he said, his blade pointing at Mordred's neck. "It will be no gain to you to fight."

But Mordred tossed his head contemptuously, his chin hard and his grip tightening. Did they think he would give in to them now?

The captain shrugged. "So be it."

He flicked his own weapon up, catching Mordred's, and Mordred was hard put to it to hold the blow with only one leg to balance on. Sweat began trickling down his face as he lunged forward with a harsh, ill-timed stroke at the other's arm.

Landing square on his right leg, he crumpled with a gasping cry. Out of a red hazy cloud he felt Captain Alétun pulling the sword from his hand and twisting back his arms. He tried to struggle, but for that he drew a string of curses from the captain, and someone brought the flat of a blade heavily across the back of his head. Darkness fell.

~

Day passed away into eventide, and into night. The patrol of twenty-five trotted back into the Runnicoran camp, harness creaking and jingling, and sent for the Paraki.

He came out to them. "What news is so urgent you must call me from my tent? Make haste, speak!"

Captain Alétun dismounted and nodded toward a figure slung across the bow of a saddle. Someone lit a brand and shone it over the unconscious young man as two soldiers lifted him down.

The leader's brows snapped together in surprise and he strode forward, staring at the white, clear-cut face. "Mordred Kenhelm," he muttered.

He turned to Captain Alétun. "Well, this is a fine catch. Perhaps something is beginning to go right after all. Get that arrow out of his leg, and bring him to a tent. I will come shortly."

~

Sounds lapped around his consciousness, dim and wavery, then clearer. At first he did not care. His leg burned, his head was aching, and those things were all that seemed to matter.

"What do you mean, he is still asleep? Have you tried to rouse him?"

The voice, brusque and familiar, jerked him aware. He heard a garbled reply, too faint for his exhausted head to focus and distinguish the words.

"He ought to have come around by now. I do not wish to be kept waiting."

All Mordred's confusion fell away into a single thought: he must keep the leader thinking he was asleep. He felt the presence bending over him, held himself still, breathed with light regularity—but he did not anticipate the kick that struck him with winding agony in the ribs. His eyes flew open and he stifled back a cry.

"Ah, so it seems he *is* awake," said the leader, the impatience in his voice replaced by satisfaction. "You may go, Pacra."

He leaned forward over Mordred, one side of his mouth curling in a faint sneer. "Our paths cross again, Richardson, or Kenhelm; unexpected, is it not?"

Mordred's head felt feverishly light, the air thick and heavy. He wanted water.

The leader bent down on one knee, frighteningly close, his breath gusting over Mordred's already hot cheeks. "Come, you are awake and you have a voice yet. Tell me, Private Kenhelm, why did you leave Orden and whither were you sent?"

Too dazed to summon a disdainful attitude or scathing answer, Mordred shook his head.

The leader's mocking smile deepened. "Nay, I will not press you. I had no need to ask at all; I merely wished to see if you would acknowledge the truth. But the sealed missive in your jerkin told all that I need know."

Mordred's breath escaped in a small, sobbing sigh. The pain pulsed harder in his head, and in his weakness and utter wretchedness he longed to weep. He clenched his teeth, harder, harder, until it hurt.

Cern Dersturi stared down at him with scorn in his piercing dark eyes. "What a touching plea your general wrote. A pity the king of Fearnland will never see it."

So he did not know about the other riders.

"Of course," the leader continued, coolly, "he will have sent out more than one rider. But we will not let them get far."

And the steady, calculated certitude in his voice, his terrible, accurate knowledge, were too much. Mordred's hope died painfully.

He shut his eyes in blind endurance, waiting for the worst of the nightmare to end.

Another light kick nudged into his side. "You had best set yourself to enjoy a long and well-earned stay here; all your wit and your tongue will avail you nothing with that leg wound. I think I shall relish wringing your secrets from you, young spy."

Mordred would have told him not to bother with such a useless attempt, but he could not find the words; everything was losing itself in a swimming, dissolving mess of fever and pain.

"Try to recover yourself over the next day," came Cern Dersturi's dry tone. "I shall be occupied elsewhere, and I will appreciate it vastly if I can question a prisoner not on the verge of delirium when I return."

His footsteps whisked away and faded. Mordred sank into sleep, deep sleep, but it was hot and airless and full of foul, twisted dreams.

~

Mordred's eyelids fluttered and he stared up at the woven ceiling of a tent, wondering why his leg pained him so intolerably. The memories sorted themselves out one by one: riding, thrown, shot, waking, Leader; and he shut his eyes with a sigh, feeling drained and oddly, grimly resigned.

His head was much clearer than it had been last night, and he evaluated his situation in a calm, thorough manner.

The aforesaid situation held little comfort. He was injured, captive, facing torture and death. "*It is always death for spies . . .*" The only point of consolation was that the leader thought of him as Richardson, plainly did not connect him to the Rehirnish peddler Damachrus who had led his army to disaster in the pass of Mirech.

Of course, Jedediah Crayes was still spying in the camp, thought Mordred. If he heard of his capture, he would certainly rescue him.

But would he hear? At any rate Mordred did not feel disposed to put faith in maybes.

"You are awake." The gruff remark with the accent of Runnicor drew his attention to a soldier who stood nearby him, leaning on a spear.

"What an observation," said Mordred scornfully. His voice scratched in his throat, hoarse from thirst.

"You need water?" The man was young, about Ahearn's age.

Mordred told himself he would not say yes. Let the stupid boy see for himself whether Mordred might need water or not. But he knew he was wrong, that his resentment was wrong, and he was ashamed of himself. "Yes," he said, and shut his eyes again, hiding his face in the crook of his arm, hating his pride and stupidity. Scalding tears slid out and wet his sleeve.

He heard the rustle and the faint slosh of liquid as the soldier set a cup down by him, then the grunt of resuming his stance.

It was a long time before Mordred lifted his head and drank.

CHAPTER 21

"**WAKE UP, YOUNG FOOL. OPEN** your eyes and look at me."

The boot poking into his side and the cold voice roused him. Mordred let his lips tighten visibly but did not obey.

"Open them, I said, you brat." The boot came again, this time a painful jab, and Mordred bit his lip against an involuntary gasp.

"I am no brat," he said aloud, coolly, distantly, "nor a fool, and I will not answer to it, Cern Dersturi."

"That is no way to speak to your captor," returned the leader grimly, and Mordred struggled to choke back a cry as the boot ground down heavily on his wounded leg.

I am not going to give in to him, he thought fiercely as he clenched his teeth. *He is stubborn, but I am more stubborn. He shall see that he can never get the better of me.*

Suddenly the weight left. "So be it," said the leader dismissively. "I can speak to you as well with your eyes shut. Now, do you remember this—guardian of yours, Mog Dremmag?"

"He was not my guardian," said Mordred, suddenly afraid. His eyes flew open and he looked up at the leader.

"You arrived with him, ate with him, slept in the same tent. Close enough."

"What of him?" Mordred struggled to keep his tone indifferent. "I thought that he must be in a different camp by now."

“He was under high suspicion after you escaped. However, in the report the lieutenant and captain acquitted him, repeating to me a most far-fetched tale—but I questioned him myself, and let it go. He has a very wily tongue.” He paused, staring into the distance.

“Unfortunately for him, he was discovered some weeks later to have been in consort with one traitorous Rehirnish peddler, even following him through the pass of Mirech when I had bidden another to take that place. When I learned of this, and recalled his connections with you, I realized his game.” His lip lifted, his eyes filling with a frightening hate as he mentioned Damachrus. “He was too clever a threat to chance detaining him; I dispatched of him at once.”

Mordred stared at him, suddenly no longer hot and uncomfortable but cold and faint.

“I thought you might prefer to know, lest you entertain unmerited hopes that he rush boldly in to rescue you a second time.”

He looked steadily down at Mordred, waiting for the answer. But Mordred could not answer.

He *would* not look down. He would not weep. He would not let the leader gloat upon his weakness—

His eyes burned as he stared adamantly into Cern Dersturi’s dark gaze, until at last the Runnicoran turned away.

~

The low rumbling of thunder ripped along the base of a leaden sky. The rider, cutting across the flayed, barren swathes of the Great Waste, saw the second rider and drew rein. It was his third day out from Orden; the lone man could hardly be a Runnicoran soldier. Nor one of the other two couriers, for he did not ride toward the northwest but away from it. So the courier let his horse proceed at a slow walk, curiosity welling beneath his dark, piercing eyes, until he drew abreast of the other.

"Fearn-lith keos iya rôn?" he said.

The other looked at him in surprise. "I am Ordenian," he answered in the common tongue. "Who are you?"

"I am Grant Eagle. I ride to Fearnland to seek the king's aid."

"Then you are too late," returned the first. "I it was whom they sent, and I bore the word to King Earel, and his answer was this: the Wild Men have heavily oppressed their borders, and their attacks grow fierce. 'My own men are needed,' he said. Fearnland cannot come."

"So be it," said Grant somberly. "Then we return alone and succorless."

"But Orden has not yet fallen? For you are not far out from the mountains."

"She still holds," said Grant. "For how long, no man knows."

He reined Lady and trotted back southward, and the other man rode beside him. Their pace was slow now with the heaviness between them.

"I wonder what shall become of the other two messengers who were sent with me," Grant mused aloud at last.

A shrug was his answer, and then, "They will ride to Fearnland, and hear the truth that we already know. If you know not their whereabouts, Grant Eagle, there is no way to tell them."

"Yet maybe the arrival of another will prove our urgency and persuade the king to spare what little he can," Grant said.

"Perhaps," said the other. But his face was that of a man who has set himself not to hope.

They rode on.

~

Cern Dersturi had implied that he would see to torturing Mordred when he returned, but other than his excursion to inform Mordred of Jedediah Crayes' death, he did not appear in the tent at all that day. Mordred did not know why; he only knew that he was left alone with a slowly spreading sense of grief, like a cut that widened along the stem of a tree, shearing off life little by little.

He knew that when the grief cut through the last splinter, he would not want to live any more. The memories of horror and pain, that impended over him with crushing agony, were futile to run from. He had tried, and it had sapped so much of his strength, and if he could not run from the memories they would destroy him. The general's presence was like the hand of a surgeon, lancing poison from the wound, yet only creating more pain because he could not heal the source. The faces of the people he loved—even Fenris—reminded him despairingly of the void inside him, sucking his thoughts irrevocably back into the memories. And there were other things, little things—the twisted, nagging guilt of the deaths; the grating throb in his leg; Cern Dersturi's cruelty, and the fear that he would find out about Damachrus. Soon his loss would crash down on him fully, and then t*here would be nowhere left to run.*

"You are not like a spy." It was his guard, the same as yesterday's, who spoke in his slow, careful common tongue. Mordred knew now that his name was Ebrun, for the night guard had called him that when he came in.

"What did you expect?" he asked flatly, turning his head from where it had lain buried on his arms.

Ebrun deliberated, maybe searching for the words he wanted. "You are not like a spy is supposed to be." He grinned at Mordred.

Mordred could not smile back, even though a part of him wanted to. Listlessness swamped him.

"You are young. Eighteen, maybe?"

"Nineteen." Somewhere in the siege of Mianu, his birthday had passed him by.

"So—a little one. A boy." He was regarding Mordred with a look like wonder, as if he truly could not credit the notorious feat of spying to the face before him.

Mordred's pride was pricked, but only a little. He felt, if anything, amusement. "Boy? You can't be much better."

Ebrun continued on. "And you are not evil."

"Evil?" Now Mordred wanted to laugh, and almost did; but the lingering dullness cast itself back over him, and the sound never made it out.

"You are very ordinary," Ebrun concluded.

"Most people are," said Mordred. And then, because he could not bear the kindness when there was so much shattering and dying within him, he flung his head back into the safety of his arms, and refused to speak again the rest of the day.

~

The tent flap opened on darkness, and then a tall figure. Mordred thought it would be the night guard, come to relieve Ebrun, but it was another soldier, then two more, who spoke in quiet, rapid Runnicoran to Ebrun. They looked at Mordred twice, and seemed dubious.

Then Ebrun shook his head authoritatively, and spoke louder, and Mordred heard something about a horse. After that they argued, and Ebrun's cheeks got very red, but he must have won his argument, for he slammed down his spear with an air of satisfaction as the other two departed, and when they came back they were leading a horse.

Ebrun turned to Mordred. "Get on."

Mordred stared at him, half in bewilderment over the situation and half in disbelief at the thought of trying to mount. He did not move.

"Get on the horse," repeated Ebrun, urgency and impatience seething in his voice.

Mordred caught his breath, and then blindly leaped up and lunged for the animal. One step and his right leg buckled; another and he crashed to the ground. He lay there, hot, sick anger and humiliation burning in his throat.

Someone laughed loudly. Mordred buried his face against the matted grass, his shoulders shaking. He was not going to get up, not ever again, and they could not make him.

Hands settled on him, tugging underneath his shoulders. He resisted stiffly.

"Come," said Ebrun. "Please, get up."

He was sorry for what had happened. Mordred could hear the apology in his stumbling words, and he knew it was not Ebrun who had laughed. He could defy no longer, but let Ebrun raise him to his feet and help him to the horse.

What happened after that, he did not notice or care. He sat the horse for what seemed hours, dizzy with the fever that was rising in him again, and he was cold with the night air and his head ached and burned. He fell against the horse's neck after awhile and clung to its mane, because it was the only way to keep himself from tumbling off. The rub of his right leg against the horse's flank and the struggle of gripping with his knees became a torment, and the fiery stabs seemed to squeeze all up his thigh.

At last someone's hand gripped his arm, drawing him down, and he lurched willingly from the saddle, sinking to the ground in a limp huddle. "Sleep now; it is nearly dawn," said Ebrun, and Mordred slept.

He woke hours later and to his relief the searing, inflamed pain in his leg had abated. Ebrun was tending to a fire nearby.

"Where's the tent?" It was an odd question to ask, but Ebrun did not seem surprised as he looked up.

"They stopped only for some hours so that the soldiers can rest. We will move soon."

Mordred shrank from the thought of riding again. "Why did we leave?" he asked. "Is it the whole camp, then?"

"The Paraki is moving two parts of the camp to the north," said Ebrun, stirring the fire. "The other part stays behind."

"Why?" It did not make sense to Mordred. How far north? Were there not Runnicorans already assailing the borders there?

Ebrun shrugged. "The Ordeni are supposed to think that there is no more army in the south."

"Oh." Mordred shut his eyes, understanding quite well now. The leader, frustrated yet again in his attempted penetration of Orden's defense, now made a great show of marching away to the north, all the while leaving a third of the real army behind so that they could strike at some point when the guard was down. It was clever, a chancy gamble, but very clever, and of course he had marched past the West Gate at night, when no man could definitively count the numbers.

When word was brought to the general, he could launch a strike on the southern camp—why, it was the ideal time to attack, when the army had split into a much, much smaller size—

But there was no one to bring the word to the general anymore.

Mordred's shoulders heaved, and he rolled over, trembling, trying to shut out the truth, but the barricades slipped away like water through fingers, and the last fringe was severed, and the truth fell on him, naked and cold.

He was alone.

He was alone, and so tired of holding on.

If only the pain would stop, if only everything would stop, *if only he could—*

"Do you have family?"

Not now. He could not bear questions right now. Not now, please. "Aye," he said, the word shuddering out of him. Fenris—*Fenris—*

Something snapped.

He broke into racking sobs that tore out no matter how hard he tried to muffle them. "Fenris," he gasped. "Ebrun—I can't die—I cannot die—"

The grief and desperation shook him. He had not thought of Fenris, really thought of Fenris, in so long, and now that he did, the revelation was fierce as the purging touch of a furnace iron. It did not matter whether the pain inside destroyed him, whether ten thousand men had died by his act, whether he never saw his brother again, for Fenris' sake *he must not die.*

"I do not understand." Ebrun's voice faded through to him.

Mordred lifted his tear-wet face and locked burning, reckless eyes with Ebrun's. "I cannot die."

He drew a great, shivering breath. The storm had passed. His head was a little clearer, a little steadier. "But die or no," he murmured, "I'll hold on. I'll hold on, Fenris."

~

The army made slower progress than Cern Dersturi wished. Another nightfall came and still they had not reached the distance he desired. As he stood in his tent, eyes darting grimly over the walls, a thought came to him and he called for Dovurti Atta.

"The prisoner, the spy—Richardson. Who is his daytime guard?"

"His name is Ebrun, Paraki."

"Has he been relieved yet?"

"'Tis not likely, Paraki."

"Summon his relief, and send Ebrun here to me."

Ebrun arrived, and waited in rigidly upright posture, his eyelid twitching nervously.

"You are Ebrun; you serve as the Kenhelm prisoner's guard in daylight."

"Aye, Paraki, but I was not relieved last night."

The leader dismissed it with an irritated flick of the hand. "Has he caused you any trouble?" he demanded coolly.

"No, Paraki."

A faint smile edged the leader's mouth. "Yes. It seems that you get along well with your charge, do you not?"

"I—I—yes, Paraki."

"Do not fear." Cern Dersturi watched him with that faint, sarcastic smile. "I have not rebuked you, boy, nor am I going to. Now, tell me, what has he said to you in your speech together? He is cunning, that brash lad, but not without his weaknesses. Has he let anything slip to you?"

He could see Ebrun collecting his wits slowly, attempting to remember. "Do not keep me all night, boy. We do not have it. What comes to your mind?"

"He—he said he is nineteen."

The leader snorted. "Aught better than that?"

"We discussed the moving of the camp." Ebrun spread his hands helplessly. "Some days ago he mentioned he was from Rehirne. He said he has family . . . "

The leader uttered a grunt of disgust. Yet even as he did so, his mind was following one of the boy's remarks, one that had caught his attention, though he did not yet know why.

He is from Rehirne.

Private Richardson's wide-set, grey eyes pierced his mind, matched with another keen pair—*those of a Rehirnish merchant called Damachrus.*

His breath drew in, his eyes flickered for an instant in astonishment and disbelief.

Could it be—the one who had tricked him once, tricked him twice?

The warning that he had not heeded returned to him. Damachrus' husky, accented voice spoke in his mind, but the familiar ring in it was that of the young, proud-faced man whom he had employed as spy. The baffled, boiling rage surged up in him, yearning for an outlet.

He shall pay.

"Out," he snapped to Ebrun, and the young soldier stared at him for an instant, turned, and bolted from the tent.

Cern Dersturi wheeled, his lips curling back from his teeth in a wolfish snarl of anger. He ripped open the rear flap and stormed to the tent of the Kenhelm spy.

~

Mordred started from an uneasy doze as rapid footsteps burst in. Anger filled the tent.

There was a madness in the leader's eyes as he leapt upon Mordred and slapped a hand into his shoulder, pinning him to the ground. "Who are you?"

An instinct deep in Mordred understood what he meant, and pure, cold fear took him.

"Are you Damachrus of Ralecurn?" The leader's quick, destructive fingers bit into him, his terrible dark eyes blazing with a flameless wrath. "Answer me!"

Mordred was in a horror beyond trembling or struggling. "You know," he whispered. "Why do you ask?"

"You," Cern Dersturi, in a harsh, cold voice. The madness had left his eyes; they were steel, but no less deadly than before. He struck Mordred across the face. "*Damachrus,*" he spat. "Liar, wretch, traitor, spy!" Springing to his feet, he set his boot deliberately on Mordred's right leg and bore down with all his weight.

Mordred endured it with set teeth. Physical suffering, that he could bear if he must; even when the flares of white pain seemed to be wreathing his whole body, he did not let fall a sound. But when the leader drew back his foot, and began to kick the wounded leg, again and again, with intense, controlled fury, a half-formed choke escaped Mordred's lips, and as the pain exploded higher and higher the rest of the world seemed to grow colder and colder.

The leader bent low over him, oddly dim and hazy, but the malevolence was bright in his eye. "It is not finished, Damachrus," he said softly, and then he was gone.

Mordred lay in the dark, half-conscious and delirious with pain, and thought with a flitter of an odd, rather pathetic pride, *I didn't scream for him.*

CHAPTER 22

THE THIN FIGURE GHOSTED IN a casual way amid the pitched camp. Starlight, patrols, Runnicor, Orden—none of that meant anything to him on his cunning errand. He slipped straight up to one of the tents, an imposing black triangular shape, and slit a hole in the side with the practiced hand of an assassin. He must move quickly; the camp would be astir in a matter of hours.

The guard was the first thing he noted, and the most important; a strike to the head laid him low, and the sinister figure struck a flare, directing it on the other occupant of the tent.

The young man slept, his face ashen under the prancing flame-light. As the stranger moved forward he stirred and started awake, panic raw in his eyes, and his chest rose with a vehemently determined breath. And then, as the man bent down and the light splayed across his features, the fear changed like a strike of lighting to shock and wonder. *"Jedediah Crayes?"*

"I don't know how you get yourself into these scrapes," said Jedediah Crayes in his most blackly censorious tones. "Apparently, two brushes with death are not enough for Mordred Kenhelm; he has to get himself into a third, innocuously believing that Jedediah Crayes can drop everything and come after him like a doting father on his bratty child."

"I—thought—" Mordred seemed to struggle for the words. "I thought you were dead."

"Dead?" Jedediah Crayes threw back his head in a muted yowl of laughter. "What peerless idiot told you that?"

"The leader." Mordred shut his eyes with an unexpected, violent shudder. "He said he executed you."

"He said, did he? I'm ashamed of you, you absurd boy. Giving all the credit to a Runnicoran who would lie as soon as eat his supper, and none to Jedediah Crayes of the Legean Association? All my forty-six years I've dodged death. Yes, he wanted to kill me, yes, he *tried* to kill me, but that doesn't mean he did it.

"Do you know the problem with your dear Paraki? He is too *impatient*. He never chews his plans, or, most likely, his words, ten times before he spits them out. He is far too ready to believe that something has gone his way if he wants it bad enough. And that, my—young fool, is why after chasing me to the edge of a river and watching my spectacular drowning performance, he gave up and walked away. It cost me a rather irksome, not to say painful, term underwater." Jedediah Crayes scowled, feeling his clothes as though they might still be damp. "I'm sure, if he had known I were Jedediah Crayes, he would have been a shade more diligent in rooting me out and giving me a proper death. Pity for him, he still doesn't."

Mordred smiled, but it seemed to lack its usual life. Jedediah Crayes threw him a hard look before continuing.

"I went to Mitheren with the latest news that I'd heard before my most ceremonious execution, that being the move of the army. Of course, they were on the move by the time I got back. I snooped around for a little while—not with a disguise, just slinking from shadow to shadow—hanging around that Alétun's tent mostly to see if I could hear any news of poor Mog Dremmag's untimely fate. Instead, I came across a rumor of a different sort altogether, and I began to think I should start chasing after that Paraki and his army to rescue the general's favorite spy for him."

This time the smile that flickered over Mordred's face was a little more genuine. "The *general's* favorite spy?"

Jedediah Crayes huffed and grunted. "Yes. You're his pet, didn't you know? Treats you like you're his little lapdog."

Those grey eyes were sparking at him in mischief, teasing him about some absurd notion that Jedediah Crayes made up his mind he did not know. He cleared his throat with an adroit change of subject. "Anyway, would you kindly explain what you're doing here?—besides that you have a death wish."

"I was riding to Fearnland under the general's orders," said Mordred; "that is all."

"Do you have any conception of what it means to stay safe?" Jedediah Crayes bellowed in disgust. "No, I know. You don't even have a conception of 'safe'. Mordred's idea of life—danger is fun!"

Mordred looked completely unmoved by this pronouncement.

"Now, I suppose you're all right?" Jedediah Crayes narrowed his eyes at the thin, dirt-streaked face with a swollen bruise welted across the mouth and cheek and steeled himself for the coming affirmation.

The affirmation did not come, nor did a denial. Mordred's breath quickened, the fear rising again in his eyes. "Jedediah Crayes," he said, "he knows I am Damachrus. He found out—tonight."

Jedediah Crayes studied him silently. "About time we get you out then, hmm?" he remarked and hauled Mordred easily to his feet.

Mordred took one step and crumpled.

Jedediah Crayes had him in a fast and steady grip before he hit the ground, scanning him all over. Mordred lay without resistance, sweat glittering out on his brow and his face twisted in a grimace of frantic suppression.

"You little *idiot*," said Jedediah Crayes heatedly. "Next time, tell me when you have an injury to your leg! I can't notice everything myself in this dim tent."

"I'm fine," Mordred panted, pushing against Jedediah Crayes' arm. "I can—manage."

Jedediah Crayes' eyebrows soared as high as he could send them. "You can manage?" He shook his head. "Listen, my boy, I'm not going to leave you here; you needn't fret for that. You can manage, and you shall manage, but you are going to lean on me, and once we get a safe distance I'll take a look at that leg. No buts from you."

He lifted Mordred up again and settled the young man's right arm around his shoulders, and they moved at a cripple's pace out of the slit in the tent canvas that Jedediah Crayes had made mere minutes before.

It was the pace that set a worry in Jedediah Crayes' mind. He had counted on a degree of setback from Mordred, but the little fool did not seem able to put an ounce of weight on his leg. They made a shuffling, dragging progress across the damp grass—all too noisy—and if anyone saw them, they were finished.

Or, Mordred was finished. Jedediah Crayes himself could melt away alone into the blackness, and try a second rescue later on. But they would be aware of him then, hunting for him, and by the time their watch grew lax again Mordred might well be dead.

Jedediah Crayes' mind continued working actively, exploring all possible trails and loopholes. False trail, well, if they got out of the camp alive he might have a chance to make one. Commandeer a few horses, well, if he could safely rid himself of Mordred he might have a chance to do it. Pretend he was a guard taking Mordred to Cern Dersturi—Jedediah Crayes eyed that one appreciatively. After all, it was dark, with small chance of anyone who knew his face or would connect it to Mog Dremmag. If he could just get a scrap or two of armor—

Jedediah Crayes thrust Mordred down under the shadow of a tent, muttered, "Don't move," and sprinted back to the other tent and the unconscious guard inside.

He planned to be at Mordred's side again in moments, and he was, nor did Mordred stir until he returned to announce his presence with a casual "Just me."

Several minutes later it came, what Jedediah Crayes had known was inevitable, and a sense of cool satisfaction pervaded him at his foresight in donning the armor.

"Ca unik?" the captain barked, coming up on them out of the dimness.

Jedediah Crayes bowed, as best as he could when supporting Mordred on one side, and explained smartly in effortless Runnicoran that his name was Apri and he was taking the prisoner to the Paraki; did the captain not know that the Paraki had discovered this very night that this man was the Damachrus who had brought him much ruin? The Paraki was very, very angry and desired to have much vengeance on this wretch.

Jedediah Crayes felt Mordred leaning against him, quivering tensely. He did not look at him, but fixed his eyes earnestly on the glaring pair of the captain, who was perhaps disappointed not to have caught two drunkards lolling about after midnight.

"Do you need help?" asked the captain shortly. "He looks to be a burden; the Paraki will not thank you for taking an hour with his sport."

"I can make him move if I need him," said Jedediah Crayes with relish, giving Mordred a kick hard enough to be considered mocking, and light enough to not hurt at all. The satisfaction deepened in his core as the captain stepped aside with a grunt and faded into the gnawing shadows.

"So far, so good," he murmured to himself almost inaudibly. He almost gave Mordred a reassuring thump on the back, but, after all, that smacked of affection.

Outwards they worked to the edge of the camp, awkwardly, slowly, Mordred's arm wrapped across Jedediah Crayes' shoulder and his breath coming quick and short like a desperate colt's; for he was driving himself very desperately, very hard, and Jedediah Crayes could see that his leg was taxing him. All at once he was proud of the boy, with a keen, swelling pride that made his hands gentle as he steadied Mordred's balance.

They were past the bounds of the camp now, entering the heavy woods that cloaked the feet of the Elerien Mountains, and the scent of moldering leaf and damp, thin, sweet pine was steadying.

Jedediah Crayes paused, guiding Mordred against a tree where he could lean. "They haven't missed you yet, and that's a true gift," he said. "But they will, and we're a good three days north of the West

Gate." It would be a mere day had Mordred two good legs, but he did not mention that.

Mordred nodded, his face a muzzy whiteness half turned away in the night.

"Can you go on for a few more miles? They'll have scouts circling the camp, and anyway I should like to have a few more hours between us and them before we rest a little."

Mordred gave another nod, almost invisible between them.

"I want to hear you answer me." His voice was a little harder; he meant it to be. Mordred would assent no matter what, he knew, rather than admit his weakness. But a mere nod could mean just that—a blind, half-conscious insistence on his strength, without awareness of what was asked of him.

"Yes," said Mordred, and his teeth were closed on the word in a relentless determination, and Jedediah Crayes was content.

So they pressed on.

A few hours, Jedediah Crayes had said; but it had to be only one, for at the end of that one Mordred was reeling and too weak to even cling to Jedediah Crayes in support. Jedediah Crayes laid him down and ordered him not to move, not that he believed Mordred could in that state, and searched in the ominously growing dawn for a proper hiding place. The camp would be up by now. The escape would be uncovered. Time was running out, and here they were stranded without a stick of shelter.

The overhang? Too obvious. The hollow under the creek-bank? Not if he could help it.

Then Jedediah Crayes' eyes glinted with an idea, and he laughed because it was absurd, and because it could work. And he withdrew a coil of slim rope from his haversack and began to tie it firmly under Mordred's arms.

~

Jedediah Crayes tilted his head against the peeling bark of the tree, ears alert, chest heaving like a broken-winded horse, and wiry dark hair wet with sweat. The ground yawned at him twenty feet away; beside him in the crook of three great branches Mordred lay, out cold as far as Jedediah Crayes could tell. All the better for now. The sun was high, nearing noon, and he had begun to hear distant commotion. The hunt was on.

Jedediah Crayes snickered softly and very happily to himself. This was the most reckless thing he had done in a long time, and he was delighted with it. It had also been shockingly exertive, which increased the pleasure tenfold. The effort of hauling an insensible young man slightly beyond his own size into a suitable broad-leafed tree, even with ropes, and managing thence to drag him up five feet more to the crotch without letting him fall, was something he would savor in remembrance for a long time.

Having recovered something of his breath, he turned his head to Mordred again and eyed the leg that had caused them so much trouble. The boot was still on it, but now in daylight Jedediah Crayes could see the jagged puncture hole left by what had most probably been an arrow. The leather was brittle and curling at the margins of the hole, and black with bloodstains.

He debated the wisdom of removing the boot at this moment. But the pursuit was not very near yet, and if Mordred made any involuntary noises he could stop him in time; and he wanted strongly to have a look at the wound and do what he could to treat it. So he tugged, and to his relief it came off, if with a little difficulty. The leg must not be dangerously swollen.

He had to cut away the cloth of Mordred's long pants from the injury; it was fast to the skin with a sickening amount of dried blood. At that moment Jedediah Crayes could have happily kicked Cern Dersturi, the shooter of Mordred's leg, and most importantly whoever had removed that arrow from it. The blistering idiot who had yanked the arrow loose by brutish brawn, sparing no concern for anybody's comfort, much less anybody's actual *health*—

Jedediah Crayes, with a seething intake of breath, pulled himself away from visions of visiting this unknown monster with bloody noses and jaws and broken teeth and possibly an arrow in *his* leg, and began to pry and soak the cloth and the blood loose.

~

Mordred came out of a long black fall with Jedediah Crayes' voice muttering irritably but unintelligibly in his ears, gurgling like distant water. His leg stung with spurts of pain, and felt frighteningly raw and open, as though the air were burning it. He sensed fingers on it, and instinct and fear took hold. He tried to jerk away.

"Wonderful," grumbled those irritable tones above him. "You would choose this moment to come out of it. Hold still, little fool. You do realize you're on a tree, and now that you're awake it's entirely on your own head if you crash to the welcoming soil below."

None of what he said quite made any sense to Mordred, except the command, and so he lay still, biting his lip as Jedediah Crayes probed and prodded his leg. "What—what does it look like?" he asked at a moment when the fingers paused and the edgy pains ebbed a little.

"Not too bad. Not too good. No rotting or oozing, but it's inflamed and nastily bruised. The wound hasn't closed properly yet." Jedediah Crayes paused again. "I'm very sorry, my boy, but I'm going to have to open it further to make sure that everything is in place to heal right. I may not be a proper healer, but an arrow pulled out can mean muscles and tendons twisted, and you don't want that. So hold still and I shouldn't be surprised if you faint again in a moment; you don't look like you have much of a hold on consciousness anyway . . . "

He made the first cut while he was still talking, and Mordred found himself riding a wave of knotted, stomach-turning pain, and then he slipped back into the long black fall.

~

When Mordred woke, he was clear and responsive, without a trace of fever or clouded mind. He remembered everything, and was, Jedediah Crayes suspected, quite aware of any inconvenience that he had caused. He said nothing at all except in answer to questions, and lay still, his grey eyes staring hard and keen at things unknown.

Jedediah Crayes watched him out of leery eyes. This was a Mordred like glimpses that he had seen in the one he first met—a Mordred of strange withdrawal, cold and untrusting, jaw outthrust against the world, stiff at any hint of mockery. An enigma, he had called him. Jedediah Crayes was unused to this Mordred and not at all sure he liked his return.

Ask questions, he thought vexedly. *Ask questions!*

Mordred asked one question late in the afternoon. "Have any soldiers come searching?"

"Several came this way," answered Jedediah Crayes. "They passed on without a glance upwards. They're still about, though. When night comes I'll go down and do a little hunting, for I think we'll have to stay here several days while your leg heals."

Mordred bit his lip at that until it turned white, and turned his face away.

~

Two days they lay up in the tree. The forest crawled with patrols in the day, and it was little better at night.

"The only chance we have with things like this is on horseback," said Jedediah Crayes, quelling a yawn as he stared up at the rising moon the first night. "If that leg of yours is improving—it'll be a hard ride, you know."

"I can manage." Mordred's cold wall came down for an instant, his eyes shining with a bold light. Under the moon his nostrils were flared with the promise of perilous excitement. "We'll ride. It's the only way; I'll manage."

And Jedediah Crayes hoped that openness would stay. But in the morning Mordred was the same guarded, stone-faced creature.

What was wrong with him? Jedediah Crayes demanded silently. He could not have suddenly grown afraid of Jedediah Crayes' company. Or had he? But they had grown accustomed to one another. Mordred had let himself be vulnerable, and Jedediah Crayes had grown used to it, and now he was refusing to be vulnerable any longer.

He sensed that he was very close on the truth—groping on its very edges, even—and held on to that thought. But try as he did, and he tried very hard, he could not find a certain answer.

In disgust he lay back on a limb. Who wanted to ferret out the complex ifs and maybes of someone else's mind? Send me a group of bandits to arrest, he thought sentimentally, and wondered why he had involved himself in Orden's silly mess in the first place. It would only reinforce everyone's opinion that he had an attachment to the country.

Mordred's wound did appear much better than it had the previous day, and Jedediah Crayes announced that they would flee that night. As veils of darkness gathered over the world, he climbed down from the tree and headed for the Runnicoran camp.

~

Mordred watched the stars growing white and iridescent, but his eyes fixed there so unswervingly scarcely saw them. They were seeing other things—a score of other things, some old, and some newer, all chafing with a pain that lurked close by, and would hurt much more if he let down the shield.

The worst of it was the thought that he must go back again. Perhaps, he thought with awakening sureness, it was because Inspector Dickson was near that he hated the return so much. Also, he knew, it was that he had nothing to distract him, nothing else to concentrate his will upon. But one way or another, the return always meant that the memories surged up, and the wounds reopened.

He did not want to die anymore. He had been sick then, confused with grief and fever and more muddled than he knew. Now, he was ready to fight, to fight against the memories with every weapon he had, to fight because, with his stubborn blood, he *would* not give up; and whatever it took to keep them out, so be it.

Something scuffled nearby and Jedediah Crayes sprang lightly up into the crook of the tree, carrying with him a wave of pure self-complacency. "Down you get, Mordred Kenhelm." He offered him a hand, but Mordred brushed it aside; he had already climbed down and up once—without Jedediah Crayes' knowledge—just to be sure he could. In a tree, arms are as much use as legs, and with his good leg for the odd bit of leverage he managed to swing down with an ease that Jedediah Crayes noted reluctantly.

He was waiting for Mordred at the bottom, though, and would not brook contradiction in helping him to the horse. "The dark mare's for you," he said, nodding to the near horse. "Her gaits are easier. Couldn't spare the time to find a saddle. Can you sit a horse bareback?"

Mordred balked inwardly, and then hurled his doubts aside. "I don't have a choice," he said steadily and with a firm shove from Jedediah Crayes launched himself off his left leg onto the horse's warm, squirming back.

Squirming was the way it felt, wriggling and pulsating as though it were a nest of worms he was astride and not a horse, but after a moment he began to be used to it, and it felt merely like life underneath him; and also the mare herself grew quieter, for he realized she had startled a little when he landed so rudely on her. "Sa, lass," he murmured, rubbing her neck. "Sa, sa."

Jedediah Crayes watched him in an unreadable way, his brows twitching together; Mordred was indifferently aware of his gaze. "Has anyone ever told you that you have a good hand with horses?" he said abruptly. Without waiting he leaped on his own and urged it forward under the drooping trees.

"Come," he said, looking back to see that Mordred was following. "We've a ride ahead of us—a ride to make the Flight of Galdeol and Thorgan pale by relation."

"Then let us ride," said Mordred, and he was afraid, mostly about his leg, but his fear served only to whet his senses and make him more eager for the danger ahead.

Then the voice rang out behind them. It spoke in Runnicoran, clear and uncompromising. "Who goes in the dark?"

~

Jedediah Crayes had two dozen glib retorts on his tongue for the challenger. But he never spoke them, for a torch pierced the drowsy darkness of the forest, and its long orange fingers groped nearer.

"Ride," he snapped to Mordred, and dug in his heels; his mount broke into a flying trot, and then a canter. "Stay right behind me," he flung back, hoping Mordred heard him. Even a canter was madness in the forest at night, but Jedediah Crayes had spent hours traversing the woods yesterday for a reason, and he knew exactly where he was going. If Mordred could stay directly on his trail, all was well. They could certainly afford no slower a pace, not now when all the light was with their enemies.

They broke loose of the trees into frothing stream-shallows. "Downstream," Jedediah Crayes barked and swerved the horse right.

They splashed through the water for some hundreds of yards, until Jedediah Crayes felt the bed growing grittier underfoot, and then pebbly, and turned them out onto the bank. To have either horse lose footing or catch a hoof between two stones would be disaster. Still, the shore was clear with moonlight, the trees sparser, and they ran with steady speed alongside the water.

"This should run into the Dirion River," said Jedediah Crayes above the sound of hooves. "We'll swim across when we reach it."

"How far—is the West Gate?" Mordred's voice sounded strained, either with pain, or exertion, or both.

"The West Gate? We might reach it by dawn. Let's hope so, because if not, we'll be a target for all the arrows in the world."

The pursuit had fallen behind for a little, but it was picking up again. Jedediah Crayes shot a glance down the bank and saw them swooping down, shouting emboldenment to their horses as they caught sight of the two riders ahead of them.

"Oh, drat," he muttered under his breath, the wry, passionless exclamation reflecting his cool-headed mood. It was going to be a long, hard ride.

The moon was setting when they reached the Dirion River's vast waters and Jedediah Crayes, knowing that Mordred's leg must be interfering with his grip on the horse, felt a prickle of concern.

"Can you swim?" he demanded as the water swirled around the horses' hocks.

"No," said Mordred, his voice a rough gasp this time.

"Then hold on," Jedediah Crayes ordered.

Mordred held. There was one doubtful moment when his mare seemed to be foundering under her own weariness and Mordred's weight, but she gained the far ground, and the four of them came out sodden on the other side at last, and the last sliver of moon sank into the west.

South they galloped, and now the land was clear, though the stars were the only light. The Runnicorans drew closer.

Then something moved on the grey flats, coming out of a dark mass of woods, swinging around in an arc to intercept them from the southeast.

"Oh, *bother*," said Jedediah Crayes.

It was a Runnicoran patrol.

CHAPTER 23

DARKNESS SWAM OVER HIM, WEBBED and cloudy and faintly imprisoning. But his mind had broken loose of it, and he knew that he was waking and soon his body would come free as well.

He remembered the moon, and the small, soft-eyed dark mare. "*Downstream,*" said a terse, snapping voice in his head, and then he remembered the chase, the pain in his leg growing worse and worse until his whole world became two words: *Hold on*. Crossing the Dirion River, and then—then the patrol racing out of the trees to cut them off. They were hemmed in, trapped.

Jedediah Crayes' voice, hard, cutting through to him: "Mordred, boy, are you with me?" His own answer, fiercely firm, firmer than he was. The responding order: *Stay with me*. And then Jedediah Crayes' horse leaping away in a blur, and Mordred pressing his mare after, spurring her on with every word and physical thrust he had, unable to ever quite catch up, the pain of his leg fading away to less than nothing in the intensity and rush. Passing under the nose of the foremost horse, a blade slicing just above his head—and they were away, racing down the shore, the pursuit stringing out behind them and trying vainly to gather up the lost ground. The horse flew under him like a winged thing, and as light rolled up over the sky, he felt wonderfully free, and at the same time empty of breath, weight, or even life . . .

Gathering their horses in at the West Gate, arrows arcing over their heads, but not at them—aimed at the Runnicorans behind; the gate swinging open, and the world crashing over him again in a great wave of heat and vertigo and noise. He remembered feeling sick with the heat, so sick that he might have vomited; he did not remember whether he had; but he knew he had fallen off the horse, because he remembered the mare's breath snuffling by his ear, while voices babbled dimly through the noise, which he realized now had been mostly in his own head.

And that was the last he remembered.

Where was he now? He knew he had been sleeping a long time; he remembered no dreams, but the darkness behind him felt long and unbroken. He opened his eyes, and saw a distant stone ceiling that looked like it might be cobwebbed.

Without thinking whether it might hurt him, he turned his head to the side. It did not hurt, and he saw a flat grey stone wall that shot up until it met that far-off ceiling with a join of many cobwebs. The floor needed sweeping.

What is the matter with me? he thought. *I am turning into Laufeia.*

He turned to the other side, and saw rows of rude cots stretching out to the end of a long, bare room, a figure on every one, and more figures, women mostly, moving between them. And then he knew where he was, and he felt tired and a little abandoned.

So, they had brought him to a hospice and left him there. That was all very well; of course Jedediah Crayes had his own things to be doing, but he could not help the abandoned feeling.

"Aye, lad, awake, are we?" An older woman with a sharp chin and a low, throaty voice settled her fingers over his forehead. He squirmed away.

"Hold still, lad."

He shook his head harder, dislodging her fingers. He resented her calling him "lad." He disliked everything about her.

"How's the leg feeling, aye?"

"My leg is fine," he said stiffly. He had not thought about his leg till now; it gave off a dull ache, but was almost unnoticeable.

"Not hurting none? Now, boy, you can tell it to me."

"It is fine," he said between his teeth, hating her more with every second.

She took his mounting fury for pain, and murmured soothingly, patting him on the cheek. He wrenched away again, pressing his face violently into the cot.

"Lass!" he heard the woman calling. "You come see to this boy; I can't do naught with him."

Feet patted over the stones and another hand, firm but smaller and much gentler, touched him on the shoulder. "What's the trouble?" asked the girl, and Mordred knew that she was speaking to him, not the woman.

But he knew her voice, too, a low voice that crooned easily and seemed to have a joyous laughter underneath it. "Mirda," he said, looking up; and suddenly the world was a little warmer, and he did not feel quite so abandoned.

"I declare, he knows you," said the woman, and Mordred gave her a look rather like a cat about to hiss.

"It's all right, Priscilla, you can go," Mirda said reassuringly but quite adamantly, and the older woman walked away. Mordred sighed and lay back with shut eyes as Mirda settled herself down beside the bed.

"Now, I won't bother you about how you're feeling," said Mirda cheerfully, "because I'm sure you are much more interested in hearing about how you got here. Do you know how long you've been sleeping?"

"No," said Mordred, opening his eyes and watching her as she sat with arms hugging her knees and her guileless blue eyes smiling at him. "How long?"

"A day, more or less. Several men brought you in unconscious, and one of them, a tall man—nearly as tall as you, I daresay—with a hawklike sort of face said to look after you well, and that he would come back in a day or two. You've been sleeping ever since, but it must have been a good sleep; you're looking well."

Mordred's heart stirred with a comforted happiness, and a regret for the complaints he had harbored so hastily. He had not been left forgotten at all.

But another thought invaded, and the days loomed up ahead of him like a dark prison corridor. "How long until I can walk?" he asked.

Mirda twitched her shoulders in a small shrug. "They'll probably let you leave in several days with a crutch. I expect you'll be able to walk properly in a week, or a little longer. It looks like an old wound."

He said nothing. She might think whatever she wanted about the wound; he was not going to tell her. He was also not going to use a crutch.

~

Mirda left for other tasks, and the brightness that had lifted Mordred's spirit with her sunny nature seemed to die with her going. He tossed on the cot, every small thing vexing him: an ache in his back, an ant crawling up the bed frame, someone laughing loudly. There were no windows in the room, and he hated its cold, dreary air, the feeling of ominous enclosure from the eyeless walls.

He heard the woman Priscilla more times than he could count, talking to patients near him and generally managing the ward. No one came near him again, and he was glad; he wanted to be left alone.

Early in the afternoon, he heard Priscilla's voice rise above the half-stillness again. "You there, aye, you, lad. Go see to the young man at the end, and change the dressing on his leg."

"Ma'am," muttered a voice that Mordred had never expected to hear in this place and hated beyond any other thing in the world.

"No whining!" Priscilla overrode him firmly. "Go, at once, I tell you."

The thrashing rage began to well up, slow at first and then dangerously high, and he kept it tightly, carefully covered, lest he lose control. Inspector Dickson appeared beside his bed, face wary, and Mordred let his lip curl up a little. "Come to gloat?" he asked.

He watched the bafflement sink into Inspector Dickson's face, the comprehension, the growing anger, and felt a hot satisfaction inside.

"I am here to help, not crow," answered Inspector Dickson in that hard way, his anger held back under a taut, stern mask. Mordred's fury, eased slightly, boiled afresh.

"So they have put you to work after all? Inspector Wilhelm Dickson, nursemaid to the soldiers. I hope you are not too disappointed that your leisure time in Orden was cut short."

"Have *done*!" snapped Inspector Dickson, his calm breaking for a moment. "I wish to be here no more than you wish to have me, and if I had a say in the matter I would be on the other side of the hospice! So hold your fishwife's tongue and we will part ways the quicker."

A taunting smile reigned freely over Mordred's face. "So you can insult as well as gloat. But I forgot, of course you can. You are falling from your former proficiency, are you not? I seem to recall such choice words as 'murderer'—"

"Have done," Inspector Dickson ground out roughly through a clenched and tremoring jaw.

Mordred could not stop. He did not *want* to stop. "Have done? Have I said something untrue? Do tell. Remind me and I will mend it, for Inspector Dickson's word is beyond reproach and what he assures me must be true."

"Listen," spat Inspector Dickson, "I have had enough. Why must you believe me so incapable of good? Why are you so insistent to forget what you owe me? I could have left you to rot, a dozen times. It was not *me* the werevulture wanted revenge on."

Overcome with rage, Mordred would have spoken, but Inspector Dickson plunged on. "I suppose I never learned why he wished revenge. Maybe he had a good reason."

Mordred bit on his lip, forced his trembling to still; for his fury had completely blinded him and the world might have turned upside down for all he knew.

"I have yet to see anything good in you, after all," said Inspector Dickson, mocking a little in fierce retaliation, knowing he had the upper hand now.

"Then that is two of us," said Mordred, almost desultorily, and he was bitter because his voice shook with anger and Inspector Dickson would not know it was anger and would scorn him for weakness. Inside him seemed to be a great throbbing, bruising storm, and he was lost in it. His hatred was the only real thing in the world, the only thing left he had to hold to, and yet it was killing him.

"Go," he said viciously, not caring whether his voice shook or the whole house crumbled around his ears. "If you lay a hand on me I will—I will—" He did not know what he would do, and that was the worst thing yet, and as Inspector Dickson stood there he whirled away and flung his head against the thin mattress, the straw poking through the coarse linen into his hot, dry-eyed face.

Someone touched his leg a long, long time later. He shied like a deer, but it was not Inspector Dickson, only Priscilla.

His whole body ached and trembled as he lay back down again. His jaw hurt. His leg hurt, too, as Priscilla changed the dressings, but it did not matter. He thrust his arm across his eyes and clamped his jaw shut again, despite the rough, dragging pain, because the anger was still there and if he did nothing with it he would go mad.

~

Mordred had three visitors at different times the next day. The shadow of Inspector Dickson was still thick and ugly over his thoughts, and afterwards when he thought of the visitors he could only remember parts, little things which were jewel-like against the haziness of the whole.

The first was Jedediah Crayes. He talked a great deal about many things, from how well Mordred was looking to what had been going on in the war councils—and had to catch himself, before he let slip certain things that would be better for the whole hospice not to hear.

"I stopped by the barracks on my way here," he mentioned, "and ferreted out your division. Found out someone called Fenris Kenhelm, a thin stripling of a lad, and told him your whereabouts."

Mordred could not let that remark pass, even from Jedediah Crayes. "Fenris is strong," he said fiercely.

Jedediah Crayes blinked at him, and threw up his hands with a pained expression. "I'm sure he is! Good grief, a simple observation and the boy wants to kill me. Anyway, I expect he'll come see you tomorrow, and I suppose I deserve no thanks for all the trouble I went to on your behalf, since I have so malignantly insulted your brother's appearance."

Mordred gave the most wan of smiles, and said he was glad that Jedediah Crayes had looked.

Jedediah Crayes got up and bent over him then with the deep, steadying sobriety in his face that only rarely came to it. "Boy, something's eating at you, and I don't pretend to know what. But it's not going to stop eating at you if you lock it away inside." And then he walked swiftly across the room and was gone, as if to stay after such a blunt, gentle moment might be somehow mortifying.

The second visitor was Ahearn. There was quite a stir about the halls when he came in, for though he was wearing nothing particularly distinguishing beyond ordinary nobleman's apparel, someone must have recognized his face. Mordred was not sure that he wanted to see him, but he waited quietly for his coming and did not avoid the eyes of the slender young man who came through the doorway.

They greeted one another awkwardly, their last meeting between them like an unpleasant secret that everyone knew but no one wanted to speak of. Mordred noticed the plain silver circlet binding back Ahearn's hair, and for some reason it hurt more than if he had been wearing a crown.

Yet Ahearn for the first time did not seem very kingly at all. He seemed like the brother who had walked at Mordred's side on their journey from Rehirne to Dirion; even like the adaptive, resourceful, half-assertive brother who had skipped stones and taught Mordred to read before the orphanage. Now it seemed to be Mordred who was different, and Mordred was miserable because of it.

"Mordred," said Ahearn at last, and he sounded afraid to speak. "Is there any way you could—come back?"

Mordred had known, the instant he began, what Ahearn was going to say. "No," he said, and then, because he did not want to be unkind to Ahearn, "please—no." He hid his face away.

"Mordred, forgive me." Ahearn touched Mordred's shoulder, his words heavy with remorse.

"You do not understand." Mordred's voice was raw with a pain that he did not try to hide. "You did nothing wrong, nothing, Ahearn. There are just some things in which I am older than you will ever be."

"Can you tell me—"

Mordred was already shaking his head. "You cannot help, Ahearn. Leave me, please leave me."

And Ahearn left.

The third visitor caused nearly as much stir as Ahearn had, and people began to look at Mordred a little strangely. It was Captain Rhodes.

He was the one of the three that stuck clearest in Mordred's mind, for reasons that could not be said for certain; but when he came in, his boyish smile seemed to light up the room. And he sat down with his cloak folded across his knee, and began to talk about Ceristen, and that seemed to Mordred the most wonderful thing that had happened in a long time.

"The first time I came—no, 'twas not the first time, but one shortly after—the Staffords' eldest daughter was being married to a weaver from Orden City. The family had exerted their full persuasions to make him practice his craft in the village itself, and were still doing it as the two were pledged together into marriage, but he would not be dissuaded and they departed for Orden City amid much laughter."

"I never knew that the Staffords had another daughter," said Mordred.

After a little a lull came, and Mordred spoke into it suddenly.

"What is between you and Captain Murray?" He startled himself by it, but he had been wondering ever since he saw their cold greeting on the bloody field of Adun Cerien.

Captain Rhodes threw him a quick, surprised, almost measuring look—not as though he were surprised that Mordred noticed, but surprised that he had asked and wondering what to make of him. Then the odd wariness—for it had been a certain wariness—snapped into a rueful acquiescence and a half-laugh.

"There is much," he said, "and it is not a thing I like to speak of—but, well, why should you not know? You are as near a friend I have as many a man in Mitheren who does not know the whole."

He paused and linked his hands behind his head. "The resentment is old," he said finally. "He saw me when we were in our captain's training together, and I think he hated me because I seemed a mere child, a spoiled brat, he called me, though he is but a year my elder. As for me, he was rough and unmannerly, at least to me; he had not the ease and grace of courteous speech amid which I was raised. He has the pride of the poor, I of the rich—" He shrugged. "It does not mesh well together."

"No," said Mordred softly. "It does not."

"But I could not do right in his eyes. Still, I cannot. And I care—I do not even know why I sometimes care—but why should I want his approval? We despise one another, and I cannot bear his company; yet, sometimes, I do yearn for it."

And Mordred was silent, but he thought that he understood. For Captain Rhodes was a follower, as his words betrayed him; he looked up to Captain Murray, even as to the general, though in a lesser sense. He needed sanction and favor from the one above him in years and wisdom.

"But that is not all," said Captain Rhodes softly. "Would that it were all—but do you know of the traitor Halin Rhinehart? He was a captain among us, but he turned upon Orden and would have seized the throne for himself. It was a very brief assay, that is why it is little known; for he sprung it while the general was away, but when the general returned he acted swiftly and put an end to it.

"And it was known that Captain Murray and Captain Rhinehart were close to one another, and it was whispered afterward that he had known of the treachery, and had aided Captain Rhinehart in it. For those who remember, some still think it of him."

Mordred looked quietly, not at Captain Rhodes but at the ceiling, and his heart burned with the pain of another.

"The general"—Captain Rhodes' voice caught—"the general never credited the rumors. He trusted him with his whole heart. But I believed it. Mordred Kenhelm, to my justification, the old Captain Rhinehart himself accused Dunstan Murray to me when the rumors began, for he was all too glad to drag another man down with him, and Dunstan Murray is not a man to speak words or give reasoning in his own behalf. I believed it, and I spoke harsh words to him, words I would not have spoken another day."

Now it was for Captain Rhodes that Mordred's heart cried out, for he knew the agony of words spoken without hope of recall. He reached out impulsively and took the other's hand, and in that moment Captain Rhodes seemed the younger.

"The matter passed away down the currents of time; he was neither officially tried nor officially vindicated. But the shame is still mine, and he has not forgotten. Now, tell me," he said, as suddenly as Mordred had spoken earlier, with a light that was half teasing and half commanding in his eye, "what is between you and that Inspector Dickson?"

Mordred's eyes jerked upon him, wavering; but caught between an obligation fairly due, a story that bore a strange half-similarity to his own dark feud, and the violent words of yesterday still tearing at him, his resistance shivered into nothing. He told.

He told Captain Rhodes everything, everything he had ever told anyone and some things that he had told no-one. He told it quietly, flatly, ignoring the ceaseless, deep-rooted pain that contracted with every word. When he was done he turned his face aside, and he was shuddering with regular, gasping breaths like a person who has been weeping a long time, except that he had not shed a tear.

At last he turned to Captain Rhodes again, and spoke with a diffident lightness. "You are the first to hear all that."

Captain Rhodes looked as if he might reply in kind, but he did not. "If I had known—if I had understood what I was asking, I would not have asked you. I am sorry that I loosed such pain. Yet if I am indeed the first to hear, then maybe you will rest easier now."

Mordred shut his eyes, and saw Inspector Dickson behind them. "Aye, it will be better. It is already a little better."

It was, and he could not deny it. His heart felt loosed of a great looming darkness that he had not even known he was teetering on for so long.

"And yet—" It was not a cure. The pain was still within him, a little cooled, a little settled. He met Captain Rhodes' eyes again, and the other man put his hands on Mordred's and shook his head.

"I understand," he said. "Some wounds, even when cleaned, are too deep for healing."

"What do I need?" Mordred asked in a sudden, fierce plea. Having now had a taste of respite, he longed for more. He felt he would do anything for it. "Is there any healing for me? What more do I need?"

"I do not know," said Captain Rhodes.

"You speak as one who does know," said Mordred harshly.

Captain Rhodes looked at him, a conflict in his gaze. "If indeed I know anything," he said, stuttering the words a little, "it is what you know already in your heart."

And then he got up and swiftly strode away, the third of the visitors to leave so abruptly, and Mordred, who sensed in an unerring yet formless way his meaning, recoiled from the bare inkling and trampled on it, building up a wall of hate and anger around the small nubbing thought.

That, whatever form *that* might take, and he dared not let it acquire shape and meaning—*that* was something he could never do.

CHAPTER 24

FENRIS STOOD BY QUIETLY AS Sergeant Garin spoke with another officer who had come past and bided a moment for pleasant discourse. As they laughed a final time and parted ways, Sergeant Garin turned and caught sight of him.

"Fenris Kenhelm! Lad, how long have you been standing there?"

"About a quarter of an hour, Sergeant," he answered, softly—he could never utter the clipped, resounding tones that were expected of the men.

"I am sorry I overlooked you. Is it urgent?—Nay, I know. You're wanting permission to see your brother, is that not it." He gave a reassuring grin and clapped Fenris on the shoulder. "I promised you that you might leave today, and that you may. Return by noon; and give him my greetings. I hope his wound won't trouble him long."

"Give him mine as well!" called Marcus, passing through the tent. "Tell him I have instigated a rumor that he will be returning here shortly, so he had better make haste to fulfill it."

"Marcus," said Bardrick sternly, but his brother laughed.

"'Tis only a jest, Bardrick. When will you learn to like them?"

"'Tis nothing about jests as jests, my brother," answered Bardrick. "It is when they come from your mouth that they cease to be enjoyable."

Marcus covered his snort of delighted laughter with a tragically offended pose. Bardrick shook his head at his brother and turned to Fenris.

"Give him all our greetings, Fenris, though I beg you not to pass on any of Marcus' absurd stories. We miss him sorely."

Therelane also glanced up and nodded, saying nothing; but Therelane rarely spoke these days. He had healed fully, his wound a mere scarred stub now, but he was thinner now, too, a lean, knotted look to his slight body, and the softness seemed to have gone out of his eyes. Not that he had ceased to be gentle; but that old unsure, innocent look was gone. But though he threw himself wholeheartedly into their daily training, he was also more wont than before to lag, and forget himself, and daydream.

Fenris found Mordred easily. A tall, sandy-bearded physician directed him there with a low rumbling laugh. "That one, eh? They say he had the king of Dirion here to see him yesterday!"

Fenris turned to look at him in astonishment.

"I wonder what one is to make of that. Nothing particular in the boy—a ragged soldier like any dozen others . . . " The man shrugged and turned again to the bloodied instruments that he was washing, and Fenris slowly left, his thoughts in turmoil.

Mordred looked well, if a little worn with illness. His face lighted at Fenris' approach, and he greeted him eagerly. And Fenris thought that some of the strain that had been surrounding him when they last parted was gone.

"Mordred," he said, a little hesitantly, not wanting to break the peace in his brother's face, however fragile and impermanent it might be. "You have seen Ahearn?"

Mordred threw him a startled look, which changed to understanding and the warm, absurd pride that always flashed out when Fenris discovered something himself. "I have seen him twice," he answered, the look fading into something graver. “I should have told you, Fenris, but I did not think of it. Forgive me.”

“I do,” Fenris answered swiftly, earnestly, filled with love at the deep, anxious plea in the grey eyes he knew so well. He was not hurt, not in the least, and his one concern was to ease Mordred’s heart.

“So—” Mordred sighed, and dropped his eyes. “It is all right, Fenris, with Ahearn and me. It is well between us. You must be easy in your mind. We are no longer angry at one another.”

“Then?” said Fenris, his heart aching as he heard the dispirited tone in Mordred’s words and knew that there was more unsaid.

“He wants me—to—to come back. And I cannot.” Mordred lifted his eyes again, and to Fenris’ grief and astonishment there were tears in them. “I cannot choose that yet. And I—I cannot bear to hurt him, not now, not after I have hurt him so already, but I cannot come with him either. At least not yet. Fenris, it is not only me of course that he wants—he wants all of us to return, and you may, if you wish, I—I will not stop you.”

“Mordred, no.” His voice trembled.

“Fenris!” Mordred sat up and reached for him. “Nay, what have I done—do not weep, Fenris—”

Fenris shook his head and struggled for the words—struggled to say that it was not himself his voice shook for, but for Mordred. For the pain that tore his brother, and the sacrifice that he would still make to see Fenris glad, while the thought of deserting his side filled Fenris with the deepest anguish. “Mordred,” he pleaded, “where you go, I will go, and where you do not go, do not ask me to go there. You know that you are more to me than any other thing.”

"I do know it," said Mordred softly. "And I will not ask it, nor will I send you away, Fenris. I only had to be sure, this once." And he caught Fenris in a firm embrace.

"Mordred?" Fenris said as they drew apart. He was afraid to ask, but he had to know. "When you are healed, when you leave—where will you go?"

Mordred looked up. "I'm coming back with you, Fenris," he answered simply, and the burning dread in Fenris' heart evaporated into speechless joy.

"You're coming back," he repeated at last in a whisper.

"Aye." Mordred gripped Fenris' hands, his eyes steady and assured. "I'm not leaving you, Fenris. I'm never leaving you again."

~

So Mordred came back to Sergeant Garin's company once more, after a month and a half of absence and only one brief visit between whiles. His leg was mending rapidly, and by the time he returned to the barracks he walked merely with a slight hitch—though even this he grudged, and he did not walk in the presence of other people when he could help it. Only for the sergeant and for Fenris would he stir himself.

There was no difficulty about explaining his wound. Everyone presumed as a matter of course that he had acquired it in some battle in a different division, perhaps in the north; and Mordred let them think that. If he told them that he had been riding to Fearnland, then he would have to tell them of his capture, and the leader was something that he wanted to put far behind him. At times he woke in the night having dreamed of Cern Dersturi's rage-distorted features snarling over him. He never dreamed of the werevulture.

Captain Murray still came by to observe while they trained on the open field. Mordred gathered that he considered it his place to follow the progress of the new soldiers. Mindful of Captain Rhodes' words, Mordred watched the captain, his harsh, stony features and the deep-graven lines about the mouth and between the brows, and he sought to speak to him whenever he could. Even if it were only a greeting, the gentle pity that had awoken so deeply in him yearned for an outlet. He knew the other man's pain as if it were his own: it *was* his own. And he could not but reach out.

Once, in a fragment of leisure time, Mordred came upon a man a little distance from the main barracks, firing arrows into a stacked pile of feed-sacks. He watched him, fascinated in a new way by the supple stance of the man's feet on the ground, the smooth rhythm of the hands and fingers, the dark eyes flickering keenly in practiced aim. When the man had drained his supply he went to retrieve the arrows, and Mordred stepped forward as he returned.

"Will you let me try?" he asked candidly, motioning to the wrist-thick, half-height bow upended against a stump.

The man looked curiously at him, but did not seem irked or impatient. "Have you ever shot a bow before?" he asked.

"Never," answered Mordred easily. "I saw you practicing, and I liked the way it looked. I have a good eye for throwing stones."

"You cannot just pick up a bow and shoot," said the man a little gruffly. "Though an eye for aim will stand you in good stead."

"I should like to learn," said Mordred.

The man sighed, and rubbed his coarse, dark-brown beard. "Then pick it up and I will show you."

"Thank you," said Mordred. "What is your name?"

"Grant Eagle," returned the other.

"Mordred Kenhelm; I am with Sergeant Garin."

"Are you?" Grant Eagle showed sudden interest. "Then you will know Braegon King?"

"I know him well."

"So; and I have grown to know him well myself these past weeks. It is Braegon King's doing if I have more joy in life than I did a month ago; though still I wonder whether it was worth the trouble." He shook his head. "Nah, why speak on it at all? Fetch that bow, if you want to learn."

Mordred grasped the principles quickly, and he had, as he stated truthfully, a good aim; so by the end of a half hour Grant Eagle called him a fair bowman.

"You are good enough to join the ranks of the archers, at least; any man can get into those who knows which way to turn the bow. But do not expect it to save your life yet."

Mordred smiled a little. He thought of laughing, but laughing did not come easy to him just now. "I do not care to be a master of the bow," he said. "But I am glad that I can draw one at need now, and still gladder to have made your acquaintance, Grant Eagle. I shall tell Braegon that I met you."

"Do so," said Grant, "and if you want to practice your aim another day, my bow is yours."

So they parted friends, of a sort, though there was no deep bond made between them. And Mordred saw him now and again, and spoke to him, and learned to handle the bow; he liked it better than the sword, which seemed to him so alien and difficult to wield. He could have requested a transfer to the archer ranks, as Grant had remarked, but he did not really consider that. To do so would mean to leave his brother's side again.

~

"Therelane Grey! You're falling back, man. Keep up with the rest!"

Therelane whipped back into awareness, and quickened his pace. At moments like these he felt that he could not possibly be the same person who had lived in a large, dim house cut off from the world, the blood of a curse surrounding him; lonely, privileged, the son of a wealthy man and accustomed to no privation, yet not content. Now his days were filled with arduous labor, whether he wanted it or not; he had no status, no recognition; he had got used to sleeping with only a blanket and the ground, to the sharp twinges that seemed to shoot past his wrist and into the palm and fingers that were no longer there, and to always feeling a little hungry.

But it was none of these things that distracted him, and made him lag in the marching. It was a face that had rested in his mind for the past fortnight and more.

He had never known anything like what he felt for Mirda King. It was so many things that had fallen together at once, that lost his heart to her; it was her beautiful, forthright manner, her shining joy, her wholehearted enthusiasm, and most of all the way she had reacted to his missing hand—as though he were still Therelane to her, not a whit changed. She had given him sorrow, but not condescension or awkwardness. All this from a girl he scarcely knew, and the gale of adoration blew him wonderfully, hopelessly away.

If he had had other women around him, the passion might have dwindled and been forgotten. But there were no women in his world right now; it was the world of men, harsh, exacting, unyielding. And so the memory of Mirda stayed fresh and living in Therelane's mind, and his mind returned to her unbidden and longing, dwelling on her clear smile and wide blue eyes, her softness and femininity. He loved to think on her, even though there was no thought in his mind that it would ever come to anything. After all, he had no chance to see her, and she certainly did not love him in that manner, and she would never think of wanting him, a man without two good hands.

But he cherished her image, and there was a secret wish, in the very depths of his mind, that she might come to notice him one day.

~

"Mordred!" Braegon exclaimed, coming upon him as he sat burnishing the edge of his sword. "Fred and Daren are back!"

Mordred looked up, surprised. "They left?" He had seen nothing of Fred, now that he thought about it.

"Their division departed several weeks ago to the north, but they returned this morn. We shall go see them as soon as the sergeant lets us; will you come?"

"Yes," said Mordred, "I will come." Why, in truth he had not seen Fred since the horse sale. So much had happened since. He wondered how Fred had felt parting from Fiona, lovely, compassionate Fiona with so much love to give. It had been hard for Mordred to leave his own sister . . .

The reunion was a cheerful one; the men from Sergeant Garin mingled with those of Sergeant Dendath in pleasant companionship. And then, in the middle of it all, to Mordred's surprise, Fred drew him away, saying quietly, "I would speak to you, Mordred."

Mordred accompanied him outside and waited, half-defensive and bewildered.

But Fred was silent a little, as if ordering carefully what he wanted to say. Finally he turned to Mordred, his gentle brown eyes meeting Mordred's squarely. "Ten days ago," he said, "there was a small skirmish in the north, a little foray on the enemy's part. Some of our number died, but others were taken prisoner. I was one. I learned that our side has a number of Runnicoran prisoners, and they were seeking grounds for an exchange; and I was glad at that, of course, for it meant that I would return shortly. But while we waited, the leader of the Runnicoran army came among us—his name is Cern Dersturi, and he moved through the prisoners and asked questions. I did not pay heed to what he asked, but he came to me and looked into my eyes, and he asked my name; so I told him. Then he asked if I knew a man called Mordred Kenhelm."

Here Fred's gaze grew very searching indeed, and Mordred looked away from it.

"I told him the truth. 'I do,' I said.

"'And do you know where he is?' he asked, and I was afraid because there was a great anger behind his eyes.

"And I told him that you were of my own village, but that I had not seen you since the war began, for we had not entered the same company. He seemed dissatisfied with my answer, but he did not press me. I think he would have returned and spoken with me longer, but during his absence the exchange was made and I returned to my own lines."

"And what do you want from all this?" asked Mordred, rougher than he intended. He took a low breath, striving to calm his rushing, panicked thoughts.

"I want to know how this Cern Dersturi knows your name, and why he seeks you. But I do not ask anything save what you are willing to give."

Mordred shook his head. He did not even know whether he was permitted to speak of his spy work, though he was no longer undertaking it. "Then ask of me nothing, Fred, I beg you, for I cannot give what you ask. Forget for me that you ever saw the leader. Forget his words. Do not speak of it to anyone else, please."

"I have told no one, and I will not." Fred spoke in his comforting, sure way. "Fear not, Mordred; I can guess when there is a secret to be kept. But I am anxious for you."

Mordred glanced at him, and gave a startled laugh. "Do not be. What harm can he do me here? Nay, Fred, I can take care of myself."

Fred sighed, and put his strong, calloused hand over Mordred's. "My mind is not eased. Take care of yourself, then—if you can."

~

Jedediah Crayes leaned back in his chair, studying the shrouded ceiling of the cool, dank council room. The voices droned around him, endless, repetitive and boring. They had gone on long enough.

He brought his chair legs to the floor with a dull thud that made conversation halt for an instant, and in that instant he stood and pivoted to the man he wanted.

"General, have you considered the word I brought to you more than a fortnight since?"

"I have," replied the general slowly.

"And the counsel that I recommended to you?"

"A little, aye."

"And has it been addressed in this room?"

"It has—briefly."

"Well, I'm a little fed up with all of you," snapped Jedediah Crayes. "Here you have the Runnicoran's army split, a bare third of it lying down in the forests west of here, a prime opportunity, and you sit here doing nothing! What was that you said, my dear sir, in April? 'Defense will not win us the fight, but for now it is our only path.' Quite right. Defense will not get you anywhere, and may I point out that it is now *not* your only path?"

The general would have spoken, but Jedediah Crayes overrode him. "I don't care if you're too nervous. Bah. War is about risks, you're a general, you should know that. All of you should know it! Yes, it is perfectly likely that something could go wrong. I'm not suggesting outright attack; I'm not suggesting anything in particular. All I'm suggesting is that you do something with this lump of Runnicor that's dozing south of its mother. The opportunity is not going to last forever, you know. Why did they split? So that you would *think* all their army was in the north and they could make an unexpected move from the south. You'd better hurry up before they make it."

Jedediah Crayes rested his palms coolly on the table and surveyed the silent faces around him.

At last the general rose, and bent his head to Jedediah Crayes. "I beg your forgiveness for my inaction," he said gravely. "You are right. It is time to strike back."

CHAPTER 25

THE GENERAL PACED SWIFTLY IN front of the window. "Captain Rhodes!" he called again.

Hurried footsteps sounded, and the captain rushed in. "Aye, my general. What is it?"

"The plans have been drawn up for the attack. Our main strike will be at the leader's southern camp. We have not the strength to rout them from it, and we shall not try; we shall be merely taking and burning their provisions from the supply tents, which they greatly need for their large army, as well as destroy their shelters. A decoy is planned to the north, as many men as we can muster.

"I ride with the decoy. You will lead the attack on the camp, Captain Rhodes. Choose three contingents, no more than a hundred fifty men. Remember that we mean to work through speed and stealth, not numbers. Alert them that we will be leaving within two days."

"Aye, my general."

The general nodded, touched Captain Rhodes' shoulder, and turned to the table and the parchments scattered across it. Captain Rhodes knew he was dismissed.

~

By the following dawn they were ready. The sky was still dark and starry when the small company set out to march. Among the amassed soldiers were Sergeant Garin and his men.

If the surprise foray went ill, it would be a massacre, of course. Yet despite the danger—perhaps because of it—Mordred's mood seemed alive and reckless and almost cheerful.

"'Tis practical," he said, "that we are close to the leader, is it not? We have no concerns of three-month marches with our shoes wearing out, our food running low, and disease spreading among us. One must give credit to this Runnicoran, after all. Not everyone can be so kind to his enemies."

Someone laughed. Braegon smiled wryly. Marcus Segelas, eyes glimmering with mischief, whispered loudly and solemnly about 'treasonous sentiments'.

Mordred shot him a scornful glare.

Fenris glanced at his brother, a slight line of worry across his brow. "You do not think they would believe you really think treasonously, Mordred?"

Mordred looked at him. The bright mood was gone, crushed by whatever Marcus' words had meant to him. "And what if they do? Let them think it; let them hate me. It will hardly make a difference one side to the other."

Fenris did not understand the meaning of this, and he mulled over it the rest of the morning, an uneasiness twisting his heart at the dark look in Mordred's eyes.

Noon was upon them as they approached the camp. It was almost invisible from three sides, surrounded on the north, west, and south by heavy forest; only on the east it lay opened to the plain beyond where the trees had been cut away.

"It is quiet," murmured Captain Rhodes to his second, Eckhard, as they drew near.

Eckhard nodded. "You do not think they could have known of our coming?"

Captain Rhodes cocked his head, listening again. "I cannot see that even a waiting camp could make such a dead silence," he said.

And indeed, when they sent two scouts ahead, the men came back with word that though the tents were still pitched, there were no fires nor sign of any living creature.

"Search it thoroughly," ordered Captain Rhodes. He motioned to the leader of the first of the three divisions. "The rest of us will remain here until you have scoured the camp."

"Aye, Captain Rhodes," Sergeant Garin answered. With a brief bow he turned and led his men into the silent rows of dusty tents.

Back and forth they worked through them, the only sounds the wind, the soft footsteps of soldiers and the rustling of tent flaps lifting. There was something dangerously oppressive about the silence, a silence that should never be resting over a large camp. Could they have truly left? Fenris constantly glanced over his shoulder, feeling phantom eyes upon him.

"'Tis all right, Fenris," said Mordred when he passed by him briefly, seeing his worry. "They've surely deserted it, for whatever reason." But uneasiness murmured in his own words. It did not sit well with anyone, this tense searching. They only wanted to get to the end of it, to prove indisputably that they were all alone. If they could but do that . . .

"Here, come this way." It was a man Fenris did not recognize standing behind him in the dim light of the tent. He was stocky, his brown beard trimmed close, and he wore no armor save a leather jerkin and a broad belt. His eyes glinted impatiently as he waved Fenris over.

Fenris came, slowly. "What is it?"

The man led the way quickly out of the tent and toward the outskirt of the camp. "I saw something moving," he said, heading into the surrounding trees. "I didn't dare come closer, but it looked like it might have been one man, maybe two."

"Where?" asked Fenris softly, struggling to steady his frightened breathing.

"Somewhere around here." The man took a step back next to Fenris, peering around the sun-shot greenness of the forest.

Fenris made himself stay where he was. He did not like the nearness of the man, his instinct would not let him be so close to a stranger, someone who might suddenly turn and hurt him. But this man was not one to dread, only a fellow soldier. Fenris shut his eyes and looked away, trying to force back the shrinking fears.

"Round here somewhere," the man was muttering.

The blow came quite abruptly. He had never known such pain since the bear's claws had torn his forehead open in the Wilds; but it was over in an instant, and everything was black.

~

"Sergeant. Sergeant Garin!"

Garin started at the raised voice and turned. "Marcus?"

The young man pressed his lips together a moment before speaking. His teasing tone was strangely sober. "I cannot find Bardrick anywhere, sir. And before you say it's only my brother, sir, I can't find Fenris either."

"It's a large camp," said Sergeant Garin.

"I—I've been looking for him at least half an hour, sir."

Garin frowned doubtfully into space. At last he nodded. "All right. I shall make a head count."

~

A short while later a grim-faced Garin addressed Captain Rhodes. "We are four men short, my lord."

"What has become of them?" Captain Rhodes demanded.

Garin shook his head. "No one knows."

"Yet you have not been attacked?"

"Nay, my lord."

A thick, puzzled stillness reigned, the unspoken questions dancing in the air between them. Was the army hidden somewhere near? And if not them, then who? Why would they capture instead of attack the many?

"Surely you have no noblemen among your force, Sergeant," said Captain Rhodes—"such as might be ransomed?"

"Nay, my lord. Of course not." Garin's tone was as bewildered as his. "Save that, well, Therelane Grey I understand is of higher lineage, though he joined as a footsoldier like the rest."

"Who else was taken then?"

"Mordred and Fenris Kenhelm," Sergeant Garin answered, "and Bardrick Segelas."

Those watching saw Captain Rhodes start a little, his face tighten. "*Mordred*," he murmured.

"But surely he could not know, sir—" began Marcus, but fell silent at a sharp look from the captain.

"My lord," said Sergeant Garin. "What orders?"

Captain Rhodes was silent for a little. "Proceed into the camp," he said at last, "and carry out the plan; set fire to the tents, take what supplies you can carry. But no man must go alone. Work swiftly, and keep a wary eye for any sign of the enemy." He lifted his hand, and the company of one hundred twenty edged out of cover of the trees.

Then came a wild shout—a clashing of weapons—and the trap was sprung.

"Retreat!" cried Captain Rhodes aloud. "Retreat!"

But it was useless. They were utterly hemmed in, a small knot in the midst of a roaring, weaponed maelstrom. The outer edges shrank; men fell like grass to a scythe.

Captain Rhodes knew quite clearly that only a few minutes more, and every one of them would be dead on the battlefield.

Suddenly the press seemed to be thinning. Captain Rhodes strained his eyes through the tangle of bodies toward the mounted men who had appeared on the edge of the fray.

~

The proud array of cavalry and footsoldiers moved northwards. At their head, King Ahearn of Dirion turned to the general.

"Do you hear that?" he asked.

"The hoofbeats? Aye, I hear them." The general leaned forward in the saddle, listening to the erratic thud half-masked by their own drumming.

"Is it one?" Ahearn asked, frowning.

"Impossible to say amid all this noise."

Out of the trees in front of them, a horseman galloped into the path. Handling his horse with expert grace, he whipped around directly in front of the general's mount.

The horse let out a startled, snorting whinny and reared up as the general pulled him to a halt.

"Out of the way, man!" Captain Thurgild directed an angry glower at the intruder. "Do you realize you are stopping an army on the march?"

"Keep your tongue out of this," the rider snapped back and nudged his horse further into the general's path.

"Peace, Captain," said the general. "What do you mean by this?" he asked the lean, hawk-nosed rider.

"Just this," answered Jedediah Crayes. "You will find no battle waiting for you ahead, your attack on the leader's camp is going to fail, and you had best turn around if you wish to pull them out before it is too late."

"Explain," said the general, wheeling his horse. "Give the signal to turn about," he bade the horn-bearer beside him.

Jedediah Crayes snorted. "What is there to explain, hmm? It is very simple. I have been trailing a man I suspected of spy work for some time, only to have him slip through my fingers yesterday morn. What else, I thought, could he have dashed away to do but warn the leader of an upcoming attack on his camp? When I rode ahead to see whether they took your bait for the decoy—which they did not—the answer was plain enough. Now you must move in haste; Finley Rhodes' men cannot have come to the camp yet, but it will take us several hours to reach them."

~

The noise of battle rolled to their ears through the deceptive peace of the standing trees. Cries, thuds, the crash of metal on metal.

"Quickly," said the general.

As they broke out into the fight, the Runnicorans drew back startled, their tight current of attack dissipating. In the middle of the confusion was a desperate knot of soldiers, half-scattered and fighting madly. Captain Rhodes, helmetless, his armor dented and his cheek streaming blood, looked towards them and narrowed his gaze, trying to see who they were. Then recognition dawned, and his eyes widened in relief.

The general rode forward, closing the distance between them. "What happened?" he asked Captain Rhodes.

"It appeared deserted when we came," Captain Rhodes said briefly. "I sent out a few to search it better, and they came back with four men missing. I gave the order to continue with the attack, and we had just moved out when the enemy struck."

The general nodded. "Very well. It will be spoken on more elsewhere. Give the order to your men to retreat, and we will cover you."

Slowly the Ordenians began to move back, away from the onrushing tide of the enemy. The Runnicorans sought to cut them off, but they continued to withdraw, gradually yet unstoppably.

Ahearn had been pushed to the right wing of the retreat, losing the general and his own men. In the midst of the fighting, his horse suddenly shuddered and swayed as a spear took it through the breast.

He kicked his feet loose of the stirrups, leaping off and landing heavily on his shoulder. He rolled onto his back and stood, barely in time to counter the attack of the same spearman who had killed his horse.

Ahearn was armed with a sword, but the other man handled his spear with surprising skill, using it as both blade and stave. Their fierce exchange carried them all the way to the outskirts of the fighting, where Ahearn at last landed a clean blow on the handle of the spear, snapping it in two. In another moment his adversary lay dead on the ground.

Ahearn let out his breath in a gasping sigh, feeling the tight pain of his wrenched shoulder. The next instant, a hurled stone came flying out of the battle sound to his left and clipped the back of his head, and he dropped like a felled tree.

~

Ahearn came to consciousness with a half-familiar face bending over his and an irritated, urgent voice muttering in his ear. He stirred, and grunted involuntarily at the sharp pain in the back of his head.

"Up you get, sir King," said the voice shortly, and the lean face came into focus above him.

"Jedediah Crayes," said Ahearn, sitting up slowly with his rescuer's help.

"Wonderful observation. Now I'd get up. Your head is not bad, just a brief stun. And there's a limited distance I'd be able to drag you on my own. Contrary to popular opinion, I am not invincible."

He dragged Ahearn up to his feet and led the way rapidly through the soft rods of sunlight that were lancing through the trees. "You should be glad I happened along you," he grumbled. "Lying there just like that for any Runnicoran to find you and stab you to death. Then where are your subjects? An unhappy bereaved people, with an equally unhappy Mordred Kenhelm to rule over them."

"Do not speak of my brother like that," said Ahearn sharply.

"You Kenhelms are all the same," Jedediah Crayes said hopelessly. "'Don't talk about my brother like that.' 'Don't talk about *my* brother like that!'"

He seemed to know precisely where he was going, and Ahearn, who did not, could do nothing but follow him and hope he was right. "We could not rejoin the army?" he asked.

Jedediah Crayes sputtered. "*What*? He gets completely separated from the retreat and knocked upside the head and lies unconscious for a quarter of an hour, and *what*? Excuse *me* for not trying to fight through half a mile of Runnicoran soldiers for your preference."

"I see," returned Ahearn stiffly. "And may I ask what acquaintance you have had with my brother, that you seem to know of his existence at all?"

"Acquaintance? I'm his tutor." Jedediah Crayes smiled smugly at his inscrutable remark.

"What does that mean?" Ahearn snapped back.

"Tutor in spy work. Now you can't tell that to anyone, especially considering that the war's not over and he might well go back into it if necessary. The only reason I tell you at all is that you're a high-ranking personage who would've known sooner or later."

"Mordred is—a spy?" The thought was completely unexpected and bewildering.

"Is, was," said Jedediah Crayes cheerfully, ducking under a branch. "Not serving actively in that regard at present. And I hardly need tell you he's been doing an excellent job of it. You remember the Runnicoran man Blackthorn they caught back in April? That was his doing. And the failed attack through the pass of Mirech? That was him again."

Ahearn, who thus far had known Jedediah Crayes only as a vain and thoroughly haughty man, was taken aback to hear him bragging about someone else. "I see," he said slowly.

"Hullo, now—what's this?" Jedediah Crayes bent down, running his fingers over a faint rut in the undergrowth. "Looks like a cart wheel track. And here's the other," he added, moving a little ways further.

"Does it matter?" asked Ahearn impatiently.

His disinterest only served to make Jedediah Crayes give more painstaking attention to his deductions. "Of course not," he retorted. "I'm merely interested. Who was driving a cart in this secluded area of the woods? Ha! footprints beside it, see? Two people, hmm, perhaps three, hard to tell in this light. The cart ruts are deep, though. Must have been carrying quite a load. Maybe a wood-gatherer. But was it a farmer, or a Runnicoran soldier? Not many farmers around here, probably even less with an army nearby. I would opt for the soldier."

Jedediah Crayes paced quickly along the tracks for a few feet, and Ahearn, following a short way behind, heard him give a surprised grunt.

"Doesn't look like they came to a very pretty end," he said to Ahearn as he approached. "See that?"

He pointed to a slight rise in the ground, which looked no more than a hillock until Ahearn joined Jedediah Crayes on its brow. There the ground broke away quite suddenly into a sheer cliff, and a ravine with a rushing river at the bottom. The wheel marks led up the slope, and then at the very brink, where the undergrowth petered out, there were marks of scuffling and sliding.

Ahearn looked into the gorge stretching down—down—

"But if it were wood-gatherers," he said, "they needn't have gone over with the cart."

"They may have escaped," said Jedediah Crayes. "But I don't think they were wood-gatherers."

He paused, looking at Ahearn's perplexed face.

"Their cart was full, but they were heading away from the camp altogether. And even if they had been fetching wood, the soldiers have been taking it from the east side, not the north." He paused again, as though thinking.

"There is one place they could have been heading for. That is the leader's other camp, the one that you were making a show upon with the decoy."

"So?" said Ahearn, questioningly, as Jedediah Crayes turned back from the cliff and led the way again through the trees.

"The tracks are quite recent. I would guess we happened upon traces of some trusty Runnicorans, bringing Cern Dersturi four Ordenian soldiers."

"The four that Captain Rhodes—" Ahearn began, and said no more.

~

"Let me in," snapped Jedediah Crayes, scowling at the face of the guards at the West Gate. "Do you mean to hinder Jedediah Crayes? Oh, if Jedediah Crayes isn't enough for you, this is Ahearn of Dirion, whom I imagine everyone has been in a tizzy over."

It was gladly then that they were admitted.

"We were almost ready to account you both as dead," said the general when the three of them, together with Captain Rhodes, met in Mitheren late that night.

Jedediah Crayes winced. "Both?" he muttered under his breath. He said aloud, "Your four missing soldiers, Captain Rhodes, I suspect we found. Or found as much of them as we will ever find."

"What do you mean?" asked Captain Rhodes swiftly, his face paling.

"They were being transported in a cart, to the other camp, I believe. Unfortunately their guards were careless or ignorant of the area, and the cart went over into a gorge."

"Who were the men?" the general asked, looking to Captain Rhodes.

"They were all from that village of Ceristen," said Captain Rhodes, staring at the wall. "Bardrick Segelas, Therelane Grey, and Mordred and Fenris Kenhelm."

Ahearn stood up, face stricken.

Jedediah Crayes straightened in his chair. "Well, in that case," he said abruptly, "they're obviously *not* dead."

CHAPTER 26

FENRIS SWAM UP SLOWLY THROUGH a murky haze of muddled, wisping dreams. His head ached, and the pain and clinging drowsiness clouded his thoughts. Where was he? Why did his head ache?

He strained to remember. The attack on the leader's camp; Mordred talking; the camp, deserted.

Aye, the camp had been deserted, they had searched it. One man had found movement, and he had gone with him. And then?

Then—nothing. Nothing until now . . .

His head hurt—something must have hit him. A rock—a branch? A falling branch could not have knocked him out. And why would a rock have hit him unless someone had hurled it?

Had they been attacked then? He could not remember—he could not remember. Panic shot suffocatingly through his chest, and he opened his eyes to look around, find out where he was.

He saw nothing.

It was all black.

He put a hand to his eyes, frantic, wondering whether they were really open. Surely he was still dreaming. But the ground under him was real—cold, gritty stone. The sickening pangs in his head were real.

Could the blow have blinded me? Horror overcame him, dizzied him, and the dread of not knowing anything. *Where am I?* he thought despairingly. *Where am I?*

He could not think clearly for a long time, but only lay in confused pain and terror, until he heard all at once a soft sound beside him, like a breath or a whisper. He waited tensely, listening, and it came again, a rustling noise and a faint, restless sigh.

"Where are you?" he called out, desperation shaking his voice. The effort of speaking sent flashes of pain afresh through his head.

"Fenris?" came a voice in answer, faint, unsure.

"Who are you?"

"Bardrick. Bardrick Segelas. Is that you, Fenris?"

"Aye—it is. Bardrick, I cannot see."

He heard a grunting, as though Bardrick were sitting up. Cold fingers brushed across his own. "There you are. Rest easy, Fenris. Not a one of us could see in this place, 'tis windowless as far as I can tell and night besides."

Fenris let out a shuddering breath, feeling as though a grip of burning iron had released him. But the other fears returned to hold him fiercer still. "What has happened, Bardrick? Where are we?"

Bardrick released a long, weary sigh. "I do not know. I followed a man who said he had found . . . found enemy soldiers. I think he turned on me and struck me, and I woke in a cart moving through the woods. There were two men hurrying beside it, talking—arguing, mostly. One said that he feared they were being followed.

"'If so,' said the other, 'then let's make a false trail going over that bluff.'

"'I think we ought to make it look like we killed the prisoners and then went over; they'll be more likely to believe that'—so said the first man, and they stopped the cart and argued for a little. It was dim and I thought to get away, but one of them saw me climbing out and leveled his spear at me, and the other one stunned me again from behind. After that I was too sick to try, and I remember nothing more until someone pulled me up and marched me here. That is all I know of what happened; and if it is the leader who has captured us, I do not know why, nor what he means to do with us."

Fenris did not know either. Surely it could only be the Runnicorans who had taken them; but what value were they as prisoners? Who could possibly find them useful?

"Bardrick," he said, "are there any others besides us?"

"One or two more, I think," said Bardrick. "I do not know who, though. I noticed that there were others in the cart with me, but I did not pay attention to them."

His last words faded out of Fenris' consciousness, and he slipped into a fitful, half-fevered sleep.

Several hours must have passed before he woke fully again. His first thought was that he could see. A stone wall enclosed him in an enormous circle; the ceiling was in shadow, but high and near to it there was a ring of slits in the wall, through which a greyish dawn light was seeping.

Fenris pushed himself upright, despite an onrush of dizziness. The round prison was perhaps thirty feet wide and maybe twice that in height; he could see no opening or door. The floor beneath him was stone, as he had felt earlier, cold and very filthy.

Bardrick was close beside him, his breath coming soft and even; the skin of his cheek was broken and bruised, and trickles of blood had dried on his face. Beyond him two more figures lay sprawled on the stones, their faces turned away from him. There was something about one of them—something familiar about those lean, broad shoulders—

Fenris sprang up, heedless of his throbbing head, and knelt down beside his unconscious brother. "Mordred!"

The tears spilled over. "Why, Mordred?" he whispered.

No answer came. Mordred lay still, his face white, almost translucent in the grey light, a strange stone-like cast upon it as though he were nothing more than a statue.

Why, Mordred? Why not me alone?

"Mordred," he repeated through his tears, longing for an answer.

Mordred's breathing deepened suddenly, caught a moment and resumed. His eyelids fluttered open. "Fenris," he murmured, sounding bewildered. Then his eyes darkened as though remembering, and his brows contracted in a frown.

Swift anxiety filled Fenris, banishing his grief. Although he had wanted Mordred to wake, he knew that his own sorrow that his brother had been captured was small compared to the guilt Mordred must feel. "Mordred," he said, seeking to reassure him in what little he could. "Mordred, I am all right."

Mordred gave a little, matter-of-fact nod. The tightness around his mouth slackened, and he spoke in a tired but sardonic tone. "I think . . . I'll take back what I said about our close proximity to the leader now."

Fenris was taken aback. "Mordred," he pleaded, "how can you laugh—about this?"

Mordred's eyes met Fenris', and there was something very far from laughter in them. He did not answer.

~

"Fool," said Cern Dersturi, his deep, dark eyes like knifing waves. "I told you to take Damachrus of Ralecurn for me. Mordred Kenhelm you would find him as, I said. And what is this you have brought me? *Four* useless prisoners!"

The man before him shrank back. "We were unable to mingle among the soldiers beforehand as you bade us, Paraki. Only after they arrived in the camp could we slip among them. I could not determine which of them this Mordred Kenhelm was, and only could guess from your description of a tall, dark-haired, light-eyed young man. We thought it best if we . . . "

"Took captive all the dark-haired young men in the army?" A mocking laugh came harshly from his mouth. "You miserable fool. And you only took four? What if none of them had been the one I wanted?"

"We could not take more," the man stammered. "They noticed our movements and withdrew."

"I do not want more, you know that. You should be grateful that you did manage in all your blundering to snare him, that lying scoundrel *Damachrus of Ralecurn*—" He drew in a hissing breath, and spat. "As for the others, I will attend to them."

"I did not fail you, Paraki," the man pointed out nervously.

"True. You did not fail me. You have only disappointed me, and I might say angered me by your stupidity. You are released from any kind of spy service, now or in the future; go report yourself as the nearest officer's servant. And do not think I have not been lenient with you. If you had not brought me Damachrus, I would have killed you now."

~

Fenris sat against the wall, staring at the shrouded ceiling. Strange patterns of light played through the narrow slots, like intangible blades of gold crossing one another. To his tired, half-asleep eyes they almost seemed to dance.

Mordred lay by his feet, his eyes open and staring absently away, small tight lines around his mouth. Bardrick and Therelane, too, lay on the stones, awake, weary, listless. No one spoke.

What did they have to say to one another? They were prisoners, injured, without help, for what reason none of them knew; or if any did, he said nothing of it. So silence reigned among the four prisoners.

A voice carried through the tiny windows above them, faint and distant, to Fenris' ear.

"Nay, I am done with him. He has the sense of a mule and the wit of an addled deer. For all that he secured Damachrus, he has also saddled me with three I did not ask for. His bungling maddens me; let us speak no more of it."

"But are they a waste of time? Surely there must be some worth to them." A second voice floated up, dispassionate, uncurious.

"Oh, I will ascertain as to that at once. But I do not want them under any circumstances; 'twas not my purpose to bargain noblemen's lives for gold in this war."

"True, true."

"Enough on that. We will see to them soon enough; but I am longing to see that *Damachrus* once again, and show to him what his last days will look like. That disrespectful knave, that insolent *boy*—"

The hatred that breathed under the last words frightened Fenris unspeakably. He looked down at Mordred, and in his brother's face there was a stranger fear—one that terrified Fenris, for he did not understand it.

"Are they coming in?" asked Bardrick as a loud grinding noise jarred on their ears and a section of the wall slid back into itself.

Mordred spoke, his voice slightly strained. "Fenris—all of you—don't let him find out I'm awake."

Two men strode into the room, both dark-haired and of proud bearing, but one of them was clad in black and silver and walked with a quick, long step across to them. He surveyed them with disdainful eye and pointed with his boot to Therelane.

"You, what is your name?"

Therelane told him.

"And what use, Therelane son of Guron, would you be to me if I let you live—supposing that I let you live at all?"

Therelane stared at him, stunned.

"None?" The man put a hand swiftly to the sword at his side.

"Nay—please!" Therelane cried. "I—my father is wealthy."

"A wealthy merchant, or a wealthy lord? A merchant's name carries no weight, no matter how much gold he can vomit up."

"The Greys are of noble blood."

"And he would buy you back, would he?" said the man, dropping his hand with an irritated grunt.

"Of a surety he would, my lord."

The man tossed an eloquently annoyed look to his companion. "So be it," he muttered, slamming his hand against the sword's pommel. "You, I suppose, are a noble's son as well?"—this uttered in a sarcastic tone to Bardrick.

"I was an Eraharian lord, sir," answered Bardrick with a touch of dignity. "Bardrick Segelas. But I have no lands any longer, nor any who could ransom me."

"An Eraharian?" The man frowned and exchanged soft, hurried words with the other. With a nod, but no further explanation, he turned away from Bardrick.

And then his gaze seemed to fix on Mordred, who was lying very still on the stones, his eyes closed and his breath shallow and even.

"What? Surely he is not still unconscious." He took a swift pace forward and shook Mordred by the shoulder, but Mordred jerked under his handling like a doll and sagged back inert.

The man's dark eyes glittered with suspicion and anger. Standing back, he delivered a violent kick to Mordred's ribs.

Fenris gasped. Surely Mordred could not endure that without a sign. Yet, somehow, Mordred's features retained their slack expression of repose. Even his shoulders drooped limply as he fell.

Fenris waited, fearing he would try again, but the man seemed convinced. He whirled away.

"You." The contemptuous boot was pointing to him now. The dark eyes were narrowed as they studied him. They flicked away from him a moment, and back again, and narrowed still further. "Who are you, boy?"

"Fenris." His voice was barely audible in his own ears. "Fenris, son of Carras." He was not sure why he did not give his last name, something in him feeling perhaps that Mordred would wish not to be identified with him. But how did Mordred know this man at all—and why did he call him Damachrus?

"And do *you* have anything that will stop me from running you through?" the man demanded coldly. He drew out his sword.

Fenris looked at him, his mind spinning bewilderedly, unable to speak, knowing that this man wanted to kill him and in the next moment he would.

"He is brother to the King Ahearn." Mordred's voice cut fierce and pain-filled into the silence. "He is a prince of Dirion. You dare not kill him."

The man turned slowly, his sword spinning in an arc to level at Mordred's neck. "What is this? So you are awake after all, *Damachrus*."

Mordred did not speak.

"A fine liar, you are. I did not expect such cowardice from you, you proud boy—could you not bear to face me like a man?" His voice cut harshly, mocking.

Mordred drew in a ragged breath. His features composed themselves into an aloof, impassive look. "I did not expect the Paraki of the enemy would be taken in by mere playacting."

The man's lips clamped together and his nostrils flared angrily. "As for your rigmarole about this lad's royal heritage, I suppose that is playacting as well!"

"It is no lie," Mordred said carefully, the iron-steady voice that he used when he was either angry or afraid. "If you ask the king, he will know."

The man sent a quick sweeping glance from Mordred to Fenris. "I doubt it," he said scornfully. "But I think he is something more. I would guess he is your brother?"

He needed no answer. Mordred's white, stricken face gave it for him.

A soft, cruel smile lifted the corners of the man's mouth. "Not often do I mistake so plain a resemblance in the face."

"No matter," said Mordred. His voice was shaking now but hard as steel. "You will not touch him. I tell you he is a prince of Dirion, Fenris Kenhelm son of Lord Carras of Kenhelm, brother-in-law to the late king Hiartho."

"Do you know what?" The man bent close down to Mordred's face and Mordred flinched away. "I do not care if he is. No persuasion will avail you. I will not let your brother go, Damachrus."

"You can want nothing of him!" cried Mordred.

"Of him, nothing. But shall I see you glad because he walks away free?"

"You cannot—" The words came from him stifled, a whisper. "You cannot kill him."

"I will kill him, Damachrus." The man stood, and turned away to the door. "Not yet, but I will kill him."

~

"Mordred," Therelane breathed as the door ground shut and dark silence was left behind. "That was the leader?"

Mordred did not answer for a very long time. Fenris wondered whether he had heard. At last—"Aye," he said quietly.

"Mordred, when did you meet him? And why does he call you Damachrus?" Therelane's tone, puzzled, horrified, and echoed all their thoughts.

Mordred flinched again, the way he had when the leader leaned close over him. A sharp pang of fear struck through Fenris at that look.

"Please," said Mordred, still very quietly, very steadily, "do not ask me questions, Therelane."

"But why would he hate you—so much?"

Emotions that Fenris could not grasp warred fiercely in his brother's eyes. He shook his head, a slight, distraught movement, and turned his head away.

CHAPTER 27

"**NAY, I DO NOT YET** know how to proceed." Cern Dersturi paced back and forth in his tent, his lieutenant listening close at hand. Mingled doubt and vexation showed in his face. "Certainly we must do nothing rash."

"If he were lying . . . "

"He was not lying. His features and accent are of Erahar. In telling me the truth, he clearly did not think it would save him, 'twas plain on his face that he expected to die. But if he is known among the Ordenians, and word of this gets to Erahar, it would be a most ticklish situation—disowned lord or no, it would not be well for us."

The lieutenant nodded silently. Despite having yet no solid alliance, it was Erahar which had supplied at Cern Dersturi's ruthless, expensive negotiations the *Adorti* expended a month prior on the walls of Mianu. A hasty execution of one of their aristocracy would be seen as very poor gratitude indeed.

"If I could but be sure that he was nothing to them, that his capture will have gone unnoticed—but I cannot. I will have to send word to the spies to determine more of this Segelas."

"And what of the other—the claim to royal kinship?"

"The boy? That is strange, yes. I can hardly make out whether it is true or not."

"Kenhelm, that is truly a Dirionian surname."

"Aye, and I had never paid mind to it. A fine riddle, though, that princes should go prating in peasant's clothes! Well, that is of no concern to me. Such a statement is hardly likely to be true, yet even if it is, we are already at open enmity with Dirion. And no ransom nor anger from any other quarter can compare with the pain that I can give to Mordred Kenhelm when I kill his brother to his face."

~

"I don't believe it," Jedediah Crayes said flatly to the general's turned back.

General Derek Winston turned to him, a question in his tired dark eyes.

"Do you know why I don't believe it?" demanded Jedediah Crayes. He did not wait for an answer. "There's not all that much to say it was them—it was an educated guess, yes, but still a guess. And even if it were them, who's to say they went over the cliff at all? Surely the enemy soldiers would know the area well enough to avoid an enormous gorge. Not to mention, it's a beautiful setup throw off any possible trackers. I don't believe it, I tell you. They are not dead."

"Let us not give King Ahearn false hope," said the general. "But if that is true, then we may look for word soon from the Runnicorans; let us hope they will bargain them for ransom."

"By your leave, General," said Jedediah Crayes grimly, "I'm going to rescue them."

~

Another dawn came in the round prison-tower. The remainder of that awful day had dragged out in piercing, twisted silence, the kind to make one cringe inside and long to speak. All of them longed to break it, and yet none of them dared: not while the presence of Mordred was so palpable, Mordred who turned his eyes from everyone and whose face was like death.

Yet now the night had passed, and now perhaps Therelane was bolder.

"Mordred," he said, his voice echoing startlingly off the sudden-broken peace.

Mordred heard, for his shoulders tensed; but he said nothing.

Therelane was satisfied. "Mordred, will you please tell us?"

"I do not wish to speak of that right now." Stiffness emanated from Mordred like a wall.

"But, Mordred—I need to understand! Why does he hate you? I want to know!"

"Of course," said Mordred violently, rolling to face him, "*you* have the time and care for such thoughts in your mind, you who do not have to fear—"

He fell silent, and the terrible words were never finished, but everyone knew what he had been about to say. Therelane turned away, tears in his eyes, his face flushed with a painful guilt.

For Therelane there was the promise of ransom. He would go free. And already it had bitten at him with a gnawing pang of unease, knowing as he did that Mordred and Fenris had no such promise. Mordred's open, vicious bitterness cut him deeper than a knife.

A Runnicoran soldier entered with food for them, as had happened yesterday. Mordred, who had eaten then, did not touch it now. The silence dwelt over them far worse than before.

Then it broke again as the door grated open; and this time it was the leader who entered.

"The word is sent to your father," he said curtly to Therelane. "We shall see perhaps to some more pleasant accommodations for you, as such formal propriety demands."

"I do not care," said Therelane, choking on further tears, aghast at being further privileged above the others.

"Watch your tongue, boy," snapped the leader. "There is only the smallest breach of rule between you and the point of a sword. I shall not be sorry to kill you and rid myself of the burdensome drag on my time, food and wine."

"I should like you to kill me," said Therelane bitterly.

Cern Dersturi looked at him with deep, contemptuous eyes narrowed in confusion. Then a sound or movement from Mordred drew his attention, and a dark smile came upon his face. "I daresay you are all wondering why you are here at all," he said. "Or perhaps Damachrus here has told you? No? I do not wonder, for it is his fault."

"What do you mean?" It was Bardrick who spoke, sharply.

The smile broadened on Cern Dersturi's countenance. "This gutter-brat took it on himself to spy on my army, twice, though he was caught both times. He brought my plans to ruin, and it is not to be wondered at if I hate him, is it? I hate him so much that I was willing to capture him directly from the army where he served. And my men, unsure of his identity, could only take those who fit my description of him. That, my young enemies, is why you are here and languishing—because that boy took it into his head that he could bring the plans of Cern Dersturi to naught."

"So you say." Bardrick's voice was still calm and assertive. "How are we to readily believe you in any of it?"

Cern Dersturi laughed coldly. "Let him deny it, then. He has heard every word—let him deny it if he can."

Mordred lay very still, without a word, his face hard against the crook of his arm; only Fenris, who was nearest to him, saw that he was trembling.

Cern Dersturi laughed again, a harsh, toneless laugh, and strode across to kick Mordred in the side. Then he left them.

"Mordred," said Bardrick, perhaps the only one of them capable of speech at that moment. And yet even he broke off then, seeming at a loss how to continue.

Mordred's shoulders shook. "He is right," he said in a strangled voice. "It is all—my doing—that you are here—hate me now as you will. Therelane—I didn't mean that—not a word of it—don't die—I could not bear to see you dead—"

His voice cracked on the empty silence of the tower, and Fenris laid his head against his brother's shoulder.

"Mordred," said Bardrick, "don't think we hold it against you. That would be absurd."

Therelane got to his feet and stumblingly crossed the distance that separated him from Mordred's side. He withdrew Mordred's arm from beneath his head, the sleeve wet with far more tears than had fallen in the past few minutes. He took his thin, unresponsive hand. "Mordred, you were a spy?"

"What does it matter?" Mordred's rough, pain-torn voice replied.

"That was brave."

"I don't want to talk about it," said Mordred desperately.

"But it *was*, Mordred, and you were helping Orden, and you brought the leader's plans to ruin—he said so. It's things like that that will change the tides of the war, not a few soldiers captured."

"Therelane," whispered Mordred, "I'm sorry for what I said earlier, and I wish my grief could take back those words, and I'm glad you want to help, but it doesn't help."

He drew his hand away from Therelane's, still trembling.

~

Jedediah Crayes ducked under a wet, whippy branch only to have it rake its water-laden leaves along his back. Another smacked into his face. He stepped over a sodden log and struck out around a patch of boggy earth, the thick foliage catching on him relentlessly and slashing at his eyes.

I don't like you either, he grumbled to himself.

Aloud, he was silent. He was near to the extremities of the camp now, and besides there were always the patrols to be concerned for. His resentment toward the rain-drenched world was a small thing beside the purpose that drove him to the Runnicoran army.

What wool had been between the general's ears when he had spoken of ransom? For one or two of them, maybe so, but Mordred? Damachrus? The leader would not bargain his prize for the Knives of Light themselves.

And though Jedediah Crayes intended of course to release all of them, in his mind Mordred was by far the most important.

He stole into the bounds of the camp, welcoming now the drip of rain that concealed his footfalls, and after navigating it thoroughly discovered it: a round, weathered stone tower, built in some distant time, perhaps garrisoned and used as a watch before the forest grew up; but it was long-abandoned now. There was a single door, and a guard who stood beside it, but no other entrance or even opening, save for the slitted windows around the rim.

This was where the prisoners were held.

~

Outside it was dusk-darkening and the world was dim, velvet grey, but in the tent the fuzzy radiance of torches illuminated the faces of the Paraki and the one who stood before him.

"What reports from the north mountains?" asked Cern Dersturi.

The messenger bowed. "Paraki. They have made some small advancements, but the Ordeni know the territory well, and defend it with valor. The progress is still slow."

"We must make a breakthrough." Cern Dersturi ground his teeth. "I cannot wait much longer. Either here in the west, or there in the north, a breach must be made." With one of his sharp, whip-quick movements, he turned to the table of maps and papers and motioned the man out.

Even as the flap of the red-woven tent swished shut, a dark winged figure darted through it, and Cern Dersturi moved forward with waiting mien and let the *eraris* settle on his hand. "You return from the Ordeni already? That was swift. Where is the message?"

He tore the parchment from the string around its talons, and read the lines from the one remaining spy in Orden City.

Bardrick Segelas, former lord of Erahar, is not known among the Ordeni.

~

The door was opening again. The shadows were so heavy in the tower, with the coming of night, that none of them could see the man's face until he took the torch from the guard outside and came forward with it. But Mordred, who lay with his face hidden in his arms, started as the quick footsteps came toward them, and Fenris felt him shiver.

The light swept over Fenris and Therelane. "You," said the ruthless voice, and Cern Dersturi motioned with gauntleted hand to Bardrick.

Mordred stirred beside Fenris, and lifted his head.

"Man of Erahar, Bardrick Segelas, disowned lord—that is you?"

"It is I," said Bardrick. He met the leader's eyes with perplexity and unsureness. "What do you want with me?"

"Only that I have no need to keep you," said the leader, and drew his sword and ran it into Bardrick's chest.

Therelane cried out violently. Mordred fell without a sound against Fenris. Fenris felt nothing, nothing at all. Like a dazed animal, he knew nothing but horror and helpless terror, but at the same time he knew that Bardrick had been killed and lay bleeding on the floor, while the leader strode out and left only the dim glow of the rising moon behind, Bardrick Segelas, whom he knew, whom all of them knew, who was a brother to Marcus, and Fiona, and Peony. It was not like Kenneth's death. That had seemed so dreadful at the time, but it was not like this—not like this.

Mordred shuddered like a wind-battered tree. No sound left him still. Fenris put his arms blindly around his brother, giving him the only thing he could.

Bardrick coughed heavily. Fenris turned his head and saw in the thin moonlight Therelane, who had dropped his head into his hands, lift his eyes suddenly with the light of hope and scramble to Bardrick's side. But Bardrick's eyes, as Therelane raised him and laid him on his back, were wide and urgent with the knowledge that he was dying.

"Marcus—Peony—Fiona," he said, his words broken with coughing and blood. "Tell them—I love them. I will—see them—again." And the struggling and breath ceased, and he relaxed against Therelane completely still.

Therelane wept, the sound muffled and strangely peaceful in the night. The strange paralysis around Fenris' mind and heart eased, and his breath no longer seemed dried up.

But Mordred's shaking was so violent that his forehead knocked against the floor, and Fenris in striving to hold him steady was shaken with him.

"He died, Fenris," he whispered, the tremors so racking him that he could scarcely speak. "He died—and you will die—and it is all my fault . . ."

"No, Mordred," Fenris said, over and over again. "No."

But Mordred would not listen. There was no comfort for him, whose greatest compulsion was to protect the brother now being torn away without hope of recovery or recall.

CHAPTER 28

BARDRICK'S BLOOD HAD NOT DRIED upon the floor when the wall scraped back in the damp, murky dawn and the guard entered with their meal. Therelane thought it was earlier than usual, but any surprise he felt was naught compared to the astonishment of the guard when he saw the corpse. "Well," he said, bending down on his knee, "what's all this?"

And then Therelane noticed that he did not have their meal at all, and his bewilderment in his weary mind was so great that he began to think he had fallen asleep and was dreaming.

"Which one was he?" asked the strange guard, rising and brushing the grit from his hands. "There's the boy, and his brother" —Therelane followed his gaze to Mordred and Fenris, both asleep and clasping one another—"so you are either Therelane Grey or—"

"I am Therelane Grey," said Therelane. "Who are you?"

"Jedediah Crayes, of course," said the man somewhat irritably. He knelt again by the Kenhelms and shook Mordred. "Wake up, you little fool. Calm down, it's just me. Didn't think I was planning to get you out of your mess this time?"

Therelane shook his head, willing it to clear from the maze of tiredness and grief and now shock. If this was Jedediah Crayes—*the* Jedediah Crayes—the man himself—he must be here to rescue them. He looked at Mordred, whose face was quivering with a variance of emotions. Mordred seemed to know him, but how?

"All right, boy, talk to me. Has he hurt you?"

"The leader—no. He—he killed Bardrick." Mordred spoke in a broken, distracted way.

"Aye, I see that. Why on earth?"

"He—he didn't want him at all. He didn't want any of them except me." A tearing shudder cut his words short.

Jedediah Crayes watched him, his thin, hawklike face clearly delineated in the sunless light. "A matter for more time than we have, I daresay. We'll talk about this later; for now, I'm bent on rescuing as many of you as are left."

"How will you get us out?" Mordred asked flatly. "It will not be half so easy with three as with one."

"What an optimist you're being," said Jedediah Crayes, looking affronted. "I am an adaptable person. Are any of your legs shot with arrows? No? The guard outside is incapacitated, and we're going to make an exciting little dash for it—or you are. After I point you in the right direction, I will return to my post and guard the empty tower until the act can't be kept up any longer. Can you manage that?" He looked now to Therelane as well, and to Fenris, who had wakened a few minutes past.

Fenris nodded.

"I think so," said Therelane. "But Mordred . . . Mordred needs to eat something. He hasn't eaten for nearly two days."

"Why?" Jedediah Crayes yelped angrily, so startlingly loud that Therelane winced.

Therelane stuttered, afraid to betray Mordred somehow by giving away the truth of the matter.

"Has that—excuse me, there's no word despicable enough to describe him—that leader been starving him to death?"

"No, no!" Therelane was growing frustrated that they could not simply deal with the thing and drop it. "We are given food; he would not eat it."

"*I* see." Jedediah Crayes rolled his eyes upward. "I see. Just Mordred neglecting in the usual manner to take care of himself. Boy, if you don't eat this I'll quit the Legean Association and hire myself out as a private assassin." As he spoke he produced several slips of dried venison and set them down with care in front of Mordred.

And then Therelane witnessed an astonishing thing, for Mordred actually smiled, small though it was, and looking up at Jedediah Crayes said, "I wonder if I should test you on it."

Jedediah Crayes' mouth flapped open and shut soundlessly, while amid his furious gesticulations, Mordred undisturbedly picked up the venison and ate it; though he gave one piece to Fenris.

"If everyone's done gorging themselves," said Jedediah Crayes, his temper vanishing, "then suppose we start moving."

~

Mordred reeled when he tried to stand, and caught at Fenris for support, but he found his balance and with a toss of his head silently forbade anyone to mention the matter.

"Hurry," said Jedediah Crayes, a certain sharpness in his voice, and Mordred sensed that something was hiding behind that sharpness. Unease?

The light washed over him, and he blinked and squinted against it. It seemed bright, far too bright, exposing him to the world and to the leader's eyes. Where was Fenris—

Fenris was right beside him, his shoulder pressing against Mordred's. Color and shape were bleeding into the world again, and

Mordred saw high treetops and small, tossing leaves reflecting the sheen of a cloudy-white sky. They were thick all around, the trees, save a small clear space directly in front of them—even hugging the outer walls of the tower, bowing the leafy arches of their boughs to brush the smooth rim.

"Move," said Jedediah Crayes impatiently. "That way, see? It's east. Go as fast as you can. Don't stop for anything. If they come chasing you and get too close, find a good hiding place." He settled his back against the door and folded his arms, the picture of a lonely, bored guard.

Mordred cast one look back at him under the fringe of the forest, some terrifying thing trying to make its way to the surface of his mind. It was something lacking, something lacking—

A disguise, that was what was lacking.

"Jedediah Crayes," he breathed, taking a step towards him again, just as two dark-clothed men strode quickly out of the northern trees and into the clearing; and Mordred froze.

Cern Dersturi halted at the door of the tower and swept back his hand as if to strike the guard for not moving out of the way quickly enough. But the blow hung unstruck, and the leader stood arrested, shoulders stiff. "Mog Dremmag?" he uttered in ominous, disbelieving tones.

Mog Dremmag, not quite as the leader must have last seen him—grey-streaked hair, a scar, a stomach over-fat. But the keen eyes saw past those superficial flourishes, to the alert-eyed, cunning, strong man beneath, and in the plain light of day he was not deceived.

"An unfortunate resemblance," said Jedediah Crayes sarcastically.

"It is you," said the leader; "how came you here?" And he whipped out his sword and struck at Jedediah Crayes. Mordred, still watching rooted where he stood, saw blood cascading down Jedediah Crayes' upflung wrist, and then the movement spun into a flurry of combat

The other man with him, the lieutenant Dovurti Atta, turned his head and suddenly his eyes narrowed into the trees. And Mordred knew that he had seen them.

"Soldiers!" cried the lieutenant aloud, running back towards the tents. "After the prisoners! The prisoners! Escaping!"

Even as he spoke, men hurtled through the trees in answer.

Mordred did not think about what he did; there was no thinking needed. It was the only thing to do. "Run," he said to Fenris, gripping his shoulders so tightly that his fingers trembled, and as soon as Fenris turned, he whirled and ran straight back into the oncoming rush of men. He fought, weaponless, hand and foot and head and nail. Far, far within he knew that it could not work, but he would not listen; it must work. Because Fenris *must* escape.

He could not see his brother die.

Block them. Halt them. Hold them off. His head knocked against someone's armored chest and he lurched, tumbling to the ground, half-stunned. He struggled, fighting for his senses through a mad swirl of darkness, and found that they had his arms. Kicking, wrenching, he knew dimly that they were bringing him back to the tower. He caught a flash of the leader, but he did not see Jedediah Crayes.

And then they flung him onto the stones, and he saw Fenris and Therelane huddled beside Bardrick's still body, and he lunged at the door, tore at the unyielding stone with his fingers, hurled himself at it again and again until the world faded into empty blackness.

~

"This will not happen again." An angry snarl rested on the leader's lips. "Thrice now has that Mog Dremmag intervened to deprive me of Damachrus, and he shall not do so a fourth. Set guards in a ring around that tower, and bid them on pain of death to admit no one save myself and Lieutenant Dovurti Atta, and the man who brings food to them, whom I shall choose myself."

"Paraki," came the dutiful assent.

Dovurti stepped forward. "So Mog Dremmag is not slain?"

Cern Dersturi spat. "I wounded him, but he slunk away and I did not kill him. Mark my words, though he is wounded, he will return."

"I doubt it not," said Dovurti. "He is a wily one."

"Like that Damachrus himself." The leader spat again. "I will kill them both."

~

Jedediah Crayes crouched under the shelter of a vast tree-root tangle, holding his wrist in the cold running stream to slow the persistent bleeding of the long scratch that traced up his forearm. "You're a fool," he muttered to himself. "A blind, mulish fool."

There was a much worse scratch along his ribs, one that would probably have him limping, but it was not bleeding so heavily for the present, though it hurt rather more.

Jedediah Crayes tipped his head back and stared up at the gnarled roots, his eyes hard and narrow, his mouth a grim, angry line.

But he was not angry at Mordred, or Therelane or Fenris; he was not even particularly angry at the leader. He was angry at himself.

"One of them is already dead; and I suppose before the next day's gone another one or two of them will be. Leader doesn't want them, says Mordred. And that's killing *him* more than anything else, it's plain to see. Meanwhile, I'm tied up here nursing my injuries and watching the leader surround his prison with two dozen men."

He ought to have thought the plan through more.

He snorted. He *ought* to have done a dozen things, but mooning over them wouldn't turn time back.

If only it would.

~

Therelane stared up at the yawning reaches of the tower, shivering. It might have been from fear, or cold, or both. Since he had been thrown into the stone tower again he had not stopped feeling the cold, perhaps because he had known the warmth of the outside air and the sun, even if the sun were veiled. Now the sky darkened further outside with storm clouds, and by the smell in the air rain was on the way.

Therelane's gaze flickered over Mordred. Mordred had seemed mad after they brought him back in—had knocked himself senseless against the door. He slept still, and Therelane was glad; he was afraid for him to wake.

As for Fenris, the rough handling from the soldiers seemed to have awakened old things in him, memories of brutality maybe, and he was dangerously dazed, which frightened Therelane further. Maybe, after all, if Mordred did wake, he would know how to comfort Fenris. Therelane cast an anxious look in the boy's direction, where he sat with his head hanging low and his knees drawn up.

The tempest gathered strength outside, spraying its weapons in all directions, and rain began to spatter through the small high windows. Therelane bit down against the chattering of his teeth, wrapped his arms about himself, and tried vainly to sleep. He thought of his family, his cursed family that he had sought for so long to get away from, and wanted to see them again. If he tried carefully enough he could imagine their voices in the wind—Irene, Lewis, Cormad, Ledelia.

The rain made tiny puddles. Therelane slept.

~

He woke hours later, the tower still dim with the unreal stormlight. Bardrick's body was gone. An unnamed finality smote him hard, deep inside, and suddenly Bardrick seemed to be completely dead; and he looked away from the blood on the floor, thinking of young, lovable Marcus with his infectious grin.

"When did they take him away?" he asked.

"Not long ago," answered Fenris, his dark, sad eyes turning to Therelane.

He was better, anyway, thought Therelane, relieved. Even in the poor light he could see the blackish, swollen bruise covering Fenris' lower cheek and jaw, and a pang of sorrow shot through his heart for him. He thought of Mordred, seeing Fenris struck like that time and time again as they grew up together, and felt that he understood in a better way than he ever had Mordred's love and the anger born of that love. And even the desperation that had led him to throw himself unavailing against the impenetrable stone . . .

Mordred stirred, an incoherent murmur escaping his mouth.

Therelane tensed. "Fenris," he said urgently.

Fenris was already kneeling at his brother's side, his hand on Mordred's bruised, dirt-streaked forehead. Mordred quieted, opened his eyes, and looked up at Fenris. Instantly his breathing began to quicken erratically and his face grew panicked.

"Mordred, no!" Therelane sprang to his side. "You must stay calm—listen to me, you *must*." His voice was so fierce and hard that it startled him, and it must have startled Mordred, too; he stared at Therelane, eyes wide and dilated, motionless except for his rapid breaths, looking almost like he might recklessly ignore him.

But he did not. He pushed aside Fenris' arm and got up, and stood with his head leaning against the wall, his eyes cast down and his jaw set in that stubborn way that meant the pain was locked away inside.

Therelane sighed and sat down, bowing his head on his knees. When he looked up Mordred had left the wall, and was crossing the shadow-swathed stones of the tower.

"Mordred—where are you going?" He felt an uncertain fear, without knowing what he was afraid of.

Mordred did not answer. He angled back to the wall and made a circuit of the tower, stopping for a long time at the door. Therelane came over to him and caught his arm.

"Mordred, what are you looking at?" he demanded.

"The door," said Mordred. He ran his hands over it; it was solid, scarcely distinguishable from the rest of the stones except that it was cut back so as to slide into the wall when opened. The inside had no handle, only a chipped place where there might have been one once.

Mordred shook his head and went on his way around the wall with an attitude of grim purpose. Therelane trailed him, feeling a little like a dog to a master. Then Mordred stopped, tracing a gouge scooped out of the stone at about chest height.

"It's a step," he said.

"What!" Therelane pressed his palm against the abrasive, shallow depression, scarcely as wide as his hand. "Impossible, it's just a mistake in the shaping or something of the sort. Besides, there's none below it!"

"But there are above it," said Mordred; and raising his eyes, Therelane discerned in the gloom more faint shadows on the stone, rising in a steady line around the circle of the wall until they faded from his vision.

"I think this was a storehouse," said Mordred, rubbing at the step absently. "Because there's only the one door, and no other sort of room—not even a second floor; it might have been a stable, but it's much higher than anyone would need to build a stable. And then they must have needed to get to the top of the tower, and they added these steps to make it easier; see how much rougher they are than the careful shaping of the rest?"

"They might not even go up to the top," said Therelane nervously.

"I think they do go up to the top," said Mordred. "And if not, I can come down again."

"Mordred, no, you can't!" cried Therelane. "You'll break your neck, and it's not as if—"

But Mordred had already made the leap, hauling himself with a wavering strength onto the slim ledge, teetering, and then gaining his balance as he set his other foot on the next step up and leaned hard against the wall.

He moved up, steadily, clinging to the stones with his arms—one foot on one narrow hold, the next foot on the next narrow hold. Therelane was dizzy watching, really dizzy. *Don't fall, Mordred,* he begged him silently, and thought of Mordred leaning out and falling, headlong, spreadeagled in the air before he smashed on the floor—

He wanted to look away, and the pit of his stomach felt sick, his jaw strange and tight as if there were strings pulling inside it. But his eyes were fixed helplessly on Mordred, a moving figure so high that he was only a spidery blur, slowly being swallowed in the darkness. He passed the windows—Therelane even saw him using them for support.

And then his movement stopped.

Therelane heard a grinding noise, magnified and distorted by echoes as it reached their ears. High above them, a sliver of grey light pierced the dimness, grew to the shape of a sickle moon, and then a half moon.

"He did it," he whispered, astounded. But another swell of dizziness rocked the world around him, as he realized that now Mordred would have to come down.

~

Mordred reached out, terrifyingly far, and gripped the thick edge of the hole. He could not think too hard about this, or the stones would begin to spin, and he would lose his sense of up and down, and fall. All he had to do was pull himself out, through the hole, onto the top of the tower, and prove that it could be done—and see if the trees really were as close to the tower as he had thought . . .

He heaved up with his shoulders, his back, every muscle in his body it felt he strained. His feet threatened to leave their precarious purchase, and he knew they must not, or he would be hanging in the air with sixty feet of emptiness below him. The strength of desperation launched him forward again, and his shoulders skidded past the edge of the hole, his chest smacked on cold stone, and he wriggled frantically forward like a worm until he was lying, all of him, on the smooth, wet roof.

He picked himself up, shaking with the strain he had put on himself, but he dared not waste time in rest. The sky was wet and angry above him, swinging rain this way and that with a capricious wind. The trees whipped back and forth, their leaves meshing with one another and branches scraping and creaking.

Mordred watched them in deep, sudden-springing gladness, a wondering smile on his face. He had been right; the trees were close. Very close. Their boughs arched over the tower like sheltering wings, some high above his head, some close enough to touch. He laid his hand on one that forged straight past him at waist level, stout and strong and ending in sprays of glistening leaves, and felt the gentle bumpiness of its grey bark on his fingertips. A man could crawl along that branch—

He went swiftly back to the hole, and let himself down again.

~

"Mordred!" cried Therelane in staggering relief as Mordred slid down from the last step and leaned against the wall. "Sit down and rest."

Mordred shook his head. "Time for you to go up now," he said, heaving for breath with every word.

Therelane was speechless.

"You and Fenris." Mordred pushed himself away from the wall. "You saw me go up; you know how. I'll help you up onto the first one."

"Why?" Therelane burst out. "Do you think this is going to help us escape? We'll just starve to death up there!"

Mordred looked at him, his grey eyes flashing with an instant of anger. And then the anger quieted and he said gently, "But it will help, Therelane. That's why I climbed up. I saw the trees when we got out earlier, so near the tower, and when I found the steps I thought we might get down by the trees. And we can. Come, Therelane, you can do this."

And so Therelane found himself on the dizzying steps, trying to keep a clear head and steady fingers. He went most of the way with his eyes shut; if he opened them, he thought about all sorts of things, like catwalks and rope bridges and bones crunching. He had only one hand to steady himself by, and so he was very careful to always lean into the wall as much as he could.

"You're near the top, Therelane," came Mordred's clear, encouraging call, floating up from below. *No, don't think about how far below.* Therelane dared to crack his eyes open and saw that the open hole was right above him.

He almost panicked. Mordred must have forgotten about his hand—how could he pull himself up through that?

He shut his eyes briefly against the horrific sight and steadied himself coldly. No, there must be a way.

He reached up and braced his left arm against one side of the hole, clamped his right hand around the other side, and wrenched himself up, and out. It was not so hard after all, and he felt a strange glow of pride.

He lay on his back, breathing heavily, welcoming the cool rain as it hissed needlelike on his hot face; after a little he hauled himself up and studied the roof. It was level, and quite smooth, and a short, flat-edged parapet two feet high surrounded it. The trees swayed in the wind, a tossing, perforated canopy of green.

Therelane remembered that Fenris was coming up next, and turned back to the hole in case he should need help. The covering that had lain over the hole, he saw, was a trap-door that went back into the roof much like the door had into the wall, with a hand-hold carved into the top for opening and shutting, and Therelane looked at it and fell into wondering about the people who had built the tower, and almost dozed—he was after all tired. But then he saw Fenris' hand reaching out, and he took it and after a little scramble they were together on the edge.

"Will Mordred be up soon?" he asked when Fenris had his breath back.

But Fenris shook his head. "He wouldn't start till I was out."

So it was a long time before Mordred's hand came out through the hole.

Therelane and Fenris both helped him out—Therelane was glad of it; Mordred was heavier than Fenris had been—and Mordred came out and lay limp on the roof, gasping as though every breath were his last. He had climbed the stairs three times, once down and twice up, and had exhausted his strength earlier that day. His face, streaked with rain, sweat, and filth, was almost skeleton-thin.

"Mordred, are you all right?" Therelane asked anxiously. "Can you go on?"

"I—I'm all right," Mordred murmured. "We'll go on at dark when they can't see us."

"How will we get down a tree in the dark?" protested Therelane in dismay.

"Same way you—got up the steps," returned Mordred, and Therelane wondered if there was a teasing tone in the words, but Mordred's voice was so slurred with weariness that it was impossible to tell.

Darkness came swiftly over them, sooner than Therelane expected. Mordred got up and walked to the edge of the parapet. "It's this branch," he said, his voice scarcely audible through the relentless rain. "I'll go first this time. Just pull yourself up and crawl along it till you find the trunk."

Therelane thought of one protest, and then more, but said none of them. He had complained enough today. Mordred could not help the fact that he had one hand. This was the only way out, and they had to take it.

It was eerie, aye, to inch along a limb in the dark, but he quickly trained himself to think of it as Mordred had put the matter, the way he had climbed the steps. He let his body think for him and not his eyes. And after he had reached the trunk of the tree safely, and got a little way down, he began to almost like the competent sensation.

He had one bad moment, when he could not seem to find footing anywhere. Hanging from a branch, kicking out in any direction, his toe finally brushed something directly below him; he cast caution aside, wrapped his arms around the tree bole, and slid down to a welcoming, solid surface that he realized in surprise was the ground.

"That you, Therelane?" murmured Mordred's voice close at hand.

"Aye," said Therelane.

"*Shh*," said Mordred urgently; "look, the soldiers are over there."

Therelane cast his eyes back and saw the tower scarcely five yards away, a hazy ring of men around it. "I suppose they're having a miserable night," he said, "out in the rain."

"They'll have a worse morning," said Mordred. "Come, we're all here now."

"Where are we going?" asked Therelane.

"I don't know," said Mordred. "East. Stay beside me. Fenris—there you are."

Therelane wondered how Mordred could know which way was east, and then he knew that Mordred had probably been thinking about it all afternoon while they waited; and, too, Jedediah Crayes had pointed them eastwards that morning.

Only that morning?

They stumbled through the endless dark and endless rain. Hunger grew inside Therelane, and the cold edged deeper into him.

Ahead of him there was a sudden plunging splash, and Therelane jumped in alarm. "Mordred!" he called.

"I fell into a stream." He heard the sound of Mordred climbing out onto the bank. "I'm all right. Look, there's a light down that way."

Therelane peered both ways and caught a glimpse of something, fire, leaping behind a screen of bushes or branches. "You're not going—Mordred, don't—"

It was too late. *He never listens,* thought Therelane, irritation heating the shivering cold in him. He chased blindly after Mordred, tripping into the stream twice, catching up to him finally at the edge of the firelight. Through the lattice of twining roots he could see one dark figure, leaning forward with his keen-eyed, sober face cupped in one hand.

"Well, are you going to come out?" the figure demanded snappishly. "You're either the usual brand of blundering idiot humans, or you're a wounded bear. In either case, I'd prefer to deal with you in the light. I am *not* in a good mood right now, thank you for asking."

Mordred waded around the concealing root-wall and stepped into the shifting gleam.

Jedediah Crayes took a look at him and sprang up. "How the blasted—how did you—"

A smile, tired but wider than any Therelane had seen him give in months, cracked across Mordred's face. "Well met, Jedediah Crayes."

CHAPTER 29

"GREETINGS!" THE DARK, HAWK-NOSED HEAD poked unceremoniously into the general's writing chamber, and Jedediah Crayes entered with his characteristic catlike smugness.

The general rose at once. "Jedediah Crayes! I trust then that your endeavor has met with success?"

"Oh, yes; yes." Jedediah Crayes tossed his long frame across a chair and swung his legs up to rest them possessively on the edge of the table. "Yes and no, really."

After a moment he lowered his legs to cross one over the other, and when he spoke again his voice had dropped the lazy, mocking edge. "Bardrick Segelas is dead. I tried to rescue the other three, but Cern Dersturi regrettably intercepted us and left me with a gashed flank and no rescue. However, that little Mordred brat had such a wit in his head that he managed to get them out anyway. They are now suitably ensconced in their contingent, and not too much the worse for wear."

He waved congratulations and gratitude aside with an annoyed flick of the hand. "Go tell the king of Dirion and let him fall on your neck with joy. I shan't stay around to be adulated when all I did was see them safely home."

He stood as if to make good on his word directly, but checked halfway to the door. "And how have the matters of war gone, while I was absent near a se'ennight?" Looking in his shrewd way at the heaviness upon the general's shoulders, and the fatigue that lined his face and shadowed his eyes, he nodded. “Badly, I imagine. Well, you shall see me at the war councils as usual.” He whipped around and exited the room.

~

Mordred brushed distractedly past all the welcoming words, to Marcus Segelas’ puzzled, worried eyes, obeying the impulse that made him gather the younger boy fiercely, firmly into his arms. He had always resented Marcus in a small way for his curiosity, his easy way of riding the swells of life, for the way all the other men laughed at and loved him. But not now. He needed to protect this boy, so young, younger even than Fenris, who would hear words that Mordred would rather die than hear.

“Marcus,” he said softly, “Bardrick’s dead.”

Marcus pushed away, broke out of the desperate circle of protection that Mordred had tried to give. “Bardrick,” he repeated, his stormy eyes looking up at Mordred’s, waiting for confirmation.

“I would have died for him, Marcus,” said Mordred, his voice shaking.

Marcus was not looking at him any more. He pushed away again, this time from Therelane’s outstretched hand, and ran away, out the door. No one followed him.

Mordred felt a hand cover one of his icy, trembling ones. He met Therelane’s sober gaze. “No more, Mordred,” said Therelane quietly. “It was not your doing, and you shall not lay it to your own charge. Bardrick freed you already from any blame in our captivity. Aye, he even died in peace. You must live the same.”

He halted, biting at his lip in the unsure way he had after speaking his mind so bluntly, but his eyes still met Mordred’s without a waver.

Mordred lowered his eyes. "Aye, Therelane," he answered, and knew for the first time that it was true. It would take a little time for his heart to know it in the way his head now did, but the understanding had begun.

He glanced up, afraid that he would find all eyes on him, but the other men had turned tactically away, seeming to sense that the raw grief of the returning soldiers was a thing to let be, even as Marcus'. At the same time he missed a presence strangely, one that he would have expected to come up beside him all the same. And as much as he searched the faces around him, he could not find the one he sought.

"Where is Braegon?" he asked, his low, frantic tone cutting through to all of them. He was already waiting for the awful word, but no, *no*—he could not bear that—not Braegon!

"He lives," said someone quickly. Mordred's breath left him in relief.

"Tell me, Golin," he said, just as quickly.

"They tried another raid on the enemy camp," said Golin heavily. "What madness—nay, I've no tongue of dissension. They must have hoped that the Runnicorans wouldn't anticipate a second try, and we could regain the footing we lost in that last slaughter. But this time they sent out their men to halt us, and we met them on the plains in full pitched battle. We were more in number this time—it was like Adun Cerien—but worse, for we didn't win. They drew off when they knew they had beaten us, and that we wouldn't be able to continue on; which is something, for they might have massacred us all. I bless whatever kind captain had no thirst for bloodshed that day." Golin shook his head wearily, and in a moment continued on.

"We went over the field to gather the dead and wounded, and I found Braegon. He had a spear deep in his thigh, and it was barbed, so there was no getting it out then; we tried, but I fear we only made it worse for him. But there was one with him, that friend of his named Grant Eagle, and he was trying to tend to Braegon at the time, though he was not well off himself, with both his side and his back gashed open. At any rate, we got them both to the hospice, and that's where they are now—and safer by far than any of the rest of us."

"I must see them," said Mordred urgently, remembering how glad he had been of company while he was locked away inside those solid stone doors, and also afraid, afraid for Braegon with the quick, high-stepping walk.

"You may see anyone you've a wish to," said Sergeant Garin, breaking in upon them. "The three of you won't be well enough to rejoin the regular training for several days yet, by the look of you. Recover your strength, and use your time while you have it." With a nod he stepped aside again.

~

Therelane came with Mordred to the hospice. Mordred would have brought Fenris as well, as anxious as he was to keep his brother by his side, but Fenris' slight frame was bent with plain exhaustion, and so he saw him instead safely asleep before he departed with Therelane. For himself, his body was still running on the intensity of the morning's news and the concern for Braegon and Grant. And Therelane, though he did seem weary, insisted on going.

Braegon and Grant were in the same ward, in beds not far from one another. Grant proved wakeful, if in pain, and greeted Mordred with recognition. But Braegon was in a fever, slipping in and out of consciousness, and despite his efforts Mordred could not get a certain response from him.

"It's the leg," said Grant in his hard, stoic way. "He was crazy with the pain the first day—near out of his head with it. He thrashed all around and didn't know himself. He does better now."

Something inside Mordred shuddered, as he looked at Braegon's dark, taut face, and he wondered what it would be like to be crazy with pain.

But the nurse who passed by and checked Braegon agreed with Grant—a pale, flax-haired slip of a girl with a small flat nose. "He does much better than yesterday or the day before; he will soon be on the mend. The fever already is less." She gave them a comforting smile that transfigured her wan face and moved past.

Mordred stared after her with an odd yearning. It was not as though he felt attraction to her, as a man to a woman, but there was a hunger in him for delicacy and gentleness; for beauty, and for light, soft things that did not hurt or kill. What he wanted, he realized with a great swell of that yearning ache, was Laufeia; for Laufeia, with her stern, feminine sense and quiet steel-strength, seemed an epitome of all the goodness and perfection that was left in the world.

He came out of his thoughts to see that Therelane had left his side and was speaking to another girl—Mirda, in fact, he saw. Wondering what they were discussing, he meant to join them, but instead he looked at Therelane's face again, and wondered why he was so flushed, and seemed to be stumbling so over his words. And even as he watched, Mirda made some soothing reply and Therelane's silly sheep-grin spread over his face, only more so.

Mordred's eyebrows slowly climbed up his forehead. He felt an odd desire to laugh. At the same time he felt a little deserted, a little left-behind.

He told himself not to be silly. He would not grudge Therelane and his love-starved heart any of the love he deserved. Still, the feeling remained.

In spite of his better urgings, he moved a little closer to the two of them, wanting to hear what was being said. However, all at once a whirlwind descended on them and broke up the conversation entirely—a whirlwind in the person of Irene Grey, who spun between them and asked Therelane tartly what he was doing here, and was he sick?

Therelane's stuttered reply was in the nature of, "I thought you were in Mianu."

"Seems there's more for me to do here than in Mianu," she responded. "Well, answer me; I haven't all day. Were you admitted to the hospice? You look poorly."

"It's—it would be too long to explain now, Irene. I'm sure you are too busy. But no, I'm not ill now."

"Then I'll be off," she retorted, tossing her head, and paused by Braegon's bed to feel his forehead. "Aye, he's improving. Hala said as much."

Mordred expected her to make comment on his appearance as well, but she passed him by without a glance. He watched her move, whippet-quick, down the rows, and thought of the time she had stood by Fenris' sick bed, months and months ago, then a hated stranger's face like all the others in Ceristen except for Braegon. Now she was a reminder of things familiar and beloved, and with her Laufeia came into his mind again. He wanted her back, he wanted days like the few they had known together in Ceristen, perfectly happy, perfectly content—before the Claw . . .

And as if the thoughts had conjured him, a despicable, horribly familiar figure appeared around the corner. Mordred snatched at Therelane and jerked him around with unwonted force. "Let us go," he said abruptly, and he set off with long, relentless strides across the ward, so that Therelane had to run after him to catch up.

He worried that Therelane would ask him why he had left so hurriedly, but perhaps his set face warned Therelane away. In any case, he said nothing, and Mordred returned to the barracks with him and slept. When he awoke, he had almost forgotten the incident, and it seemed Therelane had as well.

~

He and Therelane went to see Braegon again the following day. To Mordred's relief, when they approached his bed, Braegon's eyes were open and steady, and his forehead was no longer bright with sweat.

"Mordred!" he exclaimed, lifting a hand of greeting, and his old, joyous smile was the same. "And Therelane! Grant said that you were here yesterday, but I—I was quite unaware of it." He laughed ruefully, as though there had been a failure on his part.

Mordred shook his head, kneeling by the bed and studying Braegon's face in concern. "You didn't look nearly so well yesterday. Does the leg still hurt very much?"

Braegon shrugged. "I daresay it will not stop hurting for a long time. I can bear it; it has been worse."

He and Mordred spoke a while longer together, but Therelane wandered away, and Mordred, when it was time to leave, discovered with no surprise that he had sought out Mirda again.

"So, Therelane," he said, pausing on the sunlit steps of the hospice and looking at his friend until Therelane met his eyes, "Mirda?"

Therelane turned slowly red to the ears. "What about Mirda?"

Mordred uttered a quick laugh. "You absurd man! You know well what!"

Therelane flushed even deeper red, until Mordred wondered whether it would start coming out of his pores. "It does not matter," he mumbled, lowering his eyes and scuffing the step with his foot. "She will never feel so towards me. But she is the fairest and most loving thing I have ever seen, and every moment I spend with her she seems fairer still."

"Well, and who says that she will never feel so toward you? She appeared to be enjoying your company."

"No," said Therelane with an awkward insistence, "we were only talking about her brother—that is why she was happy. Look," he continued with a hasty change of subject, "she could not love—this." He shook up his sleeve until the stump of his left hand was revealed in the glaring sun.

Mordred turned astonished eyes upon him. "Therelane Grey, who has ever given you the notion that that matters? Have I? Has *Mirda*?"

"Oh—well, you know, it would not be right. She ought to have a, a whole man."

"Therelane, is there some logical reasoning behind this? Or is it absolute cloud-fluff?" Mordred demanded the words with some heat, half-amused and half-frustrated by his friend's strange attempts at chivalry.

Whatever Therelane's answer would have been was cut short, as he squinted down the steps against the light. "Is that not someone we know?"

"Captain Rhodes!" Mordred cried as he sprang down the steps to greet the dark-haired man with a boyish grin who was mounted on a dark bay horse.

Captain Rhodes swung down and returned the greeting with a laughing salute, an anxious strain easing out of his face. "Well met,

Mordred! I have missed your face—indeed, I feared that I would not see it again until a day past. You are well?—you look thin."

"I am fine," said Mordred, shrugging it carelessly aside. "In sun and wind like this, who could not feel well?"

"It is truly a fair day," agreed Captain Rhodes, lifting his face to the keen breeze. "But I cannot linger; I have a message to deliver. Farewell, Mordred. May our next meeting be in an hour of more leisure and greater hope!" He spoke the final words more softly, more as if to himself, and the strain returned to his face as he settled into the saddle and trotted down the street.

~

"Is there nothing we can do?"

"We ought to aim another strike at the southern camp. They have still left it open, not sending it north with the rest."

"Aye, in the hopes that we will do that very thing and expend our waning forces! That is what you said last time, Lord Galhas, and they crushed our soldiers as surely as at first. Only a fool tries a third time what has failed twice. The council would do well not to heed this course of action." Captain Murray seated himself, his stony features quivering with anger.

"Peace," said the general, rising. "This war of words goes nowhere. I agree with Lord Galhas that something must be done. We have made no headway against the enemy for nearly a month, while they have struck us and weakened us again and again. Yet as Captain Murray well observes, we have tried the southern camp twice and without results, and it is indeed probable that the enemy holds out there in the hope that we will try again to dash ourselves against them as against a rock, and end by dashing ourselves to pieces. We are desperate. What shall we do?"

The eyes of the lords and captains turned to one another, and to the general, and finally in a last desperation to the king, who sat so silent as always at the head of the council table. But no miracle happened, and the king's silence did not break, and no word of hope came.

"There is one thing we can do," said the general at last, and he spoke with reluctance.

"My lord," said several of the men at once in astonishment and eager hope. But Captain Rhodes' face turned with knowing and fearful eyes to the general.

"I have waited long to speak of this," said the general, clearly yet quietly, "for the need seemed to me not yet great enough. And I do not yet say that it is. I only put the question to you, my lords, to determine whether it seems so to you, for this is not a thing done lightly."

"Say on, my general," said Lord Galhas, and other heads nodded. "Of what would you speak? What can we do against the enemy?"

"The southern camp is still our best hope, because of its smallness. We have tried it twice, with footsoldiers, without avail. But we can still hit it from the air."

"How—my lord—" and the startled exclamations died away, as they saw what he meant. Lord Galhas spoke again.

"But that would mean—" He shook his head in disbelief.

"Not readily do we lend or jeopardize our dragons," said the general steadily. "Never would we squander them. Every dragon is of great value, and though we have bred them for tens of generations, still we have few. They are the prize of Orden. Yet dearer still are the lives of our people, and our country itself. Is it not so? Shall we risk our dragons to safeguard the land? I put the choice to you, my lords, but the situation is very desperate. There is even rumor that the leader is meditating an assault upon the West Gate, and I need not tell you that our forces are spread far too thinly at this moment to counter such an attack. Think well. Do you say aye or nay?"

Captain Murray was the first to stand. "It is aye from my lips, my general."

"And mine," said Captain Rhodes, also standing; "you know that."

Slowly, one by one, the men rose from their seats, and one by one the sober choice was made: Aye.

The general set his hands against the table. "Then let us make the preparations, discreetly and with great care. We will take our prized jewels of Orden, and rain dragons upon their camp."

~

Golden lantern-light flicked in tattered skeins over the brown wall. Mordred, his arms over his knees, felt the heavy hand descend on his shoulder and looked up in surprise, for it was not Sergeant Garin's touch.

It was Captain Murray. The light caught somewhere in his deep-set eyes, and his grim face, highlighted by the harsh shadows, seemed at once half-human and beyond human. "Will you come outside with me?" he asked.

Mordred got up, and came into the gentle air of summer's night, waiting.

"You know what is to take place in some three days?" said the captain brusquely.

"A battle," said Mordred, and winced unconsciously, almost expecting a slap if he had been too pert or forward.

Captain Murray only nodded with a scarcely discernible change of expression. "Go on."

"An attack on the southern camp." Mordred looked at Captain Murray bewilderedly, waiting for a further signal. "Five hundred march on it."

"Five hundred march on it by land; eighty more will fly into it by dragon. Yes, this is secret; speak of it to no one else. I am told that you have ridden a dragon before."

"A-aye." Mordred stuttered the word out, and his breath began to race as he understood what was being said.

"Your experience will be needed. Report on the third evening to Mitheren and the dragon run."

"Wait!" Mordred lunged forward as the man began to turn.

"What is it? Speak."

"Are—are only those who have ridden before being chosen?"

"Other suitable candidates are considered. Why?"

"I—I do not wish to ride with the dragons if my brother cannot also. I wish to be near him." He met the dim gaze of Captain Murray with defiance now, as it seemed to be dismissing him, scorning him. "I *must* be near him. I—" His voice faltered away, for there seemed to be nothing that was reason enough. "He needs me," he whispered, his throat heavy. *I'm never leaving you again, Fenris . . .*

"You speak of what you do not understand," said Captain Murray curtly. "If you are ordered to ride, you will ride. Furthermore, if your brother were chosen, you might be as far away from him as near him." He paused briefly.

"Nonetheless . . . I remember your words of greeting to me at times, though I had done nothing for you, nor did I ever hint at doing anything; yet still you greeted me with a strange friendliness. And

I, too, once had a brother. I will see whether your brother may be considered, Mordred Kenhelm."

~

"Frederick Thorne!"

Fred lifted his eyes as Captain Rhodes came swiftly across the courtyard of Mitheren to him. "A good meeting, Captain Rhodes," he said, smiling.

"It looks as though my word for you proved well, then," said Captain Rhodes with an answering smile. "You are among the riders?"

"Indeed, and I thank you; it is surely an honor."

Captain Rhodes only laughed; and then his face sobered deeply. "May this battle go well for us," he murmured. "For all our hopes hang on it. If it fails, we have made an abominable waste and a sacrifice for nothing."

Fred put out his hand and touched Captain Rhodes' shoulder. "Nothing is done for nothing, Captain Rhodes. Even the longest storms must end."

Captain Rhodes gave a tight smile. "And if they end on wracked timbers and a sunken keel?"

Their gazes held long and sorrowfully, and then Captain Rhodes broke and looked away. "You must go up to the dragon run," he said. "They are already assembling up there."

"And you, Captain Rhodes?"

"Captain Murray leads the land-bound attack; I am his second. Farewell, Fred Thorne. Greet Mordred for me; I know he is there, and I think that Fenris is also. I shall look for your face in the battle."

Fred bent his head. "You humble me with your friendship, my captain." And knowing that Captain Rhodes was right and he must make haste, he went quickly where he had been directed.

At the top of Mitheren, in the dimness of the dragon run, there was a mill of confusion. Someone took him and guided him to a dragon, and bade him mount and see whether the saddle were a proper fit. He waited there while a stable-man made adjustments and tightened this strap or that, and gradually he sensed a hush coming over them as men found their places and waited.

The run was split down the middle, with a long aisle between; and into a clear space in that aisle came a man who called for silence with a voice of authority.

"I, Captain Thurgild, am your commander as we ride out. You will keep your dragons in an orderly formation, not within ten feet of another lest you collide. Dark is coming, and soon we shall set out; we will ride as one fleet to the enemy camp. There we split paths. You, on the left: you are armed with crossbows, quivers of arrows, and oil. You will shoot burning arrows down into the camp, on the south side only: this is where the supplies are. The fighting should concentrate toward the north side of the camp.

"You, on the right: you are armed with a crossbow and one quiver of arrows, but no oil. You will fly low to the ground and shoot at any and all movement until our own men arrive and join the fight, whereupon you will not shoot any longer, lest you kill your own fellows. You will land your dragon and dismount, and send it away with a whistle, like this." He demonstrated twice. "Then you will join the fight with the others. Understood?"

A rumble of assent rose up, and the dragons, as if they were also agreeing, tossed up their heads and growled. Several men chuckled, and a spirit of excitement and hope seemed to rise into the company.

"So." Captain Thurgild turned and mounted his dragon. "Follow me!"

~

Fred waited tensely as the trees broke away beneath them and the dimness of the camp stretched out. He was uncertain how to begin, and afraid to go wrong.

The motion of the dragon was easy beneath him, and he felt no insecurity as he reached down to feel for an arrow in the quiver by his leg. Now?—later? Should he wait? He was strangely glad that he had been chosen to shoot only the supply tents, and not join the fighting. *"Even now, the wish is not in me to take the life of any man . . . "*

Around him, bright sparks were arcing down out of the sky upon the southern tents. Outcries rang out below. Still he dallied.

He had waited overlong; now fresh cries were sounding up. It was the footsoldiers, cutting into the fray and turning the camp into battle. Fred reached down again and took the flint and tinder, and the bottle of oil. Something whined past his ear as he did so, and he jerked up.

It came again, many of them, sharp hisses all around. And suddenly, his dragon lurched beneath him, and began to fall.

CHAPTER 30

FRED TENSED IN THE SADDLE as the wind tore his breath away, struggling to brace for the crash, but the instant the dragon's body hit the ground he jolted loose, flying like a hurled stone, the reins ripped from his hands. Blackness spun around him as he hit the ground, thick webs of sickness, and he tasted blood. But he was alive, and for the most part unhurt. Dazedly he staggered up.

The flat of a sword collided with his chest, and flung him backwards.

Utterly confounded, too startled to even find his sword, Fred stared up at the man who had struck him down, feeling cold metal touching his neck.

The leader held the blade there, lightly but enough to draw blood. "You," he said softly. "My friend the Thorne. You are quick to seek me out again."

Fred did not know what he meant to do with him, and he had no time to wonder. Frantically he rolled aside, shoving the sword away from his neck, and jerked his knife out. The sword came down once, twice, thrice, and each time clashed onto the smaller weapon barely in time to stay the blow. The fourth time Fred, not knowing what instinct prompted him to do it, dove up under the sword and thrust his knife blindly at the leader's body.

The sword dropped, grazing his shoulder, and the leader staggered back, his hand clamped against his thigh. Blood was oozing swiftly out, and the gash was deep.

Fred scrambled to his feet, not daring to waste a second. He snatched out his sword, but hesitated then, ready for flight yet uncertain what to do next. His gaze strayed down to the other man's weapon lying between them on the ground.

Maybe it was a sound—maybe it was the flicker of movement that made him look up and saw the small dagger leave the leader's hand.

He leaped aside and watched it fly past, shaking with the nearness of disaster; and then as the leader rushed forward he turned, and ran.

~

Cern Dersturi watched the man run. His teeth clenched in a sneer of pain and anger, and he unslung his bow and fitted an arrow to the string, releasing in a swift, fluid moment. In the dimness, however, he missed; the quarrel went too high and wide. About to draw again, he saw something large and heavy tumbling to the ground, ahead of Fred Thorne, and realized that his wayward arrow had struck a dragon instead.

Swiftly he fired at it a second time; the shaft drove into the animal's head as it hit the ground. It thrashed for several moments, and lay still.

~

Mordred guided the dragon gently towards the ground, waiting for the landing and reveling in the smooth, graceful motion beneath him. His sword lay ready on his knees, and he ran his hand over the hilt. There was a figure running near at hand, he saw—maybe too near; he laid pressure against the dragon's neck, shifting its angle to the left so that they would not collide.

He thought of Fenris, hoped all was well with him. He would find him, as soon as it was possible, and they would stay together through the battle.

One moment he felt a jolt.

The next there was a crushing weight on top of him, and his head spun wildly, and everything dissolved into a blankness with neither seeing, sound, nor thought.

~

Out of the night ahead a mass of dark hurtled towards Fred, sinking rapidly to the ground and scraping to a halt to the right of him with a thundering impact that he remembered. Casting a look back toward the leader, who was yet far back, he stepped anxiously around the slain dragon and sought for sign of the rider.

But this rider had not, like him, been thrown clear. In its death, the dragon had twisted on its back, pinning the man hopelessly beneath it. He lay a motionless form, his body concealed under the creature's carcass, his face a white blur under the starlight. Fred stared down at that still, pale face, the face of one he knew so well, and a strange reckless anger began to build in him, anger against the leader and against the war, overturning anxiety and fear, casting aside conscious thought.

His reason sought to halt him, would have had him turn and run again. *Turn back—you are not his equal, turn back . . .* But he could not hear it outside the raging anger.

He came on the approaching the leader, ran at him with a cry, and their blades rang on one another again. The leader's sword flashed in a dizzying swirl of patterns that he could not follow. He felt it strike him, how many times he did not know; but it was all outside the turmoil within him and he felt no pain.

And suddenly there was a roaring in his ears, and his own sword fell from his hands. The grass was wet and cool against his cheek. He was conscious of the leader's face over him for a second; and then came a crashing blow, and the darkness.

~

The leader looked down briefly at Fred, anger and contempt curling his lip. With a shrug he turned. But as he looked at the rider who lay pinned beneath the dead dragon, his face changed, and his eyes widened. For a moment he seemed at a loss, almost cheated, as he looked on death that had robbed him of his vengeance.

And then Mordred's eyelids stirred.

They drifted open, hazy and unfocused, and the leader leaned over him with a hard smile, his hand against the dragon's leathery flank, waiting for the recognition to come.

It came, in a swift flash, horror and shrinking fear, and the leader's smile grew, for the young man was wholly at his mercy; his left arm was buried with the rest of his body under the weight of the dragon, only his right arm outflung beside him, groping helplessly, searching for something.

The leader saw what—saw the sheen of the blade inches from the seeking fingers—and moved forward to cover it with his foot, seconds too late. Mordred's fingers closed around the hilt and he hoisted the sword up in an unsteady, ungainly swing.

Cern Dersturi's flare of irritation died away. If the boy wanted to play at defending himself, so much the better. He could scarcely lift the sword anyway.

He drew his own sword and let it dance mockingly towards Mordred's neck, letting Mordred knock it aside by a weak counter-move. The weapon shook in the young man's hand and drooped downwards.

"Come, Damachrus," said Cern Dersturi, that cold smile never leaving his lips. He ran his sword into Mordred's arm and withdrew it slowly. "Pick it up again. We are not finished."

~

Therelane Grey had lost both sword and knife in a short and heated encounter. Now he moved cautiously away from the heat of battle, keeping low and searching for a weapon. There were sounds of movement to his right, and he glanced toward them, but could see nothing save a broad shadow blotting out the dark tree line. The moon had hidden itself behind a cloud, and for the time being nearly all light was veiled.

Then the moon edged out, growing in power and clarity, and flooding the field before him with white light. A man in enemy colors, sword in hand—a slain dragon framing him—another sword rising from the grass . . .

Therelane dashed through the tall grass, covering the interval in a matter of seconds, and flung his whole weight against the enemy soldier. The man pitched forward, struck his head on one of the dragon's spikes, and slumped down to the ground. Therelane leaned on the dragon, panting, and looked down at the person whom he had saved.

"Mordred!" he gasped.

A slight smile wavered over Mordred's face and vanished. The sword drooped in his hand and tumbled into the grass. "Yes. Who does it look like?"

"Mordred, are you all right? What happened?"

He realized what a needless question it was, but if Mordred noticed, he gave no sign of it. "I think my dragon was shot down. I don't remember anything after—after the jolt. It's on top of me, isn't it?"

"Yes," said Therelane. He stared down at Mordred, frightened by the odd, crooked smile that dragged itself like a shriveled skin across whatever his friend was feeling beneath. He had never seen Mordred smile quite like that. "Can you move?" he stammered out.

"I can move my arm." He meant the sword, of course, he had been using the sword when Therelane came up. "The rest is trapped. Shall I try?"

His quiet, almost childlike attitude frightened Therelane still more. "One way or another, we've got to get you out. See if you can."

For one instant, under the silver moonlight, he saw Mordred's eyes and they were terrified. Then Mordred arched backwards, straining against the deadweight of flesh that held him fast, only to fall back with a muffled cry. He could not speak for some time after that, and but for his open eyes Therelane would have thought he had fainted. "I'm too far under," he said at last in a low, breathless way. "I daren't—even—try."

"Then I'll get it off," said Therelane with a reckless, urgent resolve. "I must try, at least. I don't think I could manage to roll it off you altogether, but if I lift it, could you pull yourself into the clear?"

The terror raced through Mordred's eyes again. "Maybe," he said. He braced himself and his face fluttered in a barely stifled grimace of pain. "Maybe. Go ahead and—try."

Therelane bent, set his hand and shoulder low against the dragon's flank, and strained. That he raised it from the ground at all amazed him. As he struggled to hold it steady, he knew nothing but the relentless weight and the thundering in his ears, and he could neither see Mordred nor summon the breath to speak to him.. However, when he could bear it no longer and collapsed onto the grass, to his relieved surprise Mordred was lying nearby, lips colorless and eyes shut—but free.

Therelane rose panting to his feet. “Mordred, are you awake?”

“Awake,” muttered Mordred in a small gasp.

Therelane looked at him with a growing sense of dismay. He did not know what to do now. Mordred couldn’t stay here, shouldn’t stay here—he glanced distractedly around for help, seeing the near glow of fire from the tents, the dragon’s bulk, the face of the man he had knocked out or killed. There was something about the face under the vague, shifting moonlight, something that tugged at him, and he was going to look back at it when he saw the other shadow very close by in the high grass. “What’s that?” he murmured.

“What is it?” asked Mordred, forcing his eyes open. An anxious light flickered in them at Therelane’s half-alarmed tone.

“I don’t know,” replied Therelane. He was thinking uneasily that they had been here a long time, at least a long time in the reckoning of a battle, and other Runnicorans might have started to spread out . . .

He stepped forward cautiously towards the crouching shadow, only to realize almost as soon as he had taken the first step that the man was slumped on his face, motionless, not crouching at all and assuredly not creeping towards them. He might be dead, or only unconscious, but by the looks of him he wasn’t likely to live. Therelane had already seen enough of battle to know that. Blood glinted in the moon off his back, legs and arms, pooling by his side. Pity edged up in Therelane as he looked at the still figure, the outstretched fingers inches from the forsaken sword-hilt, not knowing whether he were friend or adversary; and on an unwonted impulse he crossed to the man and turned him over, meaning to set the sword gently in those stilled, groping fingers.

He never thought about the sword again.

"Fred," he gasped aloud. He seized the utterly lifeless hand and slammed his fingers against the wrist, as though by force he could make a pulse begin. Panting in growing panic, he waited, shifting his hand from place to place on the blood-wet skin.

None . . . weak . . . slow.

Therelane hardly knew his relief, he was still so full of dread. He rose quickly to his feet and hurried back.

"Where . . . were you?" Mordred asked weakly when he returned, seeming to wrench the words out with a violent effort. "What happened?"

"Naught," said Therelane quickly. Mordred must not know, must not become distraught in his increasingly confused state. "Naught to worry about, at least not for you. You can't stay here, Mordred. I'm going to find help."

Mordred pressed his lips into a tense line, flinching, pulling himself back fiercely from whatever distant world he was sinking into. "Go, Therelane," he managed.

"I won't be long," Therelane promised. And he sped off into the night, the unnamed face of the Runnicoran soldier slipping into place as he did so—of course, it had been *the leader*. . .

He went towards the burning supply tents, hoping vaguely he would find some Ordenian soldiers there, watching the fires perhaps. It was a foolish risk he took, but he did not know it; and choking on the thick air, blinking against the smoke, he rounded a tent and collided with Captain Finley Rhodes.

"Therelane, what would you have me do?" Captain Rhodes asked at last, having heard the gasping, ill-cohered story through in silence.

"I—" Therelane fell silent, staring at the ground. It had been foolish to think that anything could be done. "I . . . I do not want to leave them alone in the battle," he finished at last.

There was silence for a space, and Captain Rhodes gazed somewhere beyond Therelane. His lips formed the names "Fred" and "Mordred." With a sharp movement, distress lining his features, he turned to face Therelane. "I have naught to occupy me now, but I must report to Captain Murray soon. Show me to them; there is something I may be able to do."

Therelane bowed his head in gratitude and turned, gesturing. Captain Rhodes motioned to several men and followed.

"Fred, he was alive?" Captain Rhodes insisted as they strode over the scorched ground.

"He had a pulse. At least I think he did." Remembering the broken body bleeding out on the moonlit ground, he could scarcely believe he had not imagined the movement to himself. "I—I don't know. Even if he does now—" He could not go on.

"You worry that much?" Something like a tremor wavered Captain Rhodes' words.

"Aye," whispered Therelane, not wanting to say it or think it.

"And Mordred?" asked Captain Rhodes softly.

"He was better than Fred; he was awake." Therelane struggled to piece together his thoughts and not think about Fred. "The leader had him earlier, and I don't know if he hurt him—I didn't think to ask, not then—trying to move the dragon and all. But he couldn't move an inch without pain, even though he tried to hide it like always. He—he *knew* he couldn't hide it." The memory of Mordred's strange, wry smile clenched a shivering hand around Therelane's stomach.

"Is this it?" asked Captain Rhodes sharply, halting at the dragon's carcass.

"Aye, and Mordred, by the dragon. And the leader . . . " Therelane paused and stared around. "He was here, and now he's gone." He looked at the crumpled hollow in the grass where the body had lain. "Maybe his men found him and took him away."

"No time to dwell on that," returned Captain Rhodes. "It is a matter beyond our concern now."

We might have killed him then, thought Therelane, shaken by the realization of it and astonished at his own blindness. *We might have killed him! Why did I not think?*

Mordred had been lying with his eyes shut, but he opened them when he heard Therelane and Captain Rhodes coming.

"The leader left," said Therelane softly, leaning down.

"Did he?" murmured Mordred faintly. "Oh."

Captain Rhodes went to Fred and bent over him briefly. Then he stood up, scanned the deep blue-black of the night overhead, and let loose a peculiar, sharp whistle.

~

The wind rushed softly, gently in Fenris' ears. For now, surrounded by the smoky, grey-tinged colors of the breeze and the night, he might almost forget that he was part of the battle raging beneath. Then shouts and groans from below pulled him back into the glaring speed of reality. The dragon banked and rose slowly on an updraft, waiting for the next command to come; but Fenris did not give it. He traced the still-unused crossbow, its weight and metal bracings cruel in his hands.

Suddenly the dragon came almost to a stop beneath him and plunged downward in a steep dive. Fenris, nearly thrown, snatched for the reins.

Shot! his mind cried to him, but his instinct sensed the control in the fall, the steady direction of the surging muscles under him. He did not understand *why* it had dived, but almost before he could be afraid again, the dragon swooped up and out, coming to rest in the grass, and three Ordenians strode towards him from the left. The one in the lead, Fenris saw, was Captain Rhodes; the two others lagged somewhat behind him, carrying a limp form.

Captain Rhodes started when he saw him.

"Fenris Kenhelm! I did not think it would be—He is alive, Fenris—"

Two thoughts Fenris thought, simultaneously and yet separately, sharp and clear. It was Mordred; and though the captain was trying to sound hopeful, it was bad.

"It is Mordred—isn't it."

Captain Rhodes nodded. "He . . . he was crushed underneath his dragon."

Fenris stared at him.

"He is *alive*," repeated Captain Rhodes. The insistent way he said it only carved deeper the dark fear shadowing his eyes. "Fenris—" His sharpening voice wanted an answer, wanted Fenris to understand. But Fenris could not speak.

The other men drew near, grunting under their burden, and Captain Rhodes turned to them. "Therelane! How is he?"

"Don't—know," answered Therelane, breathing heavily. "I think he's passed out for now."

Fenris strained his gaze toward his brother, needing to see, and yet all he could see was Mordred's dark hair and the faint line of his cheek as his head slumped against Therelane's shoulder. He looked back at the captain.

Captain Rhodes bit his lip, hesitating over some inner decision. "We could remove him to a sheltered place until the battle is over, but nay—we can surely manage without one dragon. Lay him on the saddle."

With a grunt the two hoisted Mordred up in front of Fenris and stepped back. Fenris put a hand on Mordred's wet forehead, looking at the white, unmarked face. More wetness trailed across his other hand from Mordred's right arm, thicker and darker. The left arm hung crooked.

He heard Captain Rhodes speaking again. "I will fetch my own for Fred. If Captain Murray will but spare me—"

"Fred," Fenris whispered, unable to take in all that Captain Rhodes meant through his stricken daze, waiting for the second nightmare to fall.

"Aye, Fred," Captain Rhodes replied, his distracted tone growing harsher. "Fred has been wounded—gravely, more gravely than your brother. Enough of this, enough talk, you must go *now*!"

He cut himself off and his voice softened to contrition. "I should not have lashed out, forgive me, I beg you. I know that I am being foolish in this, and I am half afraid it is all wrong instead of only half wrong as it seems in my mind . . . " He pressed his fingers between his eyes.

Mordred stirred faintly against Fenris. His face twisted in agony, and a sound that was half gasp, half cry escaped his lips, breaking off midway. Sweat gleamed on his brow, and his body relaxed inert.

Captain Rhodes gripped Fenris by the shoulder, the indecision washing out of his dark eyes; they burned with the desperate love and distress in Fenris' own heart. "He needs more care than any of us can give him now, Fenris. Take him to Orden City, to the hospice, and hurry!"

Fenris slapped the bridle obediently against the dragon's neck, holding Mordred securely with his other arm. The creature, with a lurch, sprang into the sky.

~

Grant leaned against the bed frame, his fingers moving with a weary tenseness to rub the bandage on his ribs.

"You ought to rest," said Braegon, looking across at him, seeing the exhaustion in his eyes. But the words were not a command, scarcely even advice. Neither of them could rest, not with the dread hanging over them like a knife poised to fall; the knowledge that out in the dark of the night, men they knew were fighting, maybe falling, maybe dying.

Their eyes met in silent acknowledgement of the wait, and suddenly Braegon jerked his away in a vehement impatience to the dusty floor of the ward. "The waiting is unbearable. I would be out there fighting, even dying, rather than sit in ignorance and fear like this."

"It is no use to wish," said Grant. He sighed, as though to say something further, but the doors swung open and Irene Grey strode briskly in.

Braegon's mouth tightened and he turned away from her. *Do not come. Do not say anything. I cannot know—*

She was muttering to herself, the usual disapproval permeating her demeanor. "So much death. So much suffering, the measure is absurd. Why will men persist in going out to hack themselves to pieces?" She twitched briefly, and her lips pinched themselves together.

"You are looking at us," said Braegon fiercely.

She was—or she had glanced his way, her eyes hard, before continuing on down the aisle of beds. "'Tis naught to tell you now, Master Braegon."

"What are you concealing? Who is hurt? I shall *know*. Tell us, or I shall get up and stamp on this leg."

"You'll do no such thing," snapped Irene, bending down to feel a man's feverish brow.

"Tell me!" Braegon begged. He flung aside the covers.

Irene was beside him at once, pushing him back to lie flat again, muttering under her breath, "Am I to have to tie you to your bed?"

"Enough, Irene. Let go!"

"Will you lie still and behave yourself?"

"If you tell me what I want to know!" Braegon cried.

"I shall not, and if you will not obey me I shall carry out my threat and tie you to this bed, for I have things to attend to and wasting my time holding an unruly patient down is not one of them."

Braegon let out a broken sigh. "I will have done, Irene."

"Good," she returned, and spun away from him. Braegon lay back with an arm over his eyes.

Irene made her round of the ward, the line between her eyes slowly deepening all the while; and at last she whirled from the side of a delirious boy and stalked past Braegon and Grant to the door.

It opened before she reached it.

Grant's breath hitched in a gasp, and Braegon sat up at the sound. A shadowed figure stood in the doorway, light from the ward glancing over his burden—Mordred Kenhelm's tall frame, pale and unconscious, blood running over the sleeve of his shirt and his jerkin.

Fenris came forward, stumbling, his legs all but giving way under him. "Irene," he stammered, his voice a whisper. "Irene—they said to find you—"

Irene lifted Mordred easily out of Fenris' arms. "Aye, well, here I am."

CHAPTER 31

IRENE LOWERED MORDRED TO THE floor, took Fenris' arms sharply, and marched him out of the room. "Sit down," she ordered. "You're about to faint, and that's the last thing I need now."

Fenris' legs seemed to be made of water under him as he sank down in mute obedience to the floor.

"That's right," Irene's approving voice came faintly to his ear. She pushed his head down in-between his knees, and through the fog of exhaustion and strain surrounding him he heard her footsteps moving away.

He sat like that for an uncounted time, and finally he became aware that things had grown clearer, the sights and sounds no longer muffled in that pale haze. He felt tired, but no longer like his senses were fleeing him.

Mordred, he thought, and got dizzily to his feet.

Irene was not in the ward, nor could he see Mordred, though he came forward and looked all around—

"Fenris!" said Braegon's voice to his left. "If you're looking for Mordred, he is not here. There's quite simply no room in the wards. She took him to a smaller room off to the side, I don't know where, but there must be someone around who does."

"Thank you," whispered Fenris, and turned to leave.

~

Captain Rhodes leaped off his dragon, noting that Fenris' dragon was also nearby, and ran lightly down the run to the keeper's quarters.

A barrage of knocking brought a man to the door, who eyed him blearily and suddenly came awake as he saw who he was.

"My lord?" he said.

"Come with me," said Captain Rhodes, nodding curtly in the direction of his dragon. "I have a wounded man, and I need help to get him to the hospice."

"I've a cart, my lord, but no horse to pull it with."

"We can carry him, then; it is not far."

And indeed they reached the hospice in little more than a quarter of an hour.

"Thank you," said Captain Rhodes, pressing the man's hand. "You may go."

He gave Fred into the care of the surgeons, and asked if they knew of Mordred.

"Someone brought a Mordred Kenhelm in not long since," answered one of them. "If you can find Irene Grey, you'll find him."

~

Irene Grey was bending over the bed with Mordred's unconscious body stretched out on it, running her hands over him and muttering swiftly.

"Hit his head falling, not dangerous but he'll have a headache for a day, I shouldn't wonder—not but that that will be the least of his concerns. What do you want?" she demanded in the same breath, whirling on him.

"I—wished to see Mordred," answered Captain Rhodes, staring at the white, still form on the bed.

"You've seen him then," retorted Irene. "I don't need *two* people watching my every move."

Captain Rhodes did not understand her meaning at first. Then he saw Fenris, standing pale and tense-faced a few feet away.

He looked back at Irene. "Where is he injured?"

Irene thinned her lips. "The question would be, where *isn't* he injured. The only thing we have to be glad of is that he must have fallen under the arc of the saddle, otherwise he'd be a mashed carcass this minute. He's broken at least five ribs, his left leg, and his collarbone. There will be scarce an inch of his body that isn't bruised by morning—"

She broke off as Mordred's body twitched convulsively, and strode back to his side. Mordred's breathing deepened, caught midway, and ended in a short, strangled cry. His face grew whiter than before, whiter than the clean sheet beneath him.

Irene placed her hands steadily on his shoulders as he shuddered again in that horrible spasmodic manner. "Mordred," she said sharply and clearly, "open your eyes and look at me."

His lashes lifted over eyes swimming in tears and pain. "Irene," he gasped.

"Mordred!" It was Fenris' cry, as he leaped toward the bed and leaned over his brother.

"Fenris?" said Mordred, faintly, an anguish in his tone that Captain Rhodes did not quite understand.

"Mordred, it's all right," said Fenris, his voice shaking.

Mordred's chest rose in another attempt to breathe, jerked. His face contorted, every shade of color leaving it. His teeth closed over his lip and bit down until Captain Rhodes saw the blood welling up under them. He took another breath—jerked—

Captain Rhodes turned around and rushed out the door, his command shattering. He leaned his head against the wall.

"Therelane Grey did not seem to think he was so bad before," he said hoarsely to Irene when she sped out of the room on another mission.

"I daresay he wasn't," said Irene. "He made himself worse, getting out from under the dragon, I shouldn't wonder. And he'd have been distracted and excited with the present danger at the time, but after a lapse like this, the pain comes on in full force."

She swept away down the hall.

Time passed achingly on. Irene was everywhere and nowhere, in the room and out of it. Doctors hauled another soldier into Mordred's room. He died before morning and they hauled him out again. Captain Rhodes was afraid for a while after that—terrified that Mordred must die as well. But he could not enter that room.

Hours later the desperation of his ignorance finally surpassed his horror. He turned the handle and came in again.

Mordred was stretched out full length as before, drawing in tiny, broken, gasping breaths. His teeth clenched repeatedly over his lip, where blood trickled down his chin in little rivulets. Irene's hands were placed on his leg.

"No use putting it off, Mordred," she said. "We must set it."

His eyes drifted shut as though with exhaustion, but his face was pulled taut from strain. "Aye," he murmured in a ghost of a voice. "Do it."

As her hands began to move his body jerked violently and he forced it still with terrible effort, sweat running over his face. Irene's hands worked steadily up the leg, finding, feeling. Then, with the incredible, practiced strength hidden in her slim body, she pressed down.

Mordred arched his back, his face drawn and twisted in agony. He uttered an inarticulate gulping sound, and not just once but over and over, little choking half-noises that were worse than screams themselves.

Faint, Captain Rhodes pleaded silently. *Can he not faint?*

But Mordred did not faint. When Irene stepped back at last he lay drenched in sweat and quivering, his short breaths weak and the faintest whimper in their inhaling, like a cat's mew. As Irene bound the splint in place he shivered and bit his lip again, and when he let it loose there was fresh blood on it.

It was too much for Captain Rhodes to bear. He turned his face against the wall and wept.

"Irene," he said when she passed him again.

"I haven't time," she snapped.

"Why does he not scream? I—"

"That's why," she said shortly, shrugging to the bedside, where Captain Rhodes saw Fenris, whom he had forgotten all this time. "He can't bear for his younger brother to know what he's suffering; he'll try to hide it as long as Fenris is there."

"Then should you not send him away? It might be easier on Mordred if he could express his—"

"Are you the physician here?" cried Irene in clear exasperation. "That boy is the only thing that's holding Mordred Kenhelm onto sanity. If he didn't have Fenris to keep him in that forced calm, he'd be so out of his mind with the pain that not a one of us could handle him. He'd have himself into seizures and convulsions and delirium!" She folded her arms. "I won't have you pestering me like this, young man. Set your mind easy on Mordred; *he's* got a two to one chance of surviving the night. Fred Thorne's another matter."

"Fred," Captain Rhodes repeated slowly.

Irene was gone.

~

"What were they saying, Fenris?" Mordred pushed the words out, trying to control his voice that shook treacherously, the searing knives in his chest cutting every word short. He did not care what they were saying; it was just an effort to take his mind away.

He must concentrate—he must not cry out—he must not let Fenris see how much it hurt—Fenris was speaking again.

"I don't know." Fenris' words were steady, but his cheeks were wet. Mordred lost the rest of what he said, his focus fading in the sea of racking pain . . .

"It's all right, Fenris." He did not know how many times he had said it.

"Yes, Mordred." Fenris' voice was trembling.

He must be strong—he must show Fenris, somehow, it was all right—Fenris, so young in the orphanage—no, this was not the orphanage—he must not grow delirious . . .

Irene's cool, strong hand was feeling his sweating forehead. "Open your eyes, Mordred."

He opened them. He did not know why she asked him to do it so many times, when it was easier to keep them shut. A bolt of pain shot without reason up his leg and he sucked in a breath, knowing in the same instant that the torture in his chest would soar. The agony flashed to blinding heights, and he braced his whole body to hold back the screams, clamping his teeth down over his lip, knowing he *must not scream . . .*

~

The knock echoed on the door and the general looked away from the window, his hands clasped behind his back. "Come in," he said.

Captain Murray entered with a stiff bow, his face sharply etched and lined with a night's exertion. "We were victorious, General. The enemy has been routed from the camp."

"Good," was all the general said in answer—but his eyes were full and a weight seemed to lift from his shoulders that he had been bearing for many weeks. "You are wearied, Captain Murray. Have you need for rest before we call the council?"

"Nay. Thank you, my general."

"Then take yourself at least a little to eat while I call them together. Captain Rhodes, where is he?"

"I know nothing of Captain Rhodes," said Captain Murray shortly. "He asked leave of me to depart the battle with his dragon, which had been injured."

The general frowned, but nodded to dismiss the captain.

A knock sounded again as Captain Murray turned toward the door. He strode forward to open it.

It was Captain Rhodes there, his shoulders straight through discipline, but a dead exhaustion in his face that was greater than Captain Murray's. He paid no heed to his rival, and walked into the room, bending his head briefly to the general. "My general—I—"

The general motioned Captain Murray from the room. "What is it, *mari*?" he said gently.

Captain Rhodes' shoulders shook. "I left the battle with a wounded dragon, my general, having already sent Fenris Kenhelm away with another. It was to my judgment that they could be spared, and if that be not so it is to my charge. I—I would not have done so, except that there were two wounded men who needed the care of the hospice at once."

"There are many who need the care of the hospice in a battle," said the general quietly. "They cannot all have it, or we would lose all our soldiers."

Captain Rhodes' head dipped in a quick, painful nod.

The general looked at him a moment, kindness in his dark eyes. "So, Captain," he said, "who were these men, that you would take a dragon for them?"

"Fred Thorne was sorely wounded," said Captain Rhodes, his voice harshly steady. "Mordred Kenhelm was crushed beneath his dragon."

In that instant the general remembered that tall, grey-eyed young man and knew fully how dear he had become to him. "Does he live?" he asked, all other questions for the moment set aside as he waited for the truth.

Again the quick, painful nod. "He lives yet, my general."

"But what hope have they of him?"

"He—he is not so bad; not as such things go. The saddle fell as a protection over his body—that was all that saved him. But he has broken so many bones—and his pain, my general, his pain—" Captain Rhodes could say no more for the moment. In his eyes was the horror of the night past.

"And Fred Thorne?" said the general.

Captain Rhodes' mouth worked, as a man sick. "Fred Thorne is dying," he said.

There was nothing that either of them could say into that silence.

Captain Rhodes suddenly swayed, stumbling dizzily as his balance failed him. The general caught him with a steady arm. "*Mari*, you must rest."

"The war councils," said Captain Rhodes with an effort.

"Nay, we will go on without you. Let you go to your bed now. I shall ride to the hospice in a little, and be assured I will not neglect to see them."

~

As he made his way through the halls of the hospice, the general came across Fenris Kenhelm sitting in a narrow corridor. He halted beside him, looking at the boy and thinking of Captain Rhodes; for Fenris' frame, too, was trembling from exhaustion, though the strain within it was not that of discipline, but of waiting. His head drooped on his knees, while one hand clenched in ragged, unconscious spasms.

The general bent and laid his hand on him with a firm touch. Fenris looked up swiftly, and away again. His chest heaved sharply and his breath came quick and uneven.

The general sat beside him. "Your brother Mordred?" he asked gently. "How is he?"

Fenris was silent for a moment; it was that, the general saw, he simply could not answer. Then he spoke, with a strange control that was almost breaking. "He tried to make a jest about it—once." His voice caught, and again he mastered it and went on. "He will start to cry out suddenly, with terrible agony—and then he will remember I am there, and stop it. He cannot move, he can scarcely breathe. Irene has nothing to help him sleep, but she says if he cannot rest his body will not heal, and days like this will kill him." The words seemed to push out of him with an effort, and as they faded into a whisper he buried his face in his hands.

"Your sister Laufeia has not heard yet, has she?"

Fenris shook his head.

"Be sure I shall send for someone to tell her." The general rose, and then hesitated, yearning to say something that might comfort the suffering boy and knowing that there was nothing he could say.

He saw Fenris leap up and spin around to face the door almost before he heard it open. Irene Grey stepped out and carefully closed it behind her, nodding curtly at the general to acknowledge his presence.

She looked well-nigh as weary as Fenris, but as she addressed him her face softened a little and her words were unexpectedly kind. "Naught more we can do for now," she said. "There now, for pity's sake don't look like that. I mean that I've finally got him to sleep: a good, wholesome, natural sleep, the likes of which I haven't been able to soothe him into all this time. If not recovering, he's at least a step closer. Now go get some sleep yourself, or you'll be in as sorry a condition as him."

Fenris reeled, almost falling, so that the general thought he had fainted; but it was only the sudden release of tension. As Irene grasped his arm firmly he righted himself and murmured something indistinct.

"What was that?" Irene demanded.

"Please, let me stay up till Laufeia comes."

The frown deepened between Irene's youthful brows. "I leave that to your own judgment," she said, and sped away down the hall.

~

A girl walked over the wide, free slope of the mountain, the wind rushing past her into the green depths of the fields below, and tugging curls from her gold coronet-braid. Her slender, fair face was turned down, and there was no joy in her dark eyes.

Five days had passed over the news of Bardrick. The truth lay like a stone in Fiona's heart, shuttering the joy out of her life, so that smiles came with only half their former brightness and even the sun's glory seemed shaded. Save for a few tears let fall in the silence of the night, she had wept little; she did not feel that kind of grief, though Peony's tears fell often and without precedent throughout the day. Fiona only knew the loss, knew that she would not feel Bardrick's rough male hand stroking her cheek with his fond older-brother pride, nor hear his low-pitched voice with its little, singular rasp that she knew so well, nor watch him rebuff Marcus' teasing with that tongue-in-cheek humor . . . The loss was relentless at her side, a constant absence that only sleep could wholly drive away.

She ducked beneath the low lintel and shut the door slowly, watching as Peony shelled the beans in the light of the wide-flung window. They had no fields ploughed and planted this past spring, as they had once thought they might; only a very small one that they had cleared and hoed themselves, and planted with seeds loaned by Mrs. Earle.

"Where were you?" asked Peony dully. Her hands moved with rapidity over the loose beanstalks, as though they were the only thing that mattered.

"I went to see Marianne." Fiona sat and took a handful of the beans, twisting away the tops. "She is so lonely; she was lonely ever since Kenneth left, but now that he will never come back—I think that she and I understand one another."

The tears began to roll out of Peony's sea-blue eyes, dripping on the end of her nose as she bent her head forward, but she continued to work steadfastly. Fiona, wishing she had left the sentence unfinished, emptied the beans into the bowl at their feet and reached for another handful from the tangle.

But she never took it, for the door flew open without a knock, and as Fiona leapt to her feet, terror striking her mute—*Marcus,* was her thought—Laufeia stood on the threshold, her eyes wide and wet, tear-tracks on her cheeks.

"Laufeia, what is it?" exclaimed Peony in a gasp, knocking the bowl over in her haste as she rose.

"Fiona," said Laufeia, her eyes fixed on Fiona's. "A man—a man, with a message sent by the general—"

"Marcus," said Fiona, scarcely knowing that the word even left her lips, her hands cold and shaking.

Laufeia shook her head. "No—no. It's Fred, Fiona. He was wounded last night—gravely."

"In what way?" her voice asked, blank and strange in her ears. She buried her face in her hands. It was too much to take in at once.

"The messenger did not know. He only said there were many wounds on him." Laufeia took a breath, and seemed to gather more command over herself. "Fiona, Mordred was hurt as well; that is how I had the word, for the general sent the man to deliver the news to me. He asks me to come down to the hospice, for Fenris' sake, he says, because he needs me—oh, he will! But Fiona, come with me. I shall be glad of your company, and you can see Fred for yourself, and maybe he will not be as bad as the messenger seemed to think. You will come, Fiona?"

Fiona lifted her head, still wrestling with the import of the tidings. "I will come."

~

"A Mordred Kenhelm, you said?" The nurse looked tired. "Aye, he was brought in last night. Nay, he isn't in any of the wards. We've no room to spare. He was put in a little chamber off on the side—one of several such that the surgeons used to sleep in. Come, this way."

"Would you know of a Fred Thorne as well?" Laufeia asked further.

The nurse shrugged. "I don't know that I remember the name, but if he was brought in it's likely he's in another of the small rooms. You might ask Miss Irene Grey, she's bound to know." She hustled them down a hall.

"And where is Irene Grey?"

"I'm not the one to tell you that. You never do know with Miss Irene. She's been in your Mordred Kenhelm's room half the night, skittering back and forth between him and other patients, but she got him to sleep, or something like, this morning. She's not likely to be there now, unless he's woken from that."

"If he's still asleep, then—" Laufeia hesitated. "We shouldn't go in to see him, I expect."

The nurse, tired already, looked distraught. "I'm sorry, ma'am, I should have thought of that. You're right, of course. Miss Irene wouldn't allow it for a minute, but now I've taken you and your friend all this way for nothing."

"Oh, Fenris!" gasped Laufeia, and ran forward.

Fenris' head was leaning on the door; he seemed to almost be asleep on his feet. As Laufeia grasped his arm he shook himself awake and stumbled against her.

"Laufeia," he murmured wearily.

"Fenris, you ought to be in bed!"

"Laufeia, Mordred . . . "

"Hush, not now." She put her hand gently across his lips, in case he should miss the message. "You're going to bed, Fenris, now. You need to rest." She shot a pleading glance at the nurse for help. "Forgive me, you've done so much for us and you are so busy, but if you know of anywhere that he could lie down . . . "

She raised her eyebrows. "I don't know. There's a little closet off his brother's room—we might be able to fit him into that."

"Could you do it without disturbing Mordred?" asked Laufeia.

"I think so. I'm accustomed to moving about sick people."

~

The kind, tired nurse had just led Fenris into the room where she had made a bed ready for him, when Irene Grey came briskly upon them, startling Fiona with her sudden appearance.

"You're here, I see," she said. "I hope you got that boy to bed."

Laufeia nodded.

"Absurd." Irene's dark locks swished about her face as she jerked her head in disapproval. "I told him to lie down, but he *would* wait for you, even though he must have not slept since the night before last and he could barely stand. I wash my hands of any ill that comes of it."

She glanced at Fiona. "I expect you're here to see Fred Thorne."

Fiona took an impetuous step towards her. "Then I could?"

"If you *want* to," Irene assured her, "I won't stop you."

Fiona wavered at the words, and the tone in which they were uttered; vivid pictures played through her mind. Then she rallied. "I do."

"Come along then." Irene walked rapidly to the end of the corridor, turned right, and stopped in front of a door. She turned to Fiona. "You don't know yet, I expect."

Something in her voice made Fiona feel cold, and very ill. "Know?"

Irene's dark-fringed, stern eyes were touched with gentleness. "There's no use in giving you false hope, my dear. His concussion alone could kill him, and his body is bled nearly dry; since he was first found on the battlefield he has not moved nor spoken once. He is as lifeless as anyone not dead can be. We cleaned and bandaged all his wounds; we put him in a bed; there isn't anything more we can do for him. In his state, he may last another few days. No more."

She was saying that Fred would die. The room spun, and Fiona's head felt light. "Another few days," a voice echoed in her head. "No more . . . No more . . . "

"Now," Irene was saying. "In we go."

Fiona followed mutely.

She had expected to see something terrible—ugly—what exactly, she did not know. A hideous disfigurement ripping across Fred's gentle features; limbs twisted out of shape; the red of blood all over his body.

But as he lay there in the darkened room, sunlight seeping through a crack in the heavy curtain across the window, it was the old Fred she saw. And her first thought was, he looked asleep.

Then she came closer and saw how pale his face was, how his breathing was faint and irregular, how very still he lay. She saw the cloth bound about his head, stained with blood, and she knew that the coverlet over him hid many, many more bandages like it. With a shudder she drew the quilt aside, knelt, and took Fred's hand in hers.

It was cold.

She held it between both of hers, chafed it, breathed on it, knowing that it could not help, but wanting to do it all the same. She thought Irene would say at any moment to stop that nonsense and let him alone, but no reproof came.

A man's voice spoke behind her, impatient. "Who is she? There is nothing she can do for him; she may as well let him alone."

"She isn't hurting him," replied Irene, and the man made no reply.

Fiona clasped Fred's hand again, remembering time after time when he had reached out and taken her hand with his firm, strong grip, willing it to do so again; but there was no movement, no pressure. The hand hung limp in hers—not dead—not yet—but barely alive.

The tears welled, brimming, spilling over. She did not try to stop them.

CHAPTER 32

LAUFEIA TWISTED A PIECE OF cloth in her fingers. It might have been a bandage. She neither knew nor cared. She did not know what to do with herself; so much was banging irrationally against her mind that she was tired from it. Fenris; Mordred lying behind that door, in a bed that had belonged to a surgeon before the hospice overflowed; Fiona walking with Irene down the hall to see a Fred who Laufeia knew, in her heart, was dying; she could not stop thinking about any of them and nothing else existed in her helpless, frustrated head.

"Laufeia!"

The light, familiar voice made her look up, and with a sob she rushed into Mirda's arms. Suddenly the daze of vicious, circling thoughts was gone, and she let herself cry again, a little, on Mirda's shoulder, while Mirda's comforting hands stroked her head and her back. No questions, no words between them.

Laufeia stepped back, dashing a hand across her eyes. "Oh, Mirda. I have missed you."

"Is it for Mordred that you came?" said Mirda, taking her hand earnestly. "I heard he was brought in."

"Yes; do you know how he is, Mirda?"

"I haven't seen him. They said a dragon fell on him, but Irene speaks as though he will pull through. I would not worry for him, Laufeia. Come, I am as busy as everyone else, but if it's company you're needing, you can talk to Braegon and Grant. Braegon will be so glad to see someone from home."

"Of course," said Laufeia, eager to do something useful. She began to feel like herself again.

~

Laufeia had been anxious for Mirda at hearing that Braegon, too, was injured. But his enthusiastic greeting he gave her, with his smile as vibrant and welcoming as ever, eased her mind at once.

"And this, Laufeia, is Grant Eagle," Braegon continued with fervor, as though presenting her to a king.

"Well met, lady," said the man, lowering his head politely; young he was, yet his eyes were weary as though he had seen many years of the world and it had been too much for him.

"A thrice-worthy man, is Grant," said Braegon with that outflashing smile again. "He saved my life when I fell with this barbed shaft in my leg."

"And do not forget you saved mine first," said Grant, a slow smile softening his hard-worn features.

Somehow, Laufeia found herself in the depths of full conversation with both of them, and enjoying it. They were enjoying it, too, she thought, glancing from Braegon's animated dark face to Grant's surprisingly pleasant smile.

They regaled her with all they knew of Mordred.

"Grant taught him archery," said Braegon.

Grant nodded. "That I did—a little."

"And, whether you can believe it or not, he and three others were taken captive by the Runnicorans, and the tale is that Mordred rescued them all by himself."

Laufeia felt a smile splaying across her face, and a laugh unexpectedly bubbled out. "Braegon, you are exaggerating now. Mirda would be ashamed of you!"

Braegon tossed his head back and laughed as well. "No, not at all! That is the way Therelane told it, and though Mordred gave him a look of ice—he would have preferred, I think, for the matter to remain dark)—he did not contradict him."

The way he spoke of Mordred's reaction was so vividly true that Laufeia laughed again. "I suppose I must believe it. Mordred's pride will not let himself be recognized for anything!"

"He also came to see us twice," continued Braegon, "here in the hospice. He has great gentleness of heart, your brother."

Laufeia smiled, though suddenly her throat was tight. "For those he loves, he will do anything," she said. She longed to see him again, her wonderful brother, full of so much pride and love and contradiction.

"Laufeia Kenhelm," said the voice abruptly beside her, and she whirled.

"Irene?"

"Aye, and I have words to speak to you." Irene led her firmly aside. "We're short-handed, lady Kenhelm. The wounded from this battle will be coming in for the rest of the day; our wards are filled, the surgeons have given up their own bedrooms to hold the patients, and soon they'll be lying in the halls."

"You want me to stay and help?" Laufeia's heart leapt gladly for the thought. She still felt the need to make herself very busy, very useful—her hands ached for a task under them.

Irene shrugged. "As I said, we're far short of the people we need to care for all these men. If you will. Any spare moments you have you are free to spend with your brother."

"I will," said Laufeia. "Oh, I surely will. Thank you, Irene."

Irene's brows rose, and she looked half-amused, as though she had not expected such a grateful response. "Well, if you feel that way."

"And Fiona?" asked Laufeia.

Irene looked sadder than Laufeia had yet seen her, though her voice was even as ever. "She's staying as well. If you'll permit me to suggest it, lady Kenhelm, I think you had best go to see her."

"Fred—" began Laufeia, afraid to hear the worst.

"I told her he's dying, and it's the truth," said Irene. "No, he hasn't yet, but she doesn't know how to go on. You had best find her." And with a nod down the hall as the only indicator, she disappeared in the other direction.

~

"Fenris Kenhelm!" Sergeant Garin Hawke barked the name with more sharpness than he meant to. "What are you doing here? Where were you yesterday? We were counting you among the wounded or the dead."

Fenris stared back at him, unresponsive, wide-eyed, and Garin reprimanded himself inwardly, knowing the heated barrage had only bewildered and frightened the boy.

"Speak on," he said more gently, "and do not be afraid. Were you wounded or separated?"

Fenris shook his head. "Captain Rhodes told me to leave with Mordred," he murmured, stumbling over the words. "I brought Mordred to the hospice."

"So it was Mordred who was hurt." Therelane Grey had said as much, but he had said nothing of Fenris. "And you stayed with him, forgetting to return here?"

"I stayed with him through the night," said Fenris, seeming dazed with the memory. "After that I slept, and I did not wake till this morning. I am sorry—I forgot to come, sir."

"Aye, let it be." The sergeant felt a nagging guilt, knowing that with anyone else he would have given at the very least a stern rebuke for such a breach of discipline, and, to be impartial, he ought to give the same to Fenris. But he could not bring himself to deliver it; not while the lad stood so quietly there, his eyes still shadowed underneath with exhaustion and anguish. And besides, his excuse was a reasonable one. "Let it be. You've returned now."

He would have liked to reach out and touch the tired, valiant boy, to be a father to him for a moment and not an officer. Something in him was quite certain that Fenris had never had a proper father. He thought of his own young son, scarcely three years old, and the longing grew stronger. But the habit of stern impartiality held fast.

"Go on," he said, jerking his head into the barracks. "Get some more rest. You'll be no good on the training ground yet. Rest well."

~

Inspector Dickson unseeingly held a soldier's arm steady as Priscilla secured a bandage around it.

He had hoped he would see the last of Mordred after the young man had finally left the hospice all those weeks ago. Why, oh why, did he have to be wrong?

He hated seeing Mordred hurt as much as he hated being near him. When Mordred suffered physically, it was then that Inspector Dickson could not help but see his vulnerability, his very youngness that was otherwise hidden by the scornful mask; and his heart would ache with sorrow and pity for him, and he would wish in spite of himself that their enmity was put away.

It had been that way, at first, the other time; well, Mordred had put a quick end to it *then*. Inspector Dickson's jaw tensed in anger. But thus far Mordred had not seen him, and he had only seen brief glimpses of Mordred. He had seen more of Laufeia; it seemed she was staying on to help the surgeons, like himself, and they had exchanged short greetings. He had not had a chance to explain to her why he was here, though he would have liked to—for his presence had shocked her, plainly, and he could not help the ugly idea that she would think he had followed Mordred here, the way Mordred had even accused him of doing.

"Thoughts on your mind, young man?" asked Priscilla as they moved on. Despite her way of ordering him hither and thither, and addressing him as she did the young twelve-year-old apprentice who ran errands—she was, after all, at least sixty—at times he liked her presence. She had become a fixture in his life, like Harris back in Bulca, neither welcome nor unwelcome, but simply there. At times he suspected that behind her nettlesome, mother-like dominance, she really was fond of him.

"Thoughts?" he repeated aloud. "Nothing, ma'am."

She tsked and thumped him lightly on the arm. "Mind how you're ripping that bandage! We're as short on cloth as winter in Arahad."

~

Fiona shut the door gently behind herself. There were two other men crowded onto the floor of the room now, but Fred still lay on the bed. The coverlet no longer lay over him; it must have gone to one who needed it more, and the myriad gashes in his clothing lay plain. His shirt was mere rags on him, showing the white and bloodied bandages that covered his body.

"My love, will you wed me when the first trees of spring are budding?"

"My love," she whispered, crossing to him and kneeling by the bed. His face was unchanged from yesterday, ashen-pale, as still as if he were already dead; his hand was still cold and flaccid. "My love, will you wake?"

"Will you be my wife tomorrow?"

"Will you wake, my beloved, *coenlag*?"

"I love you, Fiona Segelas."

"Farewell, my beloved."

She held his hand, kept silent watch on his slow breaths, waiting for the moment when they would cease altogether. She had no more tears left to weep. She faced the end dry-eyed.

~

Yesterday had slipped all through Laufeia's fingers without her knowing it. There had been Fiona to comfort—Fiona who had been so dazed, like a broken, wilted flower, seeming not to know what to do with herself. But Fiona had revived now; she went about steady, assured, no longer as one in a dream, and strangely her love for Fred seemed to shine out more through it, for it was not an empty, rigid strength that held her up. It was as though, knowing that she must let him go, she had submitted and let the love pour out and strengthen her instead.

And there had been an endless whirl of work, one that Laufeia had embraced gladly, but she had forgotten to seize the slow moments when they came, had forgotten Mordred. And she did not mean to let it go by another day.

She carefully pushed the door open.

The room was tiny, scarcely more than a cubicle for a bed; but it was bright with sunshine that poured in through a wide-open window on the opposite wall. On her left was an open closet, and on her right the bed, and on the bed—staring out the window—

"Mordred!"

He swung his head around, startled.

How different he looked! She realized that she had not seen him since the day he left Ceristen. There were tight lines of pain around his eyes and his mouth, contracting in his forehead. Dark rings of sleeplessness circled his eyes. He was so thin. Worst of all, the old darkness and suffering inside had not left him. If possible, it seemed to have grown.

"Mordred," she murmured, sorrowfully.

He studied her, a tired, quizzical look. "Laufeia? Nobody told me you were here."

"Oh, Mordred, where does it hurt?"

"Please, no, Laufeia."

"Tell me, Mordred! I want to know."

"Girls . . . " He breathed in raggedly and bit down hard on his lower lip. "Think you can kiss it and make it better. Well . . . you can't."

She stamped her foot. "Talking hurts you, I can see that."

Mordred stared coolly and shrugged the tiniest shrug, which made him catch his breath in a broken gasp.

"Is there nothing you can do without pain?" she cried, half in tears.

He answered nothing.

She flung herself onto a chair and sobbed, angry in part, in part sad, mostly miserable.

"I can see you are getting along very well in here," came Irene's voice, cutting dryly into her stormy weeping.

"Irene, go out," Mordred ordered sternly.

"I am not inclined to obey mandates coming from my patients," Irene retorted. "They rarely want what is good for them."

"Irene," said Mordred, his voice was steely and calm, "leave the room. At once. Your assistance is not required here. Laufeia will call you if it is."

"I will know if my assistance is required," returned Irene, and she went out.

No sooner had the door shut than Mordred lost consciousness and pitched back onto the bed.

Laufeia flew up in a panic and dashed over to him, putting her hand over his bloodless lips and brow, snatching his hands, but even as she gasped out his name his chest heaved violently and he came out of it with a shaken ghost of a laugh. "Little . . . goose," he told her, his words faint and breathless. "If I'd been dying, Irene—would have come back in. It was my silly self—repressing all the pain while I talked to her. She probably knew it . . . figures I'm properly punished now. Thinks I won't do it again."

"Oh, Mordred!" she exclaimed, exasperated by his willful stupidity.

His eyes drifted closed, ribs lifting in those quick, struggling breaths. He opened them again by a pitiful effort. "I'm sorry, Laufeia. I didn't want to make you—cry. It does hurt, if you want to know, it hurts everywhere, my chest, my shoulders, my stomach, my leg, my head—even my neck aches. Please, Laufeia. You know it's not easy for me to give in. I didn't want you to cry. Please forgive me."

"Of course I do," Laufeia choked out. She did know how hard it was for Mordred, how he hated to even mention an injury, much less how it hurt. She had been unfeeling herself, and put him in a situation where he was forced to give way, apologize, and try to comfort a childish sister.

Mordred's chest heaved again in a faint, hoarse cough. Laufeia sprang up.

"Let me get you some water, Mordred. Your throat must be dry."

"Oh, I'll be all right," said Mordred, relaxing against his pillow with a faint smile.

"Nonsense," said Laufeia and she rose to fetch the pitcher on a stand by the window.

The quarrel was over.

CHAPTER 33

"SO OUR DRAGON ATTACK PROVED largely a success," finished the general, bending over the many maps and diagrams on the table. The other captains in the room gathered around to study them as well.

"Excellent," said Jedediah Crayes lazily, not bothering to look, as he claimed to have all the maps memorized.

"Largely a success, aye," said Captain Murray. "But it was hardly a dent in the forces arrayed against us. We cannot hold them off indefinitely, nor can we begin to drive them away."

Jedediah Crayes shut his eyes in obvious exasperation. "Thank you, Captain Murray, for your encouraging sentiments which we have heard from several different sources a thousand times."

The room fell silent, and the informal meeting drifted away from the center of the discussion room to its edges.

"I suppose you haven't seen anything lately of that Mordred brat?" Jedediah Crayes remarked to the general.

The general looked up, his dark eyes saddening suddenly. "He is under the care of a hospice in the city. He was severely injured in the battle when his dragon fell on him."

Jedediah Crayes blinked at him briefly. With an exclamation he leaped up and dashed out of the room.

~

Laufeia reached up, stretching on tiptoe to tuck the fluttering cloth into the window frame. "There, does it not look home-like?" she said to Mordred, surveying the bit of white linen hanging over the top of the window like a curtain.

Mordred looked over as though trying to appear interested for her sake. He managed a tolerant, tired smile and stared at the wall across again.

There were footsteps banging in the hall. The door slammed open with a force that made Laufeia jump, and a lithe, hawk-faced man stormed in. "What do you think you were doing, you idiot?" he shouted at Mordred, flinging an accusing finger at him. "Getting yourself practically killed in the stupid battle, and then not telling me a word about it! No, Jedediah Crayes waits in the dark for three days before anybody thinks to *enlighten* him to what is going on. 'Oh yes, make sure Jedediah Crayes doesn't find out about this. He doesn't want to know that I was stupid and let dragons fall on top of me.' How witless can you get? What do you think you were doing? Is that *enjoyable* to you, stupidity? An enjoyable pastime?"

Laufeia took a step forward, about to tell him to stop shouting at Mordred, when she noticed that Mordred was sitting up, his eyes bright and an amused grin pervading his face.

"Are you quite finished?" he asked in his lilting, mock-serious voice, a voice Laufeia had not heard him use since his return from Delgrass.

"No! Yes!" The man swung his arm in an irritated gesture, hitting the wall.

Mordred started to laugh, but it ended in a gasp and he lay back, biting his lip until it turned white.

Jedediah Crayes' entire demeanor instantly changed, his face sobering. He came forward, twitching his head slightly in a movement of anger or disapproval. "Little idiot," he muttered, but the tone was almost gentle. "Are you all right? No, don't tell me, I know your formula. 'I'm fine.' You're not fine. Dragon fell on top of you? Do you mind explaining why you're *not* dead?"

"To begin with," said Mordred wearily, though he still smiled a little as he spoke, "the dragon was shot close to the ground. It didn't fall particularly far. Also it fell with the saddle over my chest, so I wasn't quite so crushed."

"Crushed enough, I should imagine," Jedediah Crayes muttered grimly, his gaze flickering to Mordred's chest. "Did you break every single one of your ribs?"

Mordred took a shallow breath and flinched again. "Sometimes it feels like it," he murmured faintly, the pretense down for a moment. His eyes blinked and he looked up at Jedediah Crayes. "But I'm all right." He smiled oddly. "You needn't worry about me."

"I don't worry about anyone," said Jedediah Crayes gruffly. "I have no friends to worry about."

"I know," said Mordred with that peculiarly knowing smile. He shut his eyes.

"Who are you anyway?"

It took a moment for Laufeia to realize he was barking the question at her. She lifted her chin and met his sharp gaze steadily. "I am his sister, sir."

"I believe you," he said with a careless shrug, dropping the close scrutiny. "Princess of Dirion, eh?"

"*What*? Mordred, *what did you—*"

"He made me tell him, sister," said Mordred, sounding like if he were less exhausted he would have laughed. "It is all right. I trust him not to repeat it in public settings."

Laufeia took a deep breath and let it out slowly.

~

"Mordred!"

Mordred managed a small smile for Therelane, and tried to conceal how tired he was of the level of shock that he was greeted with. Did he really look so dreadful? he wondered disinterestedly. Jedediah Crayes had been far preferable to the dull repetition that everyone else gave.

"Mordred—" Therelane stammered, coming forward into the room.

"Did you slip away just to come see me?" Mordred inquired flatly.

"Nay! Of course not! There's little going on right now. I asked leave. Are you—Mordred, are you—"

"Am I all right? Hardly. Am I suffering? Not as much as a few days ago. Am I tired of people looking at me like I turned into a werevulture? Rather. Thank you for asking."

He saw Therelane's face fall and knew how sarcastic he had sounded. "I'm—sorry, Therelane." He shut his eyes, turning his face away into the pillow. "I can't seem to keep a rein on what comes out of my mouth."

Therelane was beside him, laying his hand quickly on Mordred's. "No, Mordred. It's all right, truly. It was a lack-wit's reaction I gave, only I was surprised—but I should have known better. Besides, I behaved as bad as you when I was recovering, if not worse."

Mordred opened his eyes and sent Therelane a sheepish grin. "I doubt it. But thank you."

"If Irene comes to see you as often as she did me," Therelane went on brightly, "I shouldn't wonder you feel snappish. Five minutes of Irene is enough to set most anyone on edge."

It was an attempt to divert him, and a rather obvious one, but Mordred did not care. He was ready to talk to someone else who knew. "If only she would not come and tell me that she hopes I am getting enough sleep, that she hopes I am not exerting myself, that she hopes no-one has been exciting me or upsetting me. If only she would not prod my broken leg every single day and talk about how she hopes it will not heal crooked, and about the hundreds of young men she saw who broke their legs and never walked straight again!"

He knew he had pressed himself too far and bit his lip against the arrows of pain shooting through his ribs. His body was trembling and sweating with the strain of speaking so long and loudly. But he was glad to have said it.

Therelane's hand tightened on his own. "Aye, I know. It will be all right, Mordred. I hated to have her talking to me like that as well, but if you were really in danger of a crooked leg she would tell you straight out, not just talk about it on and on."

"I guessed that," said Mordred faintly; he had, but it felt that much better to hear Therelane say it aloud.

"You're tired," said Therelane. "I ought to go, most likely."

"Nay, don't—it will pass."

"Maybe, but I haven't long to stay anyway. Mordred—" Therelane hesitated. There was an unspoken anxiety of some kind in his soft grey eyes, something he wanted to say.

"Aye?"

"Mordred, you know the leader?"

Mordred felt a sick twinge in his stomach with the sudden, sharp return of memories he had forgotten for days. "What about him?"

"How he found you that night—and I knocked him out. How I—I failed to kill him. Mordred, I didn't even think."

Mordred could barely remember. He felt a vague hint of recollection, of a sharp pain tracing through his arm, of the leader's face framed against the stars. Therelane saying something.

Therelane was watching him, his eyes filled with worry and guilt.

"You haven't anything to blame yourself for, Therelane," he said softly. "We were both a little—shaken. Besides, what would killing him have done in the end? Someone else would have taken command of the army."

Therelane nodded, his face easing—but not completely. "Mordred, he still wants—"

"*Hush,*" said Mordred fiercely, not caring for the pain that flooded his chest at the vehement motion. "Don't talk about that to me. Who knows who might hear. It doesn't matter, Therelane."

The enemy was still outside Orden. They had not breached the defense. And he? He was trapped here until he healed. He was safer than he had been for months. And the last thing that he wanted was to talk about the leader to Therelane.

"All right," Therelane said unwillingly. "I—"

"Go," Mordred said sharply. "Please, go."

He buried his face in the pillow until the door opened and Therelane's footsteps faded down the hall.

~

There was a strange, eerie sameness to the room from day to day. Fred rested on the bed, clinging to life by a frail thread that should break at any moment. Fiona came to his side each day for an hour, or as long as Irene could spare her, watching as his face slowly hollowed and his body grew gaunt. She gave him water, small dipperfuls, and held his dry lips shut until he had swallowed it. But he never moved or made the slightest sign of consciousness.

Yet strangely, this day, a hope budded painfully in her heart.

He had already lasted beyond what Irene had expected of him. "A few days," she had said, surely meaning no more than two or three. Yet this was the sixth day, and he still lived. Could it be—

She did not want to let herself think it, did not want to let herself hope. Better to say farewell, and be at peace. But the thought wormed its way through, for in her heart she did not really want to stop it.

Could it be—that because his body had held onto life those few days longer, that a balance might be tipped? Could his frame, battered and blood-drained, begin to slowly heal?

And she thought of Fred's loving face looking upon hers, not as her betrothed but as her husband, and thought of sun on Thiranu, and a home for the two of them, and a child, all the things that she had put behind her, and knew that she wanted him to live again. And she began to cry, because while she had accepted his death, its promise had been resigned and bittersweet. But now, the grief would return tenfold.

She did not cry long. Only once had she wept with total abandon at his bedside. She only let her head rest quietly on his chest, an aching storm lashing within her.

At last she rose to go. But while she still held his hand fast, gazing down at him, she felt it stir distinctly against her own.

A tide of wild emotion surged through her so shockingly swift and powerful that she sank to her knees again and buried her head in her hands.

It was moments before she could stand. His hand did not move again, but she took it and kissed it lightly before she left, joy quivering through her whole self. She forgot even to be afraid to hope.

~

Mordred watched the sun-motes dance in the shaft that fell across his bed. For some reason, the pain was worse today; he did not know why—he had learned there was no reason to it. It was strange how when one's body hurt so much, nothing seemed to matter or be real except the pain.

Someone entered, not Irene's steps and not Laufeia's. Mordred looked up, and saw Inspector Dickson.

He fell back against the pillow, teeth shut hard. How *dare* he come now—at all the times when he was weakest, he delighted to come—

"What do you want?" he asked through tight lips, staring up towards the ceiling, refusing to look at Inspector Dickson.

"I've been told to see to the wound on your arm."

"What needs to be seen about it?" The effort needed to keep his voice and face cold and distant, free from any hint of pain, was intense. If Inspector Dickson did not go soon enough, he would end by passing out again . . .

~

Inspector Dickson looked down at the young man's hard, disdainful face, feeling more tired than ever of the fight. Maybe—maybe Mordred was tired of it, too; he had none of the usual sarcastic rejoinders.

He was close, so close to admitting how much he had been in the wrong, so close to saying the words that he almost believed—*I'm sorry.* Because, after all, he *had* been in the—

Mordred spoke, his voice heavy with bitterness. "Well, go on. Or are you wondering where you left the salt, to rub into it?"

The injury of that blow, falling as it did into his own contrite thoughts, maddened Inspector Dickson like a taunted bull. He had been wrong; Mordred was not tired of the fight, not sorrowful, not remorseful. The more he thought on it, the more unfair it seemed to him, and the more furious he became. If Mordred wanted to keep the strife alive, so be it! He would give him what he asked for. He would enter wholeheartedly into everything that Mordred called him. He would stoke the fires as hot as Mordred wished them to be.

"I seem to have left it behind today," he said deliberately in answer to Mordred's gibe about the salt. "I hope my presence will be enough to discomfit you."

With a cold restraint he set about cleaning the wound. He did not try to hurry through the task.

~

Inspector Dickson came daily to look at Mordred's arm after that. Mordred pretended that it was because Inspector Dickson had asked for the duty, though he did not believe any such thing. But he began to see a change in him, as their paths crossed again and again. For a little while he could not discern what it was.

Then he saw that Inspector Dickson was not trying to rein in his anger any longer. He no longer tried to argue his own justification from deeds in the past. More than that, he sought to provoke Mordred. He *wanted* Mordred to be angry with him.

So Mordred was glad. It had been growing hard to hate a man who did not want to be hated.

~

Fiona took Fred's hand, and a thrill coursed through her. For the first time she was sure that it felt different—the past two days she had wondered, but now she was sure. It was *warm* again.

She had not told anyone of that wondrous moment, two days gone, when his hand had pressed on hers. It was for her to remember, secret and joyful, for she knew all too well that though a sign of hope to her, it was no real promise.

But now—now—

A radiant smile of pure gladness broke free of her heart and parted her lips, and she laid Fred's warm, living hand lovingly on her cheek.

It made no movement against her, yet it felt as though it might at any moment; it was the pulsing, strong-boned thing she knew.

And then, as the love and excitement whelmed in her and took away her breath, the movement did come, and the fingers brushed in a gesture weak as summer's wind across her cheek. Her head flew up.

Fred's eyelids opened slowly, heavily, as if it were an effort to prop them up, and his gaze looked directly into hers.

"Fred, beloved, *coenlag*," she cried softly, breathless, half in tears. "Do you know me?"

"Fiona," he said, the word leaving his lips in a voice as weak as the movement of his fingers had been.

She pressed his hand to her brow and let her joyous tears fall on it.

"Fiona," he said again, and those fingers moved gently in hers.

"It is well, Fred," she assured him, lifting her eyes. "Nay, it is very well. Do not fear."

"My love," he said, and his eyes closed wearily with an expression of immeasurable peace.

"Rest," she murmured to him, and rising she stooped to set a kiss on his brow. Then with swift, decisive steps she left the room.

"Irene!" she called, the serene authority in her voice strange to herself. It was a part of the gladness overflowing through her blood, it was hers to command for the moment. "Irene, Fred Thorne is awake. You must tell us how to tend to him."

Irene's mouth opened. She put a surprised hand to her head, and slowly acquiescence dawned. "Yes—" she muttered. "You are right."

But it was Laufeia who ran across the ward and put her arms around Fiona, weeping and almost laughing for joy. "He is awake, Fiona," she repeated again and again, half questioning, half marveling. "He is awake."

"In truth, he was asleep again before I left him," admitted Fiona.

This time Laufeia did laugh in earnest, blotting back the tears with a quick hand. "That is for the best, of course."

"But he is awake." Fiona looked up to a beam of sun falling through one high window, and it seemed the most glorious thing in the world. "And he will live."

CHAPTER 34

THERELANE TRAVERSED THE CITY QUICKLY. It was a week since Sergeant Garin had last given him leave, and he was eager to visit the hospice again, for Mordred—and for the other reason that had nothing to do with Mordred.

Mordred seemed still listless, and Therelane could not easily restrain his distress at the sight of how tired and ill his friend was. Even so, his face no longer looked so death-white, and the taut lines of constant pain were eased. "Has it been better, Mordred?" he asked, coming to the bedside.

Mordred answered with an almost imperceptible shrug. "I'm fine," he said, and Therelane wished he had not, because it did not seem true or even laughable. It seemed a mockery.

"Look," he said quickly, setting on the bed the thing he had brought. "It's your sword. I took it after we saw you off to Orden City, and used it in the battle because I'd lost mine."

Mordred was not interested, and it showed in his face; he looked so unimpressed it almost hurt. "Why don't you keep it?" he said tonelessly.

"Oh, I was given another. I don't need it," Therelane explained stumblingly, wishing he had not brought the sword at all.

"It's all right," said Mordred. "Put it by the bed. I don't—care."

Therelane stared at Mordred's face, wishing, not for the first time, that he could see beyond that impervious wall. The wall was not always up—last time it had not been. And it came to Therelane: was it his own words that had thrown up the breach? Was Mordred fearing that he would speak of the leader again?

I won't, Mordred, he wanted to say. *Not now that I understand it hurts you.* But deep within he was afraid to; he was afraid to be wrong, and to be cut off again with sharp words.

He said nothing. And the silence lingered fragile and twisted between them until at last he left.

~

Laufeia was the one to put a stop to Inspector Dickson's coming.

It was a hard day for Mordred, who was feeling sick and wretched with the pain, and did not want to think of Inspector Dickson, much less endure his presence. When he arrived, Mordred hated him more than ever, and the anger swept up in him like sudden flame, familiar but no longer satisfying. No, it had never really satisfied, but once it had buried the ache within, and that it did no longer.

He lay rigid under Inspector Dickson's hands, as though it were fire touching him, loathing the helpless sensation. There were no words between them this day, as there sometimes were—only anger, vibrating thick in the air like thrumming harpstrings. Inspector Dickson removed the old bandage and wrapped the new one with painstaking care.

"Your fishwife's tongue seems to have deserted you today," said Inspector Dickson shortly as he rose to leave.

Mordred, who could not let him have the last word, flared back, "A fishwife's tongue I may have, but at least it knows the faces that deserve its lash."

He did not know why Inspector Dickson suddenly checked at the door, but when he had gone, Laufeia leaned there against the door-frame, her eyes fixed levelly on him. Her hand slipped slowly down from the frame, and clenched into a small fist at her side.

"What was *that*?" she asked.

He stared expressionlessly back at her and shrugged. Let her make what she would of it. He was not here to offer her explanations.

But Laufeia did not need explanations. "Talk to me," she said, her eyes snapping with the same hot stubbornness as his own. "And I *won't* take silence for an answer. How long has this been happening?"

"What?" he asked coldly.

"This—this madness of childish insults and scornful silence! It was like seeing you and Ahearn all over again."

"He comes every day to see to my arm," said Mordred. It was not the answer that she was looking for, but she did not know that.

"Oh?" Laufeia looked more indignant still, and he almost thought she would stamp her foot as she had when they quarreled days ago. "Well, it is going to stop at once. Why has no one taken notice of this before? Who put him in charge of you? And you, you ought to be ashamed of yourself! Are you still angry at him about that, all those months ago now—"

"Don't, Laufeia," he said, low and frantic, panic choking off his breath, afraid of what he might say to her if she went on.

Her face fell and she touched his cheek with her light, firm fingers. "I'm sorry, Mordred. I was too quick to judge the situation."

"No, you were right," he said, shaking his head wearily. "But don't—please, please do not speak of it again."

She looked at him helplessly, in sadness, anxiety, and frustration. "Mordred, I fear to rake up what I do not understand. But I cannot bear to see you like this."

"Like what?" He looked away from her.

"Bitter. Silent. Like the brother of mine who was consumed with guilt and grief after Fenris' accident, the brother who did not trust the world—not the brother who teased and laughed afterwards."

"Am I like that, Laufeia?" Stricken, sick at heart, he looked to her again.

This time it was she who glanced away, her lip trembling uncertainly. "No—and yes. You do not brood in the same tight shell you did before. You do not wall away every thought and feeling, and I am glad of that. Yet at the same time it is even worse, because it is deeper. You turn your face away from me with the look of—of one to whom joy means nothing. The only time you have smiled is when that man came, that strange man who scolded you like he would a child. You are not angry at the world; you are only dead to it. Indeed, the only person for whom you seem to have anger is that Inspector. It is as though you spend all your anger on him and have none of it left for anything else. No anger—and no joy, either."

Mordred turned his face again into the bedclothes, dumb with the impact of the words; for cruel though they had not meant to be, cruel they were to him. This was what he was to Laufeia! Bitter, silent, not like he used to be. Not how she wished him to be. And he—he could change none of it.

His throat ached beyond endurance, and a cold ache pulsed in his chest, and dry eyes he pressed unseeing against the bed. He had tried to hide the truth. He had not wanted to burden her and Fenris with his suffering and his anger. But it was all no use, it had never been any use.

"Mordred." Her small, fiercely strong hands shook his shoulders. He caught his breath and tears jolted to his eyes at the grating flash through his broken collarbone. "Come back. Are you awake? If you can only tell me all that is the matter—I understand that you bear pain from what happened in Delgrass, Mordred, I understand."

"No," said Mordred.

It came on him very quietly, with Laufeia's words, that the pain of Delgrass was dead.

Not eradicated, not healed, but quite dead. Delgrass and the Claw, their very mention once a lash in open wounds, now deflected dully off a numb scar. He saw now that that was why the anger could no longer satisfy, no longer bury the hurt; for it was other hurts that tormented him now, having heaped themselves on the old one until it died out. When exactly it had happened, he could not say. He had run from the memories so long, yet for a long time, it seemed, it had been the leader shadowing his thoughts instead of the werevulture. The Claw seemed a world away, flattened and faded against the leering patchwork of the war, its horror spent.

"No, Laufeia," he said again flatly.

All that was left was his anger. His useless, ravening anger.

And that he held, because he had held it too long. He *knew,* without daring to put it in so many words to himself, that it was destroying him, but he did not care. He did not know how or want to let it go.

~

"See how bright the sun is," said Fiona, pulling aside the coarse drapes that covered the window and letting the lone shaft of light spill into a waterfall of glory that flooded the corners of the room. "And it is hot. The days of summer grow."

Fred's eyes turned to the light, and he smiled; but they looked more gladly on her. Speech came slowly to him still, and in great weakness;

so though Fiona spent all the time she could by his side, often scarcely a word was exchanged between them. Only their gazes fixed on one another, hers with all the steadfastness and love in her heart—while his seemed often full of wonder, and he would look on her unfailingly as though drinking in the sight like a river of life, and not tire of it.

Yet now trouble crept across his features, and his lips parted as he struggled to speak.

"What ails you, my beloved?" she asked, resting her hand on his brow to soothe him.

"I know not . . . how I came here," he murmured. "Where is . . . my brother, Daren? What happened to me?"

And Fiona could not give him the answers that he sought, at least not in the fullness that he desired them. She only touched his forehead again, and laid her hands on his.

~

"Aye, Marcus Segelas. What is it?" Sergeant Garin rose and looked inquiringly at the young soldier who had entered his private quarters. Marcus had sprung back resiliently from his brother's death, though his face sometimes bore a grave look that it had rarely borne, and his laughter came a little less readily than before. But underneath he was much the same; and now his eyes were glinting with a conspiratorial light, and his whole face shone underneath with eagerness and mischief.

"I and some of the others have been talking, Sergeant," he said and paused expectantly.

"Go on."

"About Fenris, sir. He's missing his brother terribly, and it's hard on him not knowing how he is."

"He hasn't asked to see him," said Sergeant Garin, raising an eyebrow.

"And he won't, sir." Marcus took an intense step forward. "He's shy of asking favors at all, but now that, you know, he went missing after the battle—well, now he doesn't think it would be a good idea to press you about leaving. Or at least, that's what we're pretty certain is the trouble. He didn't tell us, but he can't hide everything."

"So you all—however many of you it was—schemed to come and ask me instead?"

Marcus squirmed but grinned unashamedly. "If—if it's not too much to ask, sir, and if he can be spared, you might consider giving him a few days off."

Sergeant Garin shook his head, not in immediate negation but in amusement. "You schemed that, too, did you?"

"He'll be far better on the training ground and other work if his mind is set easy on Mordred, sir." Marcus was almost quivering with anticipation of the answer.

Once more Sergeant Garin shook his head. "He has it," he said. "Three days' leave. And the next one of you that comes prying for the same trick gets kicked out the back door."

Marcus sprang away delightedly, forgetting to say so much as "Thank you."

~

Captain Rhodes dismounted from his horse and tilted his head up towards the wide front of the hospice, narrowing his eyes against the whiteness of the overcast sky. Though it had been a fortnight and more since he saw Mordred writhing in torturous pain, he was fearful of how he would find him.

But there were no moans, no stifled screams. Mordred lay quiet and calm, propped to a half-sitting position, and when he saw Captain

Rhodes his eyes lit, and the shadow of a smile darted across his face. "Captain Rhodes," he said in greeting.

"Mordred!" Captain Rhodes answered gladly. "You seem far improved indeed from when I last saw you."

Mordred reacted with confusion. "When did you see me?"

"The night of the battle," answered Captain Rhodes. "I was with you in the hospice."

"Oh," said Mordred, a little blankly, and was silent.

He was the next to speak, however. "Captain Rhodes, how go the matters of war?"

Captain Rhodes' brow furrowed. He would not have discussed such things of his own wish, but Mordred had asked. "There is rumor that the leader's injury was sore, and he has been laid by. The dragon battle was successful, and that, too, was a blow to them. But their forces are slowly gaining at the north border. I know not how this will end . . . but it is like to go on for many more months, at such a rate. And there will be small joy in the victory, no matter to whom it comes. War is an evil thing, Mordred Kenhelm."

"I thought war was swift," said Mordred softly, looking not at Captain Rhodes but away towards the window. "Swift, and terrible, and I feared and dreaded it. But now I see that there is evil in the slowness, too. It is a rot eating us away in an endless death, and that is worse than a quick flame that burns through and is gone."

Captain Rhodes bent his head. "Food grows short, with so much of our trade cut off, and it will be shorter still; for with the men taken many fields lie unsown and in the autumn there will be scant harvest. Aye, and in the north, villages have been displaced by roaming bands of the enemy—houses razed, fields salted."

Mordred's eyes were distant. "None of it should have happened," he said between shut teeth.

"Let us speak of better things," said Captain Rhodes.

"Such as?" Mordred gave a strange shrug, and caught his breath in the middle of it. "In the end, there is nothing else to speak of."

For a time they were both quiet.

"Mordred," said Captain Rhodes at last, slowly and meaningly, "how goes it with you?"

Mordred's quick upfling of the head showed that he understood Captain Rhodes' question. Their eyes held in wordless intensity, and then with a small, detached sigh Mordred lay back and stared at the ceiling. "As well as can be expected," he returned coolly.

"So you have not—" Captain Rhodes broke off, knowing the answer already.

"I have *not,*" said Mordred. "His name is gall in my mouth, he did me nameless wrong, and you expect me to make peace with him?"

"If you do not, you will never be at peace in yourself," said Captain Rhodes, longing earnestly to help the young man before him. "The past is behind you and cannot be undone; you will only ruin your life by wishing otherwise. Cease the fighting."

"You are one to talk so," said Mordred sarcastically. "*You* are one to counsel me to put amity before enmity!"

He shut his mouth swiftly on the words. Pain, contrition, and panic swept across his countenance.

Captain Rhodes merely stared at him, struck speechless by the open truth slapped into his face.

"I should not have said it." A shudder ripped through Mordred. "I should not have flaunted that at you. It was the act of—no true friend."

Captain Rhodes came fully to himself. He hurried to the bed and put a hand on Mordred's shivering shoulders. "No, Mordred. Do not alarm yourself. I—I truly do not hold it against you. They were true words."

Mordred quieted under him and looked up. "But wrongly spoken," he said simply.

"I forgive you, Mordred, nor do I think the less of you for them. I beg you, do not sorrow needlessly over the matter. But I must go now."

He wheeled and left the room with urgent step.

CHAPTER 35

CAPTAIN RHODES STRODE INTO MITHEREN and through the narrow stone-paved halls. He confronted Captain Murray in a short, arched passageway where a second corridor cut through it a short way beyond them, and catching hold of the other man's shoulder he pulled him around.

Captain Murray shrugged loose and looked at him with surprise and scarcely veiled disgust, but Captain Rhodes dropped his arm and merely looked at the older, taller man.

"You hate me."

Captain Murray's grim brows raised in wonderment. "What have you ever done that I should love you?"

The younger man looked at him blankly, in silenced helplessness, and the conversation seemed like to end there, an empty wall rearing up higher and higher between them while neither spoke.

"You sneered at my speech and my past," said Captain Murray harshly and with such suddenness that Captain Rhodes started. "You saw me as uncouth—you all but said it. And the general favors you above me, aye, he *always* has. You, the spoiled, mewlish weakling, have his trust and goodwill. But I suppose that a spoiled child is better than a traitor. That is what you called me, do you forget it? And if you have not forgotten, then it is not a wonder that the general still thinks it of me, too. And you—you speak of my hatred as if it were astonishing?"

"Dunstan Murray," said Captain Rhodes hoarsely, "do not speak those words to my remembrance. A traitor, I called you, yes, a traitorous wretch. It is true; I do not forget it. And in that moment I did hate you, too, for I believed it. But not now! I have rued it years, and if you can, I beg you to forgive me for it. It was the lies that led me to believe such evil—yet nay, I admit there was already jealousy in my heart for you that lent my ear to Captain Rhinehart's tales."

"Captain Rhinehart," Murray muttered. He stared distantly over Captain Rhodes' shoulder as if he had not heard.

"I am ashamed to have thought that you would ever take part in Rhinehart's treachery. But heed me, Captain Murray, you speak riddling words. Do not attribute my unkind thoughts to the general! He could not believe such things of you, he never has. And not always does he place me in precedence over you; what of the dragon battle? Captain Murray, he values your cool head, your strategic abilities, your composure in danger and battle. Would he so readily place one in command whom he did not trust?"

"You speak strangely, as though you would indeed encourage me," said Captain Murray, now staring directly at him. "What has come over you, that you speak thus?"

Captain Rhodes bent his head, and he spoke falteringly, feeling his way through the words. "I have come to know a young man—Mordred Kenhelm is his name. He is valiant-hearted, full of compassion, and dear to me, even as a brother. Yet there is anger, deep-struck, deadly anger between him and another man. It grieves me to see the bitterness gnawing at him, and I would that he did not become even as we are, with bitterness of years between us and not merely months. I counseled him to put his grievance aside.

"But he was angered with me, and rightly so. For how can I counsel a man to make peace, when I have not made peace myself? Therefore

. . . I will no longer uphold my end of our hatred, Captain Murray, and I will not seek to be a rival to you or scorn you for what I perceived as lack. And I beg your forgiveness again for all the wrongs that I did you in the past; I confess that all you said of me is true, and well do you despise me. I will not wonder if—if you still despise me."

"Mordred Kenhelm," said Captain Murray slowly. "That name is known to me as a young man who gave me smiles such as scarce a man has given me save for the general. It is because of him that you did this?"

Captain Rhodes nodded.

"It is in my mind that I owe him much," said Captain Murray.

Captain Rhodes looked still at the ground.

"Lift up your head, you foolish child," said Captain Murray, and yet there was a rough kindness in his tone, strained from disuse. "I know deceit and falsehood, and they are not in your face. Am I such a beast that you think I will disregard your confession and sorrow as naught?"

Captain Rhodes lifted his head. "I must beg your forgiveness again, for I was indeed unsure of your answer. And . . . I thank you that you have answered as you did. For though you may not believe it, I have longed for your approval and often sought it. If you had turned your back on me now after I bared my confession, that would have been a sore wound."

Captain Murray looked at him with ever-increasing wonder and shook his head. "I have learned more of you in these few moments than in the ten years I knew you before. You yearned for my good favor? A small way you had of showing it."

"I yearned for it more than any other's, if only because I could not have it," answered Captain Rhodes with a certain weariness. "But no, I could never express it openly. What strange, tangled creatures we are."

"I pardon you fully for your fear that I would despise you," said Captain Murray gruffly. "It was well-founded. I fear that I often was the very boor you believed me to be. And my silent hatred and cold words to you were themselves cruel; if you, being true-hearted enough to confess your own wrongs to me, can also forgive me mine, I beg that you would do so."

"I forgive them willingly," said Captain Rhodes, and tears were in his eyes. Yet he smiled. "Nor will I lift them up again. They are forgotten between us."

"As are yours, Finley Rhodes," said Captain Murray with a stern, true weight in his words. His face was grim as he said it, but the care and lines upon it seemed less than they ever had. "Listen, when you first poured out your heart, it seemed to me that you were offering me more than confession; you were offering me friendship, I who have no friend, save perhaps the general. Nay, I will not claim even that; I am too hard for him."

"The general loves every soul of Orden," exclaimed Captain Rhodes firmly, "and do you think to make yourself an exception? No man is too hard for his love. But as for me, you were not wrong. I will gladly be your friend, Dunstan Murray. I have been your unwilling enemy too long."

Captain Murray was very silent, but his jaw clenched sporadically as though he were repressing some great emotion.

"Captain Rhinehart called himself my friend," he said at last as one recalling an old and evil memory. "And I regarded him as such. I had no reason to doubt him. And for *that*, I was called his consort and ally in the day of his betrayal." He breathed in with a thick sound. "When he seized the power, he did not turn on me or seek to imprison me; I think he believed that because of my earlier trust in him I would not oppose him, and perhaps he thought to persuade me easily if he had lasted longer on the throne than he did. He called himself my friend," he repeated with a strange, tired incredulity.

Captain Rhodes listened silently. He understood, with a quiet sureness, that Captain Murray was recounting this not to cast doubt on the friendship offered him, but to unburden a dark hurt. That he told it at all was, indeed, a gesture of trust. "So it was all a lie? Even his leniency in the time of his betrayal?"

"He craved only power," said Captain Murray bitterly. "He was mad for it. When I confronted him about the lies to my name, after he had been imprisoned, he laughed at me and cursed me to his own fate. I almost laid hands on him and slew him in that moment."

He cut himself short. "It is not good to think on, or speak of. There are better things before us."

Captain Rhodes nodded. "Someone comes," he said, lifting his head toward the sound of footsteps. The general appeared out of the intersecting corridor beyond them.

He halted, and his dark eyes swept them both. "Captain Murray," he said, inclining his head toward the older man. "You are wanted."

"My general," said Captain Murray, coming forward, and they disappeared together down the hall.

~

"Here she comes again!" The young soldier on the floor laughed, but not rudely. One side of his face was wrapped in bandages; his cheek had been slashed open and he had lost the sight in that eye. "You are on time, as always, *fira luithra*; but he has been waiting for your coming."

Fiona sent a smile his way and continued to the bed. Lady of Mercy, they called her, all throughout the hospice now. "Why?" she had asked

Fred, touched and humbled. "I only do what is asked of me; nothing great, nothing extraordinary that they should give me such a tender name."

Fred looked on her with his most intensely loving look, and said, "Indeed, why would they not?" as though that were an answer in itself.

Each day he grew better, and even if it were by the most infinitesimal of measures Fiona saw it and marked it with ever-rising joy. Though he still spoke slowly, the words no longer came with effort and long pauses. When she sat at his side, his hand would tighten in a rhythmic way on hers; and at times he reached up to touch her face with his gentle gesture. Yesterday, seventeen days since the battle and his wounding, he had raised himself up to sit on his own. He did not remember the battle, nor what had happened to him. Neither of them expected he ever would.

Here, strangely, to Fiona the war seemed both very near and quite far away. Near, for she tended its casualties every day, and every day there were more. Far away, for she had her betrothed near to her and it would be a long time before the war approached to take him away again. She even told herself that the war might end first, and she was willing to believe it.

~

Jedediah Crayes perched on the edge of the wide-open window, swinging his legs. "How mends the little fool today?"

He saw the perturbed look that the boy's spitfire sister flung him, and grinned in satisfaction.

The boy himself looked better than he had—better in certain ways, at least. Jedediah Crayes did not like the oddly haunted, defensive look in his eyes and the apathetic way he smiled in answer to the question.

"Talk to me," he growled, standing up and bracing his arms against the frame of the window.

"I'm—" Mordred broke off, the defensive look growing stronger as he eyed Jedediah Crayes.

"That's right," said Jedediah Crayes. "I'm not going to take 'fine' for an answer. Very good. What are you tearing yourself up over?"

"I won't tell you," said Mordred with a stiffness that made Jedediah Crayes' brows snap together and an odd sense of hurt tug at his heart.

"Mordred," said his sister with tired sternness, placing her hand on his shoulder.

He flinched away. "Don't touch me."

Jedediah Crayes released a loud grunt of exasperation. "*Talk to me.* Is it the werevulture business? Is it the leader? Is it bed rest?"

Laufeia's eyes met his, startled. She came across to him in a flash and stretched up to whisper in his ear. "You know about the werevulture?"

"I know everything," retorted Jedediah Crayes, and repented with a sigh. After all, the woman was being serious. "Yes, I know; he told me."

"Then you know about the Inspector."

Jedediah Crayes' brow arched. "Indeed. Is he what's causing trouble?"

"He is here, helping the surgeons, like I am." She put her face in her hands in a gesture of weariness. "I managed to keep them apart, but it does not seem to make a difference in him."

"Little fool," Jedediah Crayes muttered. "If *I* can't cheer his mood, then who's going to do it?"

The door opened and Jedediah Crayes edged uncomfortably away from Laufeia, aware of the concerned and affectionate nature of his tone, face, and posture.

But it was only a thin boy whose dark forelock of hair was stuck to his face with the sweat of his hurry there. "Mordred," he said, soft voice anxious as he came into the room, and he did not pay the slightest mind to the other two.

Mordred sat up, a glint of life coming into his face. "Fenris."

Laufeia took Jedediah Crayes' arm and jerked him towards the door. Jedediah Crayes, taken aback, shook her loose. "What do you want?" he hissed.

"We're going to leave them alone," said Laufeia firmly. "That is what he needs."

Jedediah Crayes scowled and thought of arguing. Instead, he yielded and let the slight girl drag him out of the room with a grip that felt like an iron cuff about his wrist. He shut the door and leaned against it with a resigned sigh. After all, she was probably right.

He sighed again. Monitoring someone's problems, and trying to fix them, required an astonishing drain on mental resources.

It seemed slightly unfair that behind the door that stripling one-third of his age was probably bending everything into shape without even breaking a sweat.

~

Papers fluttered under the hard, sure fingers as the words rang out. "Nineteen, twenty, twenty-one, twenty-two. That is all?"

"All." The man shifted wearily, but the Paraki never sat, and certainly no-one would sit while in the Paraki's standing presence. There had been a respite from that while he was gone, over a fortnight it had been, laid low in the healing tents with his leg sliced open and a head wound, but now he was back.

"And the statistics in the north?" demanded Cern Dersturi. The messenger handed him a second sheaf of papers.

When they first brought him back unconscious, there had been near panic in the army, for they feared his death. But he had recovered fully, though his officers marked at this time or that a strange wandering light, or dullness as it were, in his eyes.

"The advancements have been slow in my absence," observed Cern Dersturi now. "Are all my captains blind beggars, that I must lead them by the hand to show them how war is done?" He turned aside and kicked a chair. "Am I to return at last to the king of Runnicor with empty hands and a depleted army? Will he be pleased that his choicest general has failed him?"

He flung the papers aside onto his writing table, settling them into a squared stack. "And what of the spies? Has the latest infiltration succeeded?"

The messenger smiled suddenly. He stepped forward and uttered several sentences low in Cern Dersturi's ear.

The leader's eyes grew narrow and bright. He held still, his head tilted to the side as though still receiving the tidings; but his hand stirred at his side and closed with a dark precision upon the hilt of his sword. "At last," he murmured, anticipation quivering his nostrils and burning on the edges of his tone, "we have an opening."

CHAPTER 36

MID-JULY SUN POURED INTO THE tent. A map was spread out on the long, inlaid table; a long, blunt forefinger was resting on the western edge of the Elerien Mountains.

Cern Dersturi traced a swift line across the parchment south, and through the West Gate until his finger halted forcefully upon the black circle of Orden City.

"It is time to break them. The reports from the north are fair, but they are not gaining ground quickly enough. We have dawdled long in the west, pressing here, testing there; at last, we shall turn the tide in our favor and join forces with them *here*." The finger tapped the parchment on the Zarethir River near to Grinaz Hall.

"Lieutenant Dovurti Atta?"

"Paraki," said the leader's close confidante.

"The Western Gate of Orden will be open tonight at the setting of the sun. There is a man who will see to that. Storm it, spare no-one. Let no word be carried on, for you will march on to Orden City with three thousands, and take them by surprise. Orden will fear us before the night is past."

"Aye, Paraki."

"The rest of you lieutenants, you are under him. Cir Harrik, take a thousand cavalry archers and lead them around the city secretly—so—and come at them from the east; open fire without mercy, and let none escape. They will be caught in the pincer jaws of a trap."

"Aye, Paraki," answered the lieutenant.

Cern Dersturi sent a sweeping glance around the tent, holding one by one the eyes of every man.

"Enter the city. Overrun it. Pillage and burn."

~

Fenris stood before the open window. A thick blue twilight was gathering in the eastern sky, but over Orden City the lingering sun cast a dusky, pinkish haze shot with rays of gold. "It is so beautiful," he whispered.

He looked to Mordred. "Is it time your bandages were changed?"

Mordred nodded.

"I will go find someone," said Fenris. He left the room.

But Mordred stared at the window after he was gone, his eyes riveted by the rosy scape, so beautiful, so quiet—so very quiet . . .

"It is like the quiet before a storm," he murmured.

Then he shook his head. The sky was clear; there would be no storms tonight.

The shuffling of footsteps came to his ear, and grew louder, and the door swung wide as someone entered. But it was not Priscilla. It was not any surgeon at all.

"What are you doing here?" hissed Mordred, voice low and throbbing with anger. His storm of fury beat inside him like the wings of a panicked bird, to and fro, back and forth, not knowing what to do with itself. His ribs began to hurt with the strain of his quick, labored breathing. *"What are you doing here?"*

"Everyone else is busy," said Inspector Dickson coolly.

"You could have waited," Mordred spat.

Inspector Dickson ignored him and strode to the bed with indifferent exterior and twitching jaw to loose Mordred's shirt and unwind the bandage on his arm.

"Where is Fenris?" demanded Mordred harshly, contriving to make it sound as if Inspector Dickson were responsible in some malicious way for his brother's absence.

Inspector Dickson's hands stiffened and he glared at Mordred. "I would not know. Maybe he went back to the army. His leave cannot last forever."

Mordred laughed in derision. "He has till tomorrow. He will not depart until he has to." But his heart misgave his scornful words, and he wondered if Fenris had thought it better to go back that night after all. Well, that was all right—he did not want Fenris to come in here, anyway, and see them.

The ugly silence dragged out as he waited for Inspector Dickson to finish, refusing to assist him by the slightest movement. "Incompetent," he flung at him, relishing the momentary discomfiture the insult brought.

"Lazy," Inspector Dickson gritted, struggling to fit Mordred's rigid arm back into the sleeve.

"Please shut the window," said Mordred with a sudden swiftness as Inspector Dickson spun away quickly with taut shoulders and a darkened brow.

Inspector Dickson wheeled back on him, eyebrows arched high in astonishment, as though of all the insult Mordred had ever done him, this was the most outrageous. He glanced at the peaceful, warm sky with one evening star pricking out in the falling night. "Shut the window," he repeated incredulously.

Mordred shrugged with a slight disdainful sneer and stiffened his chin. "Would you please shut the window," he said with careful, distant politeness.

Inspector Dickson, lips thinned, swung about and in painstaking care reached out to draw the shutters in.

He staggered and sank to his knees.

For one second all was still.

"Inspector Dickson?" Mordred sat up in a panic. *"Inspector Dickson!"*

Inspector Dickson's breath sucked in sharply and let out in a soft cry of pain. He sank down and Mordred saw the long, feathered shaft protruding from his right side. He did not turn or try to rise but knelt there on the floor, his breath hitching in short, painful gasps.

"Fenris," said Mordred inaudibly. His hands shook. "Fenris." Had Fenris gone? Fenris could not have gone, must not have gone, Laufeia—where was Laufeia? Gone, not to come again till morning—His head swirled with dizziness, his eyes frozen on the lone figure kneeling in front of the window. Fenris—

"Mordred!" The cry rang out in the doorway. Fenris' eyes were wide with alarm.

"I asked him to close the window," said Mordred dazedly, covering his face with his shaking fingers.

Fenris' footsteps crossed the room and the shutters crashed shut. Something struck the wall with a dull thud outside.

"I asked him to close the window." The dizziness washed all through him; his voice trembled like his hands. His thoughts were horribly clear, yet stifled with the enormity of his guilt.

"I can't move him myself, Mordred." Fenris was beside Inspector Dickson, looking up with hesitancy.

"You can, Fenris." Mordred struggled vainly to steady his voice. "You must."

Fenris bent and slipped his arms under Inspector Dickson's, and attempted to drag him towards the side room. But Fenris, who had carried his older brother in his arms nearly half a mile to the hospice's doors, could not summon the strength to lift Inspector Dickson now.

"I—I can't, Mordred."

"Find help then."

Fenris turned and ran out the door.

~

Fiona stared at Fenris, her legs all at once weak under her. "Shot him? The enemy is *here*?"

"Please, Fiona—please help me with him." His soft voice stumbled over the urgency of his plea.

"Inspector Dickson, yes." Fiona pushed aside the terror threatening to swamp her mind and body and started quickly down the hall, Fenris close beside her.

Together they managed to get Inspector Dickson into the little closet where Fenris had once slept. The cloths that had made his bed were still there, discarded, dusty, and they laid him there.

"Can you—" Fenris' voice was barely a whisper. "Can you get the arrow out?"

Fiona's eyes traveled down to the black shaft jutting out, its fletching mangled. Something in her balked. "I can't, Fenris! I've only tended wounds, I know naught about how to remove things . . . "

"Someone has to, Fiona."

She looked up at him and saw that his eyes were bright with desperate tears, and her own filled. She realized that as sickening as the thought of taking out the arrow was, the thought of leaving it in the man any longer was still worse.

It is only like taking out a splinter, she told herself. *You can do it, you must.*

She reached out and gripped the wood with her fingers. Inspector Dickson flinched violently and let out a hard gasp.

Fiona found that she was trembling. Willing her fingers to be still, she tightened her hold and began a steady outward pull, twisting slightly as she went to ease the passage. Inspector Dickson twitched again, writhed, and suddenly he went quite limp.

Afterwards Fiona was grateful he had fainted. She did not think, if he had remained conscious, that she would have been able to continue. Even as it was, by the time that the arrow was completely out, blood was covering her hands, the blankets, and Inspector Dickson's side, and she was dizzy and nauseated.

"Fenris," she whispered, desperately keeping command over her senses. "Find me something to bandage him with."

She pressed her fingers against the wound fiercely. The amount of blood streaming out of it frightened her. But by the time Fenris reached her with several strips of cloth, it was beginning to clot and the dark flow had lessened.

When at last it was bandaged, as tightly and cleanly as she could do, she rose from her kneeling position and felt the room tilt around her. Her legs still trembled. But in that moment she knew she could not yield. The night was far from over, and there would be much to do before it was. By some strength she had never used or known before, she pushed down the sickness and felt it fade. "Fenris, come. They will need help out there."

Fenris nodded. He glanced unwillingly at the bed. "Mordred—"

"I'll be fine, Fenris." Mordred's face was ashen, but not from fear. A great, unnamed torment stirred behind his eyes. Fiona, looking at him, could see that the calm he held in place was a facade as thin as a hair; it was that close to crashing down in panic and desolation.

"Mordred," said Fenris again. His chest heaved in one short, quick breath, and his troubled eyes held a strangely intense anxiety. "I will be back," he said, like a promise.

As Mordred looked at his brother, his mask crumbled. The fragile composure was seconds away from shattering. "Fenris—I—"

Fenris turned around and fled the room.

Fiona looked at Mordred, her heart sensing the agony within him, although she could not quite guess its nature. And she ached for him.

It is time to go—

But she slipped forward, so swiftly, like a dipping Mayfly, and bent over him and kissed him gently on the brow, even as he had set his lips on her in a desperate moment half a year ago. And she drew back and passed softly out of the room.

~

"Braegon! Braegon King! What are you doing back here, man?" Sergeant Hawke frowned in a kind of disapproving dismay. "You're not fit for action yet—not on that leg."

Braegon shook his head, leaning his weight on the doorframe as he returned the Sergeant's stare. "I'm well enough to be released from the hospice, Sergeant."

"Released or no, you're due for leave, soldier. Go back to Ceristen till you're healed."

"That might be a *long* time, Sergeant." Braegon held himself straight and still, refusing to let the pleading display itself across his features.

"Private King," said the Sergeant curtly, though the tightness around his eyes showed that he understood and hated to deny Braegon's plea, "a lame soldier is worth nothing in a battle. Go home and rest."

Braegon's chest lifted sharp and sudden. For an instant it seemed he would not dare flaunt a direct order, but he plunged recklessly on. "Sergeant, I do not want to rest. I want to fight—I want to defend my own while there is still breath left in me, Sergeant, do not make me go! Let me fight!"

"Private King, you are discharged!" Sergeant Hawke took a step forward, his broad shoulders overshadowing Braegon's slim stance of defiance. The hurt in his eyes was contested by the harsh line of his set jaw.

A dead silence had fallen over every man in the barracks. There was not a breath to be heard.

Into that silence came the hiss-*thwack* of an arrow.

Before any man could move another came ripping through the door, straight between Braegon's side and the frame. With a splintering thud it landed in the opposite wall.

Braegon hurled himself to the side, and Sergeant Hawke sprang forward and slammed the door to in a lunge.

"Shut that window," he barked, jerking a finger towards one window whose shutters were swinging wide open in the breeze. Someone obeyed.

For a little while no one spoke among them. There was a shaken look in their eyes, a stricken dread. Suddenly, the war had sprung over the threshold.

"What do we do, Sergeant?" asked a fearful voice.

Sergeant Hawke looked around, his gaze flitting from one man to the other. "We wait for orders."

"Sergeant." It was Therelane Grey stepping forward. "May I depart the barracks?"

"Why?"

Therelane hesitated. "I—I want to go to the hospice, sir."

"What?"

"They—they may need alerting, sir."

"They'll know soon enough, if they do not already."

"Sergeant, they may need help if they need to make a defense—or if they need to flee the city."

"And what do you think one man is going to do in that? Besides, we know not the situation. 'Tis more than likely that any escape is futile at this point for all save an able-bodied man with a sword to his protection."

"Sergeant, please." It was Braegon speaking up. "His sister is in there."

"Braegon King, you have made things hard enough already," said Sergeant Hawke between his teeth. "Enough now."

"We can spare one man," said Braegon earnestly.

Sergeant Hawke did not look at him. "Private Grey, the answer is no."

Therelane's eyes flashed in rebellion. Slowly he looked away.

"Prepare for departure," said Sergeant Hawke, raising his voice to the rest of the men. "Have your weapons to hand. We may be called for at any moment."

Therelane made his way to stand by Braegon. "He denied me—for no reason," he said between shut teeth. "I am going."

"Therelane, no!" Braegon gripped his arm.

"They could need help, and he will not let me go to give it!"

"Aye, but what you want to do is senseless, Therelane—bordering on desertion—don't you understand—"

Therelane was pulling away from him, slipping along the wall, running out the door.

"What was that?" Sergeant Hawke swung sharply around.

The blank silence pressed heavily for several long seconds. Then Braegon said, "Therelane Grey has left, Sergeant Hawke."

"So be it," said the sergeant grimly after a moment. "Nay, don't start after him. It is on his own head if he perishes out there, and none of the rest of you need risk your lives by bringing him back."

Braegon turned his head away, sick in his mind. Did not Therelane understand?

He had tried to make him understand, but Therelane's were not the loyalties of a soldier. He did not know—it was not in him to know or comprehend them.

And though Braegon hoped that Therelane would live through the battle, he dreaded what would follow if he should.

~

Therelane Grey ran as fast as he dared push himself through the city, very much aware that at any moment he could feel an arrow thud into his body, and there was nothing he could do to help it.

He stumbled to a halt, gulping for breath. Cries rang in his ears, and when he looked back flames were licking up the side of a wooden house. Suddenly he was terrified, and beyond terrified; he wanted to crawl away and cover his head and hide. How had they got in, so far, without warning and without opposition? The madness was too much, too much—it crashed upon Therelane that this was the beginning of the end. Orden was breached at last, caught unprepared. They were going to die.

He reeled against a wall, bent his face in the crook of his arm. What was the use of going on? What could he do? Nothing would avail in the end.

But Ceristen! Ceristen—there, on Mount Thiranu, the world was untouched and safe. He lifted his eyes and looked toward the dim bulk of the mountain growing lost in the shadows of night. And then, as suddenly as the horror and despair had come upon him, it fled. While Ceristen was safe, there was surety, there was courage, there was strength to go on.

Therelane turned his eyes away from the mountain and ran.

As he drew nearer the hospice, flaming missiles began to streak past him. He saw the flowering dots of fire springing up all around in the corners of his vision, but he fixed his eyes fiercely on the road ahead of him, would not let himself look at the city as it fell to pieces.

The hospice was towering above him, a tall, unbroken monument in the night. This, too, was still free.

For how long? his mind whispered mockingly.

He rushed up the shallow stone steps, into the door, and found himself colliding hard with a figure who was carrying an armload of boards. Therelane attempted to halt, but it was too late; the two of them went crashing to the floor, Therelane's jaw scraping painfully along the edge of one wooden lath while another clipped his elbow.

An arm grasped his and pulled him to his feet. "What is this? You are in a hurry, soldier. Did you come to bring us word of the attack?"

"Aye—and to help, if you need it." Therelane glanced at the person he had run into, who was getting quickly to his feet—Fenris Kenhelm, he realized.

Their eyes met, and Therelane had known Fenris long enough to recognize the anguished look in those eyes of his. Something had gone amiss with Mordred, and whatever it was Fenris could do nothing to mend it now.

"You have our thanks then," the surgeon who had helped him up was saying. "So far we are safe, but we cannot expect that to last through the night. Come, help us bar up the doors, if you will. We can hardly make a defense of this place, if it is attacked, but we can attempt to stop anyone from getting in for a little while at least."

Therelane nodded, and bent at once to help Fenris retrieve the boards that had gone flying. As they worked, he bent towards him and asked softly, "What happened?"

Fenris wet his lips and spoke after a moment. "An arrow struck Inspector Dickson in the side. 'Twas the first warning we had."

Therelane could scarcely remember who Inspector Dickson was. "Is that—the man that arrested—"

"Yes," said Fenris swiftly, and at the darkness in his eyes Therelane dared say no more.

~

The squad of soldiers pounded through the darkened streets. Their swords were already blood-stained, and the dark purpose driving them on thirsted for more.

"*Kurik*!" shouted one. "*Kurik, etti, turta*!"

The group stumbled to a halt, blowing hard. Somewhere off to their right fires burned yellow in the night and cries resounded near and far.

"What?" said the captain in charge gruffly, swiping a hand across his clipped beard.

"See, that one." The man waved toward the long, squared outline of a tall structure rearing up on the left. "*Co' rai int.*"

The captain shrugged. "Maybe it is good. Maybe not. It looks like an army garrison."

"It is a rich man's house," said someone else, and the rest took a liking to this idea.

The captain grunted. "We will move closer and see."

They circled to the front of the building.

"See," said the first soldier, "there is a lamp on the wall and it shines on words. It says in the common tongue that it is a home for sick people."

"Aiee! Aha!" went up the cry from several throats. "That is good pickings indeed."

"*Nitta,*" said the captain, and with a swift gesture he brought them around again to the side. They swarmed up the wall, and onto the colonnades on the upper level, and came into the hospice.

~

Two people came into the room, Priscilla and a man Mordred did not recognize.

"Come," said Priscilla, taking hold of him. Mordred bit his tongue hard as she jolted his collarbone.

"What do you want?" he asked, resisting her hold on him.

"Irene Grey has ordered all the patients moved from the outer rooms," said the physician. "You will be safer than here."

They half-carried, half-dragged him out of the small bedchamber that had been his home for three weeks, and released him at last at the edge of a dark, pillared atrium, wide and grey-shadowed. Mordred caught glimpses of a few other huddled bodies scattered across the courtyard before they let him go and he slumped against a stone column, lurching forward with a loss of bearings. His cheek rested on the dusty, cold surface of the floor.

It was when they were gone that he remembered Inspector Dickson, left behind in the tiny closet.

A shudder ripped through him, and one tear fell, trickling down to dampen the dirty stone against his cheek.

His fault.

His fault.

He saw one face and one face alone in his mind, and it was not Inspector Dickson at all: it was Fenris. Again and again. *I failed you, Fenris. I let you be hurt.* And the resolve, formed so unconsciously and hammered over and over: *Never again. Never again.*

He choked on his anguish, driving his forehead into the stone. So many failures to his charge. So much blood upon his hands.

The leader took you because of me.

Bardrick died because of me.

Two thousand men died because of me.

And Inspector Dickson was shot because of him.

Now Inspector Dickson was alone in the outer chambers, in danger, forgotten, and Mordred could not mend his mistake by the least effort. He could not even go to Inspector Dickson himself and bring him here.

With a sudden, mad exertion he lunged to his feet, swayed for an instant, dizzy. His broken leg buckled under him, and he sprawled to the floor. He did not try to get up again.

~

The Runnicoran soldiers were eager for sport. They stormed through the colonnade and into the halls, singly, in twos and threes, killing little yet, looking mostly for plunder and diversion.

Because of this, the hospice was yet unalerted to their presence. The upper floor was largely quiet, few surgeons and nurses about; most of them had gone below to secure the doors, and those who saw the soldiers did not survive to give an alarm. The men grew bold.

A threesome slunk down a narrow, twisting side stair and into the lower level. "Naught up there," grumbled one. "Maybe we shall find better spoils below."

"'Ware though," muttered the shortest of them, lifting a hand. "We are like to find more of the caretakers in these parts."

They paused at the edge of a courtyard, but it was shadowed and lanternless, and they struck out along the edge of it, keeping to the shelter of the tall pillars. It was at the end that one of them stumbled and with loud cursing fell across a body lying at the foot of one column.

"So there are people in here after all!" said the short one. "Stop your spitting, Pirta, and get away from him. He may be armed."

Pirta backed away.

"No, see," said the third—"his leg is splinted. He is one of the sick."

They stood looking down at the young man, who lay helpless on his back, staring at them with wide-open grey eyes.

"He is afraid," laughed Pirta. "I will kill him."

The change in the young man's face showed that he had understood at least the gist of what was said. He pushed himself up in a rough, quick movement and launched himself backwards so that his back was braced against the pillar behind him. With defiant face, he waited.

The short man knocked Pirta's knife aside as he yanked it out, and drew his own sword to point it at the Ordenian's chest. "Boy," he said in broken, accented common tongue, "any money in your clothes?"

The young man twitched his head in a small shake.

"Any trinkets? We let you live."

"No." His voice was clear, quite steady, a little scornful.

"Brindi," said Pirta viciously in Runnicoran, "Let me at him."

Brindi stepped back with a shrug. "Do what you like. Then, let us go find the chambers where the doctors sleep and search them. I say we will find gold there if there is any in this place."

The other two mumbled agreement. But at Brindi's last words, the young man's face whitened and a fresh agitation sprang into his eyes. Without a second of warning he pounced upon Pirta and struggled to wrest the knife from his grip.

The fight lasted barely seconds. As soon as Pirta recollected himself, he knocked the young man aside, hurled him to the ground, and set about beating him with the pommel of the knife. All the while he raged under his breath and cursed the Ordenian savagely.

"*Nin co' rai*?" demanded the gruff voice of their captain coldly behind them.

"Pirta," growled Brindi, hauling the wild-eyed man off his victim. "The *Kurik*."

Pirta spat, but as the captain's eyes fixed on him he shuffled back and ducked his head.

"*Kurik* Alétun," explained Brindi humbly, "we were just—"

The captain cut him short with a wave and looked at the young man choking for breath on the floor. His sharp dark eyes widened. "Richardson," he said aloud.

Their eyes met. The young man's breath heaved in and he turned away, his head sinking with the droop of despair.

Alétun watched him, strange thoughts boiling in his head. He could take this man back to the Paraki, as he had last time. Orders were orders. But last time he had not known that Richardson was also Damachrus. Having known him for a short time, he remembered the young Richardson oddly like a wayward son, and it had dismayed and disappointed him when the boy proved traitor. He did not want to doom him to the life of inhuman torture that the Paraki in his madness would subject him to, should he bring him back.

The three soldiers were waiting, puzzled. "*Kurik* Alétun . . . " tried Brindi cautiously.

No-one would be the wiser . . . yet the thought of disobeying orders went against the grain of all that Captain Alétun had learned in twenty years of soldiering. The two choices were before him, equally plain and equally ugly, and he could not make himself choose.

The soldiers shifted and shot looks at him and one another. Mordred, Richardson, Damachrus, lay with his head hidden against the stones.

Captain Alétun spoke harshly. "Kill him," he said, and with the sharp movement of decision he whirled and strode in the opposite direction down the courtyard.

~

"Mirda!" called Priscilla. "Mirda King!"

Mirda spun around quickly in answer, shaking back the ringlets that flew into her face.

"I sent Hala upstairs some time ago, and she's not returned." Priscilla's sharp chin was frowning downward in perplexity and the beginnings of concern.

"That's all? Don't worry, Priscilla, I'll go look for her at once," said Mirda quickly, giving a supportive smile to the older woman.

"There's a good lass," said Priscilla, patting her arm.

She did not need to tell Mirda to hurry; Mirda had worked in the hospice long enough to know that delay was never affordable and never approved. She flew up the stairs and started down the long, open colonnades that lined the upper floor of the hospice, calling Hala's name.

She had entered a small, empty ward whose vaulted shadows stretched over the floor when she saw the five figures approaching, dimly lit by the thin luminance of the moon. "Hala!" she called, but they were masculine shapes. "Have you seen Hala?" she cried out to them, hurrying closer.

One of them turned and said something strangely unintelligible to another, and they laughed. And the light glinted off their swords, and Mirda realized, too late to flee, the truth.

"You call for Hala," said the one who had spoken earlier, now in the language her ears could understand. "If Hala is a girl like you, she is dead, and you are about to be dead like her."

Murmurs of grunting laughter echoed around him.

"Maybe we should not kill her," said another man suggestively.

Mirda, looking swiftly around at their grim faces, understood in her very core they were earnest, and just how deadly in earnest they were.

"I don't want to hurt you," she said clearly, sincerely, reaching out to them because it was the only thing she could think to do. "None of us do. Please don't hurt me. Have I done anything against you?"

They stared at her. Then the spokesman took a step forward and pointed at her. "You make these sick ones well. They get up and they come back to kill us." He shrugged. "You kill us, girl."

"I would help you, too, if you were sick," said Mirda steadily. "I help them all because they are like brothers to me." She leaned forward, pouring all the plea in her heart into her eyes and words. "Would you not help your brother if he were hurt? Oh, can't you see how foolish it all is?" Her voice trembled with the intensity of her emotions, but she dared not let the tears fall. Tears were weakness here, they would not help her. "We are not supposed to fight one another. We ought to be at peace. Will you not leave this place, and take your swords to those who are not defenseless and innocent?"

"If we let you go," said the foremost roughly, "you will tell everyone. No more talk." He stepped straight up to her and snatched her, and there was a *ting* of steel as he drew his knife.

Mirda screamed, and heard it echoed by more shouts all around her. The man who held her uttered a strange cough as a sword slid through his abdomen, and his staring eyes rolled up.

His grip on her relaxed, and Mirda crumpled sobbing into Therelane's arms.

~

Therelane held Mirda gently, bewildered and alarmed and grieved all at once. He thought maybe he should be dealing with the other soldiers, but he realized that they had fled, perhaps believing that since one man had had a sword, the rest of the physicians behind him would be similarly armed. So he held Mirda, patting her shoulder to soothe her, and a part of him was happy, very happy, to be holding her like this.

Mirda came out of her tears quickly, with a half-laugh, and tucked her arm willingly under his, resting her head on his chest as her panting breaths quieted. Therelane, blind with pure ecstasy, scarcely felt Irene jerking his arm until she slapped his shoulder.

"Therelane, let go of her—she's fine now—and come here. There's things to be done. I'm afraid they got all over the hospice before we were aware of it, and they won't all flee like those did."

"Aye—aye," stuttered Therelane, coming fully back to the world. "What are we going to do?"

Irene stared far away, her youthful, hardened face frighteningly sober. "Therelane, do one thing for me, you silly, indecisive dreamer-boy."

"What?"

"Tell the girl you love her. She's waiting for the word."

"I—" he started.

"No-one cares if you lost your hand, Therelane. At any rate, she doesn't. And that's what matters. Will you tell her?"

And because she did not sweep away, rushing to the next thing that had to be done, Therelane knew she needed to hear and that he needed to tell her.

"Yes," he said, and with that promise he felt a light yet profound weight settle on him. "I will tell her."

"Good." Irene whipped away.

~

Consciousness returned to Inspector Dickson by degrees. He was first aware of his side, which throbbed with a sharp pulse of pain. Then he remembered how it came to hurt like this: the cruel force of the arrow as it struck—the peculiar clarity of Mordred's frantic words through the daze of nauseating pain—two people hauling him to a bed—a flash of blinding agony as someone removed the arrow, and merciful oblivion.

Then they had left him here, alone. Even before he opened his eyes he knew he was alone; it was something in the blank silence of the room, devoid of any other's breathing. Very well; it was not the aloneness that bothered him, but the sense of unprotection. A strong conviction rested on him that he was not safe until he found other people.

And so, despite the burning flares that shot through his side, he stood on shaky legs and stumbled out of the little closet. He reeled like a drunkard, clutched at the walls for support. His head was hot and light. One small voice said he was mad to try walking on his own, but the rest of him felt duty-bound to finish what he had started.

By the time he had gained the corridor, he felt so ill that he had to sit down. He slid to the floor and let his spinning head dangle between his knees. For the first time, he wondered where Mordred was and why he had not been in the room.

Then he began to hear the voices.

They were so garbled and meaningless that he thought they were in his mind, and then as his head cleared he realized they were real, quite real, only speaking in another language. It sounded as if they were quarreling.

Inspector Dickson sat a moment longer, turning everything over in his head. They must be Runnicorans—of course they were. That meant that Runnicorans had shot him, and Runnicorans were in the hospice, and—

He shook his head wearily. It was over. The city was being overrun. And he knew as well as anyone could that Orden did not have the strength to repel the attack.

What was the general thinking, in Mitheren, alone though surrounded, because he alone bore the full grief of his country that was falling to pieces? Would he regret as Mitheren, the final stronghold, fell, that he had not found a safer place for Inspector Dickson?

Inspector Dickson pulled his thoughts away from useless introspection and pushed up to his feet again. Though his instinct was first to flee from the quarreling Runnicoran voices, a deeper sense impelled him to follow them. He needed to find out what was afoot, if he could, and how many of these were crawling through the hospice. Was he the only inhabitant left alive?

He staggered down the hall, and peering around the edge of a wide archway he saw them—three men, glowering and shouting at one another, coming almost to blows. He drew back fractionally, but they paid him no heed whatever.

Again, Inspector Dickson thought, where was Mordred in all this dark, torn madness? Why had he not been in that room? He felt the ugly stirring of that old sense of compassion whenever Mordred was injured, and suddenly his mind was flooded with all the instances of vulnerable, tender Mordred that he had ever seen. He shoved them resolutely out. He did not need to think of that, did not need to worry about Mordred now . . .

And then he saw him, lying just beyond the arguing Runnicorans, bloodied, limp, and still like a discarded rag.

In that instant he knew what a pretense, what a stupid, childish, game that fight had been.

Why had they gone on hating each other for so long?

If only he had spoken that day. Or any of the others. If only he had not let every cutting word rankle like a festering wound. If only he had admitted how much he was in the wrong.

And now he never would.

He dropped to his knees and wept, out of anguish, out of grief, but more than anything out of the repentance for all that he had said, all that he had done, and the failure to say the words he should have said.

It was not the angry roars that halted him but the sudden hush. He lifted his eyes and one man lay bleeding on the floor. The short one who held a drawn sword grunted to his companion and gestured to Mordred's body. And Inspector Dickson, to his everlasting confoundment and joy, saw Mordred's chest jump in a quick, gasping breath.

He put a hand to his head, bewildered. Incomparable and heady gladness washed over him, mingling with the inner sorrow that still held him fast. He could scarcely make sense of up or down.

"Utinna," the second man was saying to the first with a nod. The short one strode forward, straight towards Mordred, his sword lifting high.

Something cut through Inspector Dickson's heart like a knife, one single thought, shearing away all his tangled emotions and clenching into a knowledge so pure it hurt.

Mordred must not die—*Mordred must not die.*

Mordred must live.

Inspector Dickson sprang to his feet and charged at the armed man with a shout. The sword went flying at their collision, and they thudded to the floor together, rolling, snarling, striking at one another. Inspector Dickson knew that he must win in seconds or he would not win at all, and that gave him the strength of desperation. As the soldier snatched out a knife, Inspector Dickson with another yell seized at the blade and ripped it straight out of the man's fingers—but it spun out of his own, slipping to the floor.

The wild burst of strength was fading out of him. With the last of it he flung one punch, dead sure, into the middle of the Runnicoran's throat, and slumped backwards—not knowing whether the man were dead or unconscious, and for the moment not caring, either.

Then he remembered the second man, and dragged himself painfully up, wondering why he was not already stabbed and bleeding out.

But that soldier was gone. In his place stood a slender, wide-eyed young man, a sword that was not his own stained and glittering faintly in his hand. "Mordred," he said, staring past Inspector Dickson.

And he dropped the sword and leaped to Mordred's side, raising him up with wonderful, instinctive gentleness, so that Inspector Dickson had to look away, because the love between them was too plain a thing, and one that he had no share in himself.

"I came back, Mordred," Fenris whispered. "I promised I would come back. I found your sword and I came."

Inspector Dickson looked back and saw Fenris easing Mordred down again. But Mordred's eyes were open, lucid. "You came, Fenris," he said. "It's all right." His voice was hoarse and rasping.

"Mordred, are you hurt?"

"Not much." Mordred touched Fenris' hand. "I'm all right."

All at once he stirred, his eyes widening and filling with panic. "The soldiers. Fenris, where did the soldiers go—Inspector Dickson—"

"Mordred, Inspector Dickson is right here." Fenris struggled to hold his older brother down.

Mordred's taut frame went slack as the import of the words got to him. "Here," he repeated blankly. "Why?"

Fenris looked at Inspector Dickson.

"I woke up," said Inspector Dickson tiredly. His tongue felt thick, and he ached all over, and pangs shot up and down his whole right side. He did not want to explain anything. "I woke up and left the room and followed voices here. That's all." He stared at Mordred, confusion and curiosity rising in him, and his voice sharpened unconsciously to interrogation. "What did you mean, the soldiers and me?"

Mordred's head snapped up and he locked eyes with Inspector Dickson. "The soldiers were going to search the doctors' rooms," he said very slowly, stiffly, as though the words were wrung from him against his will.

"And?" pressed Inspector Dickson, bewildered still, not sure he understood. "What did you think to do about that?"

Mordred grew cold, cold as ice, the proud, angry chin lifting high. "What do you care? I would have stopped them—I—" He broke off, his voice wavering. "Forgive me."

He buried his face against the stone.

Inspector Dickson stared at the dark head turned so stubbornly away, shutting him out, and was shaken. What an admission and what a plea! No wonder that Mordred hated him, he thought in a muddled sort of way.

His side felt scalded with heat. It was probably bleeding again, he thought dully. The pain flared up again, hard-edged and frozen hot like an iron screwing deep into his midsection, and he gritted his teeth.

"What are we going to do now?" he mumbled as the wave subsided. "It's not safe here."

"Someone will come soon." He saw the desperate hope in Fenris' face, the distress building in his eyes. "I can't leave you here. Mordred, I can't leave you again."

Mordred stirred and lifted his head a fraction. "It's all right, Fenris," he said softly. "Someone will come."

They waited in silence. Someone moaned further off in the courtyard. The battle-noise distantly reached their ears.

"Inspector Dickson," came Mordred's voice. "Did you save my life?" He said it so quick and low that Inspector Dickson was all but convinced he had imagined the question.

"What makes you wonder something like that?" he asked at last.

"They were arguing over how to kill me," said Mordred, and again he spoke in that very quick, low tone, so that Inspector Dickson had to strain his ears to understand. "Pirta wanted to kill me slowly, and

Brindi wanted to hurry so they could raid the doctors' chambers, and finally he and the other one killed Pirta. Then Brindi came to kill me, but someone fought him off. I thought it was your voice I heard."

"You heard rightly," said Inspector Dickson wearily, and wondered why he had admitted it. He waited for whatever retaliation Mordred had. Having been rescued by his worst enemy, he would be mortified. Repulsed. Incensed. But Mordred did not answer.

At last, he did speak. But though quiet, his words were clear this time. "I thank you."

And Inspector Dickson was undone at the gentleness in his tone, the more so when he thought of how Mordred must have unbent his fierce, unyielding pride to say that. And he turned his head away, lest he should see him weep.

But he did not know that Mordred had turned his face again to the stones, and pressed his eyes hard against his arm, his shoulders convulsing in long, silent heaves while Fenris sought in vain to comfort him.

CHAPTER 37

THE AIR WAS RANK WITH agitation and dread. Not a man in the small barracks was free from it. Yet they had learned discipline under Sergeant Garin; they were not the same rabble of untrained farmers they had been three months ago. They did not cave to panic, but waited silently as they had been bidden, and their sergeant too waited—face hard and masking his own fear and uncertainty, leaning his arm on the sill of the shuttered window, drumming his fingers in a quick, tense rattle.

An hour went by, and the fighting had come no nearer to them than that first slew of arrows. The sound of horse hooves drubbing the earth wildly near at hand—fading out—coming nearer—slowing—dragged them all upright as one man, eyes darting anxiously in pale faces for answers that no-one had.

"It is only one," said Sergeant Garin. His tone snapped like the crack of a bowstring. "Unbar the door."

Seconds later the freed door slammed open and Captain Finley Rhodes sprang in, his dark eyes burning with urgency. "Out, men. Sergeant, lead them in a patrol of the city streets."

"How goes it?" asked Sergeant Garin in an undertone.

"It looks ill. Our only asset is that they are acting as a riot, without organization or direction. Yet that is their strength as well, for they are so many and all over that we cannot meet them on any definite front and drive them back. We have dispatched as many patrols as we can into the city in an effort to check their progress—if even that can be done."

"Where is the general?" asked a voice out of the men.

Captain Rhodes turned saddened eyes upon the speaker. "The captains and the king have begged the general not to go out into the city. He has heeded us—for now." He glanced back to Sergeant Garin. "Go you now with your men, as I bade you." He sped out, and the clamor of hooves rose up and faded away again even as the soldiers formed ranks and marched toward the city.

The horror that sprawled across Orden City was worse than Braegon had anticipated. Buildings were awash with flame, rumbling and tottering on their foundations, and the cinders fell glowing in the darkness. Men, women and children fled all around them, weeping or calling for loved ones, stumbling, wounded, alone or in tight desperate knots of families. Braegon thought of Therelane, and wondered if his rash flight had been for anything, or if he had perished in these streets while trying to reach the hospice.

He had other things, though, to occupy his attention besides Therelane: the most pressing one that his leg was not obeying him at all like it ought. He set his teeth and kept up with the others by sheer discipline, but deep within, the truth that he had known, and that Sergeant Garin had known, set its cold claws upon his heart.

"It might be a very long time, Sergeant."

Maybe it did not matter. After tonight, they might well all be dead. And if not . . . what would happen to the soldiers of a conquered land? If they let him go, a man could still manage farming with a crippled leg; better than he could soldiering.

Braegon's breath sucked in as he stumbled painfully. He would be no good by the time it came to fighting and he knew it. He should not have come; the sergeant would not have let him. He was a liability now, but it was too late to go back.

~

Laufeia dashed under an archway and skidded to a halt. "Fenris!" she cried. "And Mordred! There you are." Her gaze flew to Inspector Dickson, to the two dead Runnicoran soldiers on the ground, and back to her brothers, the elder prostrate, his hands clenched and his shoulders hitching spasmodically, the younger with a hand on him, his despairing look fading to relief as she appeared. "What happened here?"

Then she caught herself and shook her head. "Never mind it. We need to go."

"Where?" asked Fenris, getting his feet under him and slipping his hand under Mordred's arm.

Laufeia could not answer for a moment. The import of the message stopped the words in her throat. "Irene says—that there is no more staying in the hospice. We have to run."

Fenris' eyes were wide with horror. "What about all—all the other patients?"

She shook her head again, catching him in a fierce hug while her eyes stung with tears. "They'll help as many out as they can, but we have to go *now*. The soldiers are all over."

"Where do we go?" Fenris asked again, and she wept and hugged him again because the young man emerging out of the shy, terrified boy was so strong and able.

"I don't know—I don't know."

She gathered hold of herself, knowing that there must be some right answer. "Mitheren, Fenris. We'll try to get to Mitheren. I don't think we'll be able to leave the city."

Fenris nodded once, and bent to Mordred again. "Mordred," he whispered. "Can you walk?"

Mordred, in a mute, miserable movement, shook his head.

Laufeia's mind was riven with shock. Mordred never made such admissions—never. At the least he would have said, "I can manage."

What had happened to her brother?

"Can you walk if I help you on this side?" Fenris asked in the same quiet, worried way, as though nothing had happened out of the ordinary, raising Mordred up with light, sensitive hands.

Mordred's head hung down. "Yes," he said faintly.

Laufeia turned away, forcing back the comforting words and the questions that they had no time for. "Sir?" she said to Inspector Dickson. It looked as though he had been hurt.

Inspector Dickson would not look up either. "Aye," he muttered thickly.

"Do you need help? If Fenris can support Mordred on his own, I'll take you."

Inspector Dickson pressed his hands against his eyes and withdrew them roughly. "Yes, my lady; thank you."

The four of them made their way out of the hospice, hurrying and yet painfully, perilously slow. Laufeia thought they would never reach the doors in safety.

Reach them they did. They limped down the steps, and through the ravaged streets towards Mitheren.

~

Mordred staggered, nearly losing his hold on Fenris. He clung to him instinctively, like a drowner, yet he was scarcely aware of anything, even the road beneath.

There was such a battle rending him that he felt like a rag wrung out and torn apart. His pride, humiliated and crushed, raged against the man who had saved his life. Shame lay athwart it, with guilt close behind, shame that that hated man had saved it at all, despite all Mordred had called him and thought him. All the safe, viciously pleasant lies he had forged for himself, building up a false character around his most abhorred enemy, crumbled, and he was left with the stark truth that they had been lies all along. Inspector Dickson was *not* a monster without humanity or feelings; his highest purpose in life *not* to make Mordred miserable; and the Claw business was *not* all his fault. He foundered amid the crashing waves of sharp, sure realization, while his anger frantically strove to keep its footing, vying for the place it had kept so long.

"I thank you," he had said—words that he had said in one clear moment of deep, bitter conviction, words that had been like soot and ash in his mouth; yet he had said them, knowing that he owed Inspector Dickson that much.

And what else did he owe him?

The upheaval seethed endlessly, battering and devouring him with the violence of his clashing desires and will, till he writhed inwardly under its torment and could only beg for an end of it. But no release came.

A sharp tap of pain raced through his head. "Mordred," said Fenris' voice softly, and the voice and pain brought him back to the world for a moment. Buildings towered grey above him, sky and shadows a black emptiness. Smoke stung his nostrils and Fenris' tireless hands were helping him up from the ground.

"What—" he stumbled, floundering for words.

"You tripped, Mordred."

His sound leg quivered under him. "How—much—further?"

"Two miles, I think." Fenris braced him more firmly and settled Mordred's arm around his shoulders.

Mordred met Inspector Dickson's eyes, unexpectedly and by accident, and their gazes locked for one dark, unguarded moment. Then Mordred ripped away.

He heard Laufeia's small, short gasp of alarm, and it awoke instinct inside him. He lunged up to his full height, his fingers biting frantically into Fenris' shoulder to keep his balance, as his eyes flew about in search of the danger.

Then he found it—the little band of soldiers striding out of the alleyway, the moon and faint fire-glow reflecting off their Runnicoran sigil.

The man in the lead was Captain Alétun.

Mordred felt a heavy wave of despairing exhaustion that darkened everything about him, and the ground seemed to teeter very far away. But one thing kept him on his feet, and cleared his head a little—he must keep *them* safe . . .

~

Laufeia watched in horrified bewilderment as Mordred pushed away from Fenris and crashed against the nearest wall for support, dragging himself towards the enemy soldiers. It happened so quickly that she was still trying to understand when he halted and cried out in a cracked, panting voice, "Captain Alétun—"

The men pulled up abruptly and the foremost looked at him.

"Captain Alétun—" Mordred seemed to struggle past the words. "If I—if I let you take me, will you let them alone?"

Fenris, as though loosed suddenly from paralysis, rushed forward and sprang in front of his older brother. "No," he gasped, pushing Mordred back to the ground. "No, Mordred, no."

"Fenris," Mordred choked, not resisting against his brother, yet his eyes were bright and desperate and the tears began to slip down his cheeks. "If they hurt you—I can't—Let it be me, Fenris—"

"No, Mordred." Fenris flung himself across him in a tight, pleading hug. "Please, no. Not this."

Laufeia, riveted where she was, her eyes darting over the nightmare in front of her, saw the man that Mordred had called Captain Alétun signal in some way to his men; and while they remained behind, he advanced until he was less than six feet from Mordred and Fenris.

Her mouth opened, a scream of warning about to burst out.

But the Runnicoran stopped right there. "Richardson," he said, the r's rolling clipped off his tongue. "This is your brother?"

Mordred lifted his head, dread in his eyes.

"How do you live?" There was true perplexity in his tone. "I gave orders for them to kill you not an hour since."

Mordred's mouth opened. "A man saved my life," he said hoarsely. "My brother—and another man."

Silence hung over them, thick and tense. Laufeia saw strange things flash across the Runnicoran's face—uncertainty, pity, and fear.

"Some power wills to deliver you from my hand, Richardson," he said at last. "It is a better thing to pit myself against the will of the Paraki than fate."

A light of astonished hope entered Mordred's eyes, and just as quickly gave place to another, stranger thing: earnest compassion. "If that is so," he said gently, reaching out a hand to the man who stood motionless there, "call it not fate."

Captain Alétun shrugged, made as if to turn, and checked.

"Please," said Mordred very softly. "You have done so much already. Let there this once be nothing between us. Will you not take my hand, as a friend?"

Captain Alétun slowly crossed the distance between them and closed his broad-knuckled hand around the thin, long-fingered one Mordred held out to him. "You were as a son to me in my mind," he said quickly, in his brusque accent. "If it had been different—I would have looked upon you as a son indeed, *Ett-Kéva*."

He wheeled away and roared an order to his men, and their marching footsteps rose and rattled away into the darkness.

Laufeia let Inspector Dickson go and leapt to Mordred's side. "Mordred," she cried, holding him fast and kissing his forehead, so tremblingly aware of how close she had come to loss.

The tears were brimming in his eyes again, and he held her in return. "What did he call you, Mordred?" she asked as the terror of the moment died away and the salty tears running into her mouth began to slow.

A shiver of emotion jolted his shoulders against her. "Peace-maker."

~

Fiona shifted her sweat-slippery grip on the taut cloths that bound together one end of the hastily made stretcher. Fred swayed between her and Therelane, a dead weight that had quickly grown a strain on the two of them.

"Thank you," she murmured to Therelane, knowing he would understand her gratitude, for she had already expressed it.

He nodded, but was panting too hard to answer.

They made up half of a small vanguard, the last of the nurses to flee the hospice. Irene and Mirda bore another wounded man between them close behind.

Fiona thought back with shuddering heart to those last terrible moments, listening to the pound of feet all through the halls around and lying athwart Fred, both shielding him from anything that should come their way and shutting her eyes against the sight of it.

Then Therelane had come, and told her that it was time to run.

"And Fred?" she had cried, springing to her feet, tingling with the anger of desperation. "Am I to flee without him? I will not. He shall not be taken from me again!"

And Therelane had cast about, and in bare moments, it seemed, lashed together a sling of cloths for them to slip Fred into, and suddenly they were hurrying down the steps of the hospice.

"Mitheren," came Irene's curt, steady direction from behind them. "It's like as not we'll be slaughtered trying to get there, but we may as well try. 'Tis the last stronghold we have now."

So Therelane swung eastwards.

It happened before any of them knew it. One moment they were alone in a small square of crossroads; the next, seven or eight men were running towards them, spreading out in a half-circle to cut them off.

"Oh, dear," muttered Irene, motioning to Mirda to set down the burden.

Therelane let his end of Fred's sling fall and stepped forward with a firm stance. "We don't mean any harm," he said in a carefully reasonable tone. "But if—"

"Therelane!" snapped Irene and smacked his hand away from the hilt of the sword. "You be quiet. That won't help." She turned coolly to face the soldiers, spreading her arms wide as though to hide all of them behind her. "I am a descendant of Ridith, of the house of Ithera. Werevulture blood flows in my veins! These are under my protection, and do you think to touch them?"

The men drew together in a knot, eyeing her with alarm and half-disbelief. Fiona, for her part, was astounded and filled with awe at Irene's audacious, valiant declaration. Irene knew and Fiona knew that there was no power in her that could harm these men; yet they did not know it, and the true, or half-true, assertion of werevulture blood struck fear into them.

But one man stormed out of their midst, sneering, a short throwing-spear in his hand. "If witch you be," he said, "you can turn this aside!" And he cast it, so that it struck straight into her ribs and protruded out the other side.

Her body seemed very small and slight as it folded and crumpled.

Therelane's face grew white and dreadful. With a wrathful cry that broke in the middle he plunged past her and smote the spear-man to the ground.

In the flurry that followed Fiona could understand nothing, but seconds later two more men lay dead on the ground, and Therelane was driving his blade into the throat of a third. With the terrible speed and strength of controlled rage he swung again, but there was no-one in his path. The rest had fled.

Therelane stood as though rooted to the ground, head lowered. His sword slipped away and clattered free. Like a man dazed by dreaming he turned and looked at them. "Irene," he said huskily, almost a question, but not quite.

Mirda rose from the broken, still figure with a shake of the head. "She's dead, Therelane." She laid her head on his chest and put her arms around him as he sank sobbing to his knees.

~

"I love you, Mirda." He said it through the anguish that poured out of his heart, over and over. "I love you."

"I know." She was warm and quiet against him, a well for all the tears he had to fill.

"She told me to tell you. I love you, Mirda."

"I know." She rubbed his back. "Shh, I know."

And he let her hush him, like a little child.

He stood up, still holding her fast. Fire streaked up into the sky from Mount Thiranu, masked by the aura of smoke that hung over them. "Will you marry me when this is over, Mirda?"

Her head turned, and he knew that she, too, was gazing up at the flames of war on the slopes of Ceristen. Her voice was soft, matter-of-fact, and sad. "It is over."

Therelane tightened his arms and looked into the east. The sky was paling to a bluish-silver, with a rosy haze on the very horizon. Against it, the dark spire of the last stronghold had just grown visible, reminding him of their errand. "Dawn is coming. We had best be moving on."

~

The window in the chamber faced east. As the first ribbons of sun crept over the city walls and spilled into golden light and veering trails of shadow, a second presence entered the room and the man before the window stirred.

"Orden City burns," he said quietly.

Jedediah Crayes arched a grim brow in acknowledgment. "The hour grows late, my general. You would do well to go."

The general turned towards him, the indirect light throwing a soft cast upon his face. He laid a hand on the sword girt at his waist. "It is not for me to retreat and leave my people to the wolves."

"Your place is beside the king; and there is much of Orden yet that remains free," Jedediah Crayes pointed out, unsilenced.

The general shook his head. "When this has fallen, the rest will fall. There is no more army, save a few hundreds on the northern front. If my life would save my people, I would give it to them—yea, and I will give what remains of it. What was that?" he ended as Jedediah Crayes muttered something.

Jedediah Crayes started to answer, and then strode quickly to the window. "Something afoot out there, my lord," he remarked. "Beyond the city wall. A couple hundreds of soldiers with the Runnicoran banner—come to finish the city off, I daresay."

The general looked out and was silent. "Is the queen safely away?" he asked at last.

"She is departing now," said a heavy, tired voice behind them, and the king of Orden entered, his dark hair bound back and a sword in his hand. "A guard may perhaps see her safely out of the city."

"Her, and the babe within her," murmured the general. "You have seen the enemy, my king?"

King Conrad nodded. "We go to meet them at the gate."

"Ahearn of Dirion?"

"He is already assembling the remnants of his men."

Something about Jedediah Crayes' mouth twisted at the mention of Ahearn. "I wonder," he muttered to himself.

"Sir," he said to the general. "You may recall at the beginning of this mess, I offered you my services and fealty for the duration of the war."

"I release you from that," said the general, "as does the king, if need be."

Again Jedediah Crayes' mouth twisted in that wry way. "Be that as it may, I'm not a man who likes to break faith with my own word. If it weren't for the simple fact that I'm needed elsewhere, I should prefer, I think, to go down with the ship, to put it so. As it is, I have higher loyalties calling me. Farewell!"

And he was gone.

The king and the general looked at one another. All that they held dear was crumbling around them.

The general settled his shoulders, and loosened his sword in its sheath. "Come," he said. "Let us ride down to the gate."

~

They issued from the courtyard into the streets, a small, proud cavalcade, the last of Mitheren's might emptied—less than two hundreds strong.

Across the desolated city they swept, bent on nothing but reaching the gate. It was open, swinging wide on the hinges, and they burst through, past the long shadow of the wall and into the full sunlight of the day.

The Runnicoran ranks lay massed on the open plain between the city and the Elerien Mountains. Yet, strangely, they were not turned towards them.

The general reined in sharply, bringing the small host to a skidding halt, and stood in the stirrups, straining his eyes afar off.

"There is conflict there," said the king quietly beside him as a clashing commotion reached their ears.

"Aye," said Ahearn in bewilderment. "Have they begun to war among themselves—?" He broke off with a shrug.

"My general," said Captain Rhodes hoarsely, disbelief in his voice as he, too, strained forward in the saddle. "It is in my mind that—that the banner of Orden rises among the fray."

Murmurs broke out astonished along the line where he was heard. "Impossible—it is a trick of the light—surely not."

The general leaned forward again with eagerness rising amid despair, scanning for what the younger, keener eyes had caught in an irrecoverable moment. But at last he shook himself in dismissal. "Whatever may be happening there," he said, "it matters not. Come! They are distracted; we shall strike them from behind."

And with a cry he summoned them forward again, and they rushed over the earth with a sound like wings. And they came upon the Runnicorans unexpected, and cut into them, sending them scattered like the ash that rose from the city on the morning wind.

And as the fighting swelled and came to the breaking point, the general saw a pennant through the hazing thicket of war, a pennant which bore a mountain whose shining peak was surmounted by a circlet of silver stars. "*Iriem ese loninae*!" he cried. "Behold, my people, behold!"

So a hush came as two forces met and cut the Runnicoran army in two; and at the general's side Captain Rhodes called out in renewed wonder to the man at the head of the larger company, "Ormad! Captain Ormad Keyes!"

"It cannot be," said the general half-aloud, more in joy than in denial.

The captain who had led eight hundreds of Orden's military strength south to Arahad on April fifth laughed aloud and swung his sword high in greeting. "It is a timely homecoming, my general!"

"It is Captain Keyes!" The word spread like fire. "It is the men sent to Arahad, returned!"

The Runnicorans, bereft of the impetus and purpose that drove their enemies, tried to band together afresh, but in vain. They broke at last into wild retreat, running back to the West Gate.

The Ordenians did not pursue them. They turned back to the city, now coalesced into one mighty unit, and overwhelmed the enemy soldiers running rampant through the streets. Dispersed and leaderless as they were, the thing was over quickly. Some few turned and fought like cornered dogs; but the greater part were confounded and afraid, and fled, or simply surrendered their arms and let themselves be taken.

Noon was high and passing when the two horsemen met again, this time on a cobbled, empty street with the stench of smoke and blood thick and acrid on the warm air. They said no word at first, but halted wearily and looked out on the still-burning city.

The general turned to Captain Keyes. "The West Gate?" he asked. "It is how they entered, is it not?"

Captain Keyes nodded. "The garrison were all slain when we came upon it. But they did not trouble themselves to gird it with fresh defenders. It is now retaken and safe."

"They were too confident," murmured the general. "Their leader was ever quick to judge and quick to act; and it paid him well sometimes—but not in the end."

"And if we had not returned at the time it happened," returned Captain Keyes, "it would have paid him well. By the time the rumors of war reached us, we were already near to Arahad, and afterward there were days of dispute as to whether we should go on and conclude the embassy, or turn back to our king. By the sway of a hand's breadth we stand here now."

"We had ceased to look for you," the general said simply, bowing his head. "Yet a higher power willed otherwise."

"Indeed. The Eastern Watch still stands; for that, may *Iarenad Legea* be praised." Ormad Keyes paused. "Perhaps it is not for me to say, for

I have not been here this time, but I think that with this blow we will have little more to fear from them."

"I dare not speak too soon," said the general. "Still, it may be so."

"Yes, you have endured much these past months, my general. I do not want you to hope too quickly."

They sat in grave silence again, under the shimmering blaze of the sun.

~

"Halt!" shouted the man commanding the small patrol of soldiers. "Left, into that alley! Something's moving."

They sped into it, confronting the group of four. But the four were a girl and a boy and two wounded men, coughing in the smoke and weary. The tallest looked on the verge of unconsciousness.

"Mordred, Fenris!" exclaimed Braegon, pushing aside the arm of Jared Earle that had been steadying him, and limping forward. "Laufeia! Where are you going?"

"Mitheren," said Laufeia. "We left the hospice and—lost our way." She spoke with a tenacious firmness, though faintly.

"There's still fighting about," said Braegon. "You'd best not attempt to travel any further till it's over. The streets are not safe."

Fenris lowered Mordred to the ground at once, his legs folding gratefully under him. He looked up at Braegon and the rest, and a question passed through his tired eyes. "Where's Sergeant Garin?" he asked.

Braegon glanced down, his eyes dimming with the memory of the quick skirmish's aftermath, the blood, the stillness, all the eyes turned on him. They had needed a leader; they all looked to one man, and so was the silent choice made.

"He died during the night," he said quietly. "The men voted me into command in his stead." A laughter that was more pain than humor touched his lips. "A strange sergeant I make—one who can barely walk or wield a weapon!"

"But you know how," said Laufeia, and she came over and took his hand with a firm pressure. "That's what they need—someone who knows."

"And someone who cares," said Fenris softly, his head drooping. "Sergeant Garin cared."

"I am sorry," said Braegon, and he squeezed Laufeia's hand in answer and reached forward to grip Fenris' shoulder. Then he nodded to them in farewell and turned away.

CHAPTER 38

DUSK GATHERED OVER ORDEN CITY, a summer's dusk with warm afterlight gilding the grey, insects humming fuzzily in the faintly humid air.

Laufeia passed her hands over her hair, fingers tangling clumsily in the sweat-stuck wisps around her face. She was acutely aware of everything that compounded to make her feel wretched: the dull hunger at the base of her stomach, the fluttering weariness in her limbs, the lingering smoke in the air that teased and tickled her throat, suffocating air, sweltering thirst, and the unendurable filthiness.

They were not the only ones who had sought refuge in Mitheren—far from it; it seemed that half the city had flocked to the gate of the fortress. When they had finally reached the tower, under a stifling noon sun, the courtyards were already thronged thick; now, though the city was safe and the enemy driven back beyond the mountains, they kept coming, those who had nowhere else to go. Like children, they gathered to their protector and waited for comfort and sustainment. There was scarcely room to sit.

Inspector Dickson grunted something, shifting his head on Fenris' shoulder.

"What?" asked Laufeia.

"Thirsty," he repeated. His lips were pale and his eyes glassy.

Laufeia clenched her hands, tears of frustration burning behind her eyes. She glanced at Fenris, whose face was filmed with smoke and dirt and dripping with sweat as he bore up Inspector Dickson's weight without complaint, and Mordred, who lay in some kind of exhausted swoon, though now and again his lungs heaved in a great gasp for air. She had nothing to do for any of them. *Nothing*.

"It's almost night," she said aloud, firmly and steadily. "It will begin to get cooler soon."

Inspector Dickson made a dissatisfied sort of movement and shifted weakly again. She wondered if she ought to check his wound—but no, not now, not in this unbearable press of people. She had nothing to clean it with anyway.

There were men moving among the crowd, pushing through, pausing here and there; soldiers, she assumed without interest.

"Girl." One had stopped in front of her. His tone was demanding and curt, his face set in uncompromising lines.

She drew herself up to her whole small height. "My name is Laufeia, sir."

"Laufeia." He shrugged. "Where are you from?"

"I—I live in Ceristen, sir."

"And why are you here?"

"Why, sir?" She looked back at him in puzzlement. "I, my brothers, and our other friend fled the hospice during the night."

He nodded. "So. Is the hospice torn down? Has it been burned?"

"I do not know."

"Very well, we will ask about. If it is still standing, you will have to return there."

The shock must have sheeted across her face. He explained bluntly, "It is one thing to protect the townsfolk, girl, but another to house them when the danger is gone. We have not the capacity or the food for all these people, as you surely see. Those who have a place to return to must return there."

Laufeia felt the color rising hotly up her throat. She opened her mouth, but he went on.

"And if the hospice should be in ruins, then you should go to your own home. Ceristen is not far from here. Either way, you have no warrant to stay here."

Laufeia's lips set thin and hard and her cheeks burned with anger. "Look there," she said fiercely. "Do you see my brothers? We wandered the streets half a night and half a day before we reached here. Mordred barely made it into the gate before he fainted utterly, and he has been unconscious since. Fenris can scarcely walk a step, and Inspector Dickson took an arrow to the side last night. And you want to turn us into the street again? Very well, then drag them to the gate! They will not get there on their own."

"My lady—" he protested, looking down. "I am but following my orders. I am sure that with assistance from you, they can manage—"

"You are not looking or listening," she spat at him, outraged. "Have done! If you are going to drag us out, do it."

"I shall be back," he snapped, and turned away, shouldering through the masses.

He did not come back, and Laufeia gave up looking for him. She sat silent at Mordred's side and hugged her knees as the still, airless twilight deepened. Someone's foot dug into the small of her back, and a strangely dissonant cacophony of heavy breathing grew in the air around. Laufeia did not sleep.

Miserable and wakeful as the night was for her, it seemed to pass into day quickly enough—a day which promised to be hotter than the last. The courtyard was not perceptibly emptier than it had been the night before, and Laufeia wondered how successful the attempts at eviction had been. Many had turned out much like hers, she supposed.

By noon the heat and thirst was unbearable. She had often been hungry in her young life; the gnawing that seared her stomach, discomfort though it was, she could ignore. But the craving agony that seemed to writhe through her whole body, the dryness of mouth and lips, and worst of all the sight of Fenris afflicted the same way, could not be ignored.

"Lass." A hand touched her shoulder as she rocked back and forth, trying to shut out a blinding headache. She looked up to see a kindly fair-complexioned face belonging to a broadly built, middle-aged woman.

"Lass, they're giving out food up there, towards the fore of the courtyard. You'd best get some for yourself, and your kin there." She nodded to the boys and Inspector Dickson.

"Oh—thank you," said Laufeia dizzily, and she leaned forward and gave the kneeling woman a hug.

The food was gone when she got there; it had already been distributed to nearer, quicker hands. But she carried back to her brothers one large, precious mug of water.

It was about an hour later that she looked down to see Mordred's eyes on her.

"Mordred," she exclaimed softly, relieved to see him wake at last.

"Laufeia," he answered. "Where are we?"

She told him. "And," she added, "we won, Mordred. The city is safe, and the enemy has retreated."

He took it without a word.

She lifted the mug from between her knees, where she had kept the last quarter safe, and set the rim to his lips. "Drink, Mordred."

Mordred did not open his mouth. "Give it to Fenris," he muttered faintly.

"Fenris has had his. Drink."

He drank, and closed his eyes.

Laufeia put a hand on his head as he lay there, frustrated afresh by her helplessness. Why had they come here at all? But what else could they have done? Now they were trapped here until Mordred and Inspector Dickson could move on, or until they all perished from starvation and thirst. Inspector Dickson especially, she feared, would not be able to stand the heat much longer. If only it would rain, she thought desperately.

The sun moved in its blazing white path across the blue arc of sky.

Someone came pushing through the crowd, like the soldiers had the night before, but this had happened several times in the course of the day already—not soldiers now, only inhabitants trying to get through. Laufeia watched, like everyone else, or tried to watch; she could not see over so many heads. "Make way," people were murmuring. "Make way." It must be a very important person this time, she thought. The general?

"*Laufeia,*" gasped a voice that she had not heard for seven months. She looked up into Ahearn's aghast face.

He was clean, she thought with an odd sting of envy. It was her strongest emotion in that moment. He bore himself with an authority that she did not remember, and his scruffy beard was clipped and shaven close along the jaw. He looked quite horror-stricken.

"Laufeia," said Ahearn again. His eyes passed over all of them—tired, hollow-eyed, Mordred sunk in a torpor of weariness, Inspector Dickson feverish. "You should not be here!"

"That was what the soldier said last night," said Laufeia. "I am beginning to believe him."

He looked at her uncomprehendingly. "Sister, you must not stay here."

"Last time we spoke," said Laufeia, "you would not call Mordred brother. Do you still hold that? For I will not be called sister by you if so."

Ahearn recoiled a little. "You are hard," he said, without anger, rather a wondering sadness.

"I should have been harder, that night. I was angry at you both."

"Do you know me so little, Laufeia?" he queried, his shoulders hanging in a truly hurt manner. "I regretted my words not an hour after they were spoken. I would have called you back, if I could have found you. Do you know me so little?"

She shook her head. "I have been with Mordred since then, to know his mind, but you I have not known, Ahearn. How am I to know if a kingship has changed you? Or if indeed it was greed that drove you? And though you are gentler-tempered than Mordred, you are not above holding grudges either."

"Well—it is past, Laufeia. Never mind it. Mordred and I have made things right between us—did he not tell you?—or as right as they can be made." His shoulders sagged again.

"Mordred is not one to speak of things that still hurt him," said Laufeia. "I think for him the thing is not yet over."

"Mordred, is he—" began Ahearn, looking down at his brother, and then broke off. "There are better places and times to speak of all this."

"Maybe so," said Laufeia. A strange loyalty would not let her accept help from Ahearn without Mordred's acquiescence, even though she hated his disdain for what he called "charity", and hated worse his accusations of like nature that he had made against Ahearn. She bent down to her sick, half-conscious brother and touched his cheek very lightly.

"Mordred," she said when he opened his eyes. "Ahearn is here."

She saw a deep pain twist in his face, and knew that her guess spoken to Ahearn had struck true. "What does he want?" he asked dully.

Laufeia looked up, frowning, at Ahearn, waiting for confirmation and specification to what she already knew.

"To help," said Ahearn, a whipped, pleading look in his eyes. "To take you out of this hellish place and have you housed in Mitheren—as sister and brothers of a king."

Laufeia did not repeat the words to Mordred; she saw his eyes bent on Ahearn and knew that he had heard. She did not know his thoughts, only that the silence was knife-like and that Mordred looked like a man caught between two fires.

"Do it," he said, and his tone was both intense and defeated. And to Laufeia he looked, not as though he had won a battle, but as though he had won with a terrible loss, and she knew at once that there was something she did not understand, something beyond his mere pride that he had torn down. He slumped back, drained, and said so faintly that only Laufeia heard, "Inspector Dickson, too."

"Aye, Mordred," she said, grasping even as she answered that he did not mean for anyone except her to hear. "We would not leave him."

~

Laufeia came out of the small side bath-chamber, feeling wonderfully cleansed and refreshed. Her hair dangled over her shoulder in a fresh, shining braid, catching the sunset light as it streamed through an arched window. Fenris was fast asleep on the small floor pallet; she stooped to drop a loving caress on his brow. Inspector Dickson, too, lay sleeping. He had seemed better almost directly after coming into the stone-cool halls of Mitheren. It only remained to talk to Mordred, if he were still awake—about what had happened earlier.

Mordred was not asleep, not at all. He could not be further from sleep. He was sitting up, his head bowed, his hands over his face, crying in helpless, jagged sobs, trying to restrain them and failing.

She stared at him for an instant, and crossed to him without a word.

~

With Laufeia gone and the others asleep, there was no reason to hold up the wall any longer. And yet he tried, tried with all his strength, to no avail. It shattered and he wept.

There was so much, too much for his mind to take in any longer without release. All the agony and confusion of Inspector Dickson, a turmoil still beating him. Two days of unrelenting strain, Captain Alétun, death, the tide of the war turned for good. And Ahearn.

How could Ahearn do that? How could he ask it of him?

Mordred wanted only peace, but Ahearn wanted more. He wanted the old brotherly fellowship, perfect unity, and all four of them together in the palace of Ederan. And part of Mordred yearned to give it to him, because, by all rights, he ought to give it to him.

Except that Ceristen was a home to him, and *he had never had a home,* a real home, and if he went with Ahearn he would lose it utterly.

How was one to know? Did loyalty lie in blood and brother or in a home that was like family?

Tonight, at any rate, he had chosen blood. And it tore at him like teeth in the flesh, because he had betrayed Ceristen, and because he knew that he had put hope in Ahearn's heart, hope that he could never realize, and because he did not want to hurt Ahearn—he had hurt so many people—

Arms came around him, strong and protecting. He lowered his hands and caught a flash of shimmering reddish hair, but he already knew who held him.

"I didn't—" he struggled to say through the unrelenting tears. "I didn't mean—for you—to see."

"Hush, no, Mordred." She rubbed her hand against his back.

Strangely, as he relinquished his fight against the tears, they began to slow. The sobs diminished into broken sighs.

"What is it, Mordred?"

He shook his head.

"Is it cannot, or will not?"

"There is too much—for words."

"You were so stubborn; you would not weep all the hours of agony before. Why now?"

"Ahearn," he said wearily, and it came out, in bits and pieces, all roundabout and contradictory. Ahearn, the whole story of Captain Alétun, spying, captivity, his dreadful failure.

"I could not protect him, Laufeia—the leader almost killed him. And he did kill Bardrick . . .

"I destroyed something like a tenth of the army, the second time—I pretended to be a guide, and I led him false . . . It is strange that the thing he hates me for the most is the one I regret the most—I wish those deaths had been laid at anyone's door but mine, oh, Laufeia, do you understand?"

"Yes, Mordred," she said gently.

"I am afraid of him, Laufeia—so afraid—I still dream about him sometimes, in the night. The werevulture was sane, Laufeia, cruelly sane, but him—there is madness lurking somewhere inside, and I never know when it will leap out at me—"

Only about Inspector Dickson he said nothing, because he did not even know his own mind there, and he did not want to go there and try to fathom it. He fell silent at last, spent with tears and explanations, and the silence rested over both of them for what seemed a long time.

And then Laufeia said the words that he did not want to hear.

"What happened between you and Inspector Dickson?"

"Don't, Laufeia," he gasped, flinching away from her, from the name.

"No. This once, Mordred, you will tell me."

"I hurt him, Laufeia," he whispered at last. "He was a person, a person like you—like *Fenris*—and I hurt him. I wanted to make him hurt as much as I had, with all the hate in my heart, but even after it stopped hurting me I hated him. And he never was or did half of what I pretended, and I knew it. It was wrong—it was murderous—and then it was my fault that he was shot—really it was—if I hadn't asked him to close the window—"

"Mordred, you can't say that." Her arms tightened around him, as though to quell his shivering.

"But it was a silly request, and I persisted in it—so—childishly." He shut his eyes and clutched her like an anchor. "And I think in that moment I wanted him to die. I would have liked it to happen. So it was my fault, all along . . . "

"And that was how you felt when he was shot?"

"No—no, it was so different then. It was horrible, I didn't know what to do, I *could* do nothing, and he might have been dying there—it seemed as though he was—and it was my fault. And like lightning everything seemed to be so petty and baseless, all my hate and anger and the cruel words. And after all that—*he saved my life*." The admission of greatest pain, the one he could barely manage to say aloud. "He saved it—no, more than that: he put his life at risk for mine. And what have I ever done except taunt him?"

"I still love you, Mordred." She was giving him the only thing she could, trying to comfort him, trying to ease his mind, and he felt her clasp tighten on him again. "You can do nothing that will make me stop loving you."

"That is not enough," he said flatly. "I must make it right with him." He shuddered. "But what can I ever do that will make all that right?"

There is nothing. That debt is a gap too wide to fill.

~

The Runnicoran army had lost.

They could still keep trying, keep trying to regain the ground, keep trying to open the pincer-tight defenses of Orden. But their back was broken. They had tried too long. They had bargained for speed, sudden striking and a quick victory, but the war had dragged out, weakening them little bit by little bit, and now Orden, with this fresh division of military strength, was easily their equal.

Yes, the best thing, as Lieutenant Dovurti Atta was saying, was to cut their losses and retreat with dignity to Runnicor.

"Dignity!" scoffed Cir Harrik. "Dignity in defeat, indeed!"

"Defeat may be dignified," said the lieutenant coolly. "The king would be far less pleased if we returned to him after squandering our remnant of strength on a war we had already lost."

"Nonetheless he will not be very pleased," said Cir Harrik bitterly, "at our utter failure."

All eyes turned uncomfortably to the one in highest command, the one who would bear the fullest responsibility of the defeat and have to answer directly to the king who had trusted him with this plan.

But Cern Dersturi, the Paraki, met none of their gazes, fixing his dark eyes grimly on the ground with inward-turned gaze.

Little did any of them know, he was *not* going to answer to the king. He was *not* going to return disgraced at the head of a wretched, depleted army, to be stripped of his prestige and rank and more than probably sentenced to the dungeons or serf labor. He was not going back at all.

He was going to revenge himself—and of course it would end in death, but what a vengeful, glorious suicide death it would be . . .

"Send word," Lieutenant Dovurti Atta was saying, "to withdraw forces from the north. As for the main body, we march at noon."

"Lieutenant," said Cern Dersturi harshly, drawing all eyes to him again. "There is a small patrol encamped west of here. I will go fetch them. You need not wait; we will catch up."

Dovurti Atta looked back at him with searching eyes. He would know that there was no patrol in the west; and his narrowed, thoughtful gaze seemed to see his general's intent. He gave a little nod, imperceptible to the watchers. *This is your way?* he seemed to ask.

Cern Dersturi's grim jaw pulsed in answer, his chin lifting in the slightest proud gesture.

Lieutenant Dovurti Atta nodded again, and turned away.

~

Ahearn came to see that they were doing well in the morning. Laufeia assured him brusquely that they were doing quite well. Then she snatched his hand and drew him out into the hall.

"Mordred doesn't need you hovering over him," she said plainly. "He has enough on his mind without being reminded that he's brother of the king every few hours."

"What is troubling him?" Ahearn's brow furrowed anxiously.

"More than I have time to tell you," said Laufeia impatiently.

"He is my brother, too," said Ahearn, begging in a mournful, baffled way.

She shook her head. "Another time."

"There will never be 'another time'," said Ahearn bitterly; "you need not pretend. Why must I be the outcast? Mordred would be far better suited for that office!"

Laufeia froze in mid-turn and spun back on him, furious. "Tell me you meant that in jest," she said in a low, hard voice. "And if so, a poorly chosen jest it was."

Shaken, Ahearn stepped away. "I didn't mean—I didn't think—"

"You should have. At least Mordred would rather sacrifice his pride than hurt you now." She stormed back into the room and shut the door hard.

Avoiding Mordred's eyes, the first pair she met was Inspector Dickson's; he had improved rapidly, and was standing with his right side leaning on the wall. He raised his brows with a curious frown.

Laufeia was finished with interference from any quarter. She turned her back and sat stiffly in front of the window. Gradually her indignation faded, and she stared pensively out at the morning-lit city spread below, feeling sorry for Ahearn. After all, it was hard on him.

A knock rattled the door hours later. Somehow she expected Ahearn, but it was a strange face that entered.

“I was told that Mordred Kenhelm is lodged here,” said the man, whose grim features seemed almost carven out of stone. His eyes flicked around the room.

“Captain Murray!” said Mordred.

They were the first words he had spoken all day, and a light seemed to enter his face. Laufeia watched him, mesmerized, trying to understand. He had been drawn out of his pain for the first time in days.

“I was bidden to give you a message,” said Captain Murray, “by the general.” A slight smile was playing at the edges of his stony-firm mouth, and it cracked into an ungainly grin, as though he were not used to smiling so openly. “He thought you would like to know that the Runnicoran army was seen marching south and west in its entirety. A message came by dragon that those in the north have likewise departed.”

“Truly?” asked Mordred softly. “That means—”

“It is over,” said Captain Murray. “The war is over.”

“The war is over,” repeated Laufeia, so wonderstruck she could not even feel joy, turning the words this way and that to herself. She remembered the horse sale, the general’s words of sorrowful promise, Mordred’s white, rigid face, Linda Boccin sobbing wildly.

All that over.

They would go home, all three of them.

To Ceristen.

She found that she was crying.

~

Captain Murray left. And even the news of victory could not lift away Mordred’s cloud for long. He sat quiet, staring distantly away. He and Inspector Dickson both avoided even looking in one another’s direction, and the silence between them was thicker and tenser than it had ever been.

Towards evening, Inspector Dickson heaved a sudden sigh and got up abruptly. "I want to walk a little," he said. He disregarded offers of help and limped out.

If he wanted time alone, Laufeia thought, she could not fault him. She began to think that she would like to walk a little herself—

But not alone, she decided. She would bring Fenris. He needed to hear what she had heard from Mordred last night—he, above anyone else, deserved to know it.

"Do not worry if we are gone long," she told Mordred as Fenris waited for her by the door.

He nodded. She wondered if he had really heard—so lost in his hopeless suffering.

"Mordred," she said more deliberately, cutting through to him. "Mordred," she repeated, softly. "Is there no way you can make yourself at rest?"

His face twitched in pain. "There is an immeasurable gulf of wrong between us, and an unpayable debt. I must unmake that, I must make it all right. But how can I do that? There is nothing that will cover my words. How am I to repay the unpayable?"

She spoke tenderly. "Mordred, you want the impossible. Listen to me—your wrongs cannot be *unmade,* but maybe they can be mended. Your gulf cannot be filled, but maybe it can be bridged. Mend it, Mordred, in whatever way you can."

He met her gaze intensely, drinking in every word. Silence hung between them for an instant.

Then an answer came into his eyes, and peace with it, and a confused, turbulent look that had underlain his countenance for a long time faded away.

"Yes," he said. "I will do that."

~

Inspector Dickson walked mindlessly, not noticing when his side set up a fiery ache of protest. He needed to be alone, very badly, so that he could sort through matters.

Every time he remembered Mordred's quiet, costly "I thank you" in the darkened courtyard, he struggled not to weep. He knew in a way that few people did how fierce and how inexorable Mordred's pride and anger were when aimed together at one man. That he had laid them aside—that he had repudiated them!—shamed Inspector Dickson to his innermost depths. He could not bear to think how hard it had been for Mordred to say those words.

They had come so close to apology, to reconciliation. Yet neither one had done it. Why Mordred had not done it was of less concern to Inspector Dickson; why *he* had not done it was what nagged him. And the reason was simple; he was afraid. Afraid of rejection.

He did not simply want Mordred's respect, Mordred's good will. He did not merely want Mordred's face turned to him in tranquility instead of anger. He wanted Mordred's friendship.

He wanted this strange, passionate, tender-hearted young man to like him. He wanted that bright, flashing grin that he had almost never seen to be turned on him in welcome. He wanted that sensitive heart to care for him like it cared for Fenris, Laufeia, Jedediah Crayes, the general, and even a Runnicoran captain.

He already cared for Mordred, he realized blindingly—it seemed stupid that he had not realized it before—he had cared about him for a very long time. That was why he had not wanted him to die, why he wanted friendship, why he feared rejection, the answer to *all* the whys. He wanted that brotherly love reciprocated more than he had ever wanted anything in the world.

He saw the scene in his head; he had imagined it a thousand times.

"I'm sorry, Mordred."

At best, a flat answer. Maybe a complete ignoral. Mordred had broken his pride that once for him, but would it stand for another beating? Inspector Dickson shook his head. Mordred might *barely* think that he owed him an acknowledgement of the apology. Probably not forgiveness. Certainly no further.

After all, Inspector Dickson reminded himself wearily, did Mordred owe him any of that? He needn't think that he deserved anything from that face.

Just remember what you did to him.

He remembered. His readiness to give an insult for an insult. His readiness to give an insult even where none had been given, simply on memory of earlier times. His prejudice. His resentment. He remembered it all and shrank from it with loathing.

He stumbled, and sank down on the winding, silent steps that he had been descending. A musty smell drifted up into his nostrils. And something in him snapped.

Afraid or not, he could not bear the war within himself any longer.

Whether he accepts it or rejects it is neither here nor there, he told himself harshly. *You have put this off long enough. It is time to speak.*

~

The face of Cern Dersturi was known to very few beyond the Elerien Mountains. With his distinctive Runnicoran livery exchanged for the clothes of a common Ordenian, he did not fear recognition as he mingled on the streets, or in the courtyard of Mitheren. To enter the tower itself was a tricky business, but his reckless errand made him cunning: he took a yoke of buckets, filling them with water, and slipped into the kitchens by a small side-door for servants' use. Then he wandered the passageways, his feet taking him ever upwards, toward the sleeping quarters. To kill the king and the general now, in the great throne hall—no, that was too risky for his intent, too open to miscarriage. Better simply to find their bed-chambers, and then, when they retired for the night, his knife would find its mark.

But not them only; he needed others to glorify his triumph, before he was taken down and slain. The queen, the captains, and after that, any other being who came within the reach of his arm. Yes, they would mock Cern Dersturi for many days, but afterwards they would sing of him in Runnicor—a scornful snarl curled up his lip. He must find someone who would tell him the specific whereabouts of all these chambers, so that he could strike swiftly later; and he must find one now, for it was already evening.

He sent a half-closed door swinging lightly open, his eyes raking the room for sign of life. And then he forgot the king, and the general, the queen and the captains, and all his plans . . .

~

Mordred lay against the pillow, watching as the sunset flame fell steadily through the west window, his face quiet and alight. He was simply, inexpressibly at peace.

For the first time in half a year there was no pain ripping him apart inside. There was no hatred burning him in a silent poison. No multitude of obligations and fears gnawed at him, pulling him in one conflicting direction after another till he felt torn to shreds.

He could not repay Inspector Dickson. He could not do the impossible. And since that was so, rather than grieve uselessly over what he could *not* do, as Laufeia had bidden him, there only remained to do what he could. When Inspector Dickson came back, he would speak—

With a small, contented sigh he watched the burnished light dying slowly in a curious glowing haze, while the indigo shadows reached out to swallow it up. The shadow of a bird came winging across the last blaze of gold cast on the wall, and a little smile came to Mordred's face as he watched it flit away.

The door creaked open and Mordred pushed himself up eagerly, straining to see across the bar of mote-laden light. Surely Fenris and Laufeia were not back already—was it Inspector Dickson?

"I did not expect to find you here, Damachrus," said a cold, implacable, and horribly triumphant voice, and the leader came into the light.

Mordred did not cry out or even start. He was paralyzed with horror.

"Fine quarters you keep," said the leader. "I should have thought to look for you here, a doubtlessly beloved and pampered spy—you wretched brat." As he spoke he crossed to the window and slammed the shutters shut in one swift movement.

The ice holding Mordred snapped and he leapt out of the bed, diving headlong for the open door. But his broken leg betrayed him, he staggered, and an arm caught him across the throat, throwing him to the floor. The leader kicked the door shut and slapped the bolt in place.

In those few seconds of respite Mordred was able to think very clearly, and very fast. A memory broke on him—Fenris in the hospice courtyard with a sword—and he lunged for the far wall where something was glittering dimly on the floor. He snatched up the weapon and was on his feet again in an instant, propping himself on the wall, his lips clamped together as needles of sickening pain shot up his leg. Sweat broke out on his brow, rolling down to sting his eyes. It had to hold his weight—it *had* to—

The leader was watching with his faint, wolf-like smile playing derisively over his lips. "Do you really think to fight me, boy? You weakling, you cannot even stand."

He strode forward. His kick landed in Mordred's shins and Mordred, lost in a white wave of agony, crashed to the ground. When he came fully back to himself, his hand still clutched the sword, his jaw was still clenched shut and blood was running from his lip into his mouth. The leader's foot was on his sword-arm, his face bending near, so near, and the blind terror rose up in him again.

"It will be slow, Damachrus," said the leader softly as he raised his sword.

~

Inspector Dickson dragged himself up to the door and leaned against it, breathing fast. He had walked much too far and his body was repaying him in bitter coin. In a minute he would get up, and go in there, and get it over with . . .

A happy excuse floated through his head. It would be far too awkward to make an apology while Laufeia and Fenris were in the room. If he found Mordred alone, all well and good, but if not, perhaps he should wait.

He cut off the irrational thought, disgusted with himself. Better to endure the ordeal at once than deal longer with the pain of not undergoing it! Did he *want* to wait under guilty silence?

He lingered a second longer, nerving himself to pull up his tired, pain-wracked body and open the door. And he heard it.

It was just a murmuring voice to his ears, muffled, unintelligible through the thick door. He could not have said *what* it was that made the sharp, taut sense of danger run eerily through his senses, quivering like lightning-touched metal in his fingers. But he knew that sensation, like a burned hand knows the fire. He did not open the door.

All discomfort in his side forgotten, he rose up lightly and pressed his ear to the latch-hole. The voice grew a degree louder, just distinct enough to be heard.

"—no one this time, boy. Even if they come and loose that bolt, I will kill them. There will be time later to visit the king and princes of Mitheren—in this hour, I have his spy."

What madman was talking in there—and to whom? Fenris was not a spy—Mordred—*was Mordred a spy?*

Inspector Dickson's head spun. Who was in there?

Something smacked, like a palm against flesh, only harder. Right on the heels of it, a stifled, almost soundless cry.

"It hurts, does it? I shall give you worse, Damachrus. Cern Dersturi does not take lightly those who meddle with his trust."

Rage boiled up in Inspector Dickson. His hands shook with it. That was Mordred—he did not doubt it—and whoever was striking him deserved to be hung by the neck.

Then the name snagged on his attention.

All the anger leached out of him, succeeded by shock. He had not lived in Mitheren a month to forget the name of the Runnicoran leader when he heard it. What was *he* doing here? And were Fenris and Laufeia in there as well? Had he killed them?

Inspector Dickson whirled and ran down the hall. He would be killed, too, if he went in there alone.

He wondered if he had left Mordred to his death.

~

"The general just returned from a ride out to the city—he's stabling his horse." The guard looked at Inspector Dickson in alarm.

"Thank you," Inspector Dickson managed as he sped away, not daring to halt longer; already he was limping badly.

He lost his footing and tripped into someone's path, dashing his head against the flagstones.

"Inspector Dickson?" gasped Laufeia Kenhelm's voice, and he opened his eyes, wincing, on Fenris' thin, worried face.

"What are you doing out here?" demanded Laufeia, sounding as much vexed as concerned.

Inspector Dickson shook his head. The words would not come, as hard as he tried to make them. "The Runnicoran leader," he forced out. "In Mitheren. I need—to see the—the general."

He had never seen Laufeia's face so like to Mordred's. It looked like the moment when Mordred had panicked in the gaol—except that Laufeia did not panic, not like that at least. "The leader?" she repeated in the merest stricken breath.

"Cern Dersturi," said Inspector Dickson.

"You can't mean that." She was white as death, begging him to be lying.

"I do mean it, my lady, believe me—"

"You are mistaken," she said desperately.

"He was in our chambers, calling Mordred a spy and meddler. Where is the general?" He grabbed Fenris' hand and stood swaying on his feet, looking around in the dusk.

"What do you need the general for?" It was Captain Murray's curt voice speaking out of the gloom. A dim shape moved towards them.

"You'll do," said Inspector Dickson urgently. "Cern Dersturi is in Mitheren, and who knows what harm he means. We need to get armed men up there and stop him."

"You jest," said Captain Murray flatly.

"He does not jest," said Laufeia quietly. "The leader is killing Mordred up there."

Fenris broke away from the group and ran straight towards the tower.

"Fenris!" Laufeia screamed.

Captain Murray's face changed, and he jerked about to face her. His whole demeanor grew cold and grim. "Sergeant!" he shouted as his long strides took him back to the door of Mitheren. He motioned to the guards there to follow him.

"Help me," muttered Inspector Dickson to Laufeia. His legs barely supported him any longer.

They hurried at the rear of the soldiers, never catching up until the party halted in front of the door. There was Fenris, to Inspector Dickson's relief and Laufeia's plainly greater relief. He had not tried to go in on his own.

"It's bolted," said Inspector Dickson weakly, though unheard by anyone else.

Captain Murray raised his hand to the latch.

~

If Mordred could have shrunk from the blade above him, he would have. It gleamed evilly in the faint glow from the wall-candle the leader had lit. It was the only thing left that seemed quite real, and he, on his back with the leader's foot pinning him down, was helplessly exposed to its edge.

Everything else was fading.

He tried so hard to hold on, to think, but the pain would not stop. Everywhere seemed to hurt, and the fear was choking him, and he could not think . . .

Something rattled dimly on his ear. Again, louder this time, waking him a little from the nightmare, and the leader started and glanced over his shoulder, shifting his weight—

And in that one moment of distraction Mordred wrenched convulsively away from the boot grinding down on his sword-arm.

And it was free.

The leader was turning back, features twisted in anger, swinging his sword back in a high, vicious arc, and Mordred could not make his arm lift. Could not block him. Higher—higher—not high enough—the sword was like a deadweight—

Then leader stumbled over his other arm, tripped, and suddenly Mordred was smothering, crushed under a burden like a rock. The world swirled in light and dark, and he tried to hold on, but he could not hold on anymore.

~

Inspector Dickson pushed forward as the bolt gave way and the door crashed open. He saw the dimly flickering light on the wall and an armed man standing in the middle of the room, who bent, lost his balance, and fell forward.

A sword's point jutted from his back.

"Out of the way," said Captain Murray brusquely, shoving Inspector Dickson aside. He marched into the room and hauled the slain man up—the sword came loose with a sickening sound and clattered down—flinging him to the floor. And standing there, he simply stared with drawn brow from one still figure to the other.

"What are you waiting for?" Inspector Dickson barked finally. He shoved past him and knelt beside Mordred. He *could not* be dead.

He looked it, but his pulse beat steadily. Inspector Dickson reminded himself that some of the blood glistening on his shirt must be the leader's.

Captain Murray bent down beside him with a fresh torch and shone it on Mordred's face. Inspector Dickson had not been prepared for the clearer sight. Blood streaked down from the young man's lip, and a darkening bruise splayed across his cheek, dwarfing the older ones that he had sustained the night the city burned. His white face looked strange in the yellow light.

"He's alive, isn't he?" asked Laufeia's hard, clear voice behind them.

"He's alive," said Inspector Dickson.

"And if what's on his face is the worst of what he has, he'll live," said Captain Murray.

Inspector Dickson shook his head, his eye traveling down. "He's bleeding from the arm at least, and the hand, too." He lifted Mordred's right hand carefully and swiped at the blood with his own sleeve.

"Are the soldiers still here?" he asked.

"I returned them to the gate," said Captain Murray. "They're not needed now."

Inspector Dickson shook his head in wonder, the truth settling over him. Mordred had killed the leader. Killed him with a broken leg and under torture, no less. What a thing to boast of!

"I will go find some water and cloths," said Laufeia, and her light footsteps pattered away.

"I should report all this," said Captain Murray, stepping back and rubbing his brow. "The general will want to know of it." He settled the torch in a bracket. "The girl is fetching cloths; you will do well enough now. I will be glad to hear when he wakes up."

Inspector Dickson sat back heavily on his heels as silence descended on the room. Fenris came forward and sat on Mordred's other side, and put a hand wordlessly on his brother's damp, ashen forehead.

Mordred stirred, as though at the touch. He sucked in a deep, gasping breath and was quiet again.

A part of Inspector Dickson longed to take Mordred's hand, but he did not dare to. The memory pushed back to him of how he had struck Mordred in the face. His was not a hand Mordred trusted, and he could not touch him so with that knowledge weighing on his heart.

"Mordred," Fenris murmured.

Mordred stirred again, in a more conscious way, and his lashes flickered. "Fenris," he said muzzily.

"Mordred, I'm here."

"I'm . . . so tired, Fenris." Mordred's hand groped out, and Fenris took it and closed his fingers tightly about it.

"Don't die, Mordred."

Mordred smiled, as though that were an absurd idea. "I won't die."

Then he frowned. "Why am I—not dead . . . "

"What do you mean?" asked Fenris.

Mordred's head moved from side to side, puzzled. "The leader was killing me. He knocked me down, and I got the sword, and he knocked me down again. I remember—I remember that I got my sword free after that, and then he tripped and fell on me. I remember because I couldn't breathe. I think I thought he was crushing me to death. But where is he?"

"He's dead," said Inspector Dickson. "He fell onto your sword."

Mordred's eyes flicked to him, startled. "Oh, it's you," he said, and shut his eyes with a concentrated frown as though he were trying to remember something.

"It's all so confusing," he said presently with a sigh.

"We'll get it sorted out later," said Inspector Dickson. "Don't worry now. Where—where did he hurt you?"

"He didn't get so very far," said Mordred indistinctly. His eyes were drooping. "I'm all right."

He had drowsed off by the time Laufeia returned with bandages and warm water, and he slept soundly as they worked an hour or more into the night, dressing the wounds. There were not so very many, as Mordred had implied, and they were not grave ones—painful, certainly, but superficial. The worst was, perhaps, the slice across all four fingers of his right hand. Inspector Dickson did not like to think about the way it must have happened, but he could reconstruct the picture so clearly: the sword cutting down, the hand flying up in a desperate movement to ward off the coming blow—But it was not a crippling blow, and the hand would heal.

Mordred woke again when they were nearly done, Laufeia wringing out the last of the bandages into the rusty, cooling water. He was more awake this time, and more lucid.

"Inspector Dickson," he said, "how did you know he fell onto my sword?"

Inspector Dickson balked.

"He's the one who came to fetch us," said Laufeia briskly, winding the cloth around Mordred's arm. "He overheard the leader in here and gathered what was going on."

"Then that makes twice you have saved my life," said Mordred with a funny smile, "does it not?"

He was delirious, thought Inspector Dickson. But Mordred was not acting delirious at all. "Yes," he said blankly.

Mordred looked up toward the ceiling, his face strangely serene and that funny smile quirking the edges of his mouth.

"Inspector Dickson," he remarked.

Inspector Dickson grunted acknowledgment, refusing to meet Mordred's eyes.

"I killed someone."

Inspector Dickson jerked his gaze down. What was Mordred getting at?

The grey eyes were dancing behind a deceptively sober front. "You finally have a reason to arrest me."

A strange sound escaped from Laufeia, half-laugh and half something that might have been a sob. She stood up and turned away from them, and Fenris came up behind her and put his arms around her.

Inspector Dickson stared down at Mordred, too bewildered to speak.

Mordred's smile widened into a grin. "Don't they know how to tease in Delgrass?" he said.

"Of course we do!" sputtered Inspector Dickson before he could stop. He caught himself, realized he had blundered, too late—Mordred was laughing.

Laughing at Inspector Dickson, of course, for defending himself over a jest, but it was more than that: there was a release in it, a discardment of sorrow, a joy of life. It was a wonderful, strangely contagious sound.

In the end, Inspector Dickson did the only thing he could do, and the honorable thing, since after all, he had made the bungle. He laughed himself.

"Mordred," he said when it had died away, soberly. "I *am* sorry."

Mordred looked at him. "I know," he said in that gentle way he had. "I am sorry, too. And I forgive you."

Inspector Dickson did not try to hide his tears, this time. Mordred reached out, and took his hand. "Mordred Kenhelm, I also forgive you."

CHAPTER 39

THE MORNING GLOW SEEPED THROUGH the south window, a light that seemed almost palpable in its soft pulsing brilliancy. Inspector Dickson's gaze traveled absently over it, over the stones mottled with bloodstains, and ended on the tall, sleeping figure rucking the yellow-white wool coverlet. He lay in an attitude of utterly abandoned restfulness; one hand was wedged half under his head, the other dangling loosely off the bed, the fingers all but brushing the floor. His lashes rested dark on his cheekbones, and Inspector Dickson found himself studying the hideous blackish, swollen contusion that flowered across the entire left cheek.

Mordred squirmed drowsily and blinked. An impertinent smile meandered onto his face as he noticed Inspector Dickson. "What are you looking at?" he asked teasingly.

"You," said Inspector Dickson awkwardly. "Your bruise," he added, feeling the need to be honest.

Mordred reached up to feel his face. "He slapped me with the flat of his sword," he said as though it were something that did not at all matter. "How are you?"

"None the worse," said Inspector Dickson, though he flinched as he shifted in his chair. His side was most certainly overtaxed and throbbed at the least movement.

"Don't try that on me," said Mordred with an attitude of preposterous satisfaction. "I can see it's bothering you." A wide grin stretched across his face. "Or is it your conscience?"

Inspector Dickson stared back at him. He was not used to this new, laughing Mordred, so full of life and strange humor that was beyond him to ferret out. "What do you mean, my conscience?" he asked.

Mordred's smile intensified, as though Inspector Dickson had walked straight into his prepared trap. "I was just wondering if you were regretting your apology last night."

Inspector Dickson's mouth fell open, but he stopped himself short, snapped it shut, refused to repeat last night's obtusity. "You know very well I do not regret it!" he countered forcefully. "I am glad it is said at last, and I still mean it with a whole heart."

"I am glad of that," said Mordred gently, the light banter ebbing out of sight. He hesitated. "I did not want it to be a constraint between us," he went on softly, and Inspector Dickson realized he was explaining why he had made the jest. "A concealed thing, one we could not speak of. There is no reason to hide from what is past, nor reason to be ashamed of what brought us together in the end. I do not want you to think—when I laugh at something—that it is because I think it was a light matter when it happened."

"No; I understand," said Inspector Dickson, shaking his head quickly and firmly. And he did suddenly understand, very deeply, and struggled to find the words for what he felt.

Mordred held Inspector Dickson's eyes intently, earnestly, as though asking whether he indeed understood. "I want to laugh, you see," he said. "For so long everything was festering and poisonous inside me, and I am ready to let it out and make it harmless, so it cannot burn me any longer. I am *ready* to laugh again."

"Yes," said Inspector Dickson, "that is what I meant. I am ready to laugh again."

Mordred's smile broadened out again. "That is good," he said. "Why, we have a whole war finished behind us! It is a time to laugh like no other."

~

"Are you in pain, Mordred?"

Laufeia was continually fussing over him since she had wakened, something which Mordred had never had much stomach for. The peace still coursing so freshly through him did not change that, though it did soften his mood and reaction. Throwing her a slightly perturbed look, he stared absently away as she felt his bandaged hand and tucked the coverlet in more closely.

"I'm not cold," he murmured, perversely shrugging off the folds.

"I'm not going to argue with you," retorted Laufeia, "if that's what you want."

"Girls," retaliated Mordred, a perfectly irrelevant but always satisfying remark.

Laufeia said nothing, rolled her eyes skyward, and gave his shoulder a light pat as she turned. "It's noon, Mordred," she said over her shoulder. "The three of us are going to the hall. I'll bring your dinner up shortly."

"I'm sure if Inspector Dickson can go, in the state he's in, then I should be able to go, too," said Mordred, patiently explaining the axiomatic facts and forcing his tired eyelids open.

"Inspector Dickson did not get attacked by an armed madman last night!" Laufeia said sharply, throwing up her hands.

Mordred grinned sleepily as the door scraped and clicked shut behind her.

It burst open an hour later and woke him from a doze; he sat up, refreshed and very much awake, as a tall, thin figure sprang in and thundered at the top of his voice.

"*What do you think you were doing?* You boy! You pest! You—brat!" He flapped his mouth helplessly like a fish.

"What did I do?" inquired Mordred with honest interest.

"What did you do?" Jedediah Crayes roared. "Oh yes, I know what Mordred says! 'I was only trying to kill myself again, Jedediah Crayes.' Fighting the leader with half your bones broken? Are you insane? Do you send Death regular invitations for tea every month? I'm going to be grey and decrepit before my time with your mad revelries!"

"I suppose it wouldn't make a difference if I said I didn't exactly invite the leader into Mitheren?" asked Mordred innocently.

"It would not! What business had you to be in Mitheren, anyway?" Jedediah Crayes stormed back and forth across the room. "Jedediah Crayes comes back to the city, minding his own business, and the general corners him and says, 'Mordred's here.' Why am *I* supposed to care? Then, as if this is supposed to make me even happier, 'Oh, and he killed the leader last night.' When will you learn to stop courting danger, you little *idiot*?"

"I don't know why I can't manage to stay safe," said Mordred.

"Hah!" Jedediah Crayes snorted.

Mordred lay back without answering, the contented and still-mischievous smile pulling at his mouth. "Why weren't you in Mitheren before, Jedediah Crayes?"

Jedediah Crayes dropped into Inspector Dickson's old seat in a relaxed attitude. "Oh—that! I had to abandon ship rather when this whole hullabaloo brewed up in Orden City. The Legean Association wouldn't have me throwing my life away for a glorious last stand when there's other places they need my help. So I headed south, and I was two days gone before the word got to me—word that the war *had* ended, only not quite in the way I expected it." He sent Mordred a dry grin.

"I'm glad you came back," said Mordred.

"Oh, well." A ridiculously pleased smile began twisting up one side of Jedediah Crayes' mouth. "So am I, my boy, so am I."

"Even if I can't keep myself out of trouble for a month?"

Jedediah Crayes threw him a brief glower. "Yes, my dear—young fool, even then."

"Jedediah Crayes." Mordred pinched the blanket meditatively, rubbing the prickly wool from fingertip to fingertip. He looked up suddenly. "Have you met Inspector Dickson?"

Jedediah Crayes squinted at him. "Not . . . formally." He spaced each word with separate care. "Why do you ask?"

Mordred shrugged. "I think it is high time my two friends are introduced to each other."

Few things had delighted Mordred as much as the look of absolutely confounded shock on Jedediah Crayes' face.

~

"So . . . now we can go home?" It was Therelane who spoke, lying on the grass, arms crossed behind his head. Braegon sat beside him.

The latter looked down and laughed. "Not until we have been discharged. They will remember us soon enough, and come here to dismiss us. You do not want to be branded as a deserter!"

He broke off quickly and stared at Therelane with an odd breath of a laugh. Both of them had forgotten that Therelane was, in a narrow sense, in the eyes of the army, just that.

"Braegon—" started Therelane, looking away from him and beginning to tear at bits of the yellowing, trampled grass. "Ought I—ought I to report myself to someone? I disobeyed an order outright, and I knew it—and if there's punishment due, I had best take it like a man."

Braegon did not reply directly. "Do as your conscience bids you," he said at last, his lean, dark face solemn. "That is my counsel, and no more. But I will say that Sergeant Garin was the one with the quarrel between you, and now he is no more; and if it comes to a question of who saw the act of insubordination, I do not think any man in this place will speak out against you."

"But they will not lie for me," said Therelane, shocked at the idea.

"No; but I do not think they will speak out against you, either." Braegon grinned a little at him.

Therelane tossed up his hands. "Then it will be very obvious to the commanding officer that they did see me."

"Aye, Therelane, you know nothing of soldiers," said Braegon gently. "Loyalty will do much to bend justice into mercy. They will make it very clear that they know the truth, but they will let you go. And after all, a war has ended. Men are lenient."

"You think that is how it will happen," said Therelane, still half-disbelieving.

Braegon pushed him, his grin widening. "So, try and see."

~

"First of all," Jedediah Crayes managed lamely, "I am nobody's friend. And *second* of all"—he drew himself up wrathfully—"since when has that Inspector been your friend, since last time I was aware you hated him like death and the plague warmed over!"

"That would be understating it," Mordred offered.

Jedediah Crayes scowled at him. That little impudent, outrageous boy—how pleased he looked, taunting him with those oblique, straight-faced gibes—and all the while that Jedediah Crayes behaved as furious as he believed himself to be, there was another part of his mind noticing the same things with a warm gladness, thinking that it had been a long time since the boy smiled with such remarkable animation and ease as he did now.

"Will you explain?" he demanded, snapping back to equilibrium. "You're either delirious, or drunk, or—or"—he searched wildly for a suitable alternative—"you actually forgave him for good and all!"

"Well done!" said Mordred in delight. "I knew you would guess it eventually."

"I . . . commend . . . you," said Jedediah Crayes blankly and looked around for his chair to sit down again.

"And apologized, too," Mordred went on blithely, "since after all I was quite rude to him."

"I see," Jedediah Crayes mumbled, trying to recover a semblance of poise. "And may I ask what . . . er . . . catalyzed this change of face?"

Mordred considered. "I suppose it was Fenris," he said, and the smug look on his face told Jedediah Crayes that he was going to let him figure that one out on his own.

~

Laufeia hurried into the room, cheeks warm from haste. "Mordred—"

He was sitting up, wide awake and half-laughing. "Laufeia!" he exclaimed, seeing her. "What took you so long? Jedediah Crayes and I have been talking for at least half an hour."

Laufeia glanced at the newcomer with indifference. "I was—we were detained, Mordred. The general wished to speak with us."

His brows arched. "About what?" Fenris and Inspector Dickson were entering now, and he eyed them questioningly.

"No, nothing to do with us, Mordred." She hesitated an instant. "He wants to know if you will be well enough to dine below tomorrow night."

"Why?" asked Mordred sharply. "If he wants to ask me a question, he may come here; I have not forsworn visitors."

She shook her head. "It is to honor you, Mordred."

"I'll make myself sick if I have to." He flung himself back into the bed and jerked up the blanket. "I'll run around the room till I faint. I won't go."

"What?" Jedediah Crayes sputtered, standing up. "What is wrong with you, boy? Why?"

"Because he's *stupid*," said Laufeia between her teeth, exasperated to the core.

"Are you afraid of so many people?" said Jedediah Crayes vaguely.

"No," said Mordred stiffly.

"All right, then." He manifested considerable relief. "It must be remediable."

"I just don't want to go," said Mordred obstinately, burying his head into the pillow. "I don't care that I killed the leader. It was an accident anyway. I didn't do anything worth twopence. I don't want people looking at me, pointing at me, talking about me like I'm a—a *Mogra* twenty feet tall, thinking I did something wonderful!"

"It's a wonderful thing to be humble," said Jedediah Crayes with another poor attempt at condolence and empathy.

Laufeia rounded on him in annoyance. "He's not humble!" she cried. "That's just it. He's proud, too proud to let anyone thank him!"

"Oh," said Jedediah Crayes, looking relieved again but no more enlightened. He scratched his head. "That makes no sense to me."

"I'm not asking it to, sir," snapped Laufeia and turned back to Mordred. "This was the kindness of the general, and you are not going to turn your back on it. And you will stop attributing thoughts to people you have never even seen. I'm sure that most of them are perfectly sensible men and women who will think of you and treat you as a human like themselves. Gratitude does not have to mean misconceptions and fawning servility, do you understand me?"

"All right," said Mordred tightly, not lifting his head. "I'll go. But I won't like it."

~

Mordred did not look at all happy, when, the following evening, they went down to the feast.

He had brought up another argument, that morning: he still could not walk unaided, and he said that he would not humiliate himself by coming into a great crowd with a huge bruise on his face *and* a bandaged hand *and* walking like a cripple.

Laufeia had overruled him.

Now Inspector Dickson was trying to think of encouraging words to say, but he could not think of a single one, at least none that Mordred would care to hear.

"I'm sorry," he offered at last, as Fenris and Laufeia settled Mordred into a chair on the high dais. "It'll only be a few hours."

Mordred gave a taut shrug. "Long hours." But his tone was wry; he was no longer sulking, just prepared to endure the odious trial. He glanced up at Inspector Dickson with steely-set face. "I'll manage."

And he did, since Inspector Dickson saw him conversing attentively with more than one person, and once at least he heard him laugh.

"How was it?" he asked at last when they returned late in the evening.

"Not so bad," said Mordred, stretching gladly on the bed. He seemed to realize what he had said and shot a glare at Inspector Dickson. "I talked with Ahearn."

"Yes, exchanged two words with him, from what I saw," said Inspector Dickson, grinning against his better judgment. "Any more lengthy discourse?"

Mordred raised himself up on one elbow. "I talked with a nobleman named Ludan. It was very boring."

His tone dared contradiction, so Inspector Dickson gave it to him. He raised an eyebrow.

Mordred tossed his head. "I suppose it was amusing when he tried to discover my pedigree. Only Ahearn is obliging enough to play that game."

"Then what?"

"Then he was so foolish as to bring up the subject of the leader, but I deterred him from it rather quickly."

"And not very subtly, I imagine."

"I didn't say a word," Mordred countered. "I just looked at him."

Inspector Dickson pictured the stiffening of Mordred's countenance, the icy-grey stare, and grinned again.

"You know," he said suddenly, "with all you've done, the general would give you a lordship if you asked him."

"I don't want a lordship," said Mordred quietly. "I want to go home."

He lay back again on the rumpled blanket. "There's a boy—my happiest memory is tossing him high, on a white road with snowy lattice-arches in the trees and an ivory-white sky. Just a small boy, with sandy hair and square shoulders. His brother is dead now—and he's probably a little taller—and a little wider . . .

"Will you come back with me to Ceristen, Inspector Dickson? Just for a little while? There is so much I want to see again, and show you."

~

"I know," said Ahearn. "You needn't say it."

Mordred reached out and touched his brother's shoulder. "There is a part of me that wishes none of it had happened, Ahearn. But I do not belong with you any more, whether I will it or no. And even if I could uproot myself for your sake, I could not uproot the others. I cannot let this hurt divide me any longer, Ahearn. I am ready to be whole and content."

"I understand," said Ahearn with difficulty. "You—will forget me."

"No! That is not what I mean. I will remember, and it will hurt—it must always hurt a little, I think. But one can take hurts like that in stride. It is not the poisonous kind."

Ahearn nodded, his breathing thick with repressed tears.

Tears in answer glimmered in Mordred's eyes. "Do not weep, Ahearn."

Ahearn nodded again, and forced in a short, resolute breath. "I will not weep. I will let you go in peace."

Mordred got clumsily to his feet, and held Ahearn fast in a long, firm embrace. "You will be strong, Ahearn. You must be strong."

"I've got a girl to be strong for," said Ahearn with a poor attempt at a laugh as they drew apart.

Mordred stared at him. "Are you in jest, or serious?"

The tip of Ahearn's nose turned pink, like a rabbit's, and he began to smile. "Mostly in jest." He added hurriedly, "After all, it has been months. And I have not even spoken to her father."

A smile started to form over Mordred's face. "You had better organize a massive celebration," he said. "It must be a wedding expensive enough and splendorous enough for the news to reach my ears!"

~

Two men stood at the foot of a small, broad mountain, the fragrance of summer-warmed trees blowing out to them. Neither very tall, both lean, ragged, and bone-weary; one whose left hand was gone, the other halt in the leg with a marked, catching limp.

"Braegon," said Therelane, looking not at his friend but up at the steep wooded slope. "If you were ever to tell someone that you loved his sister—supposing he didn't know—how would you go about it?"

Braegon turned swiftly to look at him, one dark brow springing quizzically up his face. "That's something I have never thought on," he admitted with wry frankness. "I am happy for you, Therelane. Who is it?"

Color drowned Therelane's entire face. "Mirda," he blurted.

Braegon's head whipped up. "Therelane? Truly? But that is wonderful!" He flung an arm around Therelane's shoulders, nearly knocking them both over, and drew back again with his flashing, joyous grin wider than it had ever been. "Is it my blessing you want? You have it, without reservation. It will be a glad thing to have you as my brother!"

"So, that is over," said Therelane with a vast sigh. "Perhaps it will be easier to tell everyone else."

"Nay, nay," said Braegon with a laugh. "Do not trouble yourself with that. Mirda will do all the telling!"

"Aye," said Therelane with a slowly growing smile, "she will do that."

An absent silence fell and he looked back up at the mountain, his brows frowning into one another. "I wonder what we shall find up there."

"What do you fear to find?" asked Braegon quietly.

Therelane looked away, filled with memories of holding Mirda while distant tongues of flame blazed up on Thiranu's flanks. "The effects of fire," he said.

CHAPTER 40

A SENSE OF FAMILIARITY, OF circles, came over the general as the grim-faced, dark-eyed young man stood before him again, his head bowed in deference this time.

"What have you to say to me, Grant Eagle?" he asked gently—always the compulsion was strong upon him to be gentle toward this bereaved, broken man so weary of life.

"I must thank you, my general, for giving me a place to live and a purpose to serve while this war lasted. That is all."

"That place need not be closed to you now," said the general. "Nor need your life be empty of purpose. Will you remain with us, at this hearth, even as you have till now?"

Grant shook his head. "I must go," he said. "I have a horse to bear me, and a sword for my protection, and a restlessness within that no man can fill. I want no mere, empty soldier's life. I am not of Runnicor, and not of Orden; I do not know what to do but wander."

"If you will tarry—" said the general. "A place will be shortly empty among the captains, and it would cheer me to see you take up such a mantle, one well-fitted and well-deserved."

But Grant again shook his head.

The general touched his shoulder. "Go," he said. "May you find the purpose and the peace you seek."

~

Captain Rhodes shut the heavy wooden door with a soft click and turned questioningly. "What is it you wanted to say, my friend?"

Captain Murray's face relaxed in the hint of a smile at the address. "Do you remember the day that you confronted me and offered me your friendship?"

"How should I forget it? It was not a fortnight past. But you, Captain Murray, are not one to recall memories without purpose."

"Nor do I," agreed Captain Murray. "And you remember the village of Ceristen?"

"Of course; say on."

"The repairs of the castle were completed months ago, but at the start of the war all such things fell by the wayside. It is ready for a lord to come and establish his holding there. The day in which our rivalry ended, the general spoke to me and asked if I would take the office. He will put it to the council tonight; but I thought that I would tell you first."

"So," said Captain Rhodes; for there seemed nothing else to say. At last he said, "Do you think you shall be happy?"

"I know what you are thinking," said Captain Murray drily. "'He fought his way to the position of captain, fought to keep it, and now he will leave it!' But it is promotion rather than demotion, is it not? And besides—to prove myself to the world no longer seems as important as once it did. Aye, I think I shall be happy enough."

"Then I am glad for you," said Captain Rhodes. "But I shall miss you."

"Ceristen is not far." Captain Murray cracked an unaccustomed laugh. "A few minutes' ride on dragon! I think you will make time for a good many visits, to me and to all your other peasantry friends who live there."

Captain Rhodes nodded, the pensive uncertainty on his face melting into acceptance. Suddenly he broke out into his boyish grin. "So, Captain Murray—now Lord Murray!"

"If it passes the council vote," said Captain Murray. "It will be puzzling to many, I doubt not. And not a few will say I belong in my current office more than the other; though there is more than one fair candidate who may fill the gap."

"And supposing it does pass, when do you think you will depart thither?"

"Within the month, I expect. Things have been long in readiness." He paused in somber thought. "It is time to begin again . . . "

Captain Rhodes leaned on the swinging window's deep-cut sill, contemplating the swathes of fallow fields and distant ridges of faded blue under the clean torrents of sharp, morning-lit air. How fair seemed a thing that had been almost lost! "To begin again; yes, we are all doing that."

~

A little swell of wind puckered the current in the slow brook, and washed in welcome coolness across Fred's face. The trees were scattered far here, and as they halted again, and Fiona settled him to lie down in comfort, the view south across the sweep of the mountain was vast and full of green.

"The sky greys," said Fiona, and Fred's eye was drawn, not to the dull cast of the heavens, but to her poised, thoughtful face, lovely in its gravity.

"Maybe it will rain at last," he said.

"Maybe it will rain on us," she returned, and suddenly those changeful features sprang to life in a glimmering moment of joy. "Do you like to walk in the rain, Frederick Thorne?"

He smiled at her teasing formal address, and answered her in kind. "With you, my lady Fiona, nothing can be distasteful."

Her vivid, dark eyes were full of tenderness and laughter as they bent over him. "I think that we are close upon the village now. Are you ready to go on? Do your eyes tire you?"

"I am ready."

And so they entered Ceristen again, with Fred leaning upon his lady, and a door rattled frantically and swung wide into the dusty street, and a slim, brown-haired woman came running out to fling her arms around Fred.

"Marjorie, Marjorie." Fred held her gently, stroking her back. "I am here, and whole." He feared to ask, but it was a question that must be spoken. "Charles?"

Marjorie stepped back, wiping away the silent tears from her eyes. "Oh—Charles? No, he is in the house. Let me call him. He returned yesterday—" She was turning, flying back in with her light step. Fred reached back, and Fiona slipped again under his arm for support.

"Fiona, lass!" It was Mrs. Earle's bright-eyed, dumpy figure that bore down upon them. "And Fred Thorne with you! You're looking the worse than you did leaving, young man—but content, aye, content. Now Jared, when he came back last night, he was all upset. Downright fretting, he was, that he'd find the mountain in cinders. Said he saw it all ablaze. Jared's a good boy, but he has it in him to exaggerate now and then—"

"But I saw it, too," Fiona broke in. "There was fire on the mountain, wasn't there?"

"Oh, there was! No soldiers, but there was fire. They set a few things alight—I don't know *what* did it, exactly, but some say it was birds." Mrs. Earle shook her head judiciously. "Birds, to my way of thinking, don't have it in them to strike flint and tinder together, let alone drop them on a house. But 'twas only here and there, and all of it was put out by sunrise. No one's the worse." Mrs. Earle patted Fiona's arm. "So, dear, is your brother back?"

Fiona flinched, the look gone in a moment; but Fred saw it, and knew that for a moment she had thought of Bardrick, and not Marcus. He drew his arm closer about her.

There was much still to heal from.

~

"I am glad we shall not have to go through the village itself," muttered Mordred.

Fenris had gone up to Ceristen, very early in the morning, and brought down Smoke, the sturdy, dark-coated young stallion so full of spirit, that the Earles had kept for them all the months since the horse sale. Mordred had almost forgotten him, and had gladly made reacquaintance with the curious, feisty little beast.

He would have been far gladder if that were all he had to do.

"How else do you think you are going to get home?" snapped Laufeia. Her patience was wearing thin with his remarks, but Mordred was not ready to stop making them.

"She's right, you know," Inspector Dickson put in unhelpfully.

Mordred scowled down at him. "If the rest of you were mounted, it would not be so bad. As it is, everyone must either think I am some prig of a nobleman, or know that I am injured."

"A true horror," snorted Inspector Dickson.

Mordred thinned his lips, his glare burning harder. "You should be the one up here. Not me."

"If you think you can walk two more miles with a broken leg, you're welcome to prove it," returned Inspector Dickson.

Laufeia whirled around. "No, he is not! Mordred, if I see you make one move off that horse—"

Mordred tossed his head, a grin pushing out in spite of himself. "You don't think I would do that, do you, Laufeia?"

"I *know* you would," said Laufeia grimly.

Mordred brushed aside a thin branch clawing across his path and narrowed his eyes into the distance. "There, ahead, Laufeia, it's the road!"

He urged Smoke forward, his eyes tracing the winding, half-obscured pale ribbon, and the dark, jutting corner of something that he was sure—sure—it was the edge of the house—

They came out into the open, and there it lay, the small, peak-roofed cottage, sheltered by the trees, its square chimney smokeless and lonely. The dark wooden door was firmly shut, the windows shuttered; Laufeia would never have departed with a single opening left ajar.

I want to go home, Ahearn.

He stumbled off Smoke and leaned against the lintel as Laufeia opened the door. Memories stormed through him, swamping him in their nearness, but nearest was the last time he had seen this small kitchen—the morning sun streaming in a bar of haze, Laufeia's silent, wide eyes bidding him farewell, Fenris by the door . . .

In a pincer-grip they held him, hurting him, and then they let him go, drifting away like old, shriveled ghosts. Mordred drew in a deep sigh, and let it out, staring at the empty room.

"Are you all right?" Inspector Dickson came up beside him, brow corrugated in concern.

Mordred turned. "Oh—yes, I'm quite all right." He meant it, and he saw that Inspector Dickson understood that. "Look, there," he added, sweeping his hand toward the inner parts of the house. "A veritable hovel compared to your fine quarters in Bulca. Will you manage?"

"Oh, I'll manage," said Inspector Dickson wryly. "As long as I don't have to sleep anywhere near you and your doleful declarations of humiliation." And with that shaft he walked into the kitchen.

Mordred grinned delightedly after him.

"He's learning how to manage you," said Laufeia, appearing out of the dimness and brushing past.

"That's just what I was thinking," said Mordred in satisfaction.

~

The sun was very warm, and the smell that came through the open window one of rain-wet sod. It was such a strong, whole scent that Mordred felt he could ignore his hateful, shackling injury and spring up to run the whole breadth of the mountain. At least he had Laufeia's permission not to wear the splint any longer, as long as he did not try to stand or walk. Two weeks now, until he could call it healed . . . and two weeks seemed like a short time, until one thought of how many empty hours were in them. Empty, lonely—where had Inspector Dickson gone?

"Hello, Mordred."

Mordred opened his eyes on a small, stocky boy standing with squarely planted feet just within the threshold. "Hello, Jerithan. Come on in."

There was no surprise in his mind; perhaps because Jerithan already seemed so sure of himself, so confident he was supposed to be here. *He'll go out and do things, thought Mordred, and he won't ever be afraid to do them.*

"Where's the others?" said Jerithan, shutting the door with thoughtful precision behind himself, and thrusting his hands decisively into his pockets.

"Laufeia and Fenris are out in the barn, cleaning up a stall for our horse to use," answered Mordred. "There's another man with us, though I haven't seen him about."

"I know," said Jerithan.

Mordred arched an eyebrow at him. "You do? So the word is all over town, is it?"

"Marianne's mother told her," said Jerithan gravely.

"And what did she say?"

"That you have a foreigner in your house." Jerithan pronounced the verdict promptly and without any particular interest.

Mordred laughed. He threw back his head and laughed. He had not laughed with such abandon even the night the leader died.

"I suppose it is funny," said Jerithan seriously, causing Mordred to go off afresh and apologize breathlessly to Jerithan between spasms.

"What is afoot in here?" demanded Inspector Dickson's voice, and Mordred sat up straight, swallowing the last of his hilarity.

"*There* you are, Inspector Dickson! Nothing—you wouldn't understand, I promise you. It isn't even really funny. At any rate . . . this is Jerithan, Inspector Dickson."

"Hello, sir," said Jerithan.

"Inspector Dickson is from Delgrass," Mordred explained simply and candidly. "He arrested me by mistake when I was down there, but it all turned out well in the end."

Jerithan frowned in thought, seeming to turn this over in his mind. "I see," he said. "Is he your friend now?"

"Yes," said Mordred, "quite. Now, come sit down, Jerithan; the both of you, in fact, or I'll get a crick in my neck. How is Marianne?"

"She's all right." Jerithan sat, swinging his legs. "She has a baby inside her."

"I hadn't heard that," said Mordred, surprised.

"It's making her very fat," said Jerithan. "Not all over, just on her stomach. The rest of her is still quite thin. Her mother tells her she needs to eat more. And," he added, "sometimes the baby kicks. I felt it."

"It's curious, isn't it," said Mordred, understanding the deep fascination behind Jerithan's burst of words, blunt and matter-of-fact though they were. "A curious and wonderful thing."

Jerithan nodded. "And Marianne says, the baby is made part of her and part of Kenneth. So when it comes out and we can see it—we'll have something to remember him by." The last words came out in a forceful rush, proud and sad all at once, and Mordred, looking at him with swelling sorrow in his heart, saw the new oldness behind the hazel eyes, a depth and breadth only loss could bring into such a young face.

But he could not get up, and he did not think Jerithan would willingly come to be touched; and, perhaps, physical comfort was not what the seven-year-old boy needed right now.

"I'm glad for you, Jerithan," was all he said, softly. "I'm very glad."

~

"There you are." The biting, peculiarly arrogant voice was filled with undisguised triumph.

Mordred glimpsed a flash of Laufeia rising, the look on her face plain: *Not this man again.*

"Did you think I was hiding from you?" he inquired as a smug-faced Jedediah Crayes ducked under the door.

"My boy, don't try to protest your innocence," retaliated Jedediah Crayes with a disdainful sniff. "Slinking away to little nondescript hamlets and rude hovels—oh yes, I *know* you were giving me the slip. Nobody ever wants to stay around Jedediah Crayes, he's such a nasty, disagreeable person, isn't he? Oh yes, I understand. As long as you remained undisturbed by my loathsome presence, you were happy to remain in Mitheren, but once I showed up—*then* it was time to run!"

"Let me see," said Mordred composedly. "We were there for about one and a half days before you arrived, and after . . . "

"I don't *care*," Jedediah Crayes declared, raising his voice. "Just—just be quiet, why can't you, you saucy, long-winded rascal!"

"I don't know," said Mordred in a pretense of genuine perplexity, the provocative twitch around his mouth belying his wide, guileless eyes.

"Hmph," said Jedediah Crayes. His mood vanished and he dropped uninvited into a chair with an air of elegance. "Looks as if I scared your sister away."

"I do believe she finds your presence irksome," said Mordred.

Jedediah Crayes snorted. "Well, I don't need her to find it congenial."

"Jedediah Crayes," said Mordred absently, scarcely listening to the last part. "Where will you go now?"

"Go? Well, I have an appointment with an acquaintance to keep. After that, I expect I shall attend the assembly of the Legean Association—they hold it every few years, but with members scattered so wide, it is rare that we have more than two-thirds attending. Dull place anyway, full of reports and retirements and assignments and whatnot. They shall *all* want my report on the events of the war, of course; if I tried not to attend they would probably send Finath after me to bring me back hog-tied to the gathering." He leaned back, stretching.

"And then? The world is full of problems and peril. I shall go where I am needed."

He brought the legs of his chair to the floor with a crack, and looked at Mordred intently. "But I will come back here. Look for me in a year, or two, or three—I'll come back, and bring whatever news of the wide world you care to hear."

"I shall like that," said Mordred.

~

"How do you like it?" Mordred put the question airily, hands clasped behind his head and a lazy grin flashing out at Inspector Dickson.

"Ceristen?" Inspector Dickson cast his mind back over the past few days. "I like it—very well. It has been pleasant, restful; not to mention interesting. Do you often have so many visitors in a day?"

Mordred laughed, as he did so often now, his head flung back and his eyes alight. "Well, Jedediah Crayes is gone, and he will not be back again for a long time by his own account! But we have all just come back, and everyone wants to welcome us home again—and welcome you, of course. I daresay many of them think you plan to stay here."

"They have been very welcoming," admitted Inspector Dickson. "Yes, I could even say this feels like home, more home than Bulca does. It has a warmth and closeness that I have not felt since—well, for a long time." He looked out idly over the clean-swept floor, the scoured walls, the long gold fall of sunshine through the open window.

"Suppose you did stay," said Mordred in a different tone—quiet, earnest.

Inspector Dickson's head jerked up. "Stay? Mordred, I could not! I have to return to my king with a response that I was barred from delivering for months—and besides, I have a position, things to oversee, everything that has been on Harris' shoulders alone while I'm away." He turned up his hands with a gesture of closure. "You see?"

"You could send the response to your king by a different courier." Mordred leaned forward. "And you could send a request with it, a request to be released from your position, as long as they can find a replacement for you. It could work, don't you see? And you could have the same sort of job as in Delgrass, only here in this village. I'm sure the new lord of the castle will find some useful capacity for you."

Mordred's quick, leaping reasoning swept by too swiftly for Inspector Dickson to follow and grasp. He shook his head, helplessly bewildered. "I *could*—but why would they say yes?"

Mordred was not bemused, or agitated. He had never appeared so cheerfully calm. "Why not try it? The worst they can do is refuse. Anyway, it's not a decision to make in one day. Think on it for awhile and be sure it is what you want. It was just an idea, but if you do want to stay here, we ought to try to make it happen."

"Of course." Mordred's logic was beginning to sort itself out in Inspector Dickson's mind. "Aye, I'll think about it."

"At any rate, you are required to stay for at least one thing," said Mordred with a certain satisfaction.

"And what is that?"

"I hear," remarked Mordred dreamily, "that there is supposed to be a Thorne wedding soon . . . "

CHAPTER 41

FIONA STIRRED, WITH THE SOFT embrace of the blanket warming her cheek, and the sense of having slept very deeply, though perhaps not long.

"Fiona! Are you awake?"

Peony's intense half-whisper startled her upright, and in the mid-light between darkness and dawn she remembered why she was so fully awake, why she had not slept till the waning hours of the night, while Peony held her hand and the sinking moon lit the bedroom. And why such a consuming expectancy filled her being, and underneath it a quivering, twisted unease, as though unforeseen ruin might again fall on the day before the morning was come.

"Oh, *Peony,*" she whispered, clenching her hands around one another, the fear and the expectancy and the joy all melding into one nameless emotion that hurt with its strength. "I am so—so glad—or maybe it isn't gladness—I don't know what to do with myself."

"There, there." Peony's lovely, sea-blue eyes were warm with understanding. She tucked stray ringlets of hair back into her braid and sat up, leaning forward to stroke Fiona's entwined fingers.

"I lost him," Fiona murmured. "Now it is the culmination of all I thought I had lost. Oh, Peony, the wonder of it is breaking me."

"What's the wonder to me," said Peony briskly, "is that you slept at all when you said you couldn't even close your eyes. I must have been more excited than you after all! Come, I know what's to be done even if you don't. Make something out of your tousled hair, to start with."

Fiona laughed, and began to comb her fingers loosely through her tumbled, heavy curls; and the tightness bursting her heart seemed to slacken, and reality rushed over the world again, though wonder still tinged the edges.

Together they smoothed it into a rippling, heavy curtain, muted-gold under the growing light, and Fiona braided it around her head, while Peony darted out to forage for flowers in the woods, coming back with her arms full of cockles and bluebells. “These will make a fine wreath,” she averred, plumping down cross-legged on the floor. “Nothing complements your eyes so well as bluebells, Fiona.”

Fiona only laughed again as she slipped into a fresh kirtle and knotted a strip of leather about the waist. She did not care whether her head were bare, or crowned with all the wildflowers in the woods. She cared not whether her garments were undyed wool and linen, or the deepest crimson that pigments could yield. She bent her head and let Peony weave the blossoms into her braid, but the only thing in her mind was the knowledge that today she was one man’s, forever.

Sitting there, busy as they were, they did not notice the intruder until he cleared his throat in a slight, affected cough. Peony squeaked, flowers flying out of her hand, and Fiona looked up. There was Marcus, hair ruffled, feet planted apart and mouth puckered in a look of bashful masculinity.

“I truly hate to disrupt the bride’s toilet, but, er”—his tone grew plaintive—“is there anything to eat?”

“Oh—you!” Peony shooed him away. “There’s bread in the cupboard, and scrape out the last of yesterday’s lentils if you need more. Don’t come asking me to cook anything this morning!”

Marcus dutifully disappeared.

"So, that's done," said Peony exuberantly, straightening and kicking aside the stray stems. "Do you want any breakfast yourself?"

Fiona shook her head and stood up, panting a little in her impatience and excitement. "I want to go."

~

"Help me, Daren," Fred murmured, fumbling with the buckle of his boot. His hands were not quite steady, and ever since his awakening his eyes had not seen with their old clarity, especially in such dimness.

"Someone open the window for goodness' sake," said Sandy, slamming open the shutters even as Fred's brother hurried to his aid. "You would think this was a funeral."

Daren uttered a half-chuckle and knelt by Fred. "Lean back and rest a moment, my brother. You need not exert yourself on this of all mornings."

The buckle was settled in a trice. Daren fitted on the other boot and helped Fred to his feet. "The day is hot already. Come, let us make for the green!"

They passed Runa, the cow, who was picketed and grazing placidly outside the house, and slowly covered the open, hilly stretches between them and the woods rising up on higher ground.

"What a wonderful morning," said Sandy, breathing the air in deeply. "We haven't gone somewhere all together like this since—"

"Since before the war," said Daren.

"Yes," said Sandy. "The horse sale."

Gwenda's small fingers crept into Fred's, closing tightly on his hand. He enfolded hers in answer, looking down at her silent, staid little face. "I am here, Gwenda," he said, sensing a need for reassurance in the sudden gesture.

She nodded, a contented half-smile easing back into her face. "I know," she said. "I like your hand. It is so big and strong, and safe."

Fred smiled back, his heart swelling and humbled by her trustful love.

"Don't get tired," she added.

Daren laughed. "True womanly caution speaks! Your sisters are raising you well."

They passed through a belt of trees, and as they came out of it and crested another rise, the path swung left and the scattered buildings of the village proper were spread out before them. Miry puddles from yesterday morning's rain dotted the road, cracked at the margins; the lake lay on one hand, full and glittering, the green on the other, a flat sward cleared of trees and brush. Already knots of people gathered on the dew-dripping grass.

"Fred!" Marcus cried, tearing toward them with a gangling, incredibly rapid gait. "If you were half as excited as Fiona was to get here," he said reproachfully, pulling up in front of them, "you would have been here at the crack of dawn."

"Fiona," Fred murmured, his heart suddenly tripping in his breast, his eyes searching the small crowd.

Her shining head broke free of the rest, her slender figure came thudding against him in a moment of impetuosity unusual for her. He laughed softly, holding her fast as she buried her head on his chest and the uncertain fragrance of the flowers in her hair drifted up to him. "Could you wait no longer, my love?"

She raised steadfast dark eyes to his. "Not a moment longer."

"Then we will stay right here." Fred drew her head against his shoulder and settled his arm around her waist. "The time for waiting is truly past."

~

Fiona, tense with happiness in the circle of Fred's arms, felt the hush overcome the crowd and knew that the moment was upon them. She turned and saw the people drawing up in a rough ring around them, eager faces waiting.

"Who binds this man to this woman?" The slow, measured question rang out from Edrach Stafford's tall, blonde-bearded figure.

"Arad Earle," came the murmured answer from several throats among the crowd. Braegon King stepped into the center.

"As an elder man of this village," he declared, his clear, clipped voice carrying over the green, "and the one wisest and most respected among us, it is the duty of Arad Earle to bind this man and this woman."

Mr. Earle stepped gravely forward as Braegon retreated. "Fred Thorne," he said, his patient face tender. "Will you take your bride's hands in love?"

"Fiona Segelas, I love you."

Fred's strong-boned hands closed securely around hers, firm and gentle. "I will."

"Will you be her protector?"

"I will."

"And you, Fiona, will you be his helpmeet?"

"I will," she answered, wondering at the steadiness of her own voice.

"Will you, Fred, be strength where she is weakness, and cherish her above all else? Will you walk with her faithfully, in love, sufferance, and humility, as husband and wife?"

"I will," Fred responded, and this time his voice trembled.

"And you, Fiona, will you do likewise?"

"Will you wed me when the first trees of spring are budding?"

"Will you be my wife tomorrow?"

Fiona lifted her gaze to Fred's, and now, at last, the tumultuous joy pouring from her eyes could find expression on her lips. "I will."

The moment when Mr. Earle looped a cord about their hands and lashed them fast together, she never knew. Fred's face had already bent down to hers, and the long, painful eons of fear, hope, and expectation had at last become reality.

I will never, never let you go.

~

"I never saw a couple kiss so long!" Mrs. Earle tittered fondly with her sister, Lissa Boccin.

Lissa nodded very fast. "Methought he would faint in another moment—not that he'd be to blame, the poor lad, what with all his war wounds. Ah, but they've waited long for this."

"That they have. And who do you think will be next to go?"

"Aliria, sister, is that even a question?" Mrs. Boccin was the one who giggled now. "Look at Therelane there, blushing like a maiden! He hasn't taken his eyes off Mirda the whole morn."

"Indeed not! I am glad you are so observant, my dear . . . but it is good, very good, to see the young so happy now."

Food, dancing, gossip—it was the sum of all that the day had been, and all that it would likely be till evening. Mordred shifted, trying to subtly work the cramp out of his leg. Another week till the promise of healing was reached; for now, he was still not permitted to walk on it, and Smoke had borne him again to the wedding, much to his chagrin.

"Mordred!" Linda Boccin came flying toward him, black-haired, red-cheeked and bright-eyed, holding her hands out coquettishly. "Come—dance with me? They're starting the next."

He frowned up at her, surprised that she was unaware of his broken leg. "I don't want to dance," he said a little coldly, which was true as far as it went.

"Oh—" She stared at him, turned unwillingly, and wandered away with a dejected slump.

Mordred watched her go, wondering if all her queries had been so rebuffed. Then another voice exclaimed his name from behind, one both more familiar and more welcome.

"Braegon," he answered gladly, turning his head as his younger friend sat down with a deep, relieved sigh. "Is it the leg bothering you?"

Braegon shrugged for answer. "Aye, rather."

"It has been a long time since you took the wound," said Mordred, an unspoken question in his words: the question of the thing he had feared, ever since the moment he had heard of his friend's injury.

Again, Braegon's slim shoulders twitched in a shrug. "They say I will not walk straight on it again." His dark eyes met Mordred's frankly. "In a battle, a soldier expects that much and more. It might have been my life."

Mordred nodded, struggling to take it with the same forthright ease that Braegon did; but he could not stop thinking of Braegon's quick, high-stepping stride that had been such a part of him, now another thing twisted and stamped on by the war . . .

The hurt and the feeling of ugliness stayed with him all afternoon, and he found that he could not bear the thought of displaying his physical limitation to all eyes again. When Laufeia next passed by him, he stayed her.

"Laufeia, will you help me onto Smoke? I can leave now, while everyone is still busy, and go home on my own. You and Fenris needn't come with me. Stay as long as you like."

Laufeia knew, of course, why he wanted it. A faint line of exasperation drew itself between her eyes, and then faded into a brief moment of sympathy. She patted his arm. "Whatever you like, Mordred."

~

Inspector Dickson was enjoying himself to an extent that surprised him. He had found Mordred's young friend Jerithan again, listened to his remarkably precocious observations, and readily let the boy introduce him to everyone. Jerithan did it with a child's ease and innocence, and so meetings that might have been awkward, had Inspector Dickson been alone, were passed over as though they were nothing at all.

"This is my sister, Marianne," said Jerithan proudly. "She isn't really my sister—she's my brother's widow—but she lets me call her sister now."

Marianne Denholm was small and tired, looking too frail to carry her swollen belly, with hair of an astonishingly vivid red escaping into strands around her pinched, freckled face. There was a gritty endurance in her eyes, and she managed a smile for Inspector Dickson and nodded politely.

"We'll let your sister rest," said Inspector Dickson. "Who else have I got to meet?"

Jerithan reflected. "Gwenda Thorne," he said. "She's Fred's youngest sister. See, there she is with Filian King."

"She doesn't resemble her brother," remarked Inspector Dickson mildly.

"No," said Jerithan, "I suppose not. Sandy looks more like him."

Inspector Dickson cast another absent look at the dark-haired child with a sweet face, her small hands stroking a half-grown, hairy pup as she listened earnestly to the boy beside her. His thoughts were straying from the present conversation to other, older ones.

"Do you like Sandy?"

Inspector Dickson rubbed his brow, frowning. "I wonder—where has Mordred got to?"

~

The midafternoon air was hot and stifling. Smoke ambled down the road, even his usually brisk gait sluggish under the burning sun. Mordred nudged him tiredly with his heel to pick up the pace, but Smoke snorted and shook his head as though brushing away a bothersome fly. In spite of himself, Mordred wished he had waited for the others instead of slipping away on his own.

He heard the hooves under the sound of Smoke's, striking asymmetrically like a bad echo. Even as he pulled up to listen better, they appeared over the rise ahead of him—a large horse's head with a crooked snip dribbling down under the eye, and then a girl's small head that was only more dwarfed as the rest of her broad mount came into view.

A waving mass of bright hair blew lightly back from her face, the very edges glittering in a haze of sun—a hair that was not the pure red of Marianne Earle's nor the pale reddish-blonde of Laufeia's, but something in-between: a rusty, coppery fire-gold. She reined in as she drew abreast of him.

Strands of that blazing hair curled damply around her pale features; she met his gaze with flecked hazel-grey eyes, large in a slender, pointed face. Suddenly Mordred was aware of the faded bruise on his cheek.

"Is this Ceristen?" she said.

He gave a fairly imperceptible nod, which she must have nonetheless seen for her shoulders eased and she went on:

"I am Lethira Gerisson."

"You should not be so quick to give your name to strangers." He had not meant to interrupt her. He had not meant to say that, or anything like it. Above all, he had not meant it to sound so gruff.

"I—" She regarded him as though she did not know what to make of him. He noted conscientiously that though her horse must have been two hands taller than Smoke, her head was barely level with his. "I am looking for the Earles—if you can direct me to their house? They are kinsmen of my family, and we hoped that we could come to them."

"Where is your family then?" What was the matter with him? Why could he not stop his first thoughts from spewing out of his head?

"They are . . . " Her voice trailed away. He saw how tired and wan her face was, how her frame drooped under her tattered green cloak. "They are back in my own village. But we cannot live there. The enemy came; they burned the houses and salted the fields. And Murdoch and Graeme are ill, and Firia remained to tend them. So I came alone."

"I am sorry to hear of that," he said, and was glad to find he could say something that was not absurd. "You are wearied, and our house is not far; you can rest there tonight. My sister will not mind."

He did not know what made him say that.

Her eyes widened a little in bewilderment. How *small* she was! "Thank you," she said carefully. "Thank you, but if you could only direct me to the Earles—"

"Yes—of course," he said hurriedly, inwardly exploding with combinations of fury and resentment at his memory for betraying him.

She rode on down the road a little later, the clopping sound fading as Mordred watched her go.

He was quite sure she would never want to see him again.

EPİLOGUE

THE CHILL AUTUMN WIND BLEW across the yard, rasping leaf against leaf. Runa lowed faintly from the shed. Covering the frost-hard ground in long, sure strides, Fred shouldered aside the door and dropped a load of freshly split logs beside the fire.

The door shut unexpectedly behind him. "Gwenda?" he said, turning.

But it was his wife who stood there, unwinding the scarf from her face and neck. Her radiant smile sprang out as she saw him.

Fred stepped forward to unfasten her heavy shawl, dropping a light kiss on her brow. "I did not think to see you so soon. Is all well then?"

"Aye. It went quicker than even Mrs. Earle anticipated. Marianne is well, and the baby is strong—a big, squalling boy."

"A companion for Jerithan then, mayhap."

Fiona shook her head smilingly. "Jerithan is seven years old, Fred, and more grown than most boys of such an age." She looked into the fire, a tender, motherly look overtaking her face, and the beauty of that look struck Fred to the heart. He put his arm around her.

"Maybe . . . " Fiona's voice trailed away.

"What, my love?"

She turned her face up to him, that look of love grown stronger still. "Maybe the new babe will not have to wait long for a companion of his age."

"Is Marjorie—"

Fiona laughed. "No, Fred! Not Marjorie, but *me*!"

He gasped and caught her speechlessly in his arms. A child, of *his* own—He had not felt such spinning wonder since the day he recognized his love for her.

"When, my love? When?"

"In the spring."

Fred shook his head. "That is such a long while."

Fiona laughed in a gentle, crooning way, and touched his cheek. "It will come. It may be a long while, but it will come."

THE END

AFTERWORD AND ACKNOWLEDGMENTS

Dear reader,

Thank you.

The *Ceristen Series*, in its most specific sense, is over. I see *The Journey*, *The Village*, *The Claw*, and *The War* as an individual set with their own themes folded tidily up in the final epilogue. However, the wider story is still to be completed. The *Ceristen Series* is a seedling, home to hidden promises carrying forward into the fifth, and final, book of the Ceristen Saga. This second-generational epic, *Sorrow and Song*, is currently in progress, and as I wrestle with its sweeping scope and massive cast of characters (many whom you already know, some whom I can't wait to introduce), I hold onto the joyful vision that one day you will read these words, too.

There is a strange compulsion in authors to talk about their books and what makes them special, which is probably why afterwords (along with author's notes, introductions, et al.) exist. I don't have any deep stories behind this series, just a hundred thousand mildly interesting tidbits, which if I tried to list would keep me and you here all day. Honestly, I'm tempted.

Yet in the end, I'm realizing, I have nothing to say. No final message to leave lingering in your head that the story has not already presented better than I could do. You just finished a 150,000 word novel. Let the words speak for themselves.

If this book touched you, if it brought you joy in any way, I would love to hear from you. Or if you have a question related to any part of the series. You can reach me on social media or via the contact form in my website: www.verityabuchanan.com/contact. I am friendly and I don't bite, though my sister's kitty does.

I was thirteen when I started writing *The War.* Today, I am twenty-one. These stories, these characters, are everything to me. Thank you, once again, for being here to share their experiences alongside me.

I would like to extend a special thanks to:

Mercy, my one and only co-creator. Thanks for always being there, for pushing me to finish, and for checking to make sure we had actual definitions for the Runnicoran vocabulary that I enthusiastically generated left and right. Here's to another eight years of circumventing the plot holes in our stories.

My parents, who brought the crazy pair of us into the world. My mom—you fostered a love of learning in me and showed me to look for the other side of the story. My dad—your fondness for big, unusual, or ostentatious words rubbed off on me, and I'm not even sorry.

My beta readers. You guys are the best of the best. Vanna, thanks for falling in love with all my characters before you even officially met them, for giving the best critiques, and for telling me to go to bed like any good adopted older sister. I'll write that Irene spin-off someday, I promise. Bri, vibe partner and kindred spirit . . . thanks for all those explosive 2 AM literary analysis voice chats. No rest for the weary, we die like insomniacs. Gwyn, for catching my typos, surprising me with gorgeous fanart, and creating the iconic MORDRED scream.

Stephen, an honorary werevulture. Thanks for your meme contributions and willing participation in the launch team efforts.

Melissa, Gwyn, Dante, Elizabeth, Jennifer, and Sharon: my Wattpad readers who stuck with me the whole way, through all four books and then some. You were my guinea pigs, and you even liked it, I think. I love you all so much.

The members of my discord server. Thanks for putting up with my bombardment of character ramblings and contextless quotes, for deep discussions and for absolute mayhem, and for so much pin-worthy gold that there aren't enough pins to hold it all.

The Ambassador International crew—Anna Raats and all the others at Ambassador who've contributed and will contribute your services to this series. A huge thank you for all the questions you've answered from this chronic overthinker. Special mention to my editors: Daphne, who deserves a medal for taking on my first manuscript and a very novice me; and Susie, who fearlessly tackled the longest two books of the series without having even read the rest. You're a gem, Susie.

P. E. Ace, whose critique is always relished and whose commentary on prior drafts is frankly unparalleled.

Julianne, my fellow *Silmarillion* geek and one-time sensitivity reader. Stay strong, queen.

Cayli, who tagged along the beta read and became an unexpected fan.

Benjamin, without whose intervention Fenris would not have been scarred.

All of you—ARC readers, launch team members, regular ol' readers, silent fans and vocal fans, names I've forgotten and names I never knew, everyone who has ever had a part in this story of my stories. You matter to me. Thank you.

And to God Almighty, the One Who dwells in light, be praise forevermore.

Verity A. Buchanan

August 2021

Soli Deo Gloria

GLOSSARY OF TERMS

Runnicoran

Adorti | *noun, plural* | Runnicoran name for the mountain trolls of Fearnland and Erahar

Ca unik? | Where are you going?

Co' rai int | It's a good one

é | *2nd person pronoun singular* | you

etti | *2nd person pronoun plural* | you, you all

Etti rai! Ca corrik etti? | You there, who are you?

Ett-Kéva | Peace-maker

Ittik atti Ordeni | We are Ordenians

Kurik | *honorific* | captain

Nin co' rai? | What's going on here/what's the problem

nitta | *verb, imperative* | come

Paraki | *honorific* | leader, general

stag | *demonstrative pronoun, used as command* | there/that place

turta | *verb, imperative* | halt

utinna | *verb, imperative* | finish/take care of it/do the job

Thiredanian

eraris | *noun, singular* | a type of sentient creature which appears like a large raven

Fira luithra | Lady of mercy

Hiaro | *honorific* | Lord

Iarenad | Ruler *[typically used with Legea (of Rodronian origin) to reference the Ruler of the Worlds]*

Iriem ese loninae! | Behold the stars!

Luenna | Thaw *[an official season recognized in formal dating. Ordenians use both the Rodronian calendar system, based on lunar cycles, solstices, and equinoxes, and their own seasonal method]*

mari | *noun, singular* | son

Mogra/Mograre | *noun* | monster/ogre/Ordenian name for the mountain trolls of Fearnland and Erahar

Other Names, Terms, and Titles

coenlag: Eraharian term of endearment translating loosely to "beloved," typically romantic.

Legean Association: A body of men formed for the preservation of good in the world at large. Established by Rodronian king Terlar IV. Follow a loose hierarchy based on duration of service in the body; younger members typically take assignments from older members, often having a designated figure to report to, though until retired, every member is considered on call and should step in where needed with or without assignment. Work in collaboration with the local law enforcement whenever possible and are forbidden to infringe their authority. Retain individual citizenships and loyalties, but do not answer directly to any authority aside from the Association in matters pertaining to active duty.

Ordenian captain: Not to be confused with an ordinary army captain status, Ordenian captains are the second-highest ranking military position in the country. Typically hereditary, though when a captain dies childless the selection is referred to the council. Captains are restricted in the amount of land they are permitted to own, and most of them are quartered at Mitheren, though some choose to have secondary homes.

Ordenian General: The general is over the entire army, directly above the captains in the military chain of command. Typically hereditary, like the office of captain; when a general dies childless the selection is referred directly to the king and approved by the council. At the time of Conrad III, the general had begun to oversee duties that were historically the governor's jurisdiction in addition to his own responsibilities. Conrad III, a notably indecisive and retiring monarch, preferred to defer certain own tasks to the general as well. This was almost a direct reversal from the original aim in instituting the offices of Governor and General, which was to redistribute the king's absolute power. That it came about can be attributed to the unfortunate neglect of previous councils and monarchs to maintain their offices and prepare future generations for them. General Derek Winston was hailed as the man who "bore Orden on his shoulders", a most apt remark and one that very few saw the implications of.

Runnicor: An arid land of fairly high altitude. Comparable in size to Orden but more sparsely populated. Renowned for their robust military, their iron deposits, and the wool from their shepherding industry.

For more information about
Verity A. Buchanan
&
The War
please visit:

www.verityabuchanan.com
www.facebook.com/VBuchananWrites
www.instagram.com/verityb.writes

For more information about
AMBASSADOR INTERNATIONAL
please visit:

www.ambassador-international.com
@AmbassadorIntl
www.facebook.com/AmbassadorIntl

If you enjoyed this book, please consider leaving us a review on Amazon, Goodreads, or our website.

www.ingramcontent.com/pod-product-compliance
Lightning Source LLC
LaVergne TN
LVHW020515100826
845148LV00010B/1243

* 9 7 8 1 6 4 9 6 0 3 5 2 4 *